PRAISE FOR *THE INGRE*

"The tension builds nicely . . . Readers will enjoy the heroine's journey of self-discovery and the recipes for the lemon tarts, brownies, scones, chocolate Bundt cake, and other treats she bakes along the way."

—*Kirkus Reviews*

"*The Ingredients of Us* is a literary confection filled with multifaceted characters and a compelling story line. Gold's bittersweet look at love will satisfy any contemporary women's fiction reader's sweet tooth."

—*Booklist*

"A delightful and delicious read, *The Ingredients of Us* delves into the fabric of marriage and what happens when some ingredients in the relationship are missing. Gold has crafted a smart story line with memorable characters and mouthwatering recipes that are sure to appeal to fans of Jenny Colgan and Amy E. Reichert."

—Kerry Lonsdale, Amazon Charts and *Wall Street Journal* bestselling author

"Come for the story of a baker facing a crisis in her marriage. Stay for the recipes—lush, beautiful things, filled with life lessons. From that very first recipe for passive-aggressive blackberry jam, you know you're in for something special."

—Erica Bauermeister, author of *The School of Essential Ingredients*

"Take a marriage in crisis, add a heroine you can't help but root for, and toss in an ending you won't see coming: voilà—you've got *The Ingredients of Us*. Jennifer Gold's debut is deliciously fun."

—Camille Pagán, bestselling author of *Woman Last Seen in Her Thirties*

"*The Ingredients of Us* is a delightfully original novel filled with love, regret, and recipes that are themselves like little short stories. You'll want to cry for Elle as she navigates the breakup of her marriage and flashes back on the earlier, happier days. And then you want to follow her to her kitchen and feast on her buttery concoctions as she finds healing and strength."

—Maddie Dawson, *Washington Post* and Amazon Charts bestselling author of *Matchmaking for Beginners* and *The Survivor's Guide to Family Happiness*

"A mouthwatering tale that takes you inside a complicated marriage, raising questions about love, fidelity, family, and when career takes over. This book provides a unique take on a perennially interesting topic."

—Elyssa Friedland, author of *The Intermission*

KEEP ME AFLOAT

ALSO BY JENNIFER GOLD

The Ingredients of Us

KEEP ME AFLOAT

A NOVEL

JENNIFER GOLD

This is a work of fiction. Names, characters, organizations, places, events, and incidents are either products of the author's imagination or are used fictitiously. Any resemblance to actual persons, living or dead, or actual events is purely coincidental.

Published by Lake Union Publishing, Seattle

www.apub.com

ISBN-13: 9781542015813
ISBN-10: 1542015812

Cover design by Pepco Studios

Cover photography by Chrissy Wiley

Printed in the United States of America

For Port Townsend, cetaceans, and David Attenborough

FEBRUARY

2018

I met Dennis, my once husband, the love of my life, by accident—a car accident eighteen years ago.

Tonight, I'm following the winding, wooded 104 highway, familiar like a childhood memory. My U-Haul's high beams cast the bordering trees in a golden lick of light, elongating the roadside shadows. I watch for deer, raccoons, coyotes. How quickly could I stop if something jumped out of the forest? I probably couldn't stop at all, and the truck would just barrel into the unsuspecting nocturnal body, practically unhindered—or I'd swerve into the embankment, a skid mark made permanent on the faded blacktop.

It's not hard to imagine. I draw on my own experience, that moment of impact and the ringing that happens in your ears when you smack your head against car window glass. It's one of those things I can't help but picture, a nagging feeling of dread tucked between my ribs for another mile or two. I haven't seen Dennis in four and a half years, but I can picture him as easily as I can picture veering off this road into the night.

But before anything tragic like that can happen, branches open up to a velvet sky, and pavement turns into the grated deck of the Hood Canal floating bridge. I crack my window, breathing in the cleansing scent of salt water. A beam of moonlight glitters frigidly on the black expanse; the whitecaps are waltzing. The snow-dusted silhouettes of the Olympic Mountains to the west are crowned with stars. It's early February, and the trees on the other side of the bridge sparkle with frost. I take a sip of the coffee I bought back in Tacoma, a gas station brew that's as weak and watered down as I feel.

Two months ago, I was on a research vessel off the coast of San Diego, dipping a hydrophone into the water to listen to humpback whale songs. Then I was in the Scripps Institution of Oceanography lab observing hours' worth of recordings. A week ago, the senior researcher on the project, Dr. Amelia Perez, broke the news that our grant had not been renewed and our study was over. She gave me leads for a few other researchers who might want me on their projects, and while googling them, I went on Facebook and accidentally saw a birthday picture of Dennis, and all my ambitions, my new life in California, my career—everything came to a grinding halt.

It's amazing what a memory can do.

Home—the Olympic Peninsula of Washington, the place I'm charging toward in this obnoxious truck—is the first and last place I want to be. I haven't been home since my life with Dennis ended. That fateful night—my mind foggy with uncertainty, his breath sharp with alcohol—when I left the perfect husband. But distance hasn't helped the hurt; time hasn't healed. No matter how hard I try to escape the ghosts that haunt me, they never really go, and so five days ago, I figured I might as well face them on my own turf.

I've been driving for eighteen hours straight (twenty-two if you count yesterday, before sleeping in that motel past Bakersfield), and my foot is made of lead. I yawn, realizing I have no place to sleep tonight, having made no arrangements. I dial my parents' number. It's nearing one a.m., and when my father answers, his voice is gravelly with sleep.

"Abby, what is it?"

"I'm just past the Hood Canal."

"You're—?" There's some rustling on the other end, the sound of sheets wafting.

I say, "I didn't think to get a hotel."

"You don't need a hotel, Babs. I'll unlock the door."

"I'm sorry."

"It's fine. Is everything all right?" His voice is gentle. I hear his bare feet hitting hardwood, the sink running, and the rising octaves of a glass being filled.

"I'm sorry I didn't tell you sooner. I . . ." Approaching the turn toward home, I tap my brakes and flip my blinker on, even though there's no one behind me. "I wasn't thinking." It's like I've been in a trance since San Diego.

"No explanation needed," Dad says. "It'll be nice to see you."

"I won't wake you."

"I'll wait up. I turned on the porch light."

I'm almost thirty-five, and somehow my parents always bring out my inner seventeen year old. "I've been driving all day; I might sleep in."

"Whatever you need."

"Thanks, Dad."

"We're your parents, Abby. This is what we're here for." I hear sheets again, my mother's voice turning up in question.

"See you soon, Dad."

"Drive safe."

I end the call.

I've been homesick in a ragged, embarrassed sort of way. I finally found the success I always wanted, yet I've been drawn back home like a fish to a luminescent lure. I can't escape its pull. My parents still live in my childhood farmhouse; my best friends, Chrissy and Nick, have settled into marriage; and chilly salt air still wafts up from familiar bluffs, familiar beaches, familiar bays. Evergreens sway over old playgrounds and make-out spots. My favorite ice cream place still churns homemade flavors like vanilla lavender and tangerine chocolate chip. The promise of my parents' hugs and my best friends' laughter—paired with the devastating blow of a lost research stipend—has been the perfect wagging, pulsing temptation out there in the deep, dark, and very vast ocean.

At least, that's what I keep telling myself.

There's also my unresolved feelings for Dennis. And Eli—the other driver in this car crash that is my love life. Successful in photography and the ruin of my marriage. I'm not so certain the pros of coming home outweigh the cons, but it's too late now, because I'm almost there.

The road is snaking more drastically; I've reached Chimacum Valley. The truck doesn't take turns well, and I drive a little under the speed limit. The half moon is still high enough to cast the hayfields and cow barns in silver-blue light. I pass the new fire station, the diner, my old high school. I turn onto West Valley Road; then I'm in my parents' driveway. The clock reads 1:29 a.m. All those miles of pavement are balled up inside me, weighing me down. Whatever lightness I felt when I rented the U-Haul has been replaced with the necessity of sleep. I put the truck in park behind my dad's Chevy and climb out of the cab. My legs are weak, hips stiff, butt numb.

My parents still have a wreath on their door, even though it's well past Christmas. Tiptoeing across the gravel drive, I see my parents' dog, Cooper, in the window. His tail is wagging furiously, and when I turn the doorknob, I crouch down so he doesn't get out. He's a mix of Australian shepherd and Lab, brown with gray and white speckles. I hold him back, burying my fingers into his soft coat, lifting my chin against the barrage of licks and lunges. Coop and I—we always got along. My parents got him around the time Dennis and I were engaged, nine years ago, and Coop—at first too much puppy to be trusted out on the farm with Dad—spent many afternoons with my mother and Chrissy and me looking at bridal magazines.

I stand up and push him back, trying to diminish his excitement. "I know, I know," I whisper. "I missed you too. I'm sorry."

His toenails tap-tap-tap on the floor, making a racket. *"Shhhhh,"* I urge. "You have to be quiet."

My father comes around the corner, rubbing sleep from his eyes. His beer belly is rounder than I last remember. "My Babby," he says and pulls me into a hug.

My mother arrives then, too, collared-pajama clad, hair mussed. "Sweetheart." She joins the embrace, bouncing with sleepy excitement, and my limbs turn to jelly. Their embrace is akin to the little-kid feeling of getting lost in the grocery store and then spotting your mother at the far end of the cereal aisle: relief, thankfulness, and shame over getting lost in the first place.

When we pull apart—too soon, though my mother's hand lingers on my shoulder—I tell them, "You didn't have to wait up."

Dad waves away the comment. I can't think too hard about the years gone by without tears threatening the corners of my eyes.

Mom says, "You must be exhausted."

I nod, however, not wanting to leave their company just yet but also drawn to the promise of bed. "We'll catch up more tomorrow?"

My mother frowns, an uncommon expression on her naturally bubbly face. "I hate this, but I have work in the morning, dear. I won't see you until tomorrow evening."

"I'll be here," I console.

"You better." She kisses my temple. "The guest bed sheets are clean."

"Perfect," I say.

Dad reaches past me to turn off the porch light and lock the dead bolt. He says, "See you in the morning, Babs," and it feels almost as if I never left. Almost.

2000

I met Dennis in high school, but we weren't high school sweethearts. He was a grade ahead of me, and he didn't go to rural Chimacum High but to Port Townsend, the touristy peninsula town about ten miles away. We met at a party my junior year. It was at some house on Hastings Avenue, tucked into the woods in one of those new-new homes that looked cheaper than the old farmhouses and Victorians that most of my friends lived in.

It was a Saturday night in April, and everyone was itching for summer. The music was blaring, and I'd never had that many beers before, so my head was fuzzy, and I was in the kitchen with my very best friends—Chrissy Porter and Nick Harris, both of whom I'd known since kindergarten—pigging out on chips and onion dip. Dennis was in that kitchen, too, but I didn't know it yet. He was getting another Mike's Hard Lemonade for his girlfriend at the time, Amber. Dennis dated her for a long while, but that's a whole other thing that doesn't matter now. The point is, had Dennis and I met in that kitchen, things might have gone very differently.

As the night slowed down and the party thinned out, the kids leftover got restless. Small towns morphed into strange places when teenagers got bored. Some smoked pot, but this wasn't that kind of party. Among the "country kids" in Chimacum, drive-by mailbox smashing was a crueler extracurricular, but most of us just drank Buds in basements. Kids in PT liked to do doughnuts in the shipyard or make out at the ends of dead-end roads. That night, we wanted to go driving. James McCallum claimed he could do a one-eighty in his car, and well, some other guy didn't believe him. Nick, all hopped up on four beers, was curious if James could pull it off, and he was my ride, so I went along.

I ended up crammed in the back of Nick's two-door car with three other kids I didn't know. Chrissy took shotgun. A bag of Doritos sat between her and Nick up front, just behind the gearshift. I tried reaching for it a few times without any luck. I was wedged sideways against a tall skinny guy whose knees were practically level with his chest, and I didn't want to rub up against him any more than I had to.

I couldn't remember if I'd had three beers or four. I stared ahead, the yellow road lines zipping by like stars stretched by hyperdrive. Was Nick swerving? Or was my own dizziness betraying me? The world raced toward us and flew past.

We drove out to a wide dirt road, where James and the other guy were about to take turns speeding ahead and yanking the e-brake, going for that one-eighty. The rest of us hung back, three other cars total. About ten minutes passed without much action. James and his competition were parked side by side, still discussing stretches of road. Nick cranked his window down and yelled out to another car of spectators. The driver was Wesley Baker, and he yelled something back. His girlfriend was in the front seat, still sipping a beer, and her blonde ponytail swung back and forth as she looked between Wes and Nick.

The kid beside me squirmed, and his elbow pressed into my breast. "I gotta get out. My legs are asleep."

I tapped on Chrissy's shoulder, but she wasn't paying attention. Nick and Wes were arguing now—or, really, *posturing*. Wes was a good kid but had started hanging with the crowd that liked to destroy mailboxes.

"Can I get out?" the tall kid beside me whined. I tapped Chrissy again, but she was getting sucked into Wes and Nick's dispute, leaning across the Doritos and yelling out the window.

The tall kid's elbow pressed just above my ribs and against the underwire of my bra. I leaned forward and started fiddling with the lever on the side of Chrissy's seat. Once it shifted, Chrissy—still wrapped up in the argument with the other car—took the hint and opened her door. All of us in the back climbed out, relieved to have some personal space, but on my own two feet, I suddenly felt wobbly and a little sick.

I stared at the ground, at the dark dust and jagged bits of gravel, trying to clear my head. I must've looked ragged, because then Chrissy was at my side. "Abby, are you all right?"

"Sure, yeah," I said, but no matter how hard I tried to will myself sober, I felt frustratingly dizzy.

Chrissy urged me into the passenger seat. "Here, just relax." She patted my leg, and then she was yelling at Wes again: "Oh yeah? He could if he wanted to!"

I stared at my hands, then the Doritos, considering whether I wanted to try to eat. Maybe the chips would soak up the beer? My mouth was dry.

"Okay, fine," Nick was saying. He turned his key, the engine ticking a few times before it turned over. "Close your door, Abs," he said, and I obeyed, still trying to find my head.

We were leaving Chrissy and the tall kid and the others behind, but by the time I realized what was going on, it was too late for me to ask to get out.

Nick and Wes were driving down the road, still hurling insults out their windows.

Coming to my senses a bit, I said, "Nick, what are we doing?"

"Put on your seat belt," he said.

"I don't feel good."

"This ass clown doesn't believe I know how to do a one-eighty."

"Do you?"

"Just put on your seat belt."

I did as I was told. It was just us and that dirt road then, because even James hadn't attempted a one-eighty yet. Up ahead, Wes was turning around so we could race back toward the onlookers and maybe give them a show. In his front seat, Wes's girlfriend nonchalantly sipped her beer like this was just another Saturday night.

Then we were turning around, too, and Nick was revving his engine like some cheesy guy in a movie. I'd never seen him get so worked up before, but alcohol did different things to different people, and we had both had more than we were accustomed to. Even amiable teenage boys were sometimes at the mercy of their hormones and the desire to look cool.

I gripped the side of the door. "You sure this is a good idea, Nick?"

"I know how to skid, Abby," he said.

"I just mean, we've been drinking."

"I had all that food." He turned to me. "Don't worry. I won't let anything bad happen."

And yet worry twisted up in my stomach, tangled and dense like a blackberry vine. Wes had gunned it down the road, a plume of dust blotting out the stars. I closed my eyes, feeling Nick ease on the gas. I'd never thought driving fast was sexy, and in that moment, just the two of us, I hated Nick for thinking this was a viable way to show everyone he was a man, or whatever he was trying to do.

The tires crunched, and the whole body of the car rattled like a bottle cap in a garbage disposal. I forced my eyes open—Nick was pushing forty, which might as well have been a hundred miles an hour on that bumpy dirt road. Then, up ahead, I spotted James's parked Camaro and the wagging tail of Wes's burgundy Prelude.

"Hold on," Nick said, and he jerked the wheel at the same time that he yanked on the e-brake.

There was a moment where nothing happened, and then it was all happening at once. My head knocked against the passenger window, hard. Then the car was spinning, dust flying, gravel grinding in my ears. I heard a shriek through Nick's open window, then saw James's Camaro again, then brush, the reaching arms of ferns, and the solid trunk of a tree. The abrupt crunch of metal rattled the car. My seat belt whaled on my neck, and my head whipped against the window again.

I couldn't see anything, only hear, through ringing ears, the muffled sounds of Nick panting, kids' voices, the rustling of bushes, and the cracking of twigs underfoot. My door opened, and a rush of cold night air snatched at my bare shoulders. Then I heard Wes—yes—he volunteered his pocketknife to saw at my seat belt. My world tilted sideways, and I felt hands on me, many hands. I was floating. Then nothing at all.

Then—was I in bed? I wished for bed, the soft cradle of a pillow, but . . . no. I was on my back on the hard ground. Gravel stabbed into the back of my head. I opened my eyes, and a face was staring down.

"Give her some space," someone said, but he ignored them. His hand was on my arm, his square jaw clenched. There was a dusting of acne scars on his cheeks, and his blue eyes searched mine.

"Are you all right?" he asked.

I heard Nick saying, "Oh God, oh *God*."

Then Chrissy's voice chimed in. "Abby, Abby?" She knelt on the other side of me. "Can you talk?"

"I—" My head felt as if it had been stepped on by an elephant. I couldn't think of what to say.

"Can you sit up?" the guy beside me asked.

I moved my arm, then my neck. My head throbbed. As soon as I made it partway up, I felt a rush of bile in the back of my throat. I turned, vomited. The guy had to jump back so it didn't get on his shoes.

"Give her some room," someone repeated.

Then Nick again: "Oh my God, *fuck*."

I propped myself up on an elbow and heaved again, and I felt surprisingly better.

"We called 911," Chrissy told me. "And your parents."

"I'm sorry, Abs," Wes said.

The guy with the blue eyes was rubbing my arm now, not so dissuaded by the mess. "Do you want to lie back down?"

I shook my head. I didn't want to move.

He kept rubbing my arm, and for those minutes while we waited for the ambulance, he became my anchor. His hand didn't waver, not even when the sirens finally arrived, not even when the paramedics stepped in. Finally, they asked him to move back, and only then did his hand let go.

2018

In the late morning, I awaken to a quiet house. My limbs are heavy and dull, as if filled with wet sand. After a quick trip to the U-Haul for clean clothes and a toothbrush, I conclude that no one is home, so I take an extra-long shower. The previous night feels like a vivid dream, driving in the dark down those familiar roads. I was only gone long enough for the guilt of leaving Dennis to get fuzzy around the edges—now that I'm home again, it comes zooming back into focus.

I close my eyes under the hot stream of water, trying not to think about the only thing I've been able to think about for the past four and a half years.

I'm fresh and dressed and waiting on the couch when, at noon, I hear my dad's truck putter into the driveway. Coop bursts through the front door, tail wagging. I stand and wander toward the kitchen, scratching the dog's head, grateful to be relieved of my own spiraling thoughts.

"Morning," Dad says, tossing a pair of dirty gloves on the floor beside his boots. "Hungry?"

"Starved."

Washing his hands, he asks, "Turkey sandwich okay?"

"With—"

"Extra dijon. I know." He glances over his shoulder with a grin.

I take two plates down from the cupboard, then slide onto a barstool at the kitchen island. Dad opens the fridge, then the pantry.

"Out working?" I ask.

He untwists a bag of bread. "Tractor maintenance."

My parents' living has always been a hodgepodge: Dad with the tractor repair, tending the hayfields, the twenty beef cattle; Mom teaching horseback riding lessons and, later, doing part-time hours in the grocery store floral department. It always amazed me, their ability to work day in and day out. A farm is not like a nine-to-five, where you go home at the end of the day; it's all day, every day, not even weekends to sleep in. There's an efficient and steady rhythm to it, and whenever I come home, I fall into that rhythm as easily as a leaf falls into a river. "Any way I can help?"

"Did you learn about tractors while you were gone?" He cracks another smile, calloused hands carefully laying thin slices of turkey on the bread. "You can help me with a fence, if you'd like."

Most dads bond with their daughters at things like father-daughter dances; my dad and I always bonded over fence repairs. "I'm game."

The big bay windows in the conjoined living room reveal the whole spread of the valley. Propped up on the western ridge facing east, my parents' house overlooks all forty-five acres of their property. Far in the distance, the back field is lined with the thin thread of a barbed wire fence. Chickweed has tangled up the posts, and the pasture out there is edged with emerald bull grass. Above the opposite ridge, small white clouds speckle the sky.

Dad bangs a mustard bottle on the counter, startling me out of my stare. "By the U-Haul, I'm guessing you're not just visiting."

Recalling the circumstance of my arrival, I shift on my stool. "Sorry. I just—"

"Couldn't stay away." He knows me too well—and he was never one to judge. "Do you have a job lined up?"

A wad of achy apprehension forms in my stomach. I don't know how to answer—I don't have any prospects. I should have thought ahead; I should have reminded myself that I've tried this before and that there aren't any marine biology jobs for me in town. I should have continued the career I started in California, the career I *want*—but here I am, once again pushing aside my career goals because of Dennis.

Dad doesn't press. "Your mother can ask around." He slides a plate in front of me.

"I'll find something," I say, picking up my sandwich. It tastes like childhood summers. A lump of regret forms in my throat, and it takes some effort to swallow it down with the turkey.

"Did you find what you were looking for in California?" It's Dad's kind way of asking, *How* are *you, Abby?*

I take another bite, hoping the bread can soak up the next wave of emotion. I chew, swallow, but Dad's still across from me, looking at me like he can read my mind. "I don't know what I'm looking for anymore," I say. Then my eyes are filling fast, and my chest aches, and my face is hot, and hot tears spill over.

If Mom were standing across from me, she'd rush in for a hug and say, *Oh, Abby, it's all right, it's all right*, and it would make me cry even harder. But thank goodness Dad's here instead, because he simply hands me a napkin to dab at my wet nose.

"You'll need gloves," he says, back to practicality. "And can you dirty up those jeans?"

"I'll have to change," I say, regaining some composure. "Does Mom have a pair I can borrow?"

"Her Carhartts," he says. "Finish your sandwich; I'll get clean ones."

He leaves me alone in the kitchen, and I'm tempted to cry again. *You can't run from the hurt, Abby,* my father said when I decided to move away. *I'm not running. I'm starting over,* I replied, and at the time, it was the truth. But here Dad is, years later, right as rain, yet kind enough not to say *I told you so*.

~

"Shit," Dad says, rifling through his toolbox. "I forgot the fence pliers."

We're far out in the field, replacing a stretch of barbed wire and a rotted-out fence post. Fast-moving clouds slide above us, the sun shining through in slow blinks; I can see my breath.

"I'll get them." I move the post-hole digger that's leaning against the tailgate of Dad's truck.

"You'd never find them," Dad says. "Just roll up the old stretch of wire. I'll be right back." The truck dings when he opens the door, and then he's driving back toward the barn, which looks like a Breyer toy in the distance. Even Coop is a ways off, deep in a thicket of chickweed, sniffing something out. His tail is stiff and curled up, and when the truck engine fades, I can hear his snorts and sneezes.

I turn back toward our project, the toolbox open, the hammer and crowbar lying in the grass. Slipping on Dad's welding gloves, I roll up the rusty stretch of barbed wire, the end of it wagging dangerously as I wrestle it into a neat spool.

Alone with myself, I consider my job prospects. I forgot how stifling this town could be, how long I struggled to launch my career without any results. It was only when I left that I found a job that was worthwhile. No work excited me as much as the research study in California. Our focus was recording humpback whale communication during their breeding season. Big males would bellow into the blue, their low-frequency rumbles like smooth jazz to the fertile females. I studied hundreds of whale songs, identifying patterns for the lead researcher, Dr. Perez. She was focused on understanding baleen whale communication, postulating their intelligence.

The study was the most meaningful, soul-lifting, passionate work I'd ever done. But the lure of home was strong—not just because of Dennis, or my family and friends, but because of the environment. No matter how lovely and warm the waters are in California, the Pacific

Northwest is the true marine gem. It has some of the richest waters on the planet, murky with life-sustaining green. Humpbacks aren't the only whales that thrive here, nor are they the only whales that hold a place in my heart. Washington is also home to the most studied and endangered population of orcas in the world. Back in the seventies, wild orcas were torn from their families and shipped to aquariums like SeaWorld. Due to these cruel acts, along with oil tankers, pipelines, pollution, river dams, and farmed salmon, there are only seventy-five southern resident killer whales remaining. And like the humpbacks, they are likely more intelligent than we humans know.

I pause in my fence-rolling task. Dad is driving back out, the truck bouncing through the rough field. The sun dips behind clouds again, the day dimming.

There's a research group in this area that studies the southern resident orcas: the Center for Salish Orca Research. It's perhaps the only opportunity I have to continue my career while I'm here on the Olympic Peninsula. There's a chance I can sign on to a southern resident study—but what if I can't? I'm a baleen whale expert, after all—I know humpbacks, gray whales, minkes. Toothed whales—including the dolphin family, of which orcas are the largest member—aren't my specialty, at least on paper.

With a wrench in my gut, I realize what I've done: I walked away from the start of a new life, a new career, at the first sign of a roadblock. Dr. Perez sent those leads, but then I happened upon that picture of Dennis online, forgot all about the whales, and came home anyway. How could I let my regret cloud my focus once again? Maybe my excuses aren't as justified as I thought. Maybe I'm just a fool, plain and simple.

I finish rolling the wire into a semineat spool. Dad parks the truck and gets out, waving the fence pliers. At least this work is steady; at least this part of my life makes sense.

2000

I walked away from the crash in Nick's car with a fat bump on my head, some whiplash, and a terrible headache, but not much else. My parents and I left the ER just after sunrise, the spring sky as sweet as sorbet. I was grounded, of course, but all three of us knew that was a formality—my parents were just relieved that I was all right, and I had already been scared shitless enough to vow never to get into a drunk boy's car again.

On Monday, I found out that Nick had sprained his wrist. He'd been so caught up in worrying about me that he hadn't gone to the hospital until the day after the accident; he'd woken up with numb fingers and purple-and-black bruising halfway up his arm. At school, he wore a short brace and used it as an excuse not to take notes in class.

"How's your car?" I asked him. We were standing by my locker, and Chrissy had her arm looped through mine.

"Totaled," Nick said. "My mom's pretty pissed, but I think that's because she'll miss sending me for groceries. The good news: they're thinking about buying me a new car, if I pay for half. And here I thought I was saving up for another beater."

"So *that's* why you crashed," I said.

His face contorted into a mix of horror and guilt, his eyebrows pinched and his mouth twisted up. "Wha—?"

"I'm kidding," I said.

"Jeez, Abs, I feel bad enough as it is," he said, lifting his good arm and giving me a quick hug.

Chrissy huffed. "You should."

"I *do*."

I wanted to ask them who that guy had been, the one who'd been there with me on the ground before the paramedics had arrived, the one with blue eyes. The one who'd stayed even after I'd barfed on his shoes. I'd been thinking about him since the crash, a tickle in my belly every time I pictured his face.

"Abby." The three of us turned around to face Wes. His macho persona had disappeared, and he looked as he had in junior high, no more ripped jeans or patchy chin stubble. I liked him better that way. He looked a tad sheepish now, though, shoulders hunched. "I'm glad you're okay."

"Thanks," I said.

"I worried all Sunday." He glanced down the hall, his eyes going distant. Then he shifted on his feet and met my eyes again. "It's my fault. I shouldn't have taunted Nick."

"You're both idiots," Chrissy said.

I smiled at Wes. "It's okay. I'm all right."

"No hard feelings here," Nick added.

Wes nodded and did a little hop, sliding his backpack strap higher onto one shoulder. "Well, I'm really, really glad you're okay." He walked away, down the hall toward the library.

"That was . . . nice," Chrissy said, but there was a bite in her tone.

I shrugged. I wasn't really mad at anyone—except maybe Nick, who seemed to have enough remorse on his own. But any anger that remained wouldn't last—Nick was one of my best friends, and it seemed pointless to stew on it when I could just accept his apology and let us get back to our lives. "You guys going to the job fair tonight?"

Nick and Chrissy both groaned and nodded. "Against my will," Chrissy added.

"It could be cool," I said. It was the one outing exempt from my grounding.

"No, it couldn't," she said.

"Well, I'm going to be there," I offered. As a junior, I'd been thinking more and more about the future. Unlike most of my classmates, I was good at science and math especially, but I had no idea what to do with those skills beyond high school.

It turned out that a lot of kids were there, and a lot of adults too. My parents let me take their CR-V, and I picked up Chrissy, Nick, and Nick's younger sister, Julie. We arrived after everything was in full swing, row after row of booths set up in the gym. Employers and colleges had big banners that smelled like vinyl, and people were milling around with little plastic cups. We found the snack table in the corner, and Nick tested out the cheese cubes, spearing about four onto a single toothpick. Chrissy was still grumbling about coming, so I left her and Nick with the food and took Julie into the maze of tables.

"Anything catch your eye, Jules?" I asked her, and it wasn't long before she had wandered off toward a computer-coding table, the banner adorned with confusing caret marks and lowercase letters.

I kept going down the aisle, my eyes scanning the big signs and brochures and plastic tablecloths and bowls of candy. It wasn't until I reached the end of the row that something piqued my interest. Along with brochures and business cards, the table also held a small tank of water, plus a microscope and a stack of slides. A strange, giddy feeling swept through me, making my heart pitter-patter. The blue-and-white banner had a giant octopus on it, and the letters read, **SALISH SCIENCE CENTER.**

Behind the table, a twentysomething woman wore a sweatshirt with the same octopus logo. She was rummaging around in a box underneath the table, and I considered walking right past, but my interest outweighed my shyness, so I stopped and pretended to look at the brochures.

When the woman noticed me, she stood and asked, "Do you want to try the microscope?" She had curly hair like mine, a shoulder-length tangle held back by a big clip. Maybe I saw myself in her, my future self, in that navy-blue sweatshirt with a magnificent coiled octopus on it, holding a magnifying glass in one of its tentacles. Maybe the accident had startled me into extroversion.

"Sure," I said.

She reached across the table and adjusted the microscope, setting a slide under the trio of lenses. She flipped on the light and adjusted the lever again. "Seawater," she said as I bent forward. "If it's out of focus, you can use this lever."

I felt for it and twisted, and the white light in my vision sharpened, shapes coming into focus. I saw a round green blob, unmoving; a stationary green rectangle; some squiggles.

"You're probably seeing cyanobacteria, those coiled filaments," the woman said. "Diatoms are the boxy algae."

I nodded, my eyes glued to the eyepiece.

"If you're lucky, you'll find a copepod. It'll look like a tiny shrimp. They swim fast." The slide moved, and I realized she was adjusting the microscope again.

My stomach somersaulted with excited fascination. "This . . . this is just one drop of seawater?"

"Yep. Pretty incredible, right?"

"Yeah," I managed despite my awe. I'd never seen the world like this, the *life*, right at my fingertips. I imagined the entire sea this crowded—not the vast blue you saw from a beach but this alphabet soup of organisms. If one slide was so full of life, I couldn't fathom how full the ocean was. My hands rested on the table, and I peered into that tiny world, my breath caught in my throat.

A scuttling flash of movement passed through the upper right corner of the slide. "Whoa," I breathed.

"Copepod?"

"I—I'm not sure."

"Here." She guided my hand to the lever that could adjust the position of the slide. "You can try to follow it."

I swung my little window to the right, searching desperately for the thing, but it was gone. Then—"I see it!" I exclaimed. My hands quivered with delight. I adjusted the lever, trying to follow it further, but the bug slipped out of view once again. I kept looking, my eyes starting to strain.

The microscope went dark, and I realized the woman had turned off the light. I pulled away, afraid I had done something wrong, but when I looked up, she was smiling. "Better to end on a high note."

"Oh," I said, feeling a little rejected.

"We have volunteer programs and internships."

I remembered where I was—the school gym, surrounded by people selling their professions—and felt suddenly silly.

"Do you have an interest in marine science?"

"I never thought about it," I said.

"Well, think about it." She handed me a flyer. "You'd get to spend a lot more time with the microscope."

I looked at the flyer in my hands, then back up at her. "How do I sign up?"

She walked me through their brochure and was handing me an internship application when Chrissy walked up. "Abby, *there* you are!"

"Here I am."

"Where's Jules?"

I pointed at the coding booth, but she was no longer there. After a brief panic, I spotted her a few tables down, talking to a guy wearing a Washington State University T-shirt, their big cougar mascot spread across the sign behind him.

"Oh *hell* no, we're Huskies," Chrissy said, storming over.

I turned back to the marine science lady, but she was chatting with another student, so I stuffed the brochure in my pocket and hurried after my friend.

Chrissy was dragging Julie away, but she was still clutching their flyers.

"You don't want to be a Coug," Chrissy insisted.

Nick came over, awkwardly pinching two punch cups with his good hand. "Hey, our parents were Cougars," he said, offering Julie a cup. She grinned at her big brother, then stuck her tongue out at Chrissy.

But Chrissy had already moved on: her eyes were laser focused on a guy halfway down the gym. "Heeey, Abs, look—if it isn't your knight in shining armor." She nudged me with her elbow.

With a nervous rush, the memory came: his concerned mouth, his hand brushing my arm, those oceanic eyes staring into mine. Now, he stood at a table for some sort of trade; I couldn't tell what. He wore an old T-shirt that stretched over his chest. He had a bit of a belly, but he also had strong-looking arms.

"Who is he?" I asked.

"You don't know him? That's Dennis Nelson." I must've had a blank look, because she elaborated: "My brother is dating his sister."

"Oh."

"Aren't you going to go say hi?"

My mouth went dry, and I turned to her. "Why?"

"He *rescued* you."

"Then I've given him enough trouble."

Nick and Jules had already gravitated back toward the WSU table. I started walking in the opposite direction, pretending to peruse a display on nursing. But Chrissy didn't fall in step with me. In fact, when I glanced back, I saw that she had done the opposite: she was heading straight toward Dennis. I spun on my heel, rushing after her. When I came up alongside the two of them, I felt my cheeks flush.

Chrissy was saying, "Well, ask her yourself."

Dennis regarded me with those blue, blue eyes. "How are you? Abby, right?"

I nodded. "I'm fine, just fine."

"Got some bad color."

I looked down at my shirt, afraid there was a stain.

"I meant on your head. You must've hit it hard." He tapped his temple.

"I'm sorry I threw up on your shoes," I blurted. Chrissy's hand clamped on my forearm, her nails digging in—her special way of telling me, *You're being a dork.*

But Dennis smiled, his teeth straight and white. Unlike most guys at school, it appeared as though he actually needed to shave: his jawline was textured with blond stubble. He looked like a man. "I won't hold it against you."

"Thanks."

As if remembering something, he said, "Oh," and retrieved a wrinkled envelope from his back pocket. "For you."

Stupefied, I took it. The envelope's face was blank. Chrissy's grip on my arm tightened.

He added, "I'm glad you're okay."

Out of nowhere, a girl slid up to Dennis, arm locking around his waist. She had straight, highlighted hair and pretty brown eyes, and the half moons of her breasts rose out of her low-cut top. Chrissy's nails dug deeper, and I squirmed free.

"Abby, this is Amber, my girlfriend," Dennis said.

"Hey." My stomach pitched.

Settled under his arm, Amber looked up at Dennis. "Is this the Abby from the accident?"

"In the flesh," I said, too loud.

"Dennis told me about the whole thing," Amber said, facing me now. "How scary. But I bet he was gallant."

"Yeah."

The corners of Dennis's lips turned downward. "Finding any potential dream jobs?"

"I guess." Maybe I shouldn't have agreed with Amber about his heroics. The conversation faltered. "You?"

Dennis shrugged, and Amber cut in, "He wants to go into his dad's construction business."

"That's cool," I said.

"Yeah, but Mom has other plans. That's why I'm here," Dennis said. "She told me I can't come home until I have at least five flyers in hand."

"Ugh, same," Chrissy said.

"I think it's fun," Amber said.

I didn't want to like her, but I did. "Me too."

"All the opportunities at our fingertips. I can't wait for graduation." Her shoulders rose and fell while she talked, her propped-up breasts wobbling. "Are you graduating this year?"

Caught up in looking at her, wondering how long she'd been with Dennis and whether or not he'd gotten inside that push-up bra, I didn't register her question.

"Next year," Chrissy cut in, thankfully.

"Tough luck," Amber said.

Embarrassment pricked my cheeks, and I feared I was turning red. I hadn't felt young around seniors before, but seeing Dennis and Amber together looking so adult made me feel like I was ten years old.

The conversation didn't last long after that, and I didn't listen to the small talk, only the moment Dennis said, "Well, see you around," and those eyes on me, the brief, possibly imagined linger before he and Amber walked away.

When they were out of earshot, Chrissy turned to me. "You *love* him!"

"I don't love him." I looked around for Nick and Jules, thinking we ought to leave soon too. I gripped the envelope Dennis had given me, my fingers slippery with sweat.

"You *do* love him," Chrissy said. "You couldn't take your eyes off him. And he *rescued* you—it's so romantic."

Sometimes I had to laugh at Chrissy's enthusiasm.

"What's it say?"

I stared down at the envelope in my hands, then slid a finger under the barely stuck point of the fold. He'd licked the adhesive strip—for *me*.

"Hurry it up," Chrissy said, snatching the envelope. She slid the card out, and I peered over her shoulder to see the crooked handwriting. It said, *Abby, I was worried so I bought you this card. I hope you heal up fast. Love, Dennis.*

I took the card from Chrissy and looked at the picture on the front. It was a painting of a field, with little impressionistic-looking cows in the distance.

"He wrote, '*Love*, Dennis,'" Chrissy said. *"Loooove."*

My palms grew clammy again. "Didn't you notice the girl hanging on his arm?"

"What, Little Miss I-Stuff-My-Bra? That won't last."

"Christina," I said, and she giggled. "What's in that punch?"

"Nothing," she said and laughed again.

2018

Coop is the first one to sense that Mom is home from the flower department and whines at the front door. Dad and I are in the kitchen making dinner. My mother comes in, and for a good minute there's this flurry of commotion: the dog wagging and jumping, Mom with her purse and keys and unzipped coat, and her shriek of delight when she sees me. Dumping her excess things on the floor, she wraps me up in a long hug, her kisses loud next to my ear.

"I just saw you last night," I say, laughing.

"Not the same. I'm *awake* now," she says, pulling back to look at me. "Your father had you working, didn't he?"

"She offered," he says from beside the stove. An eruption of sizzles overtakes my mother's "humph."

"How did you know?" I ask.

"There's hay in your hair, dear," she says.

After the fence, Dad and I moved a few bales down from the loft and fed the horses. I pass a hand over my hair, feeling for the hay, but Mom plucks it out and gives me an *it's been too long* smile.

"So you're moving back," she says, coming farther into the house. "Didn't like the biologist life after all?"

The truth is, I loved it. The many days waking up early with eagerness and purpose; the time spent on a bobbing vessel, the sun beating down; that unmistakable puff of breath, the sea parting open for a graceful, hulking body; and the hydrophone relaying the humpbacks' songs, my elation humming through my veins. Even the tedious work on the computer—listening to hours of recordings and writing down observations—was bliss.

It was the guilt that ate me up and spat me out.

How could I feel happy and fulfilled after what I'd done to Dennis? How could I move on with my life when I'd ruined the lives of others? In California, when things got quiet and I sat alone with myself, all those ugly, clawing, prickly feelings snaked their way up from the place I'd buried them. I was getting tired of slashing them back all by myself.

To answer my mother, I shrug, feeling suddenly drained.

"Will you pick up your research again?"

"I don't know, Mom." Unlike Dad, who doesn't push for answers, my mother has a way of putting her finger right on the bruise with just a question.

"Will you need to find a place?" she continues. "You're welcome to stay here, of course, but I know you'll want your own space eventually—right?"

"I really just want dinner right now, Mom."

Something occurs to her, and she gasps. "I saw Gwen Holland today at the store. She has a cottage she's renovating to rent out—it's almost done. Should I call her?"

"I haven't thought that far, Mom."

"It's a good opportunity, dear. Perfect timing."

"Then call her," I say, going to the cutting board again. I slice some vegetables, my lungs tightening. Housing, rent, work—it's a smack of reality. After I've basked in the simplicity of fences all afternoon, Mom's questions are too much.

"I'm pressuring you," my mother realizes. "I'm sorry, sweetheart; I know it's been hard. Home is supposed to nurture." She comes over and kisses my forehead. "How about I open some wine?"

"Now you're talking," I say.

As the evening slips by with wine and family gossip and stir-fry, I wonder if coming back was a mistake. Running away from home to live in isolation from my family wasn't ideal, but is tormenting myself with the past any better? We talk and laugh about stupid things, and Dad goes out for slices of pie from the Chimacum Diner, and I keep dreading the inevitable day when I'll drive past Dennis on Discovery Road or bump into Eli at the DMV. That's the thing about a small hometown: You can't escape your old self. Everyone is in everyone else's business, and errands are a social event.

"Have you talked to Chrissy?" Mom asks.

We're both barefoot now, curled up on the couch and facing each other with our backs to the armrests. Coop is asleep in his bed, breathing through loose lips, a soft smacking sound filling the silence between my mother and me.

"I wanted to surprise her in person," I say.

We stayed in touch while I was away, of course. Chrissy married Nick—surprise, surprise—and now she works at the hospital as an oncology nurse. She thought my moving to California was a brave thing: "escaping the town," as she put it. But it wasn't brave at all. No matter where I go, I feel like a coward.

"She'll be so glad to see you," my mother says. She's cupping her wineglass like a mug, the edges of it all smudged up. Her hair is cut short, and she's finally embraced the gray. Perfect smile lines deepen as she looks at me. "I'm glad you came home, Abby. Your father and I—we were worried about you. Most people—" She pauses. Dad has returned from his pie trip, headlights illuminating the kitchen curtains. Coop lifts his head, his tail flopping against his fleece bed. "Most people look to their family and friends for comfort during hard times." She stands up, welcoming my father home. They kiss, lingering in each other's arms before unwrapping the bag and opening the Styrofoam containers of banana-cream and apple pie.

Is it strange that I left? I wonder. Don't we all handle hardship differently? Or am I an anomaly? All those nights talking to Chrissy over the phone—the tears, the heartache—did she feel the same way? Did she wonder what was wrong with me that I'd want to gain some distance? *No,* I think. She would have told me if she'd thought I was handling things poorly. She knew I was building my career; she knew that I needed the distraction.

I stand, and Coop follows me into the kitchen. Dad hands me a fork and a container with a *B* on top. After grabbing extra napkins, the three of us settle back into the living room. The valley stretches out beyond the windows in the darkness, and the partial moon reveals pale tendrils of fog forming; I know by morning they'll be as opaque and ineffable as my thoughts.

Inside the container is a pile of white cream, pale goo beneath, a ruffle of crust on one side. I take a bite, and my eyelids fall closed as I revel in the sweet, lumpy marvelousness that is banana-cream pie. The comforting flavor is as soft and welcoming as a pillow. I realize I'm smiling.

"Good?" Dad asks.

He's seen my face, so he already knows my answer. "Good," I say, but I know it's a temporary pleasure.

2001

I worked at the Salish Science Center my senior year and the summer after I graduated high school. I went from cleaning touch tanks to working the cash register at the gift shop to leading tours of the museum. Then I was accepted at the University of Alaska to study marine biology; I would leave for Juneau in the fall. Life was moving at lightning speed, but I felt ready. My parents were proud. Chrissy was already promising care packages with cookies, and her eccentric mother was going to knit me a new hat.

One day that summer, I visited Chrissy at work. She waitressed at an Italian restaurant while attending summer classes at the community college. She'd wanted to be a nurse since she was little, and while I hated that she was so busy that summer—the summer before I left for college—she was driven and in her bliss. Her adult life was within reach. All of us—myself, Chrissy, Nick—we had that postgraduation itch. We were all so sure of our plans.

I sat at a small table near the kitchen with Nick. He and Chrissy had just started dating, but it had been a long time coming. They'd been flirting for over a year, so when it finally happened, right after winter break, I was actually relieved.

"So you haven't heard from Kevin?" Nick asked, sipping his Coke.

I shook my head. "Thank goodness." Kevin Granger was that tall guy from the back of Nick's car the year before. After I'd watched Dennis graduate—and witnessed the big smoochy kisses he'd given Amber after the ceremony, the two of them cap-and-gown clad—I'd decided to abandon my crush. Kevin was kind and brainy. I'd lost my virginity to him, but afterward, he'd gotten clingy. Sometime around my own graduation, I'd realized that we had nothing in common, and—though I wouldn't have admitted it at the time—I still occasionally thought about Dennis. I kept his card in my underwear drawer and sometimes would push back the cotton and lace and stare at the way he wrote *Love, Dennis*. Just picturing his face made my cheeks burn. I didn't see how things could work with Kevin once I went away to college, so I broke things off.

"It makes sense," Nick said. "You wouldn't want to do long distance."

"What's this about long distance?" Chrissy asked, sidling up to our table. She wore black slacks, and the heart-shaped locket that Nick had given her was centered over her V-neck. "Something you want to tell me?"

Nick pinched her leg. "I'm not going anywhere."

I rolled my eyes. "We were talking about Kevin."

Chrissy cocked a hip. "I saw him in here the other day."

"You did?"

"He asked about you," she said. "I told him you were fine."

"How'd he seem?" I asked.

"Mopey," Chrissy said. "Do you guys know what you want?"

I ordered a personal-size pepperoni pizza, and Nick got the Alfredo. It was 4:30 p.m., right between the lunch and dinner rushes, and the place was dead. Chrissy brought our food out in no time, and after setting down the plates, she lingered at the table.

"I get off at five," she said.

"Yeah, you do." Nick winked.

Chrissy and I both groaned.

"Anyway"—she glared at Nick—"Mom gave me a Pete's Sweets gift card for my birthday. Ice cream on me."

"You're the best," I said, picking up a slice of pizza.

"I know." Chrissy grinned, spun, and shuffled back into the kitchen.

Nick and I ate in relative silence for a while, aside from brief intermissions when Chrissy came to fill up our waters or relight our candle or some other excuse to chitchat. So when Dennis walked in with his girlfriend, Chrissy was close enough to shoot me a look. I hadn't seen Dennis since he'd graduated a year before, and Chrissy had lost track of him after their siblings had broken up, but she always referred to him as my "one who got away," much to my outward displeasure—but maybe, secretly, I agreed with her.

As if her exaggerated glance weren't enough, Chrissy passed by and said, "Look who . . . ," drawing out the *o*'s in a singsong tone.

"Shush," I said. "He's here with his *girlfriend*." The hostess had seated them in a booth across the room, right behind Nick; I could see them plainly.

Nick glanced over his shoulder, shook his head, and went back to his Alfredo. "Give it up, Chrissy. She's leaving soon."

She shrugged. "Say the word, and I'll spill this pitcher of water on her lap."

"Chrissy," I hissed.

"Kidding," she said.

I watched her approach Dennis's table, pour them water, and take their drink orders. His girlfriend, Amber, wore an orange sundress and high wedges that showed off her tan legs—they glowed bronze even under the table. I thought of my own pale legs, jean shorts, unflattering T-shirt. My breasts weren't small, but they weren't shapely either—why hadn't I worn my good bra today?

I nibbled on my pizza, unable to quit looking past Nick's head to watch Dennis and Amber's date unfold. She gestured and he laughed;

he spoke and she nodded; they brushed hands; they shared an appetizer. They seemed happy. I told myself not to care—I didn't even *know* Dennis, not really—but it got under my skin. Not even Kevin was around to keep me company anymore.

After we paid, Chrissy came out of the back with her jacket and purse, and we left before Dennis and Amber saw us.

"Don't you want to say hi?" Chrissy prodded.

"No," I said.

Nick led the way outside. The sun was still bright, but in the shade, the air was cool. "Leave her alone, Chrissy. She's going to be in Alaska by the end of the summer."

"Right!" Chrissy said, as if just realizing. "You'll get to date college guys."

I laughed. "Yeah, college guys."

We walked over to Pete's, ordered cones, and settled into a booth. Chrissy told us about her classes; Nick expressed his interest in attending community college for graphic design. I retold them about seeing orcas last week on a boating afternoon with the Salish Science Center, rattling off facts and remembering new details.

After our cones, we wandered down the dock near Pope Marine Park, enjoying the last bit of warmth. A few seabirds loitered on the neighboring dock, but the sun was too bright for me to identify their silhouette bodies. Beyond the Coupeville ferry and the paper mill steam and the curve of our town, the Olympic Mountains rose in chiseled blue. The pale sky was the color of custard, and long clouds slid high, high over our heads.

Chrissy and Nick held hands, and I had my arm looped through Chrissy's, and for a moment I was reminded of when we were children. Making mud pies in Nick's backyard, sharing a single pair of Rollerblades with Chrissy, watching cartoons after sleepovers. When we were twelve, we took turns driving my dad's truck during hay season, the seat scooched all the way forward to accommodate our short legs. We rode my horse, Cinnamon, bareback and climbed the freshly stacked hay until we had red rashes on our forearms.

I smiled to myself, listening to Chrissy and Nick bicker over which movie we'd watch back at Nick's house later. On that June evening, walking side by side, I felt a deep cord connecting the three of us, tethering us together. No matter how far any of us strayed, that cord was our lifeline.

"I love you guys," I said.

"Mushy alert," Chrissy replied, but she squeezed my arm.

"I'm going to miss you."

"You won't," Chrissy said. "I'll call every day until you're sick of me."

"Like you don't do that already?" Nick quipped, and Chrissy shoved him with her shoulder.

As we rounded the bend back onto the main street, we spotted Dennis and Amber exiting the Italian place and heading our way.

"*Shit*," I breathed, knowing what Chrissy would do next.

She waved and called out, "Hey!"

Dennis waved back, but Amber looked confused. They came over, meeting us in front of the ice cream shop. My shoulders rocked forward; I felt ragged in my casual clothes compared to Amber. She had this tan, svelte body, and it was clear she wasn't wearing a bra under her halter dress.

"Abby," Dennis said when we were close enough.

Chrissy bumped me forward.

"Hey," I said. "How's it going?"

"Good," he said.

I nodded at Amber. I couldn't think of anything to say but, "I like your dress."

She smiled, as if everyone liked her dress. "Thank you."

Dennis's eyes were still on me, cutting through me. I squirmed, not wanting him to look at me when I felt so disheveled.

"Congrats on graduating." He appeared very much the same: broad shoulders, solid looking, like he could lift a whole mountain if he wanted.

"Thanks," I said.

Amber looked just a little impatient. Her manicured fingers slid around Dennis's bicep, and she smiled up at him. "Ice cream?"

"Yeah," he told her. Looking back at me, his mouth quirked apologetically. "Nice to see you—all of you." His eyes darted to Chrissy and Nick before landing on me again. "Take care."

I nodded and watched him go. The bell of the ice cream shop jingled as he disappeared inside. I stood there on the sidewalk dumbly, staring through the window, watching them draw a number, step up to the counter, point at flavors. Dennis was like one of the orcas I'd seen—even when he came near, he was still so out of reach. The sight of him was thrilling. Each time he ducked away, I lingered, wondering when I'd see him next.

"What does he see in her?" Chrissy broke through my thoughts.

"Huh?"

Nick said, "It's the boobs."

She shot him a dark look.

"What? You saw them. They're always so *out there*."

"Thin ice," Chrissy hissed.

"Yours are better," Nick said, as if that would erase the mistake.

Chrissy eased a bit. "He barely looked at us, Abby. He was *staring* at you."

"He wasn't," I said, but my pulse jittered. "I don't know why you're so focused on him. I don't know him. We've literally met three times."

"It's the way he looks at you," Chrissy said. "There's something there. I can feel it."

"Whatever," I said, but I felt it too. Like a current, I was swept up by him. The whole world melted away when I looked into his eyes. "Let's go," I said. "Did you guys decide on a movie?"

2018

At dawn on Monday, I wake to the sounds of my parents' early-morning routine: the rattle of Cooper's kibble in the bowl, the coffeepot gurgling, the shower running. My room is still dark, and I can tell the day will be overcast; everything—the dresser, the sheets, the carpeting—is shaded by gray. I hear the cattle mooing, their voices dull through the fog. The front door slams. I imagine my father wearing his big winter coat, throwing hay and opening gates, his breath billowing up toward the barn's lone light. A rooster's call pierces the stillness, shrill and echoing. Mom's car engine rumbles to life.

I roll out of bed, slip into a robe, and pad down the hall. There's one cup's worth left in the coffeepot, and I pour it into a mug and wander into the living room with those big single-panel bay windows. The poplar trees that line one fence are cast in silvery light, their bare branches shimmering. I settle into the La-Z-Boy, throw a blanket over my legs, and sip my coffee and watch the day begin. Fog slides over the fields, heavy now, obscuring the grass, but I can see the dark shadows of cattle interrupting the cloud bank.

How am I supposed to go on with my life without work, Dennis, or even a place of my own? Perhaps a job is a good idea after all—but in this town, the options are slim, and I can't bear the thought of settling for retail or customer service. Never again. The Center for Salish Orca Research is my only chance to continue the career I started.

Cooper finds me before my thoughts spiral any further. He's already exuberant from an early breakfast and trip outside, and he nudges my foot with his nose, asking for pets. I reach down and run my fingertips between his eyes and over his head. When I pause to sip my coffee, he stares up at me with a face of innocence and wisdom all wrapped into one. He lifts me out of my contemplative mood like a buoy.

"I have to take a trip to Cenex. Want to come?" Dad's standing in the kitchen, his hair wet. I can smell his aftershave from yards away, and it reminds me of being a kid.

"I should do something with the U-Haul," I tell him. "And I want to visit Chrissy."

He shrugs into his jacket. "I won't be long. You can put your stuff in the basement."

"There isn't much."

"Whatever you need, Babs."

When I'm halfway through unloading boxes, Dad returns, and he helps with the larger pieces: my mattress and box spring, my small dining table and chairs, and my love seat. Since I didn't have a car in California, Dad follows me to the rental location in his pickup so that I'm not stranded there once I return the U-Haul. I pull the truck up beside the tiny office and climb out. Dad parks around the side and follows me in. Behind the desk, a stout woman wearing a retro Chimacum High School sweatshirt greets us. The walls are lined with boxes, blankets, packing tape, foam peanut bags, tarps, mattress covers—anything you might ever need to move, mostly plastic.

While Dad mills around, I step up to the counter. "I'm returning a truck," I say.

The woman points her chin outside with a casual jerk. "That it out there?"

I nod, pull the contract out of my pocket, unfold it, and hand it over.

She types something on her computer, prepares a clipboard, then stands. "Well, let's take a look."

Dad waits in the shop while I follow her outside, circling the truck, checking the back, noting the gas and the mileage. I realize I probably should have filled the tank before returning it—don't they charge a lot for gas? The guy in California explained it all, but I didn't pay attention. I probably should have returned it yesterday—how much does an extra day cost? I wipe my clammy hands on my pants and mentally take stock: I have two thousand dollars left in my account, plus two nearly maxed-out credit cards.

Finally, she leads me back inside and hops onto her stool again. "All righty. No noticeable new damage." She clicks her computer mouse. "No rented pads." Click. "Added miles . . ." She trails off and types a number, referencing my contract. Click. "The total comes to one thousand three hundred forty-three dollars and seventy-eight cents." She meets my eyes expectantly. "Should we use the card on file?"

When Chrissy and I were fifteen, her mom once caught us pouring vodka into glasses of orange juice. I distinctly remember the feeling of when she walked into the room, that thick-throated, air-in-your-stomach rush of shame and dread and fear of punishment.

I get that feeling now, and I know I have no choice but to pay and lose most of my remaining money and possibly mooch off my parents for much longer than an almost thirty-five-year-old ought to.

I glance back toward my father, who is perusing the tarps. In a small voice, I ask the woman, "Is it possible to split it on two different credit cards?"

The woman's face pinches for a moment, a deep ridge forming between her thin, drawn-on eyebrows. My dread deepens.

When Chrissy's mother walked in, the bottle slipped from Chrissy's fingers and shattered on the floor. Her mother turned vermilion—not because we'd been drinking but because it'd been a nearly full bottle of Grey Goose.

I know the U-Haul lady will refuse me; I know it. And then I won't even be able to afford my own place or a car, and I'll have to find a shit job that'll keep me stuck in this town, barely getting by, forever. In this moment, I am certain that is my future.

But before the woman can speak, Dad slides a tarp onto the counter, along with a pack of spearmint gum. "I'll take care of it, and these too."

I shake my head. "No, Dad, it's fine. I got it." But I don't have it, and he's seen right through me, as he always does.

He hands the woman his card and signs for it, and that is that.

Back outside, in his truck, I sigh. "You didn't have to do that."

He glances into the rearview mirror and backs out of the spot. "Consider it a donation to your future."

I'm too broke and grateful to refuse him, so I simply nod, watching him watch the road. Thanks to Dad, with the money I have left, I might have barely enough to start over.

2007

The next time I met Dennis was during my last year of college in Alaska, finishing a master's program with a thesis in cetacean behavior, when I came home for Christmas. Nick and Chrissy were engaged and had just bought a house in Port Townsend, and I spent the morning with them, our own mini Christmas of sorts. They gave me a stocking and everything, and I met their new labradoodle puppy, Ginger. We sat in our pajamas beside their tinsel-covered Douglas fir, our fingers buried in Ginger's soft curls, Nick making periodic trips to the kitchen to refill our coffee mugs.

I'd missed them terribly. While I'd been off on boats studying baleen whales, life had continued at home. They told me about their wedding plans, Chrissy waving her hands expressively, her engagement ring reflecting the colorful Christmas lights, while Nick smiled contentedly. They told me about how much they missed me; the time apart had shaken loose our sentimentality. We were all so pleased with ourselves, with our new life paths, yet there was this indescribable sorrow swirling beneath the words in our conversation. Our childhoods had slipped away, and we had all been so busy enjoying our newfound adulthood that we had sort of forgotten to acknowledge it.

It was hard to say goodbye that afternoon. After making and subsequently devouring nearly an entire Bundt pan of monkey bread, we were all sluggish but happy. It had been a long while since we'd had time to just sit and talk and laugh, and then it was the clock that pierced our rosy bubble. My grandparents were arriving tonight, and I'd promised my mother I'd help with the cooking. My parents had been quarreling lately, little spats that weren't worth noticing, except for the fact that they'd sort of tainted my home-from-college visit. Chrissy and Nick had been my holiday respite.

We hugged on their new porch, and Ginger's little fluffy tail wagged as I walked toward my mother's CR-V. From inside the car, I waved. The happy couple beamed and waved back, then retreated into their home, arm in arm. Before I got on the road, Mom called me.

"Hello?" I answered, bracing for a complaint or another holiday-related disaster. She was so tightly wound during the holidays, keeping busy, my father staying out of her way, and this year had been especially bad.

But she hadn't called to complain. "Honey, are you still out? Can you pick up some espresso for me? I need it for a recipe."

"On my way home now," I said. "How much do you need?"

"Four ounces, it says." I could hear the mixer buzzing. A pot clanged, and she cursed under her breath. "Do you mind, dear?"

"Not at all."

"Thank you, thank you," she said. "See you soon."

The phone line clicked, and I tossed my phone onto the passenger seat.

Water Street, the main road through the tourist part of Port Townsend, had six or so blocks of themed trinket shops, coffee spots, restaurants, and the mouths of piers where cruise ships parked. An old Victorian town, it had once been the scene of brothels and shanghais—Owl Cigar ads still lingered on the brick walls of the ornate buildings that lined downtown. Chrissy and Nick had mentioned that there was a new coffee shop located in a retired jailhouse beneath the sidewalk. I texted Chrissy to get the exact location after I'd found a place to park.

At first, I was not sure I was in the right place—I descended a stone staircase beneath a sign that read **Under Ground Coffee** and was surprised to find a warmly lit, crowded business below the street. Three large connected rooms housed tables and upholstered chairs, all of them occupied. Faded but ornate rugs splattered the cement floor. Barred windows lined an interior wall, not imposing but instead part of the aesthetic. Chrissy had said this was a hip place, but I'd never seen anything like it. For most of my life, coffee had been an early-morning experience, a one-button coffee maker gurgling in the predawn darkness and churning out black liquid with grit toward the bottom. Here, it was an art.

I got in line behind four other people. The counter was a long slab of dark wood, and it spanned the entire front room, one end to the other. Two baristas worked behind it in an elaborate dance of pulling shots, steaming milk, zesting citrus, and dusting the foamy tops of drinks with cinnamon. The espresso machine was a candy-red Cadillac, as much a part of the baristas' dance as they were. A few people sat right at the bar, farther down from the cash register, chatting with the gangly yet graceful male barista while he poured milk into a burnt-sienna mug.

I glanced at the chalkboard hanging behind the bar, thinking about getting myself something.

"Abby?" someone said.

I turned around, and when I took him in, bit by unexpected bit, it was as if the whole world had been put on pause. The clanging of mugs and steaming of milk and the general chatter of the shop guests fell away, and I blinked like a stunned fish.

"Dennis?" I asked.

And then it all surged upon me again, the hectic din of spoons rattling on saucers and people laughing and the squeak of floorboards reminding me that we were, in fact, under an old building. It had been perhaps six years since I'd even seen him, yet all the feelings came rushing back in a flash.

"How are you?" I asked.

He looked so different—older, I realized. He'd grown up out of his high school belly, slimmed a bit, but had a barrel chest and big arms that demanded space. His hair was cut short, and he had a close, neat beard tinged slightly red compared to his blond-blond hair. The only thing that truly was the same was his eyes. I wondered if he had ended up marrying Amber.

"I'm good," he answered. "I haven't seen you around—are you in town for the holidays?"

I nodded, noticing that he was not wearing a wedding band. "I'm going to school up in Alaska."

"Alaska?" he said, drawing out the word. "What's up there?"

"Cetaceans." His blank look divulged that I'd been spending too much time with biologists and oceanographers. I clarified: "Whales. Marine biology."

"A scientist?" He sounded impressed.

A swell of pride tickled my lips. The line moved by one, and I shifted up, abashed by my own delight. "What about you? What have you been up to?"

"Construction," he said. "My dad's business. I'm going to take over for him someday."

"Just what you wanted, right?" I asked.

"Yeah."

"That's great . . ." I didn't know enough about construction to ask a follow-up question. In the awkward silence, I wondered what his arms would feel like wrapped around me. The thought startled me, the transparency of it, the way it clamored through me. And then I realized that maybe I *knew* what his arms felt like around me, because he'd done it before, pulling me out of that car.

"I know construction isn't the most interesting thing," Dennis said, and I snapped out of my reverie.

I shook my head. "Oh no, I—"

"Next?" The female barista was waiting for me, an easy smile on her face.

My mind fumbled to remember why I was here. "I need four shots of espresso for a recipe. Plus . . ." I trailed off, looking at the menu board but not really seeing the list, feeling pressured by the long line standing behind me and Dennis's gaze.

The barista leaned on the counter, no hurry. She wore plum lipstick that complemented her black skin and box-braided hair.

I regarded the chaotic menu again and picked out a word. "I'll have a . . . a borgia?"

She smiled, straightening. "Twelve ounce?"

"Sure."

"To go?"

"Yes, thank you," I said.

She typed a few numbers into the register. "That'll be nine dollars and thirty-two cents."

Dennis touched my shoulder, electric. He said, "I'll have one too," and handed the barista his card.

I protested.

"Fourteen dollars and thirty-eight cents," the barista amended and ran his card.

"You didn't have to," I said, turning back to him.

He was standing close; his chest seemed even wider as he leaned toward me, past me, and signed the receipt. We stepped aside. The red-haired barista was already working on our drinks.

"No worries," he said. "What is a borgia, anyway?"

"No idea."

He stifled a laugh, true surprise widening his eyes.

"I just picked something off the menu."

"Well, I hope it's good."

"Me too," I said.

His smile relaxed from amusement to amiable joy, his lips pressing together but his eyes still crinkled. The change—such a small one—made my breath catch.

"It's good to see you," he said. "It's been a long time."

"Years," I said. "Rescue any car crash victims lately?"

He laughed. "No, just the one."

I looked into his eyes and saw flecks of dark gray near the pupils. He stared back with the same lingering intensity, and I wondered what he saw in mine. "A waste of skill, if you ask me," I said.

"It takes *a lot* of skill to pull a girl out of a car," he joked.

"And stay with her on the ground until the ambulance shows up." I was serious.

"And avoid getting vomit on my shoes."

I wrinkled my nose and laughed. "That *does* take skill."

He chuckled.

"So no heroics since then?"

"Nah." The barista set two full to-go cups on the bar, and Dennis handed one to me. There was a heart in the foam. "You were my first and last damsel."

I took a tentative sip. It tasted like one of those orange chocolate balls you cracked open on the table. "I wasn't a damsel. I was a hostage to a brief fit of testosterone."

"Ah." He sipped his own drink, a touch of foam lingering on his beard as he lowered the cup from his lips. I thought, briefly, that I could kiss his upper lip and lick the foam away.

"These are good," he said of the drink.

"A lucky guess."

We both sipped, relishing. Then the silence stretched on a moment too long, and without thinking, I blurted, "Construction isn't boring."

"Huh?"

"You said it wasn't interesting. I—" It was just like me to linger on an awkward moment already passed, but I pressed on. "Earlier. I wasn't being critical; I just don't know anything about it."

His face brightened. "Oh."

My mother's espresso shots were placed on the bar, a stout cup filled with liquid that matched the barista's hickory-colored beard.

"Maybe I could tell you about it sometime," Dennis said. "Are you involved with anyone?"

I realized he was asking me out, and the flattery made my chest feel warm and syrupy. He liked *me*? How was it possible?

"I'm not seeing anyone, no." A fling or two in Alaska, but nothing serious.

"Can I have your number?" He pulled out his phone and typed as I spoke my digits.

Just then, my phone went off. A text: Hey.

"Just making sure it works." He smiled. He was standing close. "I'm assuming you have somewhere to be now?"

"My parents'," I said, disappointment flooding my veins. "But I'm in town through Christmas."

He touched my arm, and I craved for him to pull me close, but then someone was scooting past me. Dennis was simply moving me out of their way.

"I'll call you, then," Dennis said, dropping his hand.

The warmth of him lingered on my elbow. "I'd like that."

2018

Dad lets me drop him off at home, and after emailing my résumé and an impassioned cover letter to the Center for Salish Orca Research, I take his truck into town. If anyone can remind me why I came home—and take my mind off the job application—it's Chrissy.

On a map, Port Townsend looks like the head of a dragon, a curved peninsula tipped back and ready to roar. Chimacum—where my parents live—is located in the dragon's heart. Jefferson Healthcare is set in its jaw, on a bluff overlooking downtown, the bay, and the close-by islands. Snaking along Sims Way toward the hospital, I look for the stark white of the Whidbey Island ferry but don't see it through the late-morning mist. The island itself is shrouded, a slumbering stretch of land made practically invisible. Somewhere beyond the winter gray, the Cascades await the bald skies of spring.

I'm eager to see my best friend.

From what I know of Chrissy's schedule, she's probably just starting work. I park at the newly renovated wing of the hospital building. Inside, an electric fire shimmies behind glass panels in the middle of the waiting room; I tug at my big winter coat, suddenly uncomfortably warm. In contrast to the sterility of most hospitals, the lobby smells like new carpeting and drywall.

At the front desk, I ask, "Is Chrissy working today?"

The woman looks up. She can't be more than my age; there's a photo on her desk of a child laughing on a swing. "Chrissy?"

"Oh, I mean Christina Harris."

The woman types on the computer, scanning what I imagine is a large spreadsheet. "Do you know what floor she works on?"

I shake my head. "She's the lead oncology nurse."

"That'll be the third floor." She points. "Elevators are down that hall."

"Thank you," I say and hurry away.

The elevator opens to another hallway and, across, a door that says **Oncology**. I'm afraid to go any farther—is this an employees-only door? I peer through the window. There's a line of rooms with sand-colored curtains and bright lights overhead. It looks like a miserable place. I imagine patients getting their chemo in those cold rooms, worried about their futures.

Two nurses round the corner, talking. I recognize one: Chrissy, looking so serious and accomplished, holding a medical chart. I haven't been home in four and a half years and therefore haven't seen her at work since she was promoted. I open the door.

"Is this gynecology?" I ask, my mouth quirked.

The other nurse looks up first, her jaw clenched with irritation.

Chrissy lifts her head too. "Oh my God," she says, an exuberant whisper. Then an inappropriately loud squeal: "Oh. My. *God.*"

She runs toward me, her Nikes squeaking. We collide in a tight embrace, her petite body knocking me back a full step. She squeals again, my eardrum rattling. I laugh and hold her tighter.

When we part, she asks, "What are you *doing* here?"

"Visiting you, of course."

The other nurse goes back to work, probably well aware of Chrissy's short attention span.

"*Not* what I meant," Chrissy says, laughing, but her brown eyes search mine. For a moment, her mood takes a solemn dip. There's an unspoken *knowing* between us. Friends since we were children. Scrapes and bruises, love and heartbreak. We've braved it all together, and I feel the weight of that now. Oh, how desperately I missed her—more than I even knew. I thought her visits to California had eased the distance, but there's nothing—*nothing*—like seeing her here, at home.

"When did you get back?" She hits my arm. "And why didn't you *warn* me?"

"Saturday night, late," I said. "I didn't even warn my parents."

"Saturday?"

"I slept half of Sunday."

She folds her arms. "And the other half?"

"Shush," I say. "You know I missed you."

She hugs me again, then glances at her watch. "I missed you, too, you stinker. I have a patient—can we talk later? Want to have dinner tonight? Our house."

I'm not ready to let her go. "Sounds great."

"I'll text Nick. He'll be so jazzed to see you," she says. "We have so much to catch up on."

"I know," I say.

Her eyebrows dip with concern. "I hope this means you're all right, Abby."

I cling to the joy of our reunion, not ready to dredge up old stuff.

"This is a toxic place for you," she pushes, but I don't want to get into it now.

"What, you didn't miss me?"

"I'm serious," she says.

"Turns out you can't start over without first getting closure. Don't you have a patient?"

"Don't get me wrong—I'm glad to see you," she says. "I just hope you're here for the right reasons."

Suddenly my eyes are blurry. "I missed you."

Chrissy wraps her arms around me, a double squeeze. "Dinner," she says. "I'll have Nick make something with lots of calories."

I blink away the emotion. She's walking backward down the hall.

"Six?" I suggest.

She gives a thumbs-up, blows a kiss, and then disappears around the corner.

2008

Dennis and I never did connect again over Christmas break, but when I returned to Alaska, we got in the habit of talking on the phone. I liked the way his voice sounded through the receiver, the crackle after a long day. My cell service was bad, and some nights I had to stand outside until my toes were frozen in my boots. About twelve days after he found out that I'd been shivering in the Alaskan darkness just to talk to him, a box arrived. Inside was a sky-blue corded phone, vintage, as if he'd shipped it from the 1960s. I loved it—it meant he liked hearing my voice too. We always talked before I went to bed, and with the new phone, I could close my eyes and imagine him lying there beside me in the dark, his voice a whisper, telling me about his day.

During those conversations, he filled me in on hometown gossip, construction, and funny things he'd seen on TV. I told him about classmates, whales, and the studies I'd been reading. The moon would rise, and our discussions would deepen. Did he believe in reincarnation? Had I ever seen a ghost? And did we ever consider how small humanity was, in the big cosmic scheme of things? Our compatibility was undeniable. He poked fun at my being a science nerd, but he also called me Smarty, and I liked it—Dennis made me feel sexy-smart. And he was equally impressive to me—he could build houses, for Pete's sake.

We also had inside jokes. He was usually the one to call me (I'd never forget that achy anticipatory feeling of waiting for my phone to ring), but once I called him, and he answered, "Pizza Hut." I immediately apologized for the wrong number and hung up, and he had to call me back and explain that it was him the whole time. He'd laughed good and hard over that one, questioning my braininess after all. We finally postulated that perhaps my growing up without siblings had made me innocently gullible.

Throughout the banter, there was this unspoken heat between us. I'd never felt such intimacy with a man before, and we hadn't even touched. He told me about his alcoholic father—the reason Dennis didn't drink—and how he used to hide in the closet with his sister until the yelling died down. My heart reached out toward him over the forested miles between us, and I told him how sorry I was, but secretly, I was glad he told me intimate things and proud of his resilience. He'd managed to go into business with his father later on—once his dad had gotten sober—and as men, they worked side by side for many years.

On a night in mid-April, Dennis called a little earlier than normal. His father had died of a heart attack a few weeks prior, and Dennis had missed a few of our call dates, so when the phone rang, I sprang to get it.

"Hello?"

"Yeah, I'll take a large cheese pizza, a medium pepperoni, and a Coke."

"Delivery?" I asked, playing along.

"Please," he breathed. "Anything to see you."

"That would be one hell of a delivery charge," I said, but my pulse quickened. "How are you?"

A pause. "I'm all right. Things are finally settling down out here."

I'd wanted to attend the funeral to support him, but Dennis assured me it wasn't worth the plane ticket. We hadn't defined our relationship—let alone told our parents—and perhaps that had something to do with it. Since that conversation, I'd been wondering how serious he felt about me.

I said, "I wish I could have been there for you."

"You *were* there for me," he replied. "You always pick up the phone."

A smile twitched at my lips. "And the business?"

"My sister's helping in the office," he said. "I'm getting into a rhythm. Dad had some unfinished projects."

We were both silent for a beat.

"You called early."

"I know," Dennis said. "I missed you. I'm sorry I haven't had time to talk."

"It's understandable." It had been torture for me. Worrying about him, missing him, staring at that damn phone, willing it to ring. I couldn't be angry with him, but for the past two weeks, I had been in agony, withdrawal.

"I've been meaning to—" He stopped, hesitated. I could hear the hiss of a soda's pull tab, the squeak of a leather couch cushion. "I have to—I wanted to ask—um."

"What is it?"

"Your graduation is coming up," Dennis said. "Do you know . . . what your plans are afterward?"

"I'm still trying to figure that out." I'd spent my whole life in school, and despite talk of research programs with my professors, the concept of actually using my degree still seemed abstract, something far in the future. "Why do you ask?"

"Well . . . my dad dying got me thinking." He struggled for phrasing. "About life—about you, Abby. I can't stand you being so far away, and I'm sick of beating around the bush. I want to see you."

"I want to see you too." My ear was growing hot with the phone pressed to my face, and I shifted it against my cheek. "I'll be visiting—"

"No," he interrupted. "I want to see you every day. I want to be *with* you. Like, date you."

I could hear the blush in his voice, so I suspected he could hear the blush in mine when I said, "I want that too. Very much."

"I don't want to force you to come back to Washington," he said. "If it can't work—"

Marine biology didn't matter in that moment. "You wouldn't be forcing me."

"I want to take you out." There was fervor in his voice now. "You graduate on June twelfth, then head home, right?"

"Yes."

"I know it's a long way off, but are you free on June fifteenth?"

I laughed. "I can check my calendar, but I'm pretty sure I'm free."

"Well, now you have plans. When you get back, we're going on a real date." He sounded triumphant.

"I'll be counting down the days," I told him, and I did.

2018

Before they know I've arrived, I pause on Chrissy and Nick's porch. It's past dark, and the sky is a black haze. The sage edging their house rustles, and I can't help but glance down at the place Dennis sat that night four and a half years ago when our marriage ended. I remember his drunk eyes and my confused thoughts and sitting there beside him with our lives laid out before us. It's a moment I've mentally replayed a million times, as if I could will it to happen differently, but it always ends the same: with me telling the truth and Dennis walking away.

Nonetheless, I'm glad to see my friends again. I shake my head and roll my shoulders back, then knock.

Chrissy opens the door, and I'm met with the smell of bacon, the sound of soft rock. She squeals and hugs me, her hair damp and coconutty.

"Is she here?" It's Nick from the kitchen.

"See for yourself," she calls, ushering me inside.

The warmth of their home envelops me, and I shrug out of my jacket, leaving the bad thoughts behind.

Nick rounds the bend, wiping his hands on a dish towel. He swings it over his shoulder when he sees me and brushes his unruly hair out of his face. "She lives," he says.

I rush toward him, and his arms settle over me. Never one to be left out, Chrissy joins the hug so that I'm squished in a friend sandwich. The tension in my shoulders eases, and for a few seconds, I forget about everything altogether.

But then they release me. Nick's eyebrows crease in not quite pity, and he asks, "How are you?"

"Don't look at me like that," I say, pushing his shoulder. "I'm good."

He smiles. "Fine, fine. I have pancakes to flip." He disappears into the kitchen again.

"Breakfast for dinner?" They know it's my favorite.

Chrissy winks. "Comfort food."

I follow her into their living room. Their house is one of the many Victorians uptown, and every doorframe has intricate molding. The twelve-foot ceiling makes the small space feel big.

"I know what you're thinking," Chrissy says. "The place feels strange without a dog."

Ginger died six months ago. I found a Mexican artist who did pet portraits and sent them a painting. Now, I spot the painting hanging on the wall above an empty dog bed. It still impresses me how the artist captured Ginger's sweet nature, her intelligent eyes.

"We're thinking of getting a puppy," Chrissy says. "There are two fresh litters at the shelter right now. How soon is too soon?"

I wonder that myself. "A home isn't a home without a dog," I say and pad over the hardwood floor onto a patterned crimson carpet. I point down at the woven zigzags. "This is cool."

"My mom brought it back from India." Chrissy settles on their sectional, tucking her legs beneath her.

I sit too. "She went to India?"

Chrissy rolls her eyes. "Another saga in the endless midlife crisis."

Chrissy has never met her father, a man from Argentina who only knew her mother for a night. Her mom is constantly flitting off to other places, sometimes with no warning at all. We spent many evenings giggling in my room on school nights because her mom was out with a new man or forgot to pick Chrissy up from softball practice.

Her face crinkles with a smile. "God, it's good to see you. You look great."

I shrug. "Thanks." Chrissy is wearing a baggy sweater and a pair of leggings, and the white socks bunched around her ankles are a reminder of the nineties. She looks exactly the same as she did at fifteen. "You look happy."

"I am."

We grin at each other. I forgot what it was like to have a friend around, someone to hug and talk to and count on. Sure, I could call her up from California, but that wasn't the same as sitting on her couch.

Chrissy shakes her head, clearly thinking the same thing. "Gah, I just can't believe you're really here."

"I know," I say. "I missed—"

"The famous biologist in the flesh."

I frown. "Famous? Hardly."

"Your quote in the *Atlantic* says differently."

I shake my head. It's true—a journalist covered the study's findings for the *Atlantic*'s science section. I was quoted saying something lofty about the intellectual capacity of humpback whales. It was something I firmly believed, something I'd told Dennis, once, long before I'd even seen a humpback up close, to which he'd scoffed and said, *Smarty and her theories*. But Dr. Amelia Perez was proving those things I'd known just from listening to recordings of the whales. That they had identity, culture, tradition, family. Dr. Perez deserved the spotlight—she gave my inspirational pull quote meaning.

All that, of course, doesn't deter Chrissy's insistence that I'm now "famous."

"You've been quoted in the paper before," I counter.

"Psh. The *local* paper doesn't compare."

"Yeah, well—"

Just then, a rattling crash from the kitchen. Nick's voice: "Damn it!"

We both rush to find Nick bent over spilled hash browns.

"Oh no," I say.

"Are you hurt?" Chrissy asks.

Nick shakes his head, stands. "I salvaged most of them, but I think the cast iron dented the floor."

Chrissy stoops, inspecting the wood. "Shit, that sucks."

"Still have all my toes, though."

"Oh, good." She rises to her tippy-toes to kiss him.

Watching them, a twinge of sorrow makes my bones ache. I had that kind of love, once. A jump in the throat when something banged in the other room. A rush of relief upon finding him whole, stooped over one mess or another. I used my tippy-toes to kiss Dennis thousands of times. I knew what it felt like to have what Chrissy and Nick still have—will I ever have that again? Do I even deserve to?

2008

On June 15, I met Dennis outside a narrow hole-in-the-wall restaurant in Port Townsend. Not much had changed since I'd last been in town, but when I spotted Dennis walking up the hill toward me, it felt like nothing would be the same ever again.

Once he was within talking distance, he gestured to the café and said, "This isn't Pizza Hut."

My ribs felt like a cage full of butterflies; I was so used to hearing him through the phone that his voice in person took me by surprise. It was steadier. Sexier.

"Damn, and I was craving a medium pepperoni," I said.

"I hear this place is good too." Dennis wore jeans with black shoes, his face clean shaven. His blue button-down was tight around his big shoulders, his biceps. The fluttering in my ribs intensified.

He stopped a yard away, seemingly in hesitation. I wanted to take a step closer, but without a phone in my hand, I felt as if I didn't have a life vest. I had grown so accustomed to the safety of distance that I'd forgotten what I'd missed: expressions, gestures, attraction. Now the floodgates were open, and I feared I'd get swept away and say something stupid.

"You look beautiful," he said.

Chrissy had let me borrow a black dress that flared off my hips. "Thank you."

"I'm glad you could come."

"I've been wanting—"

He closed the distance between us in one big stride, interrupting my thought. His hand cupped my face, and the other arm wrapped around my waist. I laughed, dizzied. He drew me close, our chests pressing together, and his lips met mine. He was careful at first but grew ardent. His mouth slid over mine, and I could smell him, shower fresh and intoxicating. Right there on the street, he kissed me with an urgency I'd been feeling for months. It was one hell of a way to break the ice.

When he released me, I wobbled, panting. Self-conscious, I looked around to see who had witnessed our sudden passion, but people were going about their business: ambling down the sidewalk, parallel parking, smoking by a restaurant's back door. Dennis was regarding me, his mouth red from my lipstick, and I reached up to wipe it away. A smile formed under my fingers, and he kissed my palm.

"I'd waited long enough," he said.

He was still standing close, a hand lingering on my waist. I felt his body heat through the thin fabric between us. The taste of him lingered on my tongue, a mix of cinnamon and something else, something primal. "Too long," I said.

"I hope that wasn't too . . ."

I shook my head, and he grinned.

"Hungry?" he asked, opening his palm toward the restaurant.

"Very," I said, but I wasn't talking about the food.

2018

When Chrissy and I return to her couch, she opens a jug of orange juice and a bottle of champagne, saying, "We're doing this right."

"What's the occasion?"

"You, silly." She scoots closer until we're hip to hip.

Nick arrives, carrying our dinner plates on his arm like a waiter, and sits on the other side of the sectional so that I'm in between them in the elbow of the L-shaped cushions.

"Wow, this looks good," I say as he passes me a plate. Golden hash browns, sunny eggs, extra crispy bacon, and two pancakes bejeweled with fruit.

Chrissy pours mimosas, and when Nick says, "Dig in," we do.

The conversation meanders from childhood reminiscing to funny work stories. As more mimosas are poured, the laughter grows. I appreciate talking about anything other than how I left my husband. Since coming home, the topic has seemed to hang in the air like a fog, unsaid but *felt*—yet while we eat, the fog lifts. Chrissy updates me on her mother, ever single, irresponsibly traveling the globe, and the latest man she brought home.

"He's just another white person searching for meaning in Asia," Chrissy says, her drink sloshing with an exasperated gesture. "The poor locals. You'd think they'd get sick of teaching my crazy mother and her sixty-year-old boyfriend how to meditate. I'm not sure she's *ever* sat still enough."

"It's just her hippie phase," Nick says.

"I swear, the guy hadn't showered in a year," Chrissy continues. "He looked like she found him wandering around in the Himalayas, far away from civilization. I was surprised he was wearing shoes."

"But he spoke like an English professor," Nick adds.

"His appearance was clearly a delusional act." Chrissy pours more champagne into her glass, diluting the juice. "Later, Mom showed us more pictures from her trip. The guy was naked in every single one of them."

"Naked?" I ask, trying not to picture it.

Chrissy wrinkles her nose. "You could barely see his junk under all that hair."

I laugh, good and deep, my eyes watering. They laugh, too, until we're all cackling and gasping for breath. Sitting cross-legged on the couch, it's like we're back in high school. I half expect the conversation to turn toward homework. But instead, Chrissy looks at me.

"So what about you, Abs—any stories from California?"

I shake my head. "You've heard all the good ones."

"I don't mean with the whales; I mean the people. You haven't told us *anything* about the people, except Dr. What's-Her-Face and all her amazing theories."

"Dr. Perez," I correct, "and her hypotheses are a significant part of—"

"Oh, I know, I know." Chrissy waves her hands. "But c'mon. There had to have been interesting people working with you—or hot locals! No surfer heartthrobs?"

I smile, but it's a mask now. I'm not her mother, content with jumping from guy to guy. Of course there weren't any heartthrobs, or any flings at all. How could I, after the mess I'd made here? Chrissy knows all this, talked through all this on the phone, but perhaps the mimosas have awakened her true feelings.

In a muffled tone, I say, "Just assistants to Dr. Perez."

"Pasty scientists out on the town?"

Nick seems to notice my turn in mood. *"Chrissy."*

She regards me with more clarity, her cheeks all flushed and eyes sparkling but her mouth pressed into a thin line of understanding. "I'm sorry, Abs," she says. "I didn't mean it like that."

She pulls me close, and I sigh, a long shudder. Then, unexpectedly, Chrissy sits up straighter. She looks me in the eye.

"Real talk, now," she says. "Why did you come back? I mean, I'm glad you're here, but after everything that happened . . ." She shrugs, her eyes unwavering.

The work I did on Dr. Perez's team was life changing—and then it ended, and I didn't have any distractions anymore. That day with Eli on the beach—that night with Dennis—the indecision, the alcohol . . . I'd wanted to escape all the damage I'd done. Even though I *was* far from home, the hurt had found me anyway. It didn't seem worth it to face all those feelings alone anymore. The truth is, I was lonely.

I shift my legs out straight, stalling. Chrissy and I are sharing a blanket, and I pick at the fringed edge so I don't have to look at her.

Gently, she says, "You aren't here to see Eli, are you?"

Maybe a part of me is. Dennis was my first true love, but when things turned sour, for a while, Eli was my refuge. Is it wrong to think that he's the only man in the world who truly understands me? Who related to my intellectual passions more than anyone else ever has? He showed me how to feel *awake*, *alive*. Of course I want that again. I want to take hold of that feeling and never let go. Is that so wrong?

Chrissy continues this one-sided conversation. "You didn't hear, did you? Eli is getting a divorce."

Thanks to social media, I had actually heard. In California, the news knocked the wind out of me. Tonight, it merely makes my breath catch. I ask, "Do you know why?" *That* is something I've yet to learn. It can't be my fault—I haven't seen Eli in four and a half years—but I get this nagging feeling that it's more complicated than that.

Chrissy shakes her head. "Rumors," she says. "Nothing definitive."

"Oh."

Her glance goes right through me, right into the dark corners of my mind. She wants to know if I had something to do with it, but she's smart enough not to ask.

"We haven't spoken since . . ." I trail off. My legs under the blanket are suddenly clammy. "He's still in town, though, right?" He must be, to run his gallery.

Nick nods. "I was jogging downtown and saw him getting into his car just a few days ago."

Relief spreads through me. But then, "Since when do you jog?"

Nick and Chrissy share a private look—small smiles, glittering eyes, warmth.

"We're both trying to get healthier," Nick says vaguely.

"Now's as good a time as any," Chrissy says to him, and Nick shrugs. She twists on the couch so that she's facing me. "We've decided to start trying."

It takes me a moment to process. "Trying? As in, baby?"

"Trying as in baby," Nick confirms. "Our careers have finally settled, we're stable, and well, we're getting older. It's time for that next step."

Chrissy beams at me.

My stomach drops. I should be happy for them. I should squeal with joy and ask questions. I should feel . . . something *other* than despair. I'm not ready for children, so I know it's not jealousy, but suddenly it's as if they've left me behind. When she gets pregnant, I fear our friendship will be over. It won't be the three of *us* anymore. It'll be the three of *them*. And then who will I have?

All I can think to say is, "Should you be drinking?"

"I'm a nurse, Abby." More quietly, she adds, "At this time of the month, I'm fine to indulge a little."

"Well, I'm happy for you." It comes out as a mumble.

I think of my life, Chrissy and Nick's life, and how time just keeps uncoiling like a spool of thread. If I had a partner, would I be so bothered by Chrissy and Nick's decision? They were bound to want a baby sooner or later, and we're in our thirties now. Chrissy is out of school, and Nick's graphic design business is finally steady—now is the perfect time for them. It's as if my thread is tangled around my ankles and wrists, and theirs is unspooling without me.

"It's not really news yet," Chrissy says to me. "Pre-news."

"But we wanted you to know," Nick adds. "We didn't want you to be blindsided."

I nod dumbly, already blindsided—though I know I shouldn't be. "I'm happy for you," I repeat.

"Don't worry; the baby isn't going to replace you." Chrissy wraps her arms around me, but I don't feel comforted.

"So Nick has been jogging," I say, trying to lighten things up, trying to divert the news into something more palatable.

Chrissy's arms slip from me—letting go already. "Yeah, it's quite the sight."

Nick waggles his eyebrows, and the serious moment passes. Things could almost be normal again, but there's this snag in the threads we've braided together, and I fear it will only get worse as the weeks go on. I feel frayed already, and I hate myself for that.

"So are you going to call Eli?" Chrissy asks me.

"What? No."

"Why not? Maybe he'd like to hear from you."

I shake my head.

"Well, regardless of Eli, don't you think it's time to . . . get back in the game?"

"The game?"

"Dating," she says carefully. "It's been four and a half years. Don't you think it's time to—?"

"Not particularly," I say, bristling.

"Why not?"

"Don't you think I need to get my shit together before I can drag someone else into it?" I realize my tone is harsh, and I soften. "I just feel like I need a direction."

Chrissy's eyes hold mine. "You *do* have a direction. You were in the *Atlantic*, for God's sake."

"And now I'm back home," I say. "It was a false start."

"No." Chrissy shakes her head. "No, it was a new beginning, and you left."

My eyes are growing puffy. Despite the years, I'm not over Dennis or Eli or anything that happened—in this moment, I'm not sure I'll ever heal. "How am I supposed to move on when—"

"You don't have to move on. You just have to move forward," she says. "Abby, you must be home for a reason. Promise me you'll make the most of it." I'm shaking my head, but she insists, "Promise me."

"All right," I squeak. "All right."

"Besides, nobody ever truly has their shit together," Nick says, patting my leg. "Some people are just better at faking it."

My chest floods with sudden warmth, overcome. I came home for them, too, of course. Their opinions, their encouragement, their unending support. I grasp both their hands and squeeze tightly. "Promise that when the baby comes, we'll still have nights together like this?"

"Of course," Chrissy says, squeezing my hand in return. "So long as you don't mind lactation stains on my shirt."

"I won't," I say, but I don't like the thought. A puppy, a child. I can't imagine they'll have room for me too.

2008

On our first date, Dennis and I were seated by the window. A candle flickered between us. Dennis stroked my fingers with his thumb, his hand big and calloused. I couldn't believe he was there with me in the flesh—how long had I been dreaming about kissing him? My body tingled from minutes ago on the street, being pressed against him. How solid he was.

"Normally I would have waited to kiss you until *after* dinner," Dennis said, speaking low. The restaurant, though small, was very full. "I hope I didn't ruin the suspense."

I chuckled. It amazed me how *right* it felt to hold his hand and sit across from him at dinner. We'd never done either of those things before, and yet it felt natural.

"If anything, it adds to the suspense," I said. "When will you kiss me again? I'm on the edge of my seat."

His lips spread ever so slightly. "Good."

The waitress came by and delivered our drinks. Wine for me, Coke for Dennis.

"Where are you staying?" Dennis asked.

"With my parents for now," I said. "Currently looking for a place."

"And work?"

We hadn't talked much about my future plans, and things were still uncertain. The world felt suddenly so open, and I told him so.

"You'll figure it out," he said. "I felt the same way after high school."

"Didn't you know what you wanted to do?"

He shrugged. "For the most part, but it still felt . . ." He spread his hands.

I knew what he meant—school offered a clear path. Now, the career options were so overwhelmingly endless that I didn't know where to turn.

I changed the subject. "How's your family doing?"

He released my hand and sipped his Coke. "My mother finally stopped wearing black."

"That's a step."

He nodded. "She's still pretty torn up."

"And how are *you*?"

"Oh, you know," he said. "Consumed by the business, mostly."

"You've had to be so strong for everyone else."

His jaw clenched. "I'm all right."

Our waitress returned. "Are we ready?"

I glanced at the menu—we hadn't taken time to look.

"She'll have the Greek," Dennis said abruptly, giving me a sly look. "And I'll have the Moroccan pork."

The waitress gestured at his now-empty glass. "Another?"

"No, thanks."

She nodded and moved on to another table.

"Will I like it?" I asked challengingly. I wasn't sure I liked a man ordering for me.

"The Greek? Yes." His mouth was quirked, eyebrows raised, a playful expression.

"How are you so sure?"

He leaned forward and settled his hand over mine again. "Remember when you'd just gotten back from that three-day boat trip, and I called, and you were telling me about how much you were craving pasta?"

"Yeah."

"And remember how you complained that you weren't craving red sauce, and white sauce always ends up making you nauseous from being too rich, and you couldn't think of another pasta dish you could make, so you just gave up?"

I chuckled. "I forgot about that."

Dennis sat back with satisfaction, spreading his hands. "The Greek."

"If you say so." I couldn't believe he remembered that conversation. Looking at the easy grin on his face, I knew I was falling hard for him—or maybe I already loved him. "So tell me about yourself."

"Like what?"

I scrunched my face, thinking. "I don't know. This is a first date; I feel like we should be asking first-date questions."

"What's your favorite color?"

"*That's* what you ask girls on first dates?"

"Do you want to get to know me or not?"

I looked into his azure eyes. "Blue."

"Same," he said. "Favorite comfort food?"

"Breakfast," I said.

"My mother's stew."

"I'll have to try that sometime."

He nodded. "What's your favorite childhood movie?"

"You're going to laugh."

"I won't laugh."

"You *will*," I insisted.

"Try me."

"Nature documentaries."

He laughed. "That's not a movie."

"You asked."

"Any particular documentary?"

"No, but it has to be narrated by David Attenborough," I said. "I can't stand any other voice."

"Not even Morgan Freeman? Or Oprah?"

"It's Attenborough or nothing."

He squeezed my hand.

"What's yours?" I asked.

"Well, it'll sound stupid compared to documentaries," he complained. Then, "*Aladdin*."

"I love *Aladdin*."

"You don't have to say that."

"But it's *true*."

Our waitress returned. Dennis and I both leaned back to allow her to set the plates down. "Anything else?" We shook our heads, and she spun on a heel.

We leaned forward again, from the allure not of each other this time but of the food. The Greek steamed an intoxicating blend of flavors up toward my nose. Kalamata olives, artichoke hearts, roasted tomatoes, capers. I took a bite and melted. A light feta sauce sang over my taste buds, and I closed my eyes. *Mmmm.*

"You like?" Dennis asked.

When I opened my eyes, he looked smug. I took another bite, this time groaning out loud. "Mmmm!" Maybe I didn't mind him ordering for me after all.

"That's a sound I could listen to all day," he said.

A bolt of lightning struck deep in my belly. I chewed, swallowed, unable to think of a comeback. I imagined him eliciting that same deep hum out of me, and a tingly feeling washed over my skin.

Dennis cut into his pork. "Want to try this?"

I nodded, and he slid a small cube onto my plate.

"Wait, get some of the apricots and sauce." He lifted more ingredients over.

I scooped up the whole bite he'd prepared. It was completely different from mine but delicious all the same. Tender pork, honey, spices, and the sweet burst of a warm, swollen apricot.

He watched me. "Amazing, right?"

"Exquisite."

We ate in silence for a few minutes, caught up in our food. I drank more wine, the feta sauce from my pasta mellowing the tannins on my tongue.

"We'll have to take a Sunday to watch our childhood favorites," Dennis said, returning to our earlier conversation. "*Aladdin* and—what?"

"*Planet Earth*," I said. "That's the quintessential Attenborough documentary. But it's a series, so it has multiple parts."

"You saying it'll take all day?"

"You game?"

"Definitely." His eyes bored into me, heady and warm.

We finished our dinner in no time and declined dessert. Dennis picked up the check, and then we were out on the street again. There was still light in the sky, and I wasn't ready for the night to end.

"You want to take a walk?" I asked.

In answer, he grasped my hand.

The breeze snaked through the tall brick buildings, chilly off the water. We wandered past the theater—a line of moviegoers out front—and passed Under Ground Coffee.

"I almost didn't ask for your number," Dennis said.

"Why not?"

"We'd only met a couple times. I wasn't sure how much you remembered me."

"Of course I remembered you."

As we followed the sidewalk past closed shops, we found ourselves turning onto Union Wharf, the largest downtown pier.

Few other people were out, and the sea air sent goose bumps up my legs. We stopped at the far railing. Dennis leaned his elbows on the smooth wood. I allowed my fingers to curl over his bicep, feeling the tight, sinuous muscle underneath his sleeve.

"Nice evening," he said, his eyes on the water. "What animals live out there?"

I shrugged. "Harbor seals, porpoise, salmon. In a single speck of water, you could find copepods, crab larvae, phytoplankton."

"Phyto . . . ?"

"Plankton," I said. "Microscopic plants."

"I wasn't the best at science."

"That doesn't matter," I said.

"You're so passionate." He turned to me. "You're probably the smartest person I know."

I blushed. "Hardly."

He stood tall, his hand lifting my chin. He kissed me softly, his lips a faint whisper against mine. When we parted, he brushed a curl of hair from my face. "Should we go?"

I leaned in for another toe-curling kiss. The goose bumps on my legs tightened. "Yes."

We walked back down the dock, my heels clicking on wood. Suddenly, I felt nervous. Would he take me back to his car, his place? Or would I drive home alone? I didn't want to rush into things, but then again, was it truly rushing if we'd talked almost daily for the past few months? Did he expect to take me home? Should I think it presumptuous if he did? I'd worn matching bra and panties just in case. That didn't mean nothing. I wanted him. Badly.

I'd had a semiserious relationship before college. Then two brief, alcohol-fueled flings in Alaska. Three men in my life total. How many women had Dennis been with? Worse—how could I compare to Amber? I could still picture her with him, her lithe form, her hand on his arm as mine was now. They'd broken up years ago, but the prospect of him taking me home . . . self-consciousness rippled through me. What if I—

A crack, a drop, and somehow I was on my knees on the pier planking. Red-hot pain bloomed across my scraped knees and palms, and the joint of my ankle ached beyond belief.

"Are you all right?" Dennis asked, crouching beside me. His warm hands on my arm reminded me of the car crash.

I blinked. "My knees hurt."

And my right stiletto was missing. I glanced backward to see the heel stuck in a gap between planks. I squeezed my eyes shut with embarrassment, unable to believe my own clumsiness. My ankle throbbed.

"Let's get you up," Dennis said, wrapping an arm around me.

Once hoisted upright, I took a step on my bare foot. A spike of pain made me yelp.

"Don't put weight on it," Dennis said.

I leaned against the railing while he retrieved the shoe. It was wedged in the planking, and when he yanked it out, the heel post snapped.

"Oh damn, I'm sorry," he said.

I'd borrowed the pair from Chrissy, along with the dress. "Chrissy is going to kill me."

Dennis handed over the broken stiletto, looking stricken. "I'll replace them."

"No, no, it's fine. She'll understand, klutz that I am," I said. "She knew the risk of my borrowing them."

"Those things are dangerous," he said. "Can you walk?"

"I'm not sure."

He allowed me to put weight on him, acting as a crutch so I could test my ankle. I stepped, it hurt, and I flinched.

"I guess you won't be walking on it," Dennis said. "My truck is just a block from here. Can you hop?"

"What happens if I can't?"

"I carry you," he said.

I sucked in a breath. "We'll try hobbling first."

It took a considerable amount of time, but I managed to get to his truck, applying more and more weight on my bare foot as we went. I had to remove the other shoe, and my feet were cold and black bottomed by the time I slid onto his bench seat.

He got in. I remembered my past concerns, the prospect of lovemaking. There was a chance my ankle had ruined things, and despite my anxieties, I felt a sour disappointment at the thought.

"Where are you parked?" Dennis asked.

"Up the hill."

"Are you still in pain?"

I turned my ankle, testing the joint. "Not as much. I think I'll live."

"Can you drive?"

I hadn't thought of that. "I'm not sure."

"Should I drive you home?"

I knew the real question he was asking, and I took a chance. "Your place is closer."

A flicker of eagerness brightened his eyes, just for a moment. He started the engine, and my pulse thrummed. The shyness I'd felt outside the restaurant returned, and I prayed that he'd be able to break the ice once more.

As he drove, his hand came to rest on my leg—a safe distance from the hem of my dress. I scooched a little closer on the bench seat, testing my ankle again. A sharp pain occurred when I rolled it to the left. Pointing my toe felt better.

When I caught Dennis glancing at my legs, he said, "Any better?"

"Not really."

"I have Tylenol at home, if you want."

"Sure." I watched his face as he drove, the streetlights flashing over the bridge of his nose, his jaw.

A few minutes later, we pulled into a narrow driveway. A butter-colored house was tucked between two giant cedars, and Dennis cut the engine in front of the garage. He got out and circled the vehicle, opened my door, and helped me out of the tall cab. He guided me along a small path to the front porch, then ushered me inside.

It was a small place, probably two bedrooms max, and when he turned on the lights, I saw his leather couch—the one that squeaked on the phone—and a narrow kitchen off to the right. He tossed his keys on the counter and went to a cupboard. I remained by the door, hugging myself, barefoot and chilly and coy.

He came over again, this time with a bottle of Tylenol and a glass of water. “Here, this'll help.”

I uncapped the bottle and tossed back the pills. “I like your place.”

“It's all right.”

“It's cozy.”

“You can come in farther, if you want.” Dennis took the glass and pills from my hands and set them on the counter. “Want a tour?”

“I'm not in good tour-walking condition,” I joked.

Mischief flashed in his eyes, and he bent down and scooped me up into his arms. I squealed with surprise, my hand grasping his shoulder.

“What do you want to see first?”

“The bedroom.”

He kissed me, shifted his grip around my waist, and carried me sideways down the hall. In the doorway, the big rumpled duvet looked like a storm cloud. Dennis set me down gently on the edge of the bed. The lights were off, and all I could see was his shape, the dark outline of his body.

He seemed hesitant, and his question confirmed it. “Are you sure you're—” I reached up toward his face, and he stopped talking, answering my bid for a kiss. A soft groan rumbled in his chest and against my mouth. He knelt. Fingers brushed against my ankle, under my calf. He bent his head to kiss the sore joint, my shin, my knee. He parted my thighs, pushed aside my underwear, and kissed there too. His mouth was warm and wet, and I forgot about everything other than Dennis.

Then he was guiding me back, kissing me harder. I fumbled with the buttons on his shirt until finally his torso was bare. In the silver-blue darkness, I ran my hands along the bulk of him. His hands were in my hair and then on my back and then on the zipper of my dress. Dennis grabbed the hem and pulled the dress over my head, letting it flutter to the floor. He ran his fingers over the exposed skin, kissing new places, teasing me with his tongue. I closed my eyes and tipped my head back, reveling in his fervor. I scooted back on the bed to lure him off the floor, and realizing what I was doing, he lifted me into a better position but in the process bumped my ankle.

I yelped, more from surprise than from pain.

He halted. "Did I hurt you?"

"It's fine."

"Your ankle?"

"It's fine." I reached for him, and his mouth met mine again.

With my head cradled by his pillow, I was enveloped in the scent of him: cinnamon and shaving cream and a little sweat. He tugged off my panties. I didn't feel so insecure, not after seeing the way he looked at me then. I ran my fingers through his short hair and along his jawline.

Then he was removing his jeans, reaching for a bedside drawer, retrieving a condom. The tear of its wrapper, the unrolling of latex. Without his hands on me, the room felt cool. I glanced up toward the window, the blinds illuminated slightly.

Finally, Dennis leaned forward again. His hands roved all over me, bringing me back from my thoughts. He slid inside, and I actually gasped. He started slow, moving gently. I moved against him, breathing hard. Rocking together, we picked up speed. I couldn't believe we were there together, after all that time spent wishing and hoping and wondering and suppressing the feelings I should have never ignored. I thought about all our encounters at once, and then I *stopped* thinking and simply gave myself over to him. My body let go in a warm, cascading rush before he came too.

We panted for a few beats, and then Dennis disappeared into the bathroom. I heard the water running, the trees rustling outside. I closed my eyes, my skin cooling. Then he was back, settling the covers over both of us, pulling me close in the quiet darkness.

"Did you get there?" he asked, barely audible. His fingers played idly with my hair. With my ear to his chest, I could hear his heartbeat gradually slowing.

"Yeah, you couldn't tell?"

He sighed, sounding relieved. "Just making sure. I was afraid your ankle . . ."

"I forgot all about it."

"You're so beautiful. You know that?"

The compliment surprised me. "I'm glad you think so." I paused, overjoyed just to be in bed with him—then I thought of Amber. "Are you sure?"

"You're the most beautiful woman I've ever met—inside and out."

I stretched up to kiss him, all my apprehension dissolving. "Want to know a secret?"

"Is it a good one?"

I settled my cheek on his chest again. "I still have that card you gave me."

"What card?"

"The one you gave me after the crash."

"No way."

"It's true."

"Do you remember what I wrote?"

"'Abby, I was worried so I bought you this card. I hope you heal up fast. Love, Dennis.'"

He laughed. "'Love, Dennis.'"

"That was my favorite part."

"That *is* a good secret," he said. "Want to hear mine?"

"Hell yeah."

"I spent over an hour in Don's Pharmacy picking out that card. And another half hour trying to figure out what to write. I got in a huge fight with Amber about it."

"You did?"

"Yeah, I think she felt threatened."

"Why?"

As an answer, he squeezed me close. "'Love, Dennis.'"

I nestled against him, reveling in the feeling of his arm wrapped around me. "Well, this was a nice date."

He chuckled, my head bouncing with his breaths. "I'd say it was a success." His hand rubbed my back. "Do you think we'll have a second date?"

Now I laughed too. "I think the chances are good."

We drifted off with my body pressed against his. I knew deep down that he was special. I felt this desperate yearning to spend more dinners across from him, more nights naked with him. Back then, I wanted to hold on to him forever.

2018

I fell asleep on Chrissy and Nick's couch with a pillow clutched to my chest. Now my neck hurts, and I sit up. Someone is making coffee; other footsteps suggest they're both still home. I pad into the kitchen to find Chrissy in a bathrobe, Nick in navy pajamas.

"Morning, Cinderella," Chrissy says.

"Don't you mean Sleeping Beauty?" I ask.

"Have you *looked* in the mirror?"

I nudge her with my hip, opening a cabinet to find a mug.

Nick's rummaging in the fridge for a carton of milk; he pours himself a bowl of cornflakes. "Was the couch comfy enough?"

"I don't even remember falling asleep. Did we finish the champagne?"

Over a bite of cereal, Nick says, "*You* did."

I groan, sipping the too-hot coffee, desperate for the caffeine to bring me back to life. "You guys are bad influences. I haven't had that much fun in . . . I don't even know."

Chrissy hugs me from the side. "What are friends for?"

I glance at the clock—8:50 a.m. "Shit," I say. "My dad needs the truck in ten minutes." I set down my coffee and spring into motion, searching for my sweater, coat, and purse.

Chrissy hands me my keys, and they walk me to the door.

"Will we see you soon?" Nick asks.

"Of course," I say. "Maybe we can meet up again tomorrow?"

"Nick's working, but I'm off at noon," Chrissy says. "Lunch?"

"It's a date," I say.

The three of us hug briefly.

"I'm lucky to have you two," I say, then rush down their porch steps into the rain.

On the road, I lay on the gas. Rain spatters the windshield, the wipers wagging at sixty swipes a minute. My parents' house is about fifteen minutes outside of Port Townsend. As I enter the valley, fog distorts the road, and I slow down. Few other cars are out, their headlights on despite the hour. Darker clouds hover in the distance.

When I arrive, the dash clock reads 9:07 a.m. Gravel crunches under my feet as I rush toward the house, afraid I've made Dad late for a job. Inside, the house is quiet.

"Dad?" I call.

Nothing.

"Dad?"

Coop runs up, his fur flat along one side of his face—clearly, he's been sleeping. Did Dad get a ride some other way? I pat Coop's head.

Lifting my hood, I jog outside, around the house, and down the hill toward the barns. The cattle are huddled along the fence line; the horse pasture is empty, and I suspect they're still in their stalls.

Rounding the bend, I notice a car I don't recognize. Two people are just inside the horse barn's open double doors, shrouded in dim gray shadow. They're embracing. When I step in from the rain, they both turn, startled. The man is my father. The woman is *not* my mother. She has an angular face and is likely my parents' age, but she's bundled up in clothes that are too nice for the barn. Even her hat, which has fur around the edges, appears expensive. Dad is wearing his work clothes and has a bundle of twine in his hand as if he's just fed the horses. I can hear them munching, an idle snort. It's late to be feeding them.

"I brought the truck," I say to Dad. "Are you going to be late?"

He looks at his watch. "Yes." His eyes flicker to the woman.

A prickly, dark feeling nestles in my chest.

"This is my daughter, Abby," my father says to her.

"Oh, the scientist. I've heard great things about you, Abby." The woman's voice is breathy.

"I'm Wendy."

"Wendy was just leaving." Dad lifts a trash can lid and shoves the twine inside.

Down the line of stalls, Nutmeg—a chestnut mare—pokes her head out of her window.

"Babs, can you throw Nutty a flake of hay?" Dad asks.

Wendy steps aside as Dad bustles around, gathering another strand of twine off the floor. I know I walked in on something, but I'm not sure what—I can't stop noticing how beautiful the woman is.

"I should be going," Wendy says. "John, I'll hear from you?"

He doesn't look at her. He shoves more twine into the can.

She nods at me, turns, and walks out into the rain. I watch her from the doorway, her zigzag route to her Lexus, avoiding puddles and mud. Her tires hiss over the wet gravel as she drives off.

Dad's still rushing around. I bend toward the open hay bale and lift a good-size pat of hay. Nutmeg nickers when I approach, a low *huh-huh-huh*. She stretches out for a nibble as soon as the hay is within reach, and I toss it through her window.

"Who was that?" I ask Dad, brushing hay off my arm.

"Wendy. I'm going to be late."

I follow him out into the rain. His breath swirls, and he picks up the pace.

We go the rest of the way in silence. Turning questions over in my mind, examining the scene from all angles, I can't guess who Wendy is. I fear the answer.

At the truck, Dad touches my shoulder. "Your mom wanted me to tell you: She talked to her friend Gwen. The rental is yours if you want it."

"I don't even have a job." How can he even talk to me about Mom, when he hasn't explained what was going on in the barn?

"She wants to take you to see it this afternoon. She should be home from work in a couple hours."

I nod stiffly. He closes the door and pulls out of the driveway, taillights disappearing. I watch until he's completely gone from view. The rain is letting up, but another cloud is brewing in the distance.

2009

The beginning of Dennis and me was a free fall of laughing and lovemaking and spending every minute together. I fell into everything he had to offer: stability, comfort, humor, love. A suitable beginning for a love-of-my-life relationship. You never recognize the good times until they're behind you.

After searching for a place to live in town after college, I finally moved straight in with Dennis. When I wasn't writing the occasional article for a local environmental journal—an easy way to make a little money while I applied for research programs—I added decorative pillows and framed pictures and books to Dennis's place. Suddenly, life was filled with "we" and "our" instead of "me" and "my." We spent Christmas Eve with my family and Christmas Day with his and kissed at midnight on the New Year. We returned to our first-date restaurant for Valentine's Day, and I marked him as my plus-one for Chrissy and Nick's wedding.

I was Chrissy's maid of honor, and the weeks before the wedding were hectic. Between dress fittings and practice makeup, I'd applied for a research trip through my alma mater, working alongside students as a visiting scientist. It wasn't glamorous, but if I was accepted, I'd be tracking salmon up in Alaska, and I was desperate for something more adventurous than wasting time in my hometown. The study could be the start of my career, and I was eager to hear back.

Chrissy's bridal shower was on a bright May afternoon, the spring sun not quite sweltering. Chrissy had a family friend who owned a historic Victorian home on the bluff; it overlooked the ferry dock, inlet, and neighboring islands. I clutched my phone, periodically checking the blank screen to make sure I hadn't missed a call from an Alaskan area code. And then, finally, while I was chitchatting with one of Nick's cousins, my cell started buzzing, and I abandoned the conversation to answer the call.

I had been accepted. *Accepted!*

I imagined Dennis's reaction when I told him later. He'd probably pick me up and spin me around, insisting we go out to celebrate. He'd tell me he was proud. Dennis had been nearly as impatient to hear the news as I was—Chrissy was a close third.

In a blur, I searched the house for her. I found Chrissy in the green room—a lush, tiled, potted-plant-filled space made of windows—chatting with Nick's mother, and I rushed over.

She looked up, her eyes wide, clearly already privy to my news just based on my expression. "Yes?"

I nodded vigorously, my chest convulsing with excitement. Even my fingertips pulsed.

Chrissy—aglow from a facial and her upcoming nuptials—leaped up, her arms outstretched. "Yes, yes, yes!"

Nick's mother looked confused, and Chrissy explained: "She just received the opportunity that will launch her career!"

"Hardly," I said, bashful, but maybe her words were true.

"That's wonderful, Abby," Nick's mother said.

A few other guests came in, curious about the hubbub.

"I don't want to steal your thunder," I whispered to Chrissy, but she was already reaching for her champagne glass.

"A toast," she said. "To my best friend. Abby got some good news, and I want us all to wish her luck. It's a study in . . ."

As Chrissy spoke, I glanced around the room and spotted Dennis's sister, Jackie, who, despite having broken up with Chrissy's brother after high school, was still enough of a friend to be invited to the wedding and therefore the prewedding girl stuff. She was a bulldog of an older sister—protective of Dennis—but we'd grown to like each other. I smiled in her direction, and she returned it with a congratulatory nod.

With Chrissy's lead, all the women toasted, and I sipped from my glass. Again, Chrissy was swept away by her guests, so I wandered over toward Jackie. We leaned together in a light, shouldery hug.

"Congratulations," she said.

"Thank you. I'm still kind of in shock."

A tight expression distorted her face. "I'm surprised you applied."

"I figured it was worth a shot."

"It must be prestigious."

"Kind of," I said. "More of a stepping-stone, really."

Her expression turned hard, red lips cast in a clenched frown. I shifted on my feet, wondering what I had done to rub her the wrong way.

"But how are you?" I asked. "I love your dress."

"Have you told Dennis yet?"

I faltered. "No, I just got the call. I'll tell him later in person. Is something wrong?"

"Not at all," she said. "He'll be happy for you."

"He's always so supportive," I said.

The comment didn't seem to ease her chilly demeanor. "Well, good for you." She walked away, her shoulders tense under the fluttery floral sleeves of her dress.

"What was that about?" Chrissy asked, returning to my side.

"No idea."

"She didn't say anyth—"

Just then, Nick's sister, Julie, came over. "Congrats, Abby."

"Thanks, Jules," I said. "How's college life?"

As we talked, Jackie's presence burned a hole in my back. I couldn't imagine why she had been so harsh toward my news. Still, I shook with glee—I couldn't wait to tell Dennis.

~

Having stayed late after Chrissy's bridal shower to help clean and pack away the gifts, I returned home in the evening. Excitement vibrated through my body like a drumbeat. The sky was still light, but tucked into the trees, our house was already dark. Inside, the living room was dim as a cave, and I tossed my keys on the counter.

I called, "Dennis? You home? I have good news!" and flipped on the light.

He was sitting on the couch, his figure hunched. He looked pale.

"Dennis, why were you sitting in the dark?" I went to his side, sat close, and rubbed his back, my fingers curling at the base of his neck. "What's wrong?"

When he looked up, his eyebrows were pinched together. "Did you have a fun time at the party?"

"What's wrong?" My pulse elevated with worry. "Dennis, what's going on?"

He reached for the soda on the coffee table and took a sip. "Last week, I had that checkup at the doctor's, remember?"

"You said everything was fine."

"Well, she detected a murmur." Seeing my expression, he added, "I didn't want to worry you. The doc said it was probably nothing, but upon later inspection—" He broke off, glancing away.

Dread was pooling into every corner of my being. "What?"

"She wants me to come back in. There's an irregularity, and they want more tests."

"What could it mean?" I asked, shaking. "How bad is it?"

"Don't know yet," Dennis said. "It could be anything from high blood pressure to heart surgery."

"Surgery," I said, unbelieving. He was too young to have heart trouble. Dennis had a strong, healthy body. He ate well, had a physical job—aside from some fatigue and light-headedness, there hadn't been any sign of something wrong.

"She said it's unlikely but wanted to be up front."

I shook my head. "So now what?"

"I have an appointment tomorrow," Dennis said. "We'll get more answers then."

I felt an odd sense of desperation coursing through me, but before I could speak, Dennis said, "You mentioned good news?"

I stared into his eyes, those blue eyes I loved so much, and wanted so badly to hold on to him forever. "I love you."

"That's the good news?" He smiled and kissed me.

Tears streamed down my face, but he only kissed me harder. His hand cupped my cheek, and then his fingers tangled with my hair. When he pulled away, I felt even more ragged than before.

"You heard back from the research trip, didn't you?" Dennis asked, his hand lingering on my face.

I nodded.

"You got in?"

"I don't have to go," I said. "I don't think I want to, if you're having health problems."

Dennis sat back. "Of course you're going."

"Not with you—"

"It's your dream, Abby. I'll still be here when you get back."

I shuddered, my eyes brimming, my voice high with emotion. "Will you?" I squeaked.

"Always," Dennis said, pulling me into his arms again. "I promise."

2018

The clouds have broken, and I'm pacing the house, Coop following me back and forth, back and forth, his tail wagging worriedly. I analyze the situation I just witnessed with my father and Wendy, angry and curious and baffled all at once. What even *was* that? And then Mom is walking through the door, oblivious and cheery. She's explaining that she talked to Gwen.

The rental. Right.

Setting down her purse, she says, "I'm so excited—can we go see it now?" She cradles a bouquet of cherry-red carnations. Before I can answer, she continues, "Aren't these flowers lovely? I *had* to bring them home. We need a bit of color in all this soppy gray weather." After trimming the stems, she arranges them in a vase. "Gwen's renovation is perfect timing. The stars must've aligned."

I swallow. I get the urge to tell her—but tell her what? *Mom, I saw Dad holding a strange but gorgeous woman in the barn this morning.* The words rattle around in my head, unbearable but also unspeakable. There has to be some kind of explanation.

And then we're swept up by the day: farm chores, work stories, driving to town. At Gwen's, I find new distractions.

Gwen is an old friend of my mom's, and I haven't seen her since I was in elementary school. She lives just a few blocks from Aldrich's

Market in uptown Port Townsend—a convenient location. The rental is Gwen's former candle-making studio, renovated by her partner, Lorraine, and smelling of essential oils and soy wax.

"We're two weeks away from finishing," Gwen tells us as she shows us around.

It's located in the far end of her backyard garden, tucked between two giant rhododendrons. An efficient five hundred square feet, it's clean and private and well lit with skylights. It even comes with a roommate: a gray tabby, Taffy (whom I only meet for a darting moment, as she's preoccupied with chasing something through the thicket of tangled rhody branches). Gwen will even hold it for me while I search for work.

It's a generous offer.

As my mother and I drive away, Mom says, "What a great deal! Aren't you excited?"

Indeed, a spark of hope glimmers in my chest. "I'm glad you ran into her, Mom."

"Me too, dear, me too."

Impulsively, I pull out my phone to check my email. It's unlikely that the Center for Salish Orca Research would've responded to me in just a day's time, but I check anyway.

While I'm scrolling through emails, Mom continues, "It's a beautiful space. I wish your father and I had bamboo floors like that."

I pause on an email from Penny Shelton, a name I don't recognize. But the address domain is familiar: penny@CSOR.org. It's a reply to my résumé email. *Abby, thank you for your inquiry. Unfortunately . . .*

Is it worth reading further?

. . . your skillset is not something we're looking for right now. If you would still like to get involved, we have volunteering and unpaid internship opportunities available all year round.

Mom is still talking about the rental. She lifts her hands from the wheel in an enthused gesture. "Oh! And the *price*—you really won't find anything cheaper, dear."

A thick sense of doubt makes my head swim. I knew it. I knew they would reject me. My experience is with humpbacks, not killer whales—and besides, all the studies on my résumé were cut short. They probably think I'm noncommittal or just have bad luck. I've found myself in the same predicament I was in five years ago: job searching in a dead-end town. Rejected by the Center for Salish Orca Research. Without the CSOR, my options here come down to the paper mill or customer service. Without the CSOR, I have no direction. A cold panic grips my intestines, squeezing.

"Oh, Abby, what are the chances I would run into Gwen just as you're in need of a place? Isn't it just perfect?"

How can she not read the hopelessness on my face?

"I don't have a job," I say, muffled. "I don't have any money left." The research program ended; the Center for Salish Orca Research rejected me without even an interview; I blew off Dr. Perez's recommendations; I could apply for grants myself, but that could take months and—no. I'm out of options. The guilt of success after leaving my husband has brought me back here, back to where I feel stuck. I could blame Dennis, but the truth is that it's all my fault. My career dreams never thrived in this town—I was delusional for pretending it might be different this time.

"Oh, sweetheart, that doesn't—"

Suddenly I'm sobbing so violently that Mom has to pull over to make sure I'm okay. She rubs my back up and down, up and down.

"It's okay, it's okay," she says. "It'll all work out."

A new wave throws me against the rocks. I bury my face in my hands and rest my head on my knees and try to suck in air. Mom hands me a McDonald's napkin, and when I blow my nose, the paper turns to mush in my hands. It's like no time has passed at all.

After I blow through six more grease-splotched napkins, my mother puts her car in drive and pulls onto the road again. I keep my forehead on my knees, my sobs becoming shudders. The tires roar over asphalt, the sound penetrating the silent cab. Then a new sound: the crunch of gravel. The car turns and stops, and my mother puts it in park.

I lift my head, hair in my face. The sky has cracked open, and the sun shines brightly through charcoal, fast-moving clouds. We're at Point Hudson, near the marina. The maritime center looms behind us, a wind blockade. Docked sailboats bob wildly, the wind gusting outside the car.

My mother touches my shoulder. "I have errands to run," she says apologetically. "Why don't you get a cup of coffee?"

"In the maritime center?" I ask, glancing backward. Through a set of tall windows, I spot a group of teenagers sanding the upside-down hull of a small wooden boat.

"Yeah, there's a new coffee shop in the bottom, overlooking the water." She smiles with kindness in her eyes. "Just sit and drink coffee and watch the water, and I'll come get you in an hour."

"Okay." I get out of the car. "Thanks, Mom."

She blows me a kiss, I close the door, and then I'm all alone in the parking lot with the wind snapping at my clothes. I'm not sure a cup of coffee will make me feel any better about my fuckups, but maybe the caffeine will make me feel a little more human again on this dreary afternoon.

I hurry down the short corridor between the two buildings of the center, heading toward the beach. The wind bursts off the water and through the open hall, even more chilling than in the parking lot. Up ahead, the coffee shop is located in the western building, right on the edge of a cobblestone courtyard leading to the mouth of a pier. Beyond the abandoned summer benches and mandala-like paving, past the wood slabs and creosote-coated pylons, the ocean is a frothy, angry cobalt monster, hissing and shrouded in mist. I pull the heavy door of the shop open and slip inside, the cold clamoring in after me.

But the weather is no match for the heat and bustle indoors. Chatter fills every corner of the small, well-lit space. Customers have shed their layers, wool and fleece and waterproof shells all draped across chairbacks. Spoons clatter on saucers, people sip frothy latte tops, and the espresso machine squeals with joy.

A tall, long-haired man with a neat hickory-colored beard stands behind the bar, a dirty rag strung through his belt loop. Our eyes meet, and he says, "Welcome to Energy Coffee. What'll it be?"

I glance at the laminated menu on the counter but don't really see it. Too preoccupied by today's woes, I'm in no mood to decide. "Dealer's choice," I say.

The man's eyes widen, but then he folds his arms and sizes me up. "Feeling adventurous?"

It's not like he could make this day any worse. "Go for it."

He grins, ducking below the counter for supplies. He comes up with a few shakers—I can't see their labels—plus a squeeze bottle of dark liquid. Curiosity erodes my weary mood. He pulls espresso shots while—in an explosion of hissing, gurgling sound—he steams the milk. A cup appears. A half pour, a dash of brick-colored powder, another pour, a sprinkle, and then a fern-shaped foam pattern on top. Finally, he garnishes the mystery drink with coarse Himalayan salt.

I raise my eyebrows in suspicion.

"Just try it." He pushes the cup toward me. "You're the one who said 'dealer's choice.'"

I grasp the warm cup and lift the rim to my lips, foam tickling the roof of my mouth. At first, all I taste is the salty froth, but then another flavor appears. Spice? The kick is fierce and lively. I sip again, and this time the spice is met with the smooth sweetness of chocolate. The heat mellows on my tongue, and I savor it, licking my lips afterward.

The barista chuckles, warm and low. "You like?"

"What is it?"

"Spicy mocha," he says. "Cinnamon, cayenne, dark chocolate."

I take another indulgent sip. "Genius."

"Thank you," he says. "Name's Zack."

"Abby."

"What brings you in, Abby?"

Unhappily reminded of this day, I say, "I couldn't even begin to tell you."

"That bad, huh?" He runs his fingers through his red hair, pushing it back.

I nod.

"Well, hopefully the spice can chase away the gloom." Another customer has come in, and he slides his hand down the bar with a wink. "Take care." His attention swivels toward the new order.

"I haven't paid," I interrupt.

He waves dismissively. "On the house."

Taken off guard by his generosity, I protest, but he shakes his head. The other customer orders, and Zack continues his duties, this time prepping a pour over. I cradle the warm cup in my hands, lingering by the counter, but more customers have arrived, and Zack doesn't look over again.

A seat has opened up by the window, and I slide onto the barstool, resting my elbows on the narrow tabletop. I wonder how long the café has been open. I wonder what I'll do, now that CSOR has rejected me. I pull out my phone and consider calling my old contact at the Salish Science Center—I check their website first. She's no longer listed on their staff page; a new director smiles in her place, a man with kind eyes and a goatee, the photo taken on a beach somewhere. The footer of their website specifically says they're not hiring. I set my phone facedown and sip my mocha; my eyes sting from crying, and I close them, savoring the sweet and comforting burn of my drink. Over the next hour, the place gradually clears out, and a new rain cloud passes overhead, the sky going coal dark.

Mom texts me: 15 minutes.

I text back: Okay.

Only a few customers remain, now: one well-dressed older man, reading a thick book; a mother and daughter still wearing their hats, leaning close; and a pair of men at the counter wearing wet work boots, chatting with Zack.

Mom texts: Feeling better?

I respond with the shrug emoji, and promptly after, my mother sends the blow-kiss emoji.

I push my empty cup aside and stare out the window. The water is shrouded in a sheet of rain, little whitecaps blinking in the muddled, dimensionless gray. A chill passes over me despite the warmth of the shop, and just as my thoughts are about to take a dark turn again, Zack appears at my table. A new barista has taken his place behind the bar.

"Well, how was it?" Zack asks.

"Amazing. Thanks again, you didn't have to . . ."

He waves a hand. "Consider it a warm welcome." His brown eyes are amiable.

"Do you own this place?"

"Indeed I do. Coffee is my specialty."

"I'll say."

He chuckles. "I just wanted to thank you for stopping in. I want my customers to feel welcome."

"Thanks, I needed this," I admit. "Hard day."

He sighs, empathetic. "Did the coffee help, at least?"

"Actually, yeah."

"That's the goal." He turns abruptly, waving at the mother and daughter, who are leaving. "Nice seeing you two. Only one more month."

The mother beams, giving him a thumbs-up, and follows her daughter out into the rain.

Probably having seen the curiosity written on my face, Zack explains, "The orca countdown. They go whale watching every year, as much as possible. The season starts next month."

"Orcas in March?" I shake my head. "They're more likely to see gray whales."

Zack stands a little straighter. "Oh yeah?"

"I'm a marine biologist—*was* a marine biologist."

"Is that really something that can be past tense?"

The question catches me off guard. "The research program I was on ended recently."

"So you need a job?"

I'm starting to think he's some kind of clairvoyant, or maybe just nosy.

He continues, "I think Sound Adventures is looking for a naturalist."

"Sound Adventures?" The name is familiar.

"The whale watching company across the parking lot," he says, and I realize I've applied there before years ago, when I was still with Dennis. "Their other naturalist just told them she wouldn't be back this year, and they'll need one when the season starts. You ought to stop in. Tell them I sent you."

"Oh," I say, distracted by the memory of my last application. I withdrew my résumé back then—for Dennis.

My phone blips, and I glance down. Mom is outside. "Thanks for the job tip," I say to Zack, scooting off my stool. "I should get going."

He grabs my empty cup off the table. "Nice to meet you, Abby. I hope you stop in again."

"I'm sure I will. Thanks again for the mocha."

"The pleasure's mine." He returns to the counter, helping the other barista wash mugs.

I slip into my coat, thinking about the whale watching company. Some scientists dislike whale watching tours due to sound pollution and habitat disturbance. But generating excitement in the public, teaching them about these amazing creatures and instilling them with a love that could move them to reduce their use of plastics, quit eating farmed fish, and vote in favor of the environment—that compels me. And judging by their interest in my application six years ago, they might actually ask for an interview.

Back outside, the rain is pouring, and I rush toward Mom's car. Her headlights cut through the mist, igniting the silvery raindrops. On the opposite side of the parking lot, I spot the Sound Adventures banner on a small building—my heart catches in my throat, stinging like cayenne and cinnamon.

2009

Chrissy and Nick had a big reception just outside of town. It was a rainy day, but I don't think they noticed. Tables and chairs created a big arc around the dance floor, and three champagnes in, they danced wildly to whatever beats the DJ played. Dennis and I danced, too, my crimson bridesmaid's dress twirling as Dennis spun me round and round. He looked good in his tux—the clean cut of his collar, the tie, the long lines of black fabric—he looked sexy enough to make me swoon.

"Only one of us should be swooning," he said when I told him so, making light of his recent heart trouble. His doctor had given him a prescription, and now it was wait and see. Two weeks, and so far so good. Less light-headedness and fatigue.

As a slow song swelled, Dennis gathered me into his arms, and we swayed to the music. I rested my head on his chest, glimpsing Chrissy and Nick beaming at each other as if no one else existed. I looked at Dennis, feeling that same way. He kissed me deeply, then guided me into a slow dip.

"The deadline is tomorrow," he reminded me.

I frowned—I didn't want to think about it. My research opportunity needed an answer, but with Dennis sick, I couldn't bring myself to say yes. I was being pulled in two entirely different directions, and the closer we got to my acceptance deadline, the more it felt like my heart would just rip in two.

"I know you don't want to think about it," Dennis said, reading my mind, "so I'll decide for you."

I laughed. "Oh, really?"

"You're going," he said. "You have to. It's only a couple months, and the medication is working."

I spotted Jackie sitting at a table with her date. She glanced in my direction, and I looked away. At the bridal shower, she'd known. Dennis had told his mother about the first doctor's appointment, and she had told Jackie. Jackie had assumed I was leaving despite knowing about Dennis's heart, but it wasn't true. Even now, after Dennis had spoken to her about the whole thing, I didn't think she liked me. She'd burned the bridge before I'd had a chance to cross over and explain myself.

"Your family won't forgive me if I go," I said.

"So?"

I popped a shoulder in a half-hearted shrug. Was there a woman on the planet who didn't think about her own wedding while attending another? We'd barely been together for a year, but I didn't want Dennis's family against me—now, or in the future.

"I want them to like me," I said lamely.

"They won't understand either way," Dennis said. "And I don't want you to resent me."

Tears welled again, and he used a thumb to wipe away one that fell. "What if—"

"Don't let the what-ifs interfere with what you want, Abby," he said.

I want you, I yearned to say. *I want a career. Can't I have both?* But my throat was too watery to speak. Dennis swayed me gently, his hand nestling into the small of my back, his calloused palm catching on the flimsy fabric. I had the urge to bury my face in his chest, but I refrained.

"You're going," he said again, more forcefully. "We've done this before. I'm only a call away, remember?"

I looked up into his eyes. "I love you, D."

"I love you too, Smarty."

~

The research opportunity was a study on the ear bones of salmon (seriously). Like tree rings, a fish's otoliths told its history. Layer by layer, scientists could learn a lot about a fish's environment. Dr. Barnes at my alma mater in Alaska was leading a study on the migratory patterns of Chinook salmon, using tiny ear bones as his guide. His class of undergraduate students was helping him gather the otoliths from spawning salmon—recently dead—and I was to assist with the study, showing the students how to collect the bones and decipher the rings.

I spoke to Dennis nightly. Our conversations resembled the early days of our relationship. We discussed what we ate for breakfast, articles we'd read, funny happenings at work. Only now, we could also talk about how much we wanted each other and missed each other without leaving it implied and unspoken. I could lie in bed at night and not just imagine what Dennis felt like beside me but *know*. I even missed his snores.

He assured me that the medication for his arrhythmia was still working, despite a new adjustment in dosage. Though I tried to memorize the big words and details that Dennis relayed, I could barely focus when he spoke. The words were abstract, but the worry was real; I felt a stark relief every time he called, and my days were underpinned with concern. I had never loved someone so much.

About six weeks into the study, I ventured out with the students to gather the ear bones. The salmon were all around, spawning in the shallow water, their tails flicking over the pebbles. Many were already dead, their life cycles complete, floating in the water or rotting on shore. The students congregated with waders on, knives in hand. We were to find the freshest deceased salmon, make an incision into their brain cavities, extract the otoliths, bag them, number them, and take them back to the lab. It wasn't a glamorous process, but the results were essential.

Accustomed to our somewhat grim routine, the students joked among themselves, working in pairs to manage the cumbersome baggies, vials, and gross fish handling. Dr. Barnes oversaw the bunch—fifteen total, including myself. I was left to gather samples on my own. I didn't mind—I got to wander a little farther and liked setting myself apart from the students. It made me feel like a real biologist, even if I only received a measly stipend and a written acknowledgment at the end of the study.

I enjoyed lab work, but nothing compared to being in the field. Out here, the river meandered, collecting in crystal-clear shallow pools, rippling but not rambunctious. Fish kicked up sediment, and orange eggs sloshed in excess. The first trees were yellowing, and every time a breeze slithered along the river, a shower of leaves would glitter toward the earth. It was afternoon, and sunlight came through the canopy in narrow beams; like spotlights, they ignited patches of sandy riverbank, the twitching fins of salmon, and swarms of hovering insects. Following a trail of dead fish, I gathered as many samples as I could, listening to the students' soft voices and occasional laughter.

As I entered a slightly deeper pool, water sloshed against my waders. I spotted a female on the opposite edge of the bank and waded toward her, the ripples from my movements gently rocking her body. Once I reached her, I stooped, admiring the streak of sunset pink across her side. From fry to adult, she'd had a long journey. How many bears, eagles, and orcas had she eluded? How many humans? Like all the salmon here, she'd swum hundreds of miles, led by scent or instinct or a road map in her brain. Gone for years, only to return to her birthplace to spawn and die. The magnitude of it swayed me. The generations.

Scales came off on my glove as I turned her, preparing the incision. Her body twitched, causing me to jump. Many of these fish were near death or newly dead, and the muscle spasm wasn't a rare occurrence or the first time I'd seen it happen. But we were dedicated to humane collection. I observed her, waiting to be certain she was gone. She didn't move again; clearly the convulsion had been in death.

Bending toward her again, I reached forward with my knife, then noticed something peculiar. On the other side of her face, a strand of plastic hung out of her jaw. At first I suspected she'd swallowed a fisherman's hook, but when I looked closer, the line appeared to be floss. This region was fairly untouched by stray plastics; I wondered how far the fish had carried the pollution with her.

"Dr. Barnes," I called, and he came over, the students trailing.

He bent to look at the fish. There were little specks of water on his glasses, and when he looked at me, the sunlight glared on the lenses, so I couldn't see his eyes. "Why don't we see where it leads?"

Despite the goal of this study, I felt strange enough just cutting open the animals' heads. I didn't like disturbing nature if I didn't have to. But clearly Dr. Barnes had education in mind. I looked around at the students, who were staring down at the fish. I lowered my knife to the carcass. First, I extracted the ear bones and dropped them into the tube of a nearby student. Next, I tugged on the plastic to no avail.

Dr. Barnes said, "It'll be a lesson in anatomy, as well as pollution." His way of telling me it wasn't in vain.

Carefully, I used the knife to cut from tail to chin, right along the seam of her belly. A pang of curiosity tickled my fingertips. Silently, I apologized to the dead salmon. With medical-like precision, I sliced a little deeper, and then Dr. Barnes was opening her up for the class to see. Leftover eggs, her intestines, the feathers of her gills—it was all so neatly organized in hydrodynamic casing. Bright muscle framed each organ. Dr. Barnes tugged on the thread that came from her mouth. Something shifted in her esophagus, unseen. He cut higher on the fish and, in a spurt, identified a coil of floss. He pulled from the mouth again, and it came loose, stained pink and nearly a foot long.

Behind me, a student groaned. "It's horrible."

But my eyes had caught something else, a faint movement inside the chest. Dark and triangular, an organ constricted in slow, steady time. Her heart was still beating.

Recalling her quiver when I first found her, I gasped.

Dr. Barnes turned to me, realizing. "Would you look at that," he said. "The heart isn't quite done."

I knew from my own studies the ways that bodies still worked, even when the life light was supposedly gone. Dr. Barnes explained it further to the group, assuring them that the fish was dead, the heart too weak and erratic to take blood to her brain or other vital organs. Sure enough, as we watched, the heart stopped once for nearly thirty seconds before constricting again. Instinct, muscle memory, whatever you wanted to call it—the sight still frightened me. While Dr. Barnes spoke, I reached forward. My gloved finger grazed the heart, and it moved ever so slightly. Drawing my hand back, I stared down, watching for perhaps a minute after that last shudder occurred.

I didn't know whether to be horrified or awestruck. I looked to Dr. Barnes, who had quieted. He'd been watching me, probably trying to read the creased expression on my face. Now, his glasses made his eyes look big and inquisitive. Almost perplexed. Then his forehead softened, and his voice lifted to the crowd of students on the riverbank.

"Let's all take a moment to thank her for giving her body to this cause," he said. "It's not every day we get to see life so close up. Every one of these bodies has instinct and drive and a family tree." He paused, stood.

I rose, too, my knees aching. I stared into the treetops. Wind caressed my face, my hair, and hissed through another shower of leaves.

"Let's close our eyes and honor her," Dr. Barnes said.

All sixteen of us fell into collective silence. I heard the shift of gravel beneath rubber boots, the squeak of waders. Someone's waterproof jacket whooshing with the careful adjustment of an arm; a sniffle; my own breath seeping out of my mouth. I thought of Dr. Barnes's words, *a family tree*. What histories did this river know?

Like the fish, every human on earth had instinct, drive, family—and love. I was reminded of Dennis and his heart, the updates I so desperately looked forward to at the end of each day. A low, thundering fear ran through me then, and it stuck with me all the way back to campus.

It was late afternoon when Dr. Barnes called it a day. I stayed a little longer at the lab, helping sort and store the samples for tomorrow, when the students would try their hands at reading the rings in the bones.

"That was wild today, wasn't it?" Dr. Barnes said as we turned off the lights and locked up the lab.

"Truly," I said. "Do you think she—the fish—do you think it felt . . . ?"

Dr. Barnes stopped outside the door. We were heading in opposite directions. "No," he said. "It's just a symptom of her body's base function, is all."

I went to speak but didn't know how to form the words. I felt shaken and fascinated and humbled all at once.

"Don't feel bad about it," Dr. Barnes said. "She was gone before you spotted her, I'm sure. I've seen it before."

"Thanks," I said.

"And the class—they'll remember that forever. Part of this job is research, teaching facts. But another part is teaching reverence." He spread his hands, as if his gesture said the rest.

The school had put me up in a cottage house not far from the dorms, and I was grateful for the sunlight streaming in when I got back. I peeled away my damp, fishy clothes, leaving the outer shells at the door in a bag. Stripped down, the next thing I did was shower. In the warm water, the steam, I found my mind traveling back to Dennis and that deep rumble of worry.

When I got out, I wandered back into the small living space, my hair done up in a towel. I checked my messages, but there were none—it was still early. To occupy myself, I took a trip to the campus laundromat and bought groceries. The phone was ringing when I came back through the door. Dropping the laundry bag and my keys and slipping out of my boots, I picked up just before the call went to voice mail.

"Hello?"

"Abby." But it wasn't Dennis's low voice, the voice with love and laughter in every word uttered. It was Jackie's, cold and urgent.

"What's wrong?" I asked, my heart thundering.

"Dennis," Jackie said. "He's in the hospital."

"That's not possible," I said.

"Well, he is," she said sharply. "I suggest you come home."

MARCH

2018

By early March, I've bought a 1999 Toyota Avalon with the rest of my savings and agreed on a generous work trade with my mother's friend Gwen, weeding her huge garden to pay off the first and last months on the rental while I search for a decent job. The few times I've tried Sound Adventures, they've been closed—it's the off-season for whale watching, after all, and their voice mail says to book online or call back later. In the meantime, I've enjoyed some much-needed family-and-friend time, as if to catch up on all the hugs and laughs I missed while I was gone.

I've also stopped by Eli's gallery.

There's so much pain and guilt wrapped up in Dennis still that I figure facing Eli is simpler. Maybe he can help me make sense of everything that happened four and a half years ago—no one else has been able to. It's not like Dennis will. Perhaps something is left between Eli and me, a small seed in the barren earth. He might be my only hope in finding closure.

The first time I stopped by his gallery, he wasn't in, but according to the woman at the desk last week, he spends Mondays adjusting images in Photoshop on the gallery computer. I picture Eli biting his lip as he increases the vibrancy of foreign colors. Eli bought his own space about a year after I skipped town, which makes me happy for him—he always deserved success with his art.

Dennis was always a straightforward man. Eli was his opposite, complicated and compelling and—I admit—brooding. Years ago, Eli's art was a thousand times more interesting to me than Dennis's construction business. Years ago—us sitting at a café table, rain shimmying down the windowpane, leaning close, sipping hot coffee—conversations with Eli brought me life. I never had to explain anything to him—I could say what was on my mind, what I yearned for, and he *understood.* He didn't have to ask questions or pry for clarification—Eli simply met me where I was. And when things with Dennis got tough, I wanted someone like that.

Today is Monday, and I hover outside the window of the gallery, peering in. Big shapes line the walls, splashed with his signature taste for bold color. Photos I've never seen, photos that seem oddly familiar, photos that remind me of the past.

I cup my hands against the glass to cut the glare and get a better look—and I see him. He's nailing a hook to a wall in the far back, the familiar curves of his tattoos shifting with the sinuous effort of his biceps. The pounding of the hammer reverberates all the way out to the street. His brows are pinched in focus, and then he's turning his head . . .

I jerk back. Did he see me?

I thought he'd *want* to see me and I'd want to see him, but now I'm not so sure. Maybe my memory is distorted; maybe I'm mistaken. Maybe it's Dennis I should be visiting, after all? Things were good with Dennis once. Fond memories have haunted me since the last time I saw him, since he walked away down that dark road. The black sky twinkled with dim starlight, just enough light for me to see his shape round a corner and disappear.

I hurry away down the sidewalk. The bright near-spring sun bounces off the water and reflects on the downtown shop windows. I walk and walk until I end up by the marina. The Sound Adventures building is still locked up, but a new sign in the window tells me that the store will be open next week. **Come see gray whales!** There's a little plastic brochure box to the left of the door, and I slide one out. Inside, it details different whales and their seasons: grays, humpbacks, orcas. There's a map of the Salish Sea, the intricate waterways Washington shares with Canada. There are pictures of fur seals and harbor seals and elephant seals. Tufted puffins and murres and bald eagles.

I look up at the sky, where seagulls drift on updrafts. I fold the brochure and slide it into my back pocket. Then I turn toward the maritime center. I'm in the mood for a coffee.

2009

I returned to Dennis thirty-six hours later, and by then his heart surgery was over. After an agonized, torturous flight from Alaska, I went straight to the Seattle hospital—and then waited, waited, waited. The doctors were busy, and Jackie wouldn't speak to me, unforgiving that I'd left in the first place. Dennis's mother sat in the opposite corner of the waiting room, a purple shawl wrapped around her soft, round body, her face stricken. Neither of them would look in my direction, not really, and so I sat alone and stared at the door for hours. Nurses and doctors and patients came and went until finally a face I vaguely recognized came through.

She wore scrubs and approached Dennis's family first, and I hovered nearby, listening as if I didn't belong. I knew they'd already seen Dennis, right after the surgery, while I was still in an airport somewhere and not here for him as I should have been. The doctor was listing next steps, recovery details. He was awake, and I hadn't seen him. I hated them all for not letting me run to him.

Dennis's chest had been opened and exposed to the air just like the salmon's. I hadn't gotten that image out of my head since Jackie had called and told me to come home. Vulnerable, hanging on by a thread of instinct or muscle memory or pure will. Could I have reached out and touched his heart, still beating? Sometimes I felt as if I already had.

"Another day, Mrs. Nelson," the doctor told his mother. "In the meantime, I suggest you get some sleep. Have a bite to eat."

Jackie and Dennis's mother disappeared from the room, but I stayed. I wasn't hungry, though I couldn't remember the last time I'd eaten.

There was a little light in the morning darkness outside—perhaps five a.m.—when I awoke in the waiting room chair.

"Can I see him?" I asked the first nurse who came out of that damn sterile door. The hallway had flashed behind her, a stretch of endless fluorescent lights and light-gray tiles.

"Visiting hours start at ten, ma'am," she said, her face apologetic.

Chrissy arrived around eight and forced me to the cafeteria to eat. Over cold scrambled eggs and too-sweet orange juice, she told me, "It's not your fault."

"I never should have gone," I moaned. All out of tears, my face stung, dry.

"It's not your fault," Chrissy repeated and drew my head to her chest.

"*They* think it is," I said, referring to his family.

"*They* can go fuck themselves." She squeezed me twice. "They just want someone to blame."

Finally, finally, ten o'clock came, and Chrissy sat in the waiting room while I was taken through that dreadful door. Blue curtains and gray countertops and teal scrubs and bright lights blurred through my vision as I followed the nurse back. Outside his door, I hesitated. What if he didn't want to see me either? What if he blamed me too? But then the nurse was ushering me inside and closing the door behind me.

Dennis looked up from a cup of green Jell-O, pale but rosy cheeked. There were so many tubes coming from his body: IVs in his wrists, wires disappearing beneath his gown, and oxygen lines hooked over his ears and into his nostrils.

"Abby," he breathed, sounding more like himself than I expected.

I wavered in the doorway, not wanting to harm him with my touch. A new wave of tears filled my eyes.

"Abby, come here," Dennis said, a hand outstretched.

I took a step, wobbled. "They wouldn't let me see you until now." The water in my throat made my voice come out froggy.

"You're here now," he said. "Come closer."

When I reached him, I settled into a chair near his bedside, my hand slipping firmly into his, careful not to disturb the line in his wrist.

"Why did I go?" I asked him, my eyes squeezed shut. "Why did I leave you?"

"Because I told you to," he said. "And look, see?" He lifted my chin, and I blinked away the tears. "I'm fine, Smarty, just fine."

I rested my forehead on the edge of his mattress, and he stroked my hair weakly.

"Will you be okay?" I asked. "What have they told you?"

"The surgery was a success. They'll release me in another day," Dennis said. "I'm already walking and eating on my own."

How is that possible? I wanted to ask. How could they open him and sew him up again and have him walking in mere days? It startled me.

I shook my head. "I'm so sorry I wasn't here for you."

"You're always here for me." A shaky hand tapped his chest.

My gaze focused and refocused on his hand, the blue-speckled gown. I was quivering uncontrollably. When I looked at his face, he was smiling.

"Oh," I said.

"I'm sorry I scared you," Dennis said, shifting a little. "But I'm not going anywhere. Jell-O?"

A plastic spoon was wedged into the green wiggling lump. Suddenly, I was compelled to laugh. Such a little thing in a room weighed down by seriousness.

"Dennis," I breathed, touching his face. I kissed him gently, his lips melding with mine, his eyes still closed as I pulled back. He tasted different, sour. I didn't want to leave him ever again.

2018

The week following my almost visit with Eli, I head back down to the marina. It's late afternoon, and bundled-up baby boomers idle along the shore, their dogs on leashes. Someone is teaching a wooden-boat workshop inside the maritime center. A bell on a sailboat chimes in the dim grayness, gulls squabble on a rooftop, but otherwise, the harbor is hushed.

Sound Adventures hasn't posted the naturalist position on its website, and rather than cold-emailing, I figured I'd apply the old-fashioned way—it's easier for them to say no via email than in person. Plus, small-town businesses appreciate that face-to-face connection, and I have to make a good impression.

I lean against my car, trying to calm my sudden nerves. There's a dent in the driver's-side door, where the blue paint is chipping, and I run my hand along its jagged edge. In my other hand, my résumé flutters, crisp white in the breeze. I stare at the side of the whale watch building, the yellow letters on the window now crowded by flyers and photography and gummy window decals. The whale watching season starts soon.

I know I shouldn't be picky, but for a brief moment, I waver. While the local marine life is threatened by larger issues—pollution, declining food sources, and noise from larger ships—the tour boats don't help.

Is it hypocritical to apply for a company that intentionally disturbs the whales, even minimally?

What if they don't even want me? What if, like the CSOR, my skill set is "not something we're looking for right now"? I need a job. Any job that's relevant to my passions. I know there's some good in tour companies, too, like fostering knowledge, appreciation, and awareness. Sound Adventures is not counter to my ideals, not if it's the type of place to impart wisdom and encourage change. My pulse races and my throat feels tight. I swallow, just to make sure I still can.

Rolling my shoulders back, I try a smile, take a deep breath, and push myself forward. Through the door and inside, the space is friendly and warm, cluttered with stuffed animals, T-shirts, calendars, and shot glasses. After all my peering through the windows for the past month, the place seems nicer all lit up.

A blonde-haired woman behind the counter says, "Welcome." She's around my mother's age, and for some reason, that's comforting.

I walk straight toward her. "Hi. I'm a marine biologist. I just moved here—well, I used to live here—anyway, Zack at Energy Coffee said you might have an open naturalist position?" I slide my résumé onto the counter and notice my fingers are shaking.

"He's right; we do," the woman says, grasping the bright-white page.

"I'm good on boats," I go on. "And I'm familiar with the local wildlife."

"Public speaking?"

"Not really, but the museum required . . ."

"Oh yes, I see," she says, her eyes on my résumé.

I feel embarrassed watching her peruse my credentials, my life. I've wanted to be a marine biologist since I was a teen. I have the degrees, but what do I have to actually show for it? The research study with Dr. Perez only takes up one résumé item, cut short, and Dr. Barnes is the other. Those two, plus the Salish Science Center after high school, barely fill up a whole sheet of paper. I don't mention my other, irrelevant jobs—especially not the one I quit four and a half years ago when I also quit my marriage.

"Abby," she says, trailing off, still reading my résumé. Does she recognize my name from the first time I applied? It doesn't seem so. "Why don't you swing by tomorrow at nine a.m. for an interview?"

"Really?" I say.

"Really," she says.

"Thank you so, so much." I shake her hand, though it's awkward across the counter. "Should I bring anything?"

"Just a smile," the woman says. "And dress warm."

I thank her again and rush out into the cold before I say something stupid. My hands are shaking as I hurry back to my car, but I can't bring myself to get in. For the first time since I arrived, my prospects seem good. The thought of being out on the water once again is enough to make me weep with joy.

2009

After the scare with Dennis's heart, I didn't go back to Alaska. I stayed home with him. We watched movies and nature docs, and I cooked him heart-healthy meals and drove him to all his follow-up appointments. Six weeks after surgery, he was cleared to drive himself and started visiting the construction office to help Jackie with the accounting. The doctors said he could even go back to light physical work after the New Year, so long as he took it slow. Jackie still held a grudge against me, and his mother was still frantic about her baby boy, but otherwise, things were good.

Actually, they were better than good. The scare with his heart had ignited our love in a way unlike before. Any reservations we'd had disintegrated, and we took more time to talk and cherish each other. The hardest part about this time in our relationship was the sex—or lack thereof. Physical activity of any kind was limited until the eight-week mark, so we did a lot of kissing and talking about anything other than how long it had been since the last time we were intimate. Of course, all this holding off made us want each other even more, and so there were times that our whole house seemed to be filled with electricity. One stray movement—a touch on my hip, a graze of fingers across his shoulder—and the static would cause the whole place to combust.

Meanwhile, my parents had been arguing, and I saw myself as a buffer. Since I couldn't find work I wanted, I often helped them around the farm. When I was around, the fighting would reduce to a tense simmer. I didn't know why they fought, only that when I asked, they denied that yelling had occurred. They were the lovey-dovey type, after all: they kissed in the kitchen for no reason, still held hands at the movies, went on "pie dates" at the diner. When I was a teenager, they were often the cause of rolled eyes, groans, and vacating the room. So not having seen them kiss since I returned from Alaska, I knew something was wrong, even if I hadn't heard any arguments firsthand.

One afternoon in mid-October, I came over to help my mother teach a horseback riding lesson. This was before she worked in the flower department at Safeway, when she spent time with the horses all day. A number of families came to learn from her, and today she was teaching a triple—hence needing my help.

I arrived on time, parked at the house, and walked in without knocking. To my dismay, I heard muffled arguing, my mother's high-pitched voice and my father's low and booming one. I followed the sound into the basement and spotted them on the threshold of the laundry room. Mom leaned against the doorframe with her arms folded, while Dad gestured and paced in the hall. They hadn't seen me. Backing up, I sat on the stairs and waited.

"You're not listening to me, Martha. You never *hear* me."

"I hear you, John; I hear you. You're saying I don't do enou—"

"That's not fair," my father said. "Listen to me: I can't keep us solvent on my own."

"You said we were *fine*."

"Because I can never tell you how things actually are without you getting upset and giving me the silent treatment."

"Well, I'm talking to you now, aren't I?"

"Hardly."

"Hardly?"

Watching a moth fluttering around the ceiling light at the base of the stairs, I had the sudden urge to duck my head and cover my ears.

"Martha, I'm not taking out a second mortgage. I'm not. You going to work—"

"I *do* work. I work every damn day."

"You getting a real job—"

"Teaching children isn't real?"

"You're not listening," my father said, louder than I'd ever heard him. His voice shook me, and I couldn't imagine how it shook my mother.

"You have to get a real job, Martha. A steady, nine-to-five, real job."

Silence. No: sobbing. The moth landed on the bulb cover, its wings turned translucent by the light. I bit my lip.

My father's voice softened. "Even part-time minimum wage would make a difference, cover a few bills."

"What about Dean? What about all the extra work he was supposed to give you?"

"I'm only one man, dear. Tell me you'll start looking?"

"And what am I supposed to do with my riding families?"

"Part time," my father said. "You'll still have time to teach."

"Oh, sure," my mother said. "I'm fifty-one now, John. I can't carry two jobs."

"Yeah, well, look at me. I work hard. My back is going to hell. I won't be able to farm forever either. But this is the hand we've been dealt."

My mother whimpered, and I tried not to break down myself (it wasn't like I could lend them any funds). I had never heard them so unsentimental toward each other. I'd never heard my mother so helpless, my father so hard nosed.

I was still watching the moth when my father came around the corner. I jumped up, pretending I'd just arrived. He frowned and looked at his watch. "You here for your mother?"

I nodded. I wanted to ask if they were okay. I glanced up at the light, but the moth had fluttered off somewhere else.

"Hello, dear," my mother said, coming round as well. The three of us stood at the base of the stairs, too close.

"I think the Calhouns are already at the barn," I said, trying to ignore my mother's puffy eyes.

My father brushed past me, heading upstairs.

Mom held a pair of socks, which she seemed to notice for the first time. Then she sprang to life, slipping them on. "Right, yes, I lost track of time. Will you head down? I'll be there in a moment; I just need to change into jeans."

"Sure, Mom," I said, lingering.

"I'll only be a moment."

Mom disappeared into the laundry room again, and I heard the soft, unmistakable sound of her blowing her nose. When she came out to the barn five minutes later, it was as if the tears had never occurred.

By the time the riding lesson ended, my father's truck was gone, so I helped feed the horses and muck a few stalls. I couldn't bring myself to ask her about their problems. I considered keeping my mother company while she made dinner, but she insisted I go. Dad would return any moment, she said, and Dennis would be waiting for me. So I drove home.

Their argument had rattled me. It unnerved me to think of my parents as anything other than steady. I told Dennis this when I got home. He muted the TV, seeing right away that I was shaken. His hugs and kisses were instant.

"I'm sorry, Abs," he said.

"I know it sounds like nothing compared to your parents." Despite staying married until the end, his mom and dad had fought all the time, only his dad had been an alcoholic for most of that time, so it wasn't just venomous words—it was broken glass and Dennis hiding with Jackie under the bed.

"Still," he said, giving me a squeeze. "By the way, my appointment went well."

I sat a little straighter. "I forgot to ask! What did they have to say?"

"I'm healing nicely." Then he smiled, a mischievous glint in his eye.

"What?"

"It's been eight weeks." Upon seeing my blank expression, he elaborated with a wink. "I'm clear for more physical activity."

"Oh," I said, understanding. It was the permission we'd been waiting for, only the stuff with my parents had thrown me off kilter.

He seemed to notice my hesitation, and if he was disappointed, he didn't show it. Instead, he pulled me to his chest, comforting, and I listened to his steady heartbeat. His hand slid under my shirt and along my back, warming my skin. I smiled into his T-shirt. Sometimes I felt lost at sea, but Dennis was my anchor. No matter how much the current tried to toss me, he kept me still.

"Why don't we turn on *Blue Planet*?" Dennis said, sitting up. He knew how the sound of David Attenborough's voice made me feel better.

"Yeah?"

"Hell yeah." He stood, grabbing the DVDs. "Which episode?"

I thought about it for a moment. By the time I actually said, "'Tidal Seas,'" he'd already closed the DVD tray. He knew my favorite.

"You never want to watch 'The Deep,'" he complained.

"Light-up squids?" I wrinkled my nose in disgust, teasing him.

He gave me a little shove as he sat back down. "Tides it is."

"No, no, we can watch the ugly creatures of the deep."

"Nope, you said tides."

It *was* my favorite, and for good reason: The episode included our own waters. It was all about the richness of the coasts, the exhilaration. Big waves, deep currents, churning up nutrients. The Pacific Northwest had some of the richest waters in the world, and I felt pride when I heard the enthusiasm in Attenborough's voice. There was something poetic about rough currents dredging up life from the cold, dark seafloor.

Dennis continued, "Besides, tomorrow's my day off, and I want you in a good mood." He kissed my nose. "I made spaghetti. I'll dish you up a bowl before it gets cold."

2018

It's forty-five minutes until my interview with Sound Adventures, and my terrible beater car has broken down in the middle of the Mill Road intersection. Cars whoosh by, the wind rocking me with each sudden pass. Some people honk, piled up behind me, not realizing I'm helpless. Finally, an older gentleman gets out of his car, and with the help of his twenty-year-old son, we push-steer the car to the wide shoulder.

My flashers pulse in the fog. Traffic resumes. The father-son duo get on their way, so I call Mom, since it's her day off. She doesn't answer, probably helping Dad with the farm chores. I call Chrissy next, who is on her way to work. She calls Nick for me.

The Avalon betrayed me, and so I don't dare get back inside; I lean against the door, hugging myself in the foggy cold. Two more Good Samaritans slow down and yell out their windows in case I need help. I assure them I'm fine, just fine, and check my cell phone again for the call from Nick that hasn't come yet. It's nearing 8:40—I'd planned to get another spicy mocha from Zack at Energy Coffee before my interview, for luck, but my hopes dwindle.

I stare down woodsy Mill Road, feeling alone for the first time since I came home.

Last night, I reviewed the Sound Adventures brochure until I had it memorized, brushing up on the local marine life and accompanying facts. For instance, orcas are apex predators that reach over twenty feet in length; our local pods, the southern resident killer whales, are endangered. I am already familiar with baleen whales, characterized by the filter-feeding bristles in their mouths: humpbacks, grays, and elusive minke whales. Dall's and harbor porpoise hang around too. Harbor seals. Steller and California sea lions. And the birds, so many I can never seem to cram them all into the corners of my brain.

My phone buzzes.

"Nick?"

"Already on my way," he says. "Did you call a tow truck?"

"I can't afford—"

"We'll take care of it."

I can hear the road speeding beneath his tires through the phone line. "That's not necessary," I say meekly.

"Don't bother refusing, Abs. We got your back."

I remember the clock. "Are you close?"

"Yep. See you soon."

The call ends.

I hate how nervous I am. Some scientists say that tours contribute to the downfall of the local marine habitat, disturbing the animals. I wonder if these scientists have ever ordered something online, only to have it barrel through the strait on a container ship? Do they put gas in their cars without thinking about tankers or oil spills? Have they ever taken a ferry to Seattle?

Something Dr. Barnes said long ago zings through my mind: "Part of this job is research, teaching facts. But another part is teaching reverence." I get giddy just thinking about sharing my excitement with others. I could make real change happen, one fun fact at a time. I can't miss this interview.

Thank goodness Nick arrives then, because otherwise I might've started to panic again.

"Need a ride, lil lady?" Nick says in his best (terrible) southern accent.

"My hero," I cry, climbing into Nick's truck. "Thanks again."

"What are friends for?"

"This, I guess."

He grins. "I'll drop you off, then come back to deal with the tow. Just leave your keys in the console. You're lucky I'm self-employed."

He pulls onto the main road, and I watch that traitorous Avalon fade from view. The dash clock reads 8:50. If I don't botch the interview, my passions might have a purpose once more—and a wonderful one, at that. A rush of adrenaline, sweet and potent, courses through me like a shock.

~

We arrive at the marina with five minutes to spare. Watching Nick drive away, I feel like a kid dropped off on the first day of school. I look toward the Sound Adventures building and zip up my coat. The breeze off the water is chilly but not unexpected; I dressed warmly. If only I'd had enough time to get that good-luck mocha.

Stepping inside, I'm surprised to find a different woman behind the counter, one much younger than the one I spoke with the day before. She smiles in my direction. "Can I help you?"

"I'm here for an interview," I say. "Abby."

"Oh!" she says, springing into action. "Linda, Abby is here for her interview." She hustles into the back room and comes out alongside the woman from yesterday.

"Lovely," Linda says. Today, her gray-blonde hair is pulled back into a ponytail. "Head straight out the door and down the ramp to the lower dock. You'll find Robin on the *Glacial Wind*. It's hard to miss."

"Thank you."

The *Glacial Wind* is the biggest boat in the tiny marina, an old fishing vessel that appears to have been fitted with viewing windows, bench seats, and fixed tables. As I step onto the floating dock, my nerves jump into my mouth, and I swallow them back down. Boarding the boat on my own seems like entering someone's house without knocking, so I hesitate on the edge of the dock. I don't see anyone inside.

"Hello?" I call. My voice sounds loud in the hushed marina, yet somehow too quiet to elicit a response. "Robin?"

"Back here," a man's voice calls over the spray of a hose.

I walk down the dock toward the stern, my eyes straining to see through the windows. A hat bobs near the back deck, and I pause. "Robin?"

He stands up, his round face beaming underneath a black Sound Adventures beanie. He points at me. "Abby," he says, matter of fact and friendly. "Come aboard."

Tentatively, I grasp his offered hand and push off from the dock; the boat barely shifts under my weight. Finding my footing on the rough white deck, I let go of his hand.

"Thank you for having me," I say.

"My mother tells me you need a job," he says, coiling the hose.

I realize he's talking about Linda. "Yes, I have a degree in marine—"

"I saw your résumé already," Robin says. "Follow me."

We duck inside and walk down the center of the boat, booths on either side. Each tabletop has a flower vase and little indents for coffee mugs. Maps are spread beneath the plastic tops; I imagine people sitting, peering out the windows, tracing the table maps with their fingers. There's room for at least fifty tourists. Up front, I spot the elevated platform where the captain sits—the wheelhouse—and, through a sliding door, the steering wheel.

"Throughout the summer, we run four-hour and full-day tours," Robin explains. "For full days, we have lunch in Friday Harbor on San Juan Island. We own two active vessels, and we acquired one more for next season. We usually go up into the islands, but on shorter trips, we'll occasionally head south, or west down the strait." He takes off his hat, scratches the stubbly hair beneath, and puts his hat back on. "This early, we advertise gray whale tours. The big rush is for the orcas, only six weeks from now."

I nod along, wishing I hadn't left my notebook in the Avalon.

"Your résumé was familiar. Did you apply before?"

"Yes," I mumble. "I had to withdraw for personal reasons."

"I remember liking your cover letter," he says. "I'm glad you're here now. Tell me, Abby, why did you become a marine biologist?"

The simplicity of his question knocks me off balance. This is the strangest interview I've ever had. Tongue-tied, I rack my brain and consider the awe-inspiring beauty and terror of the ocean, its power. The creatures that endure in its depths, frolicking, fleeing, living. The hardships and the impressive will. I don't think I can adequately articulate my feelings . . . but then I remember the last time someone asked me this question.

"Because I saw seawater under a microscope once, and I wasn't the same after that."

His forehead wrinkles and he frowns, and I fear my answer is bad. But then his expression lightens. "Good. Very good. I know the feeling."

He leads me out onto the bow, where a bench protrudes into the open space. He stands by the railing and stares off toward Whidbey Island.

"You know orcas, right?"

"Yeah," I say.

"I saw that your specialty is baleen whales."

"That's true, but I care a lot about the southern resident pods." I add, "In fact, I keep forgetting to ask: Does your tour company follow the federal guidelines for—"

"We don't get too close, if that's what you're asking." He seems pleased rather than annoyed that I asked. "Good question. Now, the salmon thing with Dr. Barnes, that was interesting work."

"It was."

"You didn't complete your time there, though," Robin says. "The dates on your résumé are wrong. The study went much longer than what you put down."

His observation makes me squirm. "My husband—ex-husband—boyfriend at the time." I cough. "He needed heart surgery, and I had to leave."

"That's a good excuse," Robin says. "The study with Dr. Perez is fascinating. I was sorry it ended."

"Me too."

"I saw that *Atlantic* article about it."

I feel my face reddening.

"Good stuff," Robin says. "Eloquent. Do you have experience with people?"

"Yes."

He pats my shoulder and sits on the bench, legs stretched out, ankles stacked. "Tourists are basically teenagers. They get bored quickly. They ask weird questions. They don't always take it seriously, but they're easily blown away."

"The whales change everything," I say.

He grins, big and wide. "Exactly." A pause, a glance outside the marina. "Are you familiar with the pods?"

"The residents? Yes: J, K, L."

"Can you tell them apart?"

I scrunch up my face. "Not easily. I mean, if I had a book and could see their markings . . ."

"That's good enough," Robin says. "Don't worry, the interview is going fine. So are you busy today?"

"No plans other than this."

"Good. We have tourists arriving at ten."

2009

After watching "Tidal Seas," Dennis and I ended up watching "The Deep" after all, and that night I dreamed of light-up aliens in a black void, circling me with their confusing colors. I awoke early when Dennis got up, and ducked in and out of relaxed, heavy sleep throughout the morning. Late-morning sunlight brightened the shaded windows when I heard Dennis cooking: the clank of pans, the ding of metal measuring cups, the crack of an egg. Dennis had a knack for making perfect pancakes: fluffy, golden, flawless circles. I had no idea how he did it; from the same box recipe, my pancakes always turned out dense, brown, and lopsided.

I smiled into the pillow, stretching the sleep out of my muscles. I knew the next time I woke up, he'd have a tray full of breakfast so we could eat it in bed.

The mattress tipped as Dennis settled on the bed, and as I woke again, my first lucid thought was of pancakes. When I turned my face on the pillow, I noticed that instead of kneeling with breakfast in hand, Dennis was just kneeling. I saw his face first, hopeful and nervous all in one. He had a tight jaw with a closed-lip smile and raised eyebrows.

I blinked. Was he having heart trouble? "What's wrong?" I asked.

"Nothing at all." He glanced at the edge of my pillow, and I followed his gaze, my eyes adjusting from his face to something much closer: a ring.

It faced me on the pillow, mere inches from my nose, a cushion-cut diamond with a silver band. I felt a lift in my stomach, which traveled up into my chest. I raised my head, my arms and legs tingling.

"Abby," Dennis said slowly, joyfully. "You're everything I want in a woman. Strong, passionate, smarter than me." He chuckled nervously. "Will you marry me?"

A strange feeling occurred inside me in the span of mere seconds, but to Dennis the pause must've felt like hours. I stared at the ring and then his face and then the ring again. My body flooded with dizzy excitement and head-over-heels bliss—and a tiny ink drop of nervousness? It was a big decision, after all. But I loved him; I loved him so much my heart could burst. I recognized that nervousness as the good kind, the kind that made you laugh all the way through a roller coaster ride, the nervousness that crept up even though you *knew* that you were strapped in and secure. This was just the initial apex—I could either scream and stop the ride or lift my hands up in the air and enjoy the thrill.

I said, "Yes!"

"Yes?" Dennis grabbed the ring off the pillow, reaching for my hand.

"Of course!"

He slid the ring onto my finger and rose off the floor, climbed into bed, and squeezed me into his chest. "Oh, Abby, oh, Abby."

"I love you, Dennis," I said, tears filling my eyes.

"I'm so happy."

"Me too."

We rocked in a tight embrace, and then finally he asked, "Do you like the ring?"

I wiped my eyes with the back of my hand and stared at it—how sparkly it was. I had always liked cushion cut. "It's really beautiful, Dennis."

He kissed me, a long, slow kiss that made me lose track of my racing thoughts. Excitement bubbled up onto my tongue, and I kissed him deeper. And then we were naked, rolling around—albeit carefully—chasing our joy all the way to its completion.

Afterward, he took my face in his hands and stared into my eyes. I counted the flecks of gray in his irises.

Pulling back a little, to bring his face into focus, I said, "I thought you were bringing me breakfast in bed."

He grinned a mischievous grin. "It was my backup plan: no pancakes until you said yes."

"Clever." I looked at the ring on my finger, how it caught the light in a million different ways. Then I smiled up at Dennis. "Well, I said yes, so . . . pancakes?"

He chuckled and led me out of bed. I noticed his clothing—cast to the floor during our impassioned lovemaking—was so unlike him: khakis and a now-wrinkled white button-down.

"You dressed up," I said.

"I wanted to—I don't know—I wanted to look nice, I guess."

Pulling on one of his old T-shirts, I said, "I like you better when you're stripped naked."

He winked and shrugged into a bathrobe, then ushered me into the kitchen. He'd prepared a gorgeous spread: a tablecloth, candles, coral carnations (my favorite), and a tower of perfect pancakes. On a neighboring plate, sausages were stacked like Lincoln Logs. There was orange juice, coffee, and a bottle of syrup.

"Wow," I said. "You were smart not to show me this first. I would've given you an ultimatum."

"An ultimatum?" He sat across from me and nudged the plate of pancakes in my direction. I forked two onto my plate, then went for the sausages.

"Yeah, like: I'll only say yes if you make me breakfast like this every day."

He smiled and touched the ring on my finger. "How about every Sunday?"

I sighed in mock disappointment. "Oh, fine."

We dished out breakfast, and I thought about how roller coasters were always more fun when you put your hands in the air.

"Does anyone know?" I asked.

"About?"

I held up my hand and wiggled my now-heavier ring finger.

"Your father and my mother, and therefore probably Jackie," he said. "Your dad was excited."

"You asked his permission?"

"He said, 'I don't know—ask Abby,' but he gave me his blessing."

I laughed. "That's Dad. But what about your family?"

He shrugged. "You know how they are. They'll get more excited as time goes on, I think."

"You don't mind that your family hates me?"

"They don't hate you," he said. "I love you more than anything. They'll just have to deal with it. You make me happy, and therefore they should be happy."

I took a big, buttery, syrupy bite of pancake. Dennis sipped his orange juice.

"Do you think your sister will ever . . ." I spread my palms, struggling with the words. The ring—a little too big—swung around to the underside of my finger. I swiveled it back in place.

"Is it the wrong size?" Dennis asked.

"It's a tad big," I said. "An easy fix. I'll get it resized."

"The jewelry lady said that might happen."

"You never answered me about your sister."

His forehead creased. "Because I don't have an answer. Jackie is . . . well, you know how she is. Stubborn."

I sighed and used my fork to cut a sausage link in half. "I'll try to make it right."

"That's not your responsibility," Dennis said. "It's her problem."

I couldn't fear his sister forever. "I'll make it right," I repeated.

He took my left hand in his and stroked his thumb over the ring. "Mrs. Abby Nelson." He smiled. "I think it sounds nice."

I squeezed his fingers. "Eat your pancakes before I steal them off your plate."

2018

At first I'm not sure I understand Robin. "I'm coming along?"

"Part two of your interview."

I follow him back inside to find a new face on board, making coffee behind a small snack setup at the base of the wheelhouse. She must be over six feet tall, her hair cropped short.

"Abby, this is Captain Kimberly," Robin says.

I stick out my hand. "Nice to meet you."

"Brand new, huh? Then you'll need this." Instead of shaking my hand, she pushes a mug of hot coffee into my grasp. "You coming along is a good sign—Robin only does that with people he's pretty sure about."

"The interview isn't over yet, though," he says.

Kimberly rolls her eyes. "Abby, unless you spit on a bird or throw a rock at a seal, you can consider yourself hired."

My lungs release in a whoosh of air I hadn't known I'd been holding. To stifle the stupid grin on my face, I take a sip of the too-hot coffee, burning my tongue. I swallow quickly and test the fuzzy, numb feeling in my mouth. *Hired.* I can't turn back now. This job will keep me afloat while I sort through everything else.

"Jesus, Kim, you ruined the suspense," Robin says.

"Thanks. I'm not good with suspense."

"See? You'd chase her away if it weren't for me," Kim says.

Someone new walks through the back door, a stout woman with brunette hair pulled back at the base of her neck.

"Abby, this is Joanne. She's another naturalist," Robin says.

"Nice to meet you," she says tightly, then turns to Robin. "Is she going to be in the way?"

"You and me today, Joanne. She's going to observe."

Joanne nods but doesn't seem appeased. "Pay attention and don't interrupt," she tells me, then brushes past. Through the window, I see her opening up the outdoor storage bench on the bow.

"Ignore her," Kim says, looping her arm through mine. "She's a sheepdog. Mad loyal to her pack, wary of newcomers."

"Not to mention she just broke up with Stephen," Robin mumbles. "But don't dare mention *that*."

"And here I was just about to tell you guys that I'm *dating* Stephen," I say.

Kim barks with laughter and slaps my back. "Good find, Robin. I think she'll fit right in."

It's nearing ten when everyone gets back to business, Kim checking the engine, Joanne checking the life jackets and other stock, Robin showing me around. Then I'm positioned by the stern to help guests climb aboard, welcoming them to the *Glacial Wind* as if I didn't arrive just an hour before they did. An elderly couple with thick accents; a young family that appears to be visiting from the city; a familiar-looking mother-daughter duo arm in arm; a few loners; and a group of nine people who are clearly extended family, already rowdy and smelling of french toast and bacon. The quiet space quickly fills with exuberant energy, a mix of ages from toddler to senior chattering and laughing and ordering coffee.

Once the last member is aboard, Joanne briefs everyone on safety: where the life jackets are stowed, no running outside, and so on. She tells them to use the clock system if they spot a whale: twelve o'clock is the bow, six the stern. Robin helps Kim get underway, and then we've cleared the marina completely, Port Townsend shrinking behind us.

While Joanne tends to the passengers, Robin takes me up to the wheelhouse. I'm grateful for the respite, a little dazed from the unexpected commotion. We sit on either side of Kim. The instruments look complicated to me, but she's relaxed and smiling. The fog is dense the farther out we get, and she slows down slightly.

"So far so good?" she asks. I'm on my second cup of coffee—third if you count the one before I left my parents' house this morning.

"Yes, definitely," I say.

"I dug up the catalogs," Robin says, handing them over.

Spiral bound, laminated, and a little dirty, the top book is a reference for local killer whales. Inside are pages upon pages of photos, all the same: the surface of the ocean and the topline of a black whale, a sharp dorsal fin cutting through the water. Below the pictures are letters and numbers.

"I'm sure you already know how it works," Robin says.

"Yes." The smoky-gray markings behind an orca's dorsal fin—called the saddle patch—are all different, like fingerprints. They're how scientists identify individuals.

"These are our southern resident pods, but we also have a reference for the transient orcas that come down the strait." He flips through more books, stopping at a gray whale catalog. "Here we are."

We spend some time thumbing through gray whale pictures. Then we pull out binoculars and survey the distant rippled waves until I feel cross-eyed. Kim steers us down the strait a ways, all three of us watching for spouts of air from whales. Below, Joanne offers facts about the area and subtle reminders that these are wild animals and sometimes they aren't where we think they are. Tourists ask questions, snack, and talk.

This being a half-day trip, the tourists seem a little ragged when two hours pass and there aren't any whales. It's early in the season, and most tour companies don't have boats out just yet, so we base our direction off of two other vessels, who, like us, haven't had a sighting. Joanne goes outside with a pair of binoculars, surveying the distant water. Against my instincts to stay out of Joanne's way, I follow Robin out there too. The mother-daughter duo is bundled up on the bench, utilizing some of the boat's itchy-looking blankets to keep warm. A couple of stragglers from the big family group are leaning against the railing despite the bitter, nipping cold, their cheeks crimson. Robin and I stand beside Joanne without a word, our eyes on the ocean.

I raise my binoculars again and survey the water. The fog has lifted and the sky is clear, but the water is the color of a storm cloud, choppy but not quite white capped. My eyes focus and refocus and strain to make out a gray back or tail or spout among the dark ripples. I sway slightly as Captain Kim steers the boat south and reach for the cold railing. As I swing my binoculars to the left, my elbow hits something solid—Joanne. I apologize, but she just glares and shuffles sideways to avoid more contact. Robin nudges me and smiles a half smile to make me feel better, and then Kim—from the wheelhouse—gestures to two o'clock.

In a spike of excitement, I peer out into the strait, expecting a gray whale but surprised to see a black fin dart briefly past my vision. Tingling, I lower the binoculars, surveying where I think it might have gone, where it might surface next. Joanne ducks inside to alert the guests, and soon we're all gathered along the railing. I step back to give someone else my good view. Robin stands on the vacated bench, and he offers a hand, helping me up to the better vantage, but he's careful not to block Kim's view.

Kim kills the engine. People mutter, and water laps the hull of the *Glacial Wind*. Joanne hovers behind me with a long-lens camera, and we all watch the water for a surfacing. When it comes, the tourists collectively gasp and point. Three black dorsal fins, straight and small. Transient orcas—not as beloved as the southern resident pods but just as exhilarating as seeing wolves in the wild. The power, the cunning.

Like a choreographed dance, Captain Kim positions us again so that the next time the whales pop up, they're right at twelve o'clock. They're fairly far away, so Joanne passes out binoculars. She explains what we're seeing: they're likely resting, surfacing at a regular cadence, and hanging around in the general area. Robin goes into naturalist mode, too, answering individual questions. I hover, feeling a tad useless, listening to people's conversations.

The elderly couple is holding hands, standing far back against the side rail. A toddler squeals, enthused, though I doubt she knows what she's seeing, with the whales so far and intermittent. The family group is huddled at the front, gesturing and jumping each time the orcas pop up. In the mother-daughter duo, the mother ducks inside, and the daughter sits down on the bench near me. I sit beside her, adjusting to the cold bench, a chill traveling up through my back and shoulders.

"Pretty cool, right?" I ask the girl.

She looks up at me—she has full cheeks that she hasn't quite grown out of yet, a few pimples. She looks a bit like I did at sixteen. Under the brim of her hat, her bangs nearly reach her eyelashes. "Yeah," she says. "Are you the new naturalist?"

I realize why she looks familiar: she's the same girl that Zack spoke to a few weeks back, the one who goes all the time. "I hope so."

The girl smiles, pointing out toward the whales. "So are they boys or girls?"

"Females so far," I say. "But there could be a male around too."

"Robin said orcas are rare at this time of year."

"Well, it's unlikely we'd see the southern resident pods right now," I say. "These are transients—a little less predictable."

Another surfacing, and the girl's breath catches, even though our view is somewhat blocked by the tourists at the rail.

"Where'd your mom go?"

"Bathroom." Her mouth pulls into a frown. "She has cancer and gets sick sometimes."

Her comment snags my words. Before I can respond, her mother returns and plops down beside us.

"Did I miss anything?"

"Orcas," the girl says. "Want to go to the railing and watch?"

The mother nods, and the daughter takes her arm. They wander over to the railing. Upon observation, the mother appears more fragile than I noticed before. I stand, too, and sidle up to Robin, who's speaking to the elderly couple now.

"Just amazing," the old man says, squeezing his wife's hand. "In all my years . . ."

A puff of breath cuts him off, and we all silence, enjoying the presence of the wild, wonderful animals. I'm impressed by Captain Kim's care to not steer us too close.

Before long, it's time we head back to Port Townsend, the trip coming to a close. People file inside, ready for more snacks and homemade apple crisp—a Sound Adventures specialty. Robin seats me at a vacant table while he fills orders, he and Joanne chatting with the guests and delivering hot crisp. Once everyone is settled, Robin slides into the booth across from me, carrying two plates of dessert. Joanne sits, too, next to me. She forks a big bite of crisp into her mouth, and for a single moment, her eyes close in bliss. At least we have that in common. I take a bite myself and revel in the warm appley goodness.

"Good day," Joanne says.

Robin meets my eyes, a friendly wink. "You having fun?"

"I love it," I say.

"Usually we have two naturalists," Robin explains. "We take turns educating and serving and, of course, help Captain Kim when she needs it."

"How many days per week?" I ask. "Is there a set schedule?"

"Three right now, but that'll increase to daily by late April."

"So I would be—" I pause, noticing Joanne, who doesn't seem to like me pushing in on the operation. I rephrase. "Is there a set script for the educational periods or a basic list of things you always cover?"

"We have a guide I can show you," Robin says. "But you likely know it all, so it's just a matter of remembering which facts to deliver and when."

I take another bite of crisp, the oat topping crunchy and brown sugar sweet.

"Mary seems in good spirits," Joanne says to Robin.

"Of course, it's the first day of the new season." Robin turns to me. "I saw you talking to Becca. Sweet girl."

My heart sinks a little, thinking of her mom.

"They're regulars," Robin explains. "Her mother, Mary . . ."

"Becca told me," I say.

"Yeah, well, they love these trips," Robin says over a bite of crisp. "They spend all their time outside on the bow, even on the most frigid days. She told me wildlife makes her feel alive."

"Connecting with people—that's what our job is about," Joanne says. "Marine biology is only half of it. No, not even half. It's about showing people why these ecosystems matter and helping them fall in love with the wildlife as much as we already are."

I bob my head. I know the feeling she's talking about, like being in love: heart pumping, exciting, awe inspiring. I knew that feeling with Dennis. I swallow a big bite of crisp and glance down at the map on the table.

"Can you excuse me?" I say, gesturing toward the restroom. I lie and add, "Too much coffee."

Joanne's face goes stony again, and she lets me out. I duck into the tiny room and twist the lock, then sit on the lid of the toilet and cradle my head in my hands. In California, I was so riddled with guilt that I had trouble focusing. I'd listen to courting humpbacks on the hydrophone and find myself thinking about my courtship with Dennis instead. As I struggled to start over in California, I couldn't break the habit of thinking about him.

But today, just now, I temporarily forgot. This job might not be the prestigious research position I always envisioned for myself, but for the first time in years, I was completely in the moment. Just the water and the orcas and the shared wonder.

Overcome, I close my eyes. I can have more days like this. Many more. It's going well, and Kim said I'm as good as hired. Perhaps this job is a turning point, a chance to start over one more time and finally take my life off hold.

I blow my nose and toss the paper into the toilet bowl, then press the flush button. The toilet sucks and gurgles. I check my teeth in the mirror, fluff my windswept hair, and pull it back into a bun.

The toilet is still gurgling when I'm ready to go back out, which seems strange. I peer in, and the bowl is dreadfully full. I notice a sign across from the toilet that reads, **Toilet paper only! Don't flush feminine products, paper towels, etc.**

I only used one tissue, so I press the flush button again. The toilet merely swirls its papery contents. Oh, what I wouldn't give for a manual marine head right about now, with a hand-cranked pump, not an electric flusher. I lift the water lever to fill the bowl and try one more time, but no luck. I've never fixed a head before, but how different is it from a regular toilet? I glance around the little room, searching for a plunger. I check under the sink and in the narrow cabinet but find only cleaning supplies and extra toilet paper.

I consider leaving the problem for the next person, but when I crack the door, I see Mary standing there, looking a little queasy, and I can't do it. I come out farther and tell her, "Don't go in. Something's wrong with it."

Mary nods and returns to her seat stiffly, as if one sway of the boat will make her sick. My heart stings. I glance around, but our table is empty. Robin is engaged with the big family, gesticulating as he tells a story, people laughing. I consider telling Captain Kim, but she's driving, for God's sake, and anyway, the door to the wheelhouse is closed. Joanne, of course, is the only one who can help: she's standing near the snacks, preparing a basket of cheese and jerky for someone.

"Joanne?" I call, quietly at first, not wanting her to actually hear me. "Joanne?"

She turns, scowls.

"Something's wrong with the head," I say.

With a huff, she shoves past me into the tiny restroom and opens the cabinet, retrieving a pair of tongs in a grocery bag. Bending toward the bowl, she lowers the tongs, and moments later, her scowl turns into a deep, rigid frown. "Seriously, Abby? You should know better," she snaps.

Over her shoulder, I see that she has pulled out a tampon, along with a big wad of paper towels. My stomach sinks into my shoes.

"Jesus," Joanne says. "Nothing but toilet paper in the—"

"I know I *did*," I say. "That's not mine."

"Are you kidding me?"

"I—" I only used one tissue. But it's not like I can tell her I went to the bathroom to cry over my ex-husband, so I simply say, "I'm sorry."

She hands me the tongs. "Try not to make it even worse."

If I had a shot at the job, it's gone now. Joanne will tell Robin, of course, and if I don't know how to use a damn toilet, how can they expect me to know how to do anything else? I close myself in the bathroom again and lower the tongs into the water. I sniffle, barely seeing anything through blurry, tearful eyes.

When I'm finally done, I try flushing once more for good measure and then come back out. We're arriving in Port Townsend, the guests seated and quiet as Kim maneuvers the boat into the marina. I watch Robin and Joanne outside, uncoiling rope, hopping onto the dock and back again. Once we're docked, Robin comes back inside to thank everyone for the great day. He leads them off the boat, helping the clumsier crowd step from deck to dock.

Robin and Joanne are chatting with a few stragglers, and I wait patiently, readying myself for them to revoke their job offer. The air feels warmer in the marina, and I break a sweat.

When all the tourists have gone back up the ramp, Joanne brushes past me completely and disappears inside the boat. Robin comes up, smiling.

"Nice work today," he says.

At first I wonder if he's being sarcastic. "What?"

"I think you'd be a valuable member of our team."

Did Joanne not tell him about the head? "You're serious?"

"I joke around, but I'm not cruel," he says. "Welcome to the team."

I should feel elated, but instead I'm timid, like a feral cat being offered food. I'm not sure whether to believe the gesture or not.

"She's hired?" Kim calls, a thumbs-up appearing behind a propped-open side window to the wheelhouse.

"If she shakes my hand," Robin calls.

It's real. I got the job. I take his hand, shake once, and grin. "I'm honored."

"You should be," Robin says. "This is the best job in the world."

2009

Dennis and I got married at the courthouse in December. It was still an organized affair—I wore white, he wore a suit, and our family and friends came—but this way, we didn't have to spend money on a big shindig. After the simple ceremony, we stepped out onto the courthouse steps and took pictures. Port Townsend is one of the most picturesque towns, and that includes the courthouse. With uniform red bricks and many steps, it looks like a castle, complete with a clock tower that gongs on the hour.

My favorite photo from that day is one of just Dennis and me. We're standing on the front steps of the courthouse, the wide slabs of marble below us and the tall red clock tower rising behind. I'm holding a bouquet of pink roses, and he's kissing me, not quite in a dip, but I'm clearly caught off guard. Nick took the picture; right before, he'd told Dennis to kiss me, and my new husband had grabbed me so enthusiastically I squealed. In the photo, we're kissing into eternity, Dennis looking like he can't hold on tight enough and me looking bewildered, my pale arms rosy against my white dress in the chilly air. An all-over blush.

That evening, we rented out part of a restaurant downtown and spent the night eating and drinking and milling about in the upstairs bar. Dennis and I were inseparable, walking arm in arm and chatting with our families. In the height of the fun, he leaned in and whispered how much he wanted me, how he couldn't wait to carry me through our doorway and consummate the marriage, and I laughed as his breath tickled my ear.

"I love you, Abby, my wife," he added, and *wife* sounded so perfect.

I'd had three glasses of wine, and my white lace dress felt hot and sticky against my back. "I love you, D, my husband," I whispered back, and *husband* felt new and strange on my tongue, but the alcohol numbed the funny feeling.

"I'll be right back," he said. "Uncle Mike bought cigars. Do you think Nick would want one?"

"Yeah," I said. "Go on."

Dennis left my side then, and I swayed a little. I watched as he tapped Mike on the shoulder and gestured for Nick to come along. Chrissy watched the men leave, then met my eyes and smiled. We felt like one big family, crowded into that tiny upstairs bar. Even my mother and father were up late and laughing, revisiting the dessert table, refilling their glasses.

On my own, without Dennis to hold me up and keep my head from spinning, I considered sitting at the long table with Chrissy but instead went for the bar. I needed some sparkling water to dilute the wine.

Of course, Jackie was there, nursing some brown liquor on the rocks. With darker features than Dennis, she looked positively mean in the dim track lighting above, her stout body a little awkward in such a fluttery, feminine dress. Dennis was big and tall, and where Jackie lacked height, she made up for it in a *don't mess with me* scowl.

"Hey, Jackie," I said. "Thanks for coming."

She threw back her drink and set the empty glass on the bar, the final ice cube rattling in the bottom. "I'm here for Dennis."

I sighed privately and nodded. "I love your brother, you know," I said, and maybe it was the wine talking, because I added, "and we're family now, whether you like it or not. You can't hate me forever."

Her brown eyes searched mine. For a split second, she looked like a little girl hiding under the bed. I thought she might say something kind, but I was wrong. "I'll *never* forgive you for leaving him. You knew. You knew his heart was bad, and you left anyway, and look what happened. He almost *died*. You don't love him."

The bartender set down the water I'd forgotten I had ordered. "He practically pushed me out the door, Jackie. I was ready to stay home with him, but he wanted me to go."

"That's Dennis," she said. "Unselfish. It's up to me to be selfish for him, to take care of him—"

"He's a grown man," I said, angered. Normally I wouldn't push, but the alcohol had emboldened me. "He doesn't need you to take care of him. He's married now. I'm his *wife*—"

"You're not his blood," Jackie spat. "You don't know what he's been through."

"Yeah, well, he didn't choose you. He chose me. So get over it," I said, and I picked up my glass and stomped over to Chrissy.

She whispered in my ear, and I pretended to listen, but my eyes were still hard on Jackie, bearing down, wishing I could ignite her with my fury. I was sick of her attitude, sick of tiptoeing. Sick of awkward family dinners and Dennis constantly having to apologize for his sister. I willed the fluttery edge of her dress to catch on fire and turn to ash.

But then the night carried on, and I got sucked into a conversation with Dennis's mother and grandmother and Chrissy, funny baby stories mostly, none of which mentioned Dennis's alcoholic, dead father. We laughed, and I had more wine after all, the encounter with Jackie too sobering, and hell, it was my wedding day, and I was supposed to have fun.

Dennis came back about a half hour later, the cold clinging to his suit jacket, along with the tobacco-sweet scent of vanilla. He kissed my cheek and grasped my hand, guiding me out of my chair.

"Thank you for joining us on our wedding day, everyone," he said, "but now it's time for our wedding night, and you aren't invited."

Everyone, tipsy by now, hooted and cheered and laughed, and Dennis swept me into his arms and carried me out. I glanced back over his shoulder, just before the door closed behind us, but Jackie had left her seat at the bar. Outside, the night air nipped at my bare legs, and Dennis carried me all the way to his truck, which had *Just Married* painted in white across the tailgate.

2018

With the news of my new position at Sound Adventures, my parents and Chrissy and Nick treat me to dinner, and the following weekend we caravan my boxes to Gwen's cottage. While Dad and Nick wrestle with my couch and mattress, Chrissy and my mother ask questions about the job that I can't answer yet: *What's your schedule? Which of their boats will you be on? What are your coworkers like?*

"I'm so happy for you," my mother adds, wrapping her arm around me.

Nick passes us, carrying a doubled-up armload of boxes. "Right behind you," he says, and Chrissy steps out of his way.

We're on the pathway between the front gate and the back of the house, where the flower beds are still overgrown. Now, the three of us head toward our cars, which are stuffed to the gills. The Avalon is parked behind Chrissy and Nick's 4Runner; after its breakdown, Nick and Chrissy paid for the base repairs so I could at least drive to the job that would ultimately allow me to pay them back. I still hold a grudge against the hunk of rust, but sometimes cooperation is the only option.

Dad is in the back of his truck, shifting things around. He passes a box down to Chrissy, who carries it toward the cottage. I stack two boxes of clothes and head back too. After loading up our cars that morning, my arms are sore. As the cottage fills up, we get less and less chatty until we're all sitting on various surfaces, surrounded by boxes, panting.

We managed to move everything by six o'clock, and when I hear Nick's stomach grumble, I say, "Pizza? On me."

After a quick trip downtown to pick up our order, I pull into the crowded driveway with warmth in my chest. Gwen's house lights are off—she's visiting her daughter in Portland—but when I step around the corner again, my new cottage is glowing. It's filled with all my favorite people, and I get a tingly feeling of home that I haven't felt in God knows how long. Seeing me with the hot, gritty pizza boxes in my arms, everyone cheers when I come back inside.

"I return bearing gifts," I say, and everybody stands up and circles the bistro-size dining table. It occurs to me that my measly handful of chipped plates is buried somewhere in the avalanche of cardboard. "We don't have plates."

Nick holds up a roll of paper towels. "Not a problem."

We pile slices onto our paper towels and return to the couch area, burning our tongues on the molten cheese. We're all so hungry that we push through the pain, the sound of chewing filling the small space. It's the perfect housewarming party.

Chrissy pipes up. "Gosh, it's been forever since I've helped someone move."

"When was it, do you think?" Nick asks.

"Abby to California, I think," Chrissy says.

"That hardly counts," Nick says. "She chucked most of her stuff."

Chrissy chews, thinking. "Okay, then, when Abby and Dennis built their house?"

His name makes me stop. I swallow my bite and lower the slice from my lips.

"It's always Abby's fault we're moving boxes," Chrissy continues, but I'm hung up on the mention of Dennis's name. I haven't heard it out loud in so long. It's as if nothing has happened between then and now, as if I'm right back here with him, and he might walk inside at any moment and grab a slice of mushroom-onion-sausage.

Chrissy says, "Abby, promise me you'll stay here for a while?"

"At least long enough that we forget how much it sucks to move," Nick says.

"No, she's staying here forever," my father interjects. "I'm too old for moving boxes."

"You work on a *farm*," my mother says.

"I'm too old for that too."

They all laugh.

"So what do you say, Abby? No more moves?" Nick says.

I nod and glance toward the door, willing Dennis to walk through it.

"What is it?" Chrissy asks.

"Nothing, just tired," I say.

"Speaking of Dennis," my mother says, and I actually flinch. "Have you gone to see him since you got back?"

"Of course not," I snap. "What would be the point?"

My mom lifts her hands in surrender. "Sorry, dear, I just thought you might . . ."

"Yeah, well . . ." I stand and get another piece of pizza from the box, even though I've only eaten half of my first. When I speak again, my voice comes out high and desperate. "Can we change the subject, please?"

"How about the Mariners this year, John?" Nick asks, turning toward my father. "You think it'll be a good season?"

They launch into sports talk, and I slump back down in my chair, relieved. I eat my pizza, listening to the conversation meander. Nick tells a funny story about a recent client, my mother updates them on the health of the horses, and they polish off the pizzas. I feel half-there the rest of the night, even after we hug goodbye and I'm left alone in my new little home, car engines fading down the road.

I close the door and turn toward all my moving boxes, the empty pizza boxes, so many boxes. And yet I feel sad that everything I own is in this cottage. I once had a home with Dennis, with dish towels and decorative pillows. Now, I've reduced myself to some marine biology textbooks, a bare-minimum wardrobe, and dishes that even Goodwill would hesitate to take.

I lie back on the bed, staring through the skylight. It's fogged up, and I can't see the stars. Fitting, I guess. My whole life feels foggy, ever since I told Dennis I was unhappy.

I sigh and close my eyes, knowing I won't sleep, but maybe I'll relax. But then I get a text from Chrissy.

Sorry to bring up D, it says.

I type back, It's ok.

I watch the little typing bubble pop up, then disappear. Finally, she responds, Maybe your mom is right about going to see him.

I don't bother to respond. Instead, I stand up and yank open a box. Its contents tink and rattle as I rip the tape away. The side says *Towels Kitchen*. I pull out a newspaper-wrapped mug, headlines from the *Los Angeles Times* fluttering to the floor. My coffee maker is also in the box, half-wrapped. I pull that out too.

My phone pings again: We just want you to be happy, Abs.

I put the dreaded thing on vibrate, facedown on the table, and continue unpacking. I unpack until the whole cottage is an explosion of stuff, with empty cardboard boxes piled on the bed. I sit on the couch then and check my phone for the time: 1:01 a.m. I missed more texts, and not just from Chrissy.

Mom: Don't stay up too late getting settled! Lunch tomorrow?

Nick: I hope you're not mad at Chrissy. And: We love you.

I text Chrissy back: I'll move forward at my own speed. Then I respond to Nick: I love you guys too. I tell Mom that lunch tomorrow sounds great.

I switch the lights off and fumble around in the dark for my pajamas, which I know I saw somewhere at some point. Finally I give up and settle for a T-shirt and curl up on the couch. I close my eyes but still can't sleep. I consider putting some things away. The mess is keeping me up, I tell myself, but I know it's also the regret. I listen to the unfamiliar creaks of the cottage, the odd-sounding refrigerator, and the gusts of wind outside.

Past two a.m., I hear a soft scratching at the door, and I bolt upright. Is it an animal, a thief? Did I lock the door? I tiptoe across the cold floor, my cheek hot from where it rested on the couch cushion. A shape, small and familiar, is waiting on the other side of the glass-paneled door. It reaches toward the windowpane again, and the scratching ensues, little paw pads squeaking against the glass.

I unlatch the door, and Gwen's cat, Taffy, bounds inside. Gwen left a can of wet food in the cottage, in case Taffy got bored of the dry food Gwen left beyond the cat door in her mudroom. I go to the pantry and open a can of Tiki Cat (chicken). Meanwhile, Taffy rubs against my leg. Gwen warned me that Taffy likes company. Her back is damp, which means it must be sprinkling outside. I glance out the window, where tinsels of rainwater trail off the roof.

"Hungry?" I ask Taffy.

Her meow is high pitched but serious.

"I know," I say.

I find my box of dishes and unwrap a salad plate, then use my finger to scoop some shredded chicken out of the can. I put the rest in the fridge, then place the plate on the floor. Taffy dives in, purring while she eats. I stroke her fur, her tail flicking through my fingers. She's a welcome distraction. I sit cross-legged on the floor beside her, and when she's done, she rubs against my knees, licking her lips.

"Good job." I stand and set her plate in the sink.

She follows me to the couch and curls up beside me. Scratching under her chin, I breathe big and deep. She kneads my T-shirt, and the next thing I know, it's morning, and Taffy is waiting by the door, ready to go out.

2011

For a while, with Dennis, things were wonderful. He *did* make me breakfast on Sundays, and we watched *Blue Planet* on days when I needed comfort. We bought lattes and took walks and ordered takeout, and everything felt so easy, the way it was supposed to feel. We made love on weekend afternoons, and afterward, still hot and panting, I'd trace the surgery scar on Dennis's chest. He still took medication, but his checkups always went well, and he was able to (lightly) work again. When I kissed his chest, the incision line felt like silk against my lips.

One rainy spring afternoon, I did this, and Dennis said, "You have my heart."

"What?" I asked, still a little dazed.

"You have it."

Dennis's arms were folded up by his head, making his biceps look extra big, and a little wave of desire pulsed through me. I tried to focus. "And you have my heart."

Dennis shook his head. "No, really. When the doctors went in there to fix things, it wasn't there. You'd already stolen it."

Getting the joke, I rolled onto my back.

"It's why they thought something was wrong," Dennis went on. He turned, leaning on one elbow, his other hand sliding over my belly. "It wasn't in there."

Thinking about that scary day and the many days I spent worried about him—what if he had a heart attack while driving home from the grocery store or while I was out with friends?—I stiffened. "It's not funny," I whispered.

"If we can't laugh at ourselves . . ."

"It's not funny," I repeated, staring up at him. His eyes looked more gray than blue in the grainy afternoon light. The rain had picked up, tap-tap-tapping on the roof.

His hand traveled up between my breasts and brushed my cheek. His thumb stroked my temple. "I know you worry about me," he said. "But worrying won't do us any good."

I leaned my cheek into his palm and closed my eyes. His warmth against me made my skin tingle. I thought of losing him, and I couldn't bear it. "I love you."

His lips brushed mine. "I know you do," he said. "And I love you too. But you have to live your life."

I opened my eyes. "What are you saying?"

"You've been out of work for months. Don't you want to get back on track?"

"All the best research opportunities are far away—"

"I know this place is dingy." He shifted against the pillows. "If we had more income . . ."

"Oh," I said, realizing what he was saying. He wanted me to get a job. Any job. "I understand."

"I know you want to pursue your dreams, Abby," Dennis continued, but I didn't bother listening anymore. I'd seen it happen to other young people in this town: as soon as I got a regular job, I was stuck forever.

But I was stuck now, too, right? I ached to be on the water, but there weren't many opportunities close to home for a marine biologist, and I wasn't willing to leave Dennis again. This conversation made me realize I'd been stuck in career purgatory for over a year already. How had that happened? Maybe I didn't have a right to be picky.

"Even something temporary," Dennis continued. "Something to pay for smaller bills, so when we go for a loan, I can—"

"I'll start looking," I said, rolling over, sitting up.

"I don't mean it like that," Dennis said, reaching for me.

I stood and shrugged into my robe. "I'm glad you're thinking about our future. You're right; I should contribute to that."

"That's not how I would put it," Dennis said.

I thought about my career and how it truly added up: a minimum-wage job at a science center—practically a glorified janitor and cashier—a few environmental articles, and part of a research study that I'd bailed on. It wasn't like I had lined up anything else, but something about a regular job felt like giving up on my dream, and it was a punch in the gut.

"I'll start looking," I repeated, slinking into the hall.

Dennis got up and followed me. "I just want to make our lives better. I want to feel like we're moving forward. Don't you?"

I turned around and looked at him, standing naked in the doorway. "Of course I do."

He smiled. "I found some land for sale, not far from your parents' place."

That *did* interest me. I missed living in the country, and Dennis's old bachelor pad wasn't always fit for the two of us. I could see where he was coming from, the sweetness of the gesture.

"I want to build you a house," he said. "Whatever you want."

My stubbornness and my concerns were melting. A part-time job didn't mean I was giving up on my dream—it just meant I was feeding another dream for the time being. "Can it have a big bathroom, with one of those Jacuzzi bathtubs?"

Dennis grinned. "Duh."

I took a step forward. "And big windows and skylights?"

"Of course."

I was in his arms again, and he was brushing the robe from my shoulders. "I want a California king–size bed," I whispered against his lips.

He lifted me up. "Noted."

2018

I meet my mother for lunch at the Chimacum Diner. We sit at a table by the window, in a booth that could fit four or even six people. The waitress seems far away just standing at the end of it, telling us the chicken-fried special. The place is empty, save for some regulars, and when the waitress returns with Mom's iced tea, she has to slide it down the table toward us.

"So how was your first night in the new place?" Mom asks.

"Good," I lie. It wasn't the place but my thoughts that made the night tough. "I did some unpacking, so I'm a little tired."

"Oh, Abby, you shouldn't have stayed up late. Were you lonely?"

I was alone in California plenty, but in my hometown? That hadn't happened since . . .

"Just restless," I tell her. "Plus Gwen's cat wanted in at, like, two in the morning."

"So you had a little company," she says.

"I guess so." I glance at my menu, already knowing what I want.

The waitress returns shortly, and we both order bacon cheeseburgers. I've been coming to the Chimacum Diner since I was little, and not once have I eaten anything other than salads or burgers. There's a whole page in the menu for various steaks and potatoes and green beans, and it always seemed out of place to me.

"When do you start work?" Mom asks.

"Robin said tomorrow."

"Robin?"

"He's the other naturalist, the guy who interviewed me."

"Oh," Mom says.

I can see the question hovering on her lips: *Is he your age?* But after last night, she probably knows better than to press. Why date when I can't reconcile with the love of my life? Maybe Mom and Chrissy and the rest have finally caught on.

"Do you need money in the meantime?" Mom asks, changing the subject.

"I'm all right." Until I get paid, I have enough gas to get me through (Chrissy and Nick took care of that) and enough money on my credit card for food.

"You sure, dear? It's no trouble."

"I'm sure," I tell her.

Mom pauses to sip her tea, and I glance around the room. There's a painting of a bull elk in the snow on the wall behind her and, below it, a picture of an old broken-down farm truck. The diner walls are covered in unframed canvases, all in the same style, hunting dogs and horses and trucks and deer. They have a Bob Ross quality, the scenes realistic but clearly imagined, not truly captured from real life. The paintings could be dreams or alternate realities. If I lived in these scenes, would I still be with Dennis?

Mom turns around to see what I'm looking at. "I always wondered where they came from," she says. "They have price tags. Who buys them?" She points to a painting of an eagle in a tree overlooking some snowy mountains. "That one has been there since I don't know when."

"Since I was little?"

She shrugs. "Probably."

Our burgers arrive, with pickles and little bags of Lay's chips on the side. Mine tastes like hay season, eight hundred bales hauled from the fields in ninety-degree sun. When I was a teen, my parents hired all the strong high school boys to haul hay, but I never wanted to be left out. After a few years, I could toss a bale as well as the next guy. My parents bought thirty burgers at the end of the week, and we sat around, hay clinging to our sweaty skin, our arms scratched up, our muscles sore, chowing down. Once, I ate three burgers all in a row and didn't even feel sick. After the boys had gone home, I went out with Dad and tossed another twenty-five bales all by myself, with him driving the truck.

"Yum," I say through an unladylike-size bite. "It reminds me of hay season."

My mother groans. "Don't say it."

I laugh. "You doing it this year?"

"It's such an *endeavor*," she says. "Your father will probably insist, though. It's income, though nominal."

"Well, I can help."

"If you're not busy with your new job."

I shrug. "Evenings, then."

"Fine, fine." My mother pops open her chips.

Another barn scene wriggles into my head. Despite enjoying the past few weeks of peaceful family time, I can't help but ask. "I'm sure it's nothing, but this has been bothering me for a while. Do you know a Wendy?"

My mother stops chewing, just for a moment, then resumes. "Wendy? I'm not sure who you mean."

"She was at the barn with Dad a few weeks ago," I say, watching my mother, whose face has turned red. She glances outside. Are her eyes watery?

"Do you know who she is?" I ask.

"What did she say to you?"

"Only hello," I say. "Dad was in a hurry." My stomach turns, and it's not from the burger. "Mom? Who is she?"

"No one, dear," Mom says. "Don't worry about it."

"But—"

"Abby," she says, then plasters a smile onto her creased face. "Tell me more about your new job."

2011

In May, for Dennis, I ended up getting a job at the bank as a teller. Because of my science degree, I was pretty good at math, and I guess the ladies at US Bank thought I'd be a good fit. It was embarrassing, though, seeing people I knew, explaining to them that yes, I worked here now, and no, I wasn't doing marine biology. Aside from the chit-chat with nice coworkers and free coffee in the break room, there was nothing I enjoyed about the position. I felt defeated.

For weeks, I'd looked for better jobs. I'd considered an assistant job at the University of Washington School of Oceanography, but the commute was long, and I despised the thought of being so far from Dennis. I'd gotten as far as an interview, but after a full day commuting to the city to meet with management in person, after missing a ferry and taking two and a half hours to return home, I'd decided it was too far. I'd hated how distance had made me helpless when Dennis had had his surgery, and I was determined to never know that feeling again. I'd taken my name out of consideration the following morning and told Dennis I hadn't gotten the job.

I'd also tried more local options: the Center for Salish Orca Research, the Whale Museum in Friday Harbor, and even the Salish Science Center—but none wanted me, or they paid too little, or they required a long commute, or, or, or. I'd spent these weeks frustrated and feeling like a failure. Dennis had been encouraging and sweet, but I could tell he was eager for me to settle into something, anything, so settle I had.

At the end of my first week at the bank, Kevin Granger's mother, Kay, came in. She had always liked me and on more than one occasion had expressed her disappointment that we hadn't stayed together after high school. Kay was short and a little top heavy, with delicate hands and a sweet face. She had the same figure, bustle, and motherly instinct as a broody hen. I was not in the mood to see her.

She went to my coworker Riya's line while I kept busy tidying the pens and sticky notes by the drive-up window.

"And how are you this morning?" Riya asked.

"I'm well, thank you," Kay said. I glanced over my shoulder as she slid a check toward Riya. "Little Abby Fisher, is that you?"

I flinched—why hadn't I just kept my head down? I turned and feigned surprise. "Kay? It's been so long."

She bounced on her feet, leaning left, right, left, right. "Oh, come here, won't you?" Spreading her arms, she waddled toward the swing gate that separated the customers from employees. Reluctantly, I came through and bent into her embrace. She was all warmth and softness. If it were any other day, any other week, any other place, I wouldn't mind running into her.

She squealed with joy. "Tell me, dear, how are you?"

We parted, and I hung back by the gate, dreading the inevitable questions. "Oh, fine."

"Married now, I see," she said. "I do wish that could've been you and Kev, but he's married now too. A timid girl, but a fabulous mother. I have two grandbabies."

I smiled and nodded.

"Are you not doing marine biology anymore?" Kay asked, to my dismay.

"No, I'm here." I tried to sound like I didn't mind, but the words came out downtrodden. I glanced at the clock; only one hour until lunch.

"Well, you look fabulous. Do you have any children?"

"No," I said, cringing.

"In good time." Riya was done with her transaction. Kay waddled toward the counter, allowing me to escape into employee territory again.

"Anything else I can help you with?" Riya asked her.

"No, dear, thank you." She rested her eyes on me. "So nice to see you, Abby."

"Take care," I said, pretending to be busy.

When she was gone, Riya chuckled. "Who was that?"

"My high school boyfriend's mother," I said.

Riya laughed even harder. "She sounds like she's still hung up on you."

I shook my head, unwilling to keep talking about it. I didn't want to think about Kevin or kids or my nonexistent career—I just wanted the week to be over.

~

That afternoon, Dennis arrived to pick me up—a surprise.

"Who's *that*?" someone whispered when he walked in.

"My husband," I answered, without turning to see who'd asked.

Dennis wore a tight-fitting waffle henley and his favorite jeans, which were worn down around the pockets and the knees but not yet frayed. He looked way too sexy, made worse by the fact that he held a bouquet of yellow alstroemerias.

It was two minutes to closing, and I came out around the counter and kissed him. "These are beautiful. What are you doing here?"

"I wanted to drive out to the property, to show you."

After the hard week, the thought of buying property together shook loose my dismay like snapping sand out of a beach towel. I glanced back at Yvonne, who was in charge of training me.

"Mind if I go?"

"Not at all," Yvonne said.

"Have a good weekend," Riya added, eyeing Dennis.

I circled into the back to get my purse and coat, then hurried out the door with Dennis. His heavy-duty work truck waited out front—he'd likely come straight from work himself—and I climbed inside, placing the alstroemerias in the low cup holder to keep them upright.

"Your first week," Dennis said, starting up the truck. "How was it?"

There was no way I could tell him how much I despised it, so I said, "Fine. Still learning the ropes."

"It's only temporary," Dennis said, placing his hand on my leg. "Next year, you'll be back to counting fish, or whatever you want to do."

I had to laugh. "Counting fish. Like Dr. Seuss?"

"That's about as much as I understand," Dennis said.

Though I knew he meant well, I was slightly disheartened by his words. I tried to ignore the niggling melancholy—it would take time for me to adjust to the new job, that was all.

I shrugged. "Yeah, well, you should see me try to use power tools."

That elicited a chuckle. "With me around, you'll never have to."

He turned on the radio, and we hummed along to Tim McGraw and Keith Urban all the way out to West Valley. We passed my parents' house and, minutes later, turned onto a dirt road that headed away from the valley and up into the trees of the ridge. The road snaked through tall pines and branched into tucked-away driveways, but still we continued. Dennis turned the radio down and shifted into a lower gear, the potholes growing progressively worse with the incline, jostling us. I grasped the flowers after the third time they tipped over. Dennis smiled over at me, but I remember thinking, *I don't want to live deep in the woods*. I loved the valley.

But then it opened up. The trees fell away, and the road flattened into a large, high clearing. Soft green knee-high grass fluttered in a faint breeze, fine as brushstrokes in a painting. We drove until the road ended, about fifty yards into the open, the tire tracks stopping with no more than a trampled patch of dirt wide enough to turn around. I set the flowers on the bench seat and climbed out. The air was fresh up here, warm. The sunshine heated my back, hinting of summer.

"The clearing is six acres, but the parcel is twenty, mostly woods."

A chilly wind rustled the evergreens surrounding us; they swayed as if their trunks were rubber, their bristled tops wagging. Then I felt the sunlight again, its gentle touch on the back of my neck. I was clear headed up here. Relaxed. It reminded me of home, but better. Tucked away down a long dirt road, it felt private. A secret that was just ours.

I spotted movement not far from us, amid the grass. The brown body, almost invisible, took a step. Her ears flicked toward us. A doe, her coat glistening cinnamon gold. I imagined that Jacuzzi bathtub we'd talked about and a wide window without any curtains. I could watch the deer from the warm water, bubbles sliding over my legs, a cup of chamomile tea cradled in my fingers, early in the morning. I imagined seeing stars through the skylights over our huge bed and getting lost in the vast sheets. Up here, the night would be country dark, not city dark. I'd have to find Dennis in that big bed by touch.

Dennis leaned against the front of the truck, watching me. "What do you think?"

Pulled out of my thoughts, I turned to him. Excitement welled in my chest and constricted my throat, so my voice came out high. "Is it really possible?" Maybe the bank was worth it, after all, if it helped us accomplish *this*.

He closed the space between us, his arms heavy across my shoulders. "Absolutely."

A year later, it was built.

2018

On my way to the grocery store, I call Chrissy on speakerphone and tell her everything: the strange lunch with my mother, Wendy, and the way Mom pretended she didn't know the name. Chrissy's on a break, and I hear her tearing an energy bar wrapper while I talk.

"I guess she could be a client of Dad's," I say. I'm stopped at a roundabout, waiting for a space to pull in. When a gap in traffic presents itself, I accelerate into the circle. "I mean, there are some bigwigs in town. She could be an owner just checking in on things." I recall her knee-high leather boots, the way her thin legs protruded from her long coat, and how she and my father were hugging when I walked up.

"It's possible," Chrissy says, chewing, but I know she's not convinced. "Perhaps she's a long-lost relative."

"But then why didn't he say so?"

"An *estranged* relative."

I know we're grasping at straws. I pull into the Safeway parking lot, turn off the car, and rest my head on the steering wheel. An ugly, awful word creeps into my head, and I refuse to think it's correct, but what else could it be? *Affair.* Chrissy is nice enough not to say it aloud.

"I'm at the store. Talk later?" I need to clear my head, anyway.

"Sure, Abs," she says. "Love you."

"Love you." I hang up and get out.

Glancing at my meager shopping list, I head through the sliding doors and take up a basket. In the produce section, I bag three Honeycrisp apples, some celery, and a green bell pepper. I can't imagine my father cheating—and my mother knowing about it—but no matter how many other possibilities filter through my mind, it's the only one that makes sense. After so much turbulence with them years ago, it's possible he strayed. It's also possible that Mom found out and stayed with him anyway, though that thought makes me squirm.

Since I moved away, the store has been rearranged. It takes me forever to find spices, rice, and yogurt, but at least the beer is obvious—I get extra. I consider calling Chrissy again, just to talk me down off my mental ledge. Wendy, Wendy, Wendy. There *has* to be an explanation.

In the checkout line, the basket digs into my forearm, and I curse the heavy rice and beer for their collective assault. The plastic handles pinch my skin, and finally I set the basket on the floor. When I stand tall again, I see someone I know. She's standing in the next line over, to my left.

And of course, she's the person in town I'm most afraid to face: Jackie.

I turn away. Maybe she didn't see me. Maybe it wasn't her. My line moves forward by one person, and I'm able to steal another glance. It's her, definitely her. The same dark eyes, dark hair, strong stature. She has Dennis's nose, and the thought of him grips me so tightly I can't breathe. Am I really hyperventilating at the grocery store? Am I really going to have a panic attack next to a stand of candy bars and gum?

I lift my basket onto the conveyor belt and turn away again. She can't possibly have seen me. I stare at my shoes and then the shoes of the girl in front of me. She's wearing these cute brown booties below cuffed dark skinny jeans. There's a little mud on the heel; maybe she cut through a flower bed in the parking lot to avoid a passing car. I force myself to wonder where she bought the boots, then take myself through every step of that process in an effort to focus and relax. But then the booties are walking away from me, brown bags and the wheels of a cart leading them out of the store.

"Ma'am?" the cashier asks.

I look up and see the back of Jackie's head, her soft ponytail, just past the smiling face of my cashier.

"Do you have a club card?" He's scanning my items, typing the codes for the produce at lightning speed. His round white face smiles at me; his brown hair appears unwashed.

"Yes," I say, finally thinking again. I type my parents' phone number into the keypad.

Jackie's bagger is setting the final paper bag in her cart.

"Card?" my cashier asks. I spot his name tag, which reads *Seth.*

I pull out my wallet and find my credit card, then swipe. The keypad beeps at me.

"Hold on." Seth hits a few buttons on his keyboard. "Try now."

Swipe. Beep.

Jackie is on the move, wheeling her cart toward the customer service kiosk opposite my line. My shoulders instinctively hunch, as if that'll hide my face.

"Try again," Seth says.

Swipe. Beep.

Jackie is chatting with the customer service cashier.

"Do you have another card?" he asks.

"What?"

"Another card?"

"This has money on it," I say defensively. "I know there's money."

"Does it have a chip?"

I hold up the card so he can see. "No."

"Maybe the strip is bad," Seth says. "Let me try."

I hand him my card, and he leans over the little counter between us and swipes slowly. Again, the card machine beeps its rejection.

"Fuck," I say under my breath, and the old woman behind me scoffs. I shuffle through my purse for my debit. The total is $63.47. It probably won't overdraft me, but it'll come damn close. I insert the debit in the chip reader, and it works, prompting me to enter my PIN.

"There we go," Seth says, sounding way too victorious. The receipt prints, and he says, "Have a nice day, Ms. Fisher."

I take the receipt from his fingers and scoop up my two bags from the end of the line. Seth starts scanning the old woman's groceries, rushing me away. Jackie has left, and with a flood of relief, I hurry out to the car. At least the card debacle delayed me enough to miss her. That's certainly worth a potential overdraft charge.

Outside, I have to shift the bags in my arms in order to retrieve my keys from my purse. I cram the key into the gritty socket and pray the car doesn't betray me again. But to my relief, I'm able to open the door. I'm practically shaking from the day's barrage of bad situations. Dropping my keys on the driver's seat, I force a deep breath.

While I'm arranging my bags on the passenger seat, my attempt at zen is interrupted by the rattle of cart tires on the pavement behind me. I'm buzzing with adrenaline and panic, and somehow the sound makes it worse. Who knew the grocery store could do that? I take another desperate gulp of air and tell myself it's nothing. Closing the door, I straighten and glance in the direction of the cart noise.

Jackie stops in her tracks not six feet away, looking just as startled as I feel. Dread, like lava, fills every inch of me and hardens into solid rock.

"You," Jackie says, faint, her hands gripping the cart handle.

"Jackie," I say.

She flinches.

"Are you well?" I ask, altogether too light and conversational, but it's the closest to normal I can manage.

Snapping out of her apparent frozen shock at the sight of me, she continues onward toward the cart stand. I watch her go, the world rushing at me from all sides. Memories of my breakup with Dennis blur my vision. Jackie's bitter words leech into my head; I can still see her hair alight from the streetlamp, the night crowding us. It was the worst night of my life.

Swaying, I catch myself on the Avalon, rust scratching my fingers. When Jackie walks back to her car, she doesn't look my way. Her mouth is pressed into a line, and her gait is hurried. She disappears down the lot, and then taillights flicker on, and a white Escalade is backing out of its parking spot, about six cars down from mine. I watch the exhaust billow and dissipate as she drives away.

2012

Building our house was enough to keep me going during that first year working at the bank. We spent all our off time working: Dennis and his crew did most of it, of course, but I supplied them with sandwiches and coffee and iced tea and used a nail gun or power saw on occasion. Despite the long days, the year flew by, and then we were moved in. That spring, on weekends, much like before, we made love midday—only the rest of our afternoons were spent putting final touches on the house: light fixtures, framed pictures, furniture, and houseplants. Come summer, our focus shifted outside: I planted flowers and an herb garden, and he installed a swing on our porch and graveled the driveway.

Autumn came, and we ran out of projects. Dennis fell into a routine with his business, hiring two more guys to handle what his heart could not. I was left with work, which I hated. This was just before our three-year anniversary. I never told Dennis this, but I spent many morning commutes resisting the urge to just keep driving. I'd be halfway through Oregon by the time I'd run out of gas, and I'd be checked into a beachside motel before Dennis even began to worry.

It was a desperate, hysterical fantasy.

Stagnancy threatened to shake me loose from my domestic joy. How could I tell him I was unhappy when he'd just provided me with a home? His heart scare had taught me to hold on and never let go. It didn't seem fair to complain about career woes when I felt lucky just to have Dennis in my life at all.

I still looked for jobs, but Dennis grew to like our routine—including my job at the bank. He didn't understand why I'd give up something steady. He knew my passion, but he didn't *grasp* it. I began applying without telling him, though local opportunities were scarce. I became less picky and applied to a whale watching tour company. It went against my hope for something scientific, but I didn't even hear back. How could I tell Dennis any of this? How could I puncture the rose-gold haze of bliss that shaded our lives together? *It's only temporary,* I'd remind myself, but I started to wonder if Dennis and I had different views of what the term *temporary* meant.

It was a crisp day in October—one of those leafy, warm-toned days when the air smelled like fermenting apples and woodsmoke—when I encountered Eli. He shifted my whole life like a tectonic plate. One little slip, turning into an underwater shelf, eliciting a tsunami.

Like most days, I was on autopilot. I cashed checks, counting twenties rhythmically onto the counter. I submitted deposit slips, little papers ephemeral in my fingers. I answered the phones, explaining overdrafts and account changes and other personal but banal banking details. I was in the middle of depositing tips for a teenage girl named Tasha when a tan, lean guy with tattoo sleeves came through the door and walked up to Riya's line. I heard him say something to her, then Riya's high-pitched giggle. I lost count of Tasha's tips and had to start over.

"Busy weekend?" I asked Tasha when I was done. She'd deposited almost $90 in ones and fives, plus an $800 paycheck; her account was creeping up toward three grand.

"Overtime grind," she said.

"Do you have your eye on something special?" I asked as Riya's giggling reached its crescendo.

"A car," Tasha said.

I stole a glance at the man in Riya's line. "Is there anything else I can do for you?"

"Nah," Tasha said. "Thanks."

I tried to busy myself, but curiosity tugged at my vision, drawing me a little nearer to Riya's station. The man wore a blue T-shirt, and scruff darkened his cheeks. His hair was a little long, unkempt, but when he pushed it back, laughing, it fell into order. Riya processed his checks. I could see why she was so flirty; he *was* an attractive man.

A new customer arrived at my counter. She must've been over eighty, her cheeks freckled and streaked with smile lines. I was in the middle of her deposit when I heard the door waft closed.

When the old woman left, too, I turned to Riya. "Who was that?"

"Althea?" she asked.

"No, the guy you were flirting with," I said.

Her chin dipped in embarrassment. "His name is Eli. And I wasn't flirting."

"You *so* were," I said. "I haven't seen him in."

"He's been in Cuba for the past few months," Riya said. "Cool, right? Before that, I think he had direct deposit, because he almost never used to come in."

"What does he do?"

"Photographer," Riya said. "I'm not sure what he used to do." Then, a little accusatory, "Why do you want to know so much about him?"

"Just curious," I said teasingly.

She stuck her tongue out at me.

I added, "I'm so used to regulars."

Riya nodded, not looking convinced. Before she could say more, though, Yvonne walked through the door, back from her break, and it was Riya's turn for lunch.

That evening, as usual, I returned home in the dark, hungry and weary. Dennis's truck was in the driveway, the lights on inside the house. I walked through the door and went into the kitchen, hoping

Dennis had started dinner, but I heard the TV on in the living room. Dishes were stacked haphazardly, and the whole kitchen smelled like an old sink sponge. Irritated, I walked toward the noise.

"When did you get home?" I asked.

Dennis muted the TV. "Oh, hey, honey. How was your day?"

I clenched my fists in frustration. "Have you been home long?"

"A few hours."

"You could've started dinner."

He twisted, his arm resting along the back of the couch. "I'm sorry—I didn't realize you'd be home so late."

"There are so many dishes in the sink," I said, turning back into the kitchen.

Dennis stood and followed me, brushing my arm with his fingers. "I'm sorry, Abby—I just didn't think of it."

"Why do *I* always have to think of it?" The weight of the day felt so heavy on me then, as if our dirty dishes were stacked on my shoulders, cast iron and silverware pressing into my neck. My legs were moments away from buckling.

"I'm *sorry*," Dennis said, clearly angered by my nagging. "Did you have a bad day? Is that what this is about?"

"Of course I had a bad day," I exclaimed. "I'm hungry and tired and sick of being polite to people."

Dennis took a step toward me. "I'll do the dishes," he said gently. "Okay? And I'll make dinner. What do you want?"

"No," I said. "No, now I feel like a bitch."

"You're not a bitch."

He reached out to touch my face, but I stepped away, toward the fridge. I couldn't stand his kindness in that moment—it made me feel like a monster.

"Do you need to quit, Abby?" he asked, barely audible.

I wanted to scream, *Of course I do!* but I didn't. How could I quit? I never wanted Dennis to be the breadwinner, never wanted to be a stay-at-home whatever. I couldn't leave for a research trip, for fear of Dennis having another emergency while I was gone, and I couldn't find work I loved in town. I was a moth caught in a spider's web, each sticky strand pulling in opposite directions to keep me stuck right where I was.

So instead of answering his impossible question, I opened the fridge and pulled out a package of chicken. "I can make stir-fry?"

Dennis took the package from my fingers. "I'll do it," he insisted. "Go relax."

Feeling a twist at the top of my chest, I nodded and disappeared into our bedroom. As I slipped out of my work clothes, I heard the kitchen sink running, the clanging of pots being washed. My feet were sweaty and sore from standing all day, arches achy, heels bruised. Knowing it would take Dennis forever to make dinner, since he needed to wash the dishes just to get to the wok in the bottom of the sink, I slunk into the bathroom and drew a bath.

Our bathtub wasn't exactly how I had pictured it, back before the house was built. I'd wanted one of those large corner tubs, with windows all around. Dennis had done his best to accommodate, but we'd had to make sacrifices. A Jacuzzi tub was out of our price range, so we'd bought a large regular tub. Dennis had done what he could to make it lovely. The faucet expelled hot, hot water and had a hose attached. He had installed a heating vent nearby, and narrow modern shelves lent themselves to scented candles.

I didn't light any tonight, but the sight of them reminded me of when we'd first moved in and tried to take a bath together. It was a big tub, but Dennis was tall, and it'd felt crowded, water sloshing onto the floor, slippery legs struggling to find a comfortable place. We'd laughed and laughed. The memory brought a small smile to my lips, then a stab to my sternum. I'd been cruel to him tonight—unnecessarily. But he was so blind to my torment, and that was its own form of cruelty.

Slipping into the bubbly water, I thought of Riya and that customer she liked. She'd said he spent his time traveling and taking photos, and that wanderlust lifestyle sounded so very exciting. And he was good looking. I rarely noticed men other than Dennis, but I'd noticed Eli. Guilt stirred inside me, but I didn't know why. With a hard sigh, I forced him out of my mind. It'd been a long day.

Tipping my head back, I sank deeper into the water, bubbles tickling up the base of my neck. Scrunching my toes near the drain, the aches melted away. The water was a touch too hot, coaxing my muscles to release, delicious warmth splaying across my wet skin. I focused on the sensation. The soap smelled like lavender, and I pictured myself on a lavender farm in summer, bees buzzing around the bobbing, purple-tipped stalks. A warm breeze tousling my hair.

A soft knock on the door disturbed the daydream. The knob turned, and Dennis poked his head in. "Dinner is ready."

"I'll be right out," I said.

"Look, Abby," he said, coming in. The cold air of the bedroom cut through the steam in my mini oasis. He knelt beside me, his hands resting on the porcelain edge. "I'm sorry if I haven't been pulling my weight around here."

I shrugged, looking past him at the window. The darkness outside turned the glass into a mirror, and I saw myself, my tired face and piled-up hair, and Dennis's hunched form kneeling on the bath mat.

He took my hand, which had grown pruney. "I'll make a change. You deserve it."

Instead of being comforted or heartened by his claim, I felt truly trapped then. Trapped in my job, in our house, in that tub, with Dennis standing in the way. I loved him, but God, had he really backed me into this? It couldn't possibly be his fault, but here he was. The spider who crafted this web.

Dennis seemed to sense my mood and stood. "I'll leave you alone. But you might have to reheat your dinner."

I said, "I'm almost done."

Dennis nodded and closed the door behind him. I dipped my head underwater and toyed with the idea of not coming back up.

~

The following day, when I got home, dinner was ready. As I walked in through the door, Dennis was placing a pan of lasagna on a pot holder; the table was made up with plates, utensils, and a bowl of salad.

I dropped my purse on the floor and walked over to him, ready to nestle into his embrace. "This looks amazing, Dennis."

He didn't hold me, though. He went to the kitchen to remove garlic bread from the oven.

"Did you have a good day?" I asked, perplexed. He rarely entertained a bad mood, and his tense quietness made me wonder if I'd gone over the line yesterday.

But then he said, "Someone from a whale watching company called today and asked for an interview."

I would've felt overjoyed if it weren't for his expression.

"Whale watching tours?" he continued. "Don't those run on weekends? I'd never see you." He placed the rolls on the table, the platter clattering.

"You'd never see me?" I asked, growing heated. "Shouldn't you be *happy* for me?"

"I didn't even know you applied."

"Well, I did."

He rested his hands on the back of a chair, leaning toward me across the table. "Is the bank so bad?"

"Yes."

"I'd never see you," he repeated.

Can you see me now? I wanted to ask. *Because I don't recognize myself anymore.* Instead, I said, "Don't you want me to do something I love? Don't you want me to be out on the water?"

"Of course I do, Abby, but you're my wife. I want to have weekends with you—is that so bad?"

I couldn't answer. I was twenty-nine and held two degrees but didn't have a career to show for it. What would happen when I turned thirty? Or forty? "I'm not trying to get away from you," I said. "I just want to *do* something with my life."

"Like you're not doing something now? Have we not built a good life together?"

"We *have*—but this isn't about you," I said. "It's about my career." Short of moving somewhere else with more opportunity, the whale watching company was perhaps my only option left.

He looked away, his temple bulging. "Does it at least make as much as the bank?"

"What?"

"What's the salary?"

That'd never mattered before, not really. It wasn't like we were financially hurting. I realized, with a sour, sickly taste in my mouth, that Dennis *liked* that I worked at the bank. He liked the consistency; he liked my being close. When had his definition of *temporary* morphed into *permanent*?

"They haven't said yet. But the salary is probably less than the bank," I said quietly.

"Less than the bank," Dennis said, straightening, his arms lifting and lowering in an exasperated sigh. "When were you going to tell me about this?"

"If I got the job," I said.

"What else have you been keeping from me?"

"Nothing—I just didn't want to rock the boat unnecessarily."

"Yeah, well, what would you call *this*, if not rocking the boat?"

My ribs were caving in on themselves, a deep gnawing of conflict in my chest. "I can withdraw my résumé."

He softened, then, like the Hulk shrinking back down to size. "No, no, if you truly want—"

"It's fine," I said, sitting down at the table. The top of the lasagna was gooey with browned parmesan; Dennis was a good cook, and I was hungry after the long day.

He sat too. "If it really matters to you, Abby, go interview. I don't want to stop you—I just don't want to never see you."

The memory of his surgery sprang to mind once again. The worry in my stomach, the guilt in my breast. I didn't want to feel that ever again. If I worked out on the water and an emergency presented itself, I wouldn't be able to return to him quickly—not like I could now, at the bank, which was barely five minutes from his office. And he was right: I'd probably work weekends and never see him. As he stared at me across the table with love in his eyes, these were the excuses I told myself. It wasn't that he didn't believe in my dreams—he was just being practical. And maybe I needed to be more practical too.

"I'll withdraw my résumé," I said.

He didn't stop me.

2018

After running into Jackie at the grocery store, I decide to try Eli again. Perhaps he wants to see me as much as I need to see him. Perhaps we can help each other heal from the damage done. We were so close once. Almost as close as Dennis and me—and in some ways more so. He always had the power of making life seem less daunting, more vibrant—I need that now more than ever.

The Avalon putters along, heading toward Water Street and Eli's gallery. I'm white-knuckling the steering wheel and reciting what I'll say. *I'm sorry* and *How've you been?* and *Can we start from the beginning?* I consider how I'll ask about his divorce, but none of the combinations of words seem right. My windshield wipers squeak at a steady pace.

I pause at a stoplight, trying to find the right phrasing. Simple must be better, right? *I heard about your divorce.* Or maybe, *I was sorry to hear about your divorce.*

And then I see it: a white six-wheel truck with the Nelson Construction logo on the side. It's across the intersection to my right. Dread swirls through me. I duck, my forehead hitting the passenger seat. Did he see me? I wait for six breaths, seven, eight. Then someone is honking. I peer over the edge of the passenger window. The truck is gone. More honks from behind tell me that my light is now green. Still quaking, I ease on the gas, my vision darting.

I'm still rattled when I finally make it to the gallery. I park, open the door, and jaywalk across the street. It's locked. I read the hours on the window; today, the gallery opens at ten. It's currently 9:50. I cup my hands against the window glass, hoping to see him inside, but the front room is empty, save for the many, many images adorning the walls.

"What are you doing here?"

I turn around, and there he is—it's as if no time has passed. He looks exactly the same—a scruffy jawline and unkempt hair—only now, his ever-present half smile is nowhere to be found. It's a drizzly day, and he's wearing a windbreaker that whispers when he crosses his arms.

"Eli—"

"What are you doing here?" I've never heard his voice so icy-stern.

I'm here to see you, I want to say. *I miss you.* But words won't come.

"I don't want to see you," he says. "Please go, Abby."

Now the words tumble out. "Can we talk, Eli? I've missed you. I want to talk."

His lips press together, and he shakes his head, brushing past me to unlock the door.

"Please, may I come inside?"

"No," he says. "No." He blocks the threshold, and I feel my resolve crumbling like brittle brick in an earthquake. There's nothing I can do, nothing left between us. Why did I allow Eli to occupy so much of my time back then, time I should've spent repairing things with Dennis? *Because he gets you,* I think. *Because he knows a thing or two about guilt.*

Before I can plead, Eli whispers, "I don't want to see you again."

Then he closes the door.

2012

Eli was a regular that winter, coming in periodically to cash checks. I learned that he had photos hanging in a number of galleries, and sales were good. People loved images of tropical places in the dead of winter, he'd quipped. Riya, always giggling when he came in, asked him all sorts of questions that I couldn't help trying to overhear. His travel stories became something I looked forward to in my dreary, boring days.

Things with Dennis remained tense. He'd found his calling—or at least a skill he liked and was good at—and trying to explain my craving for purpose was met with a "Why don't you just . . ." that always seemed to miss my point. He struggled to navigate my frustration but at the same time thrived in the very monotony that made me feel stuck. He liked our life the way it was. And though things had grown stale, I still loved him.

Sick of the stuffy indoor air, even as the weather got colder, I made a habit of taking my lunch breaks outside. The bank was close enough to the water that I could walk to a nearby coffee shop, buy a drink, and sit on a bench and listen to the waves. I felt most alive by the sea, and the small moments I spent outside were rejuvenating.

On an arctic day in late November, I was leaving the coffee shop, all bundled up and headed for my usual spot by the beach, when I saw Eli on the street. I didn't expect him to recognize me out of context—no one ever did—but he walked right over.

"Abby?" he said. "On break?"

I nodded. "How've you been?" I knew he was good—he'd brought in thousands of dollars' worth of sales in just the past few weeks. I hadn't seen his photography but could assume his work was spectacular.

"Same old," he said. "Planning the next trip, actually."

"Oh?" I said. "Where?"

We fell in step, wandering the sidewalk in the direction of the branch. I still had fifteen minutes.

"Leaning toward Morocco, though maybe I'll do Egypt, yet I desperately want to go back to Peru. It's such a hard choice, you know?" His face lit up and his hands were expressive as he spoke. I recognized that excitement: it was pure passion. "The world is such a big place, and I only have the one camera."

I laughed a little. "It must be amazing, traveling all the time." He seemed so adventurous, so free. I yearned for more spontaneity in my life.

"It has its ups and downs. It's tough being away from home." We neared my turnoff to the beach, and I hesitated. Eli stopped and touched my arm. "Am I keeping you?"

I pointed my thumb over my shoulder, toward the beach. "I usually finish my coffee by the water."

"May I join you?"

The question surprised me—I hadn't thought he'd have any interest in talking to me. "Sure," I said, leading us down the gravel path toward the beach.

The bench was occupied by a woman and child, so Eli and I walked down the beach a little ways and settled on a smooth log. I sipped my pour-over, an Ethiopian roast with warm notes of chocolate, a flavor that made me feel far away.

"What types of things do you want to shoot if you go to Africa?"

"I never really know until I get there," Eli said. "But I have an interest in the sand dunes, hence the general area. And of course the architecture. You can't beat the colors in Morocco."

"Or the pyramids in Egypt," I said.

"Exactly."

"And Peru?"

Eli shifted on the log, his knee bending toward me so he sat somewhat sideways, regarding me more fully. "The last time I was there went by too quickly. The coast, the ruins, the jungle—it's all so beautiful." There was longing in his voice.

"What about Cuba?" I wanted to know. "Did you dive while you were there?"

"I'm not much of an underwater photographer," Eli said. "I did a lot of city photos. The cars, the people, the buildings. It's all so colorful. And the beaches, of course. Those are the big sellers."

"I'll have to see your work sometime," I said.

"I'm at the Hannon Gallery until the end of the year." A touch of pride made the corners of his mouth turn up. He had a narrow, kind face with full lips.

"So you didn't get in the water at all?"

"No," Eli said. "Why do you ask?"

I looked out toward the ocean. The ferry was gliding past our little spot, hulking and oddly close to the land. The water rippled up onto shore, the waves growing more urgent as the ferry disturbed the calm.

I decided to answer his question honestly. "In another life, I'm a marine biologist."

"Really?" Eli asked. "Tell me about it."

I checked the time on my phone. "Later," I said, standing.

Eli seemed to snap out of the moment. "Back to work?"

I nodded, not bothering to hide the dismay on my face. I finished my coffee in two gulps, just to fill the silence.

"I'll walk with you," Eli said. "I was headed there anyway."

"All right," I said, and we started toward the sidewalk, sand and gravel crunching under our shoes. "So when do you plan to leave?"

"Next fall," Eli said. "My wife wants me home for a while."

I hadn't known; he didn't wear a ring on his finger.

"Our daughter just started walking, God save us."

"You took them to Cuba?"

He chuckled. "No way. I travel solo."

"Your wife lets you travel while she's home alone with a little one?"

Eli gave me a loaded, sideways look. "*Lets* is not an accurate word. *Tolerates*, maybe. But hey, that's part of the deal. She knew it when we married."

"Please tell me you were at least home for your daughter's birth."

Another laugh, sweet and warm as honey on toast. "*That's* a story for another time. But yes, I was there."

We came up to the branch and paused outside.

"This was fun," Eli said, touching my arm once more, briefly. "I hope I didn't ruin your break."

"I liked the company," I said, a little surprised that that was the truth.

"Do you usually go on break this time of day?" Eli asked. "You owe me some marine biology details."

"One o'clock."

He tapped his temple. "Noted."

He held the door for me, and I stepped past. Inside, the blast of hot air didn't seem so assaulting, though seeing me come inside with Eli had Riya shooting daggers with her eyes, her mouth pursed, tight and envious. Having learned Eli was married, I felt bad for Riya, who seemed so invested in carrying out Eli's transactions when he came in.

"Nice talking to you," I said, slipping behind the counter.

"Likewise, Abby."

He fell into Yvonne's line behind two other customers, and I ducked into the back, removing my coat and hanging up my purse.

Riya cornered me by the coin-counter machine. "You were hanging out with Eli?" she asked, clearly trying to sound more casual than she felt.

"I ran into him while walking back from my break," I said.

She brightened. "Oh. Well, dibs."

Had she thought I was interested? The idea that she sensed chemistry between myself and a man who wasn't my husband caused a black wormy feeling to coil inside me. "You know I'm married," I said, trying to lighten things.

"Exactly," she said. "You have your own hunk already."

I didn't want to hurt her feelings. Gently, I said, "You know Eli is married, too, right?"

Her face sank; clearly, she had not.

"He was telling me about his wife and daughter." I touched her shoulder, slipping past so I could get back to work. "I'm sorry."

Riya hesitated in the corner, and when I looked back, I saw her reach up to wipe her face. When she turned around, her tawny skin was tinged pink, but nothing else suggested her being upset. I felt lousy—I hadn't meant to hurt her.

Glancing down at my wedding ring, I turned my hand, watching the diamond catch the light. Eli's life was such a paradox. Wanderlust photographer with a settled homelife. I couldn't imagine traveling all over the globe without Dennis—but then again, lately, I felt thousands of miles away from him.

2018

The morning is clear and chilly, and this time, I'm early enough to get coffee before heading down to the *Glacial Wind*. It's my first official day, and I'm bundled up in boots, jeans, two long-sleeved shirts, and my warmest jacket. Having tossed and turned with nightmares about Jackie burning down the grocery store and Eli causing earthquakes, I rose early and had a chance to braid my hair into pigtails and shove them under a beanie. I spent the rest of the morning petting Taffy—who was beginning to split her time between my house and Gwen's—before I dared to drive the Avalon down to the marina.

It's eight o'clock when I step into the toasty coffee shop; I have an hour before I need to meet Robin for work. An older couple is ahead of me, chitchatting with the shop owner, Zack. I'm glad to see him—just the thought of a new coffee concoction makes my lips tingle—and he smiles at me before working the espresso machine for the folks in front. I wait patiently, admiring his finesse: a toss of a bottle, a spin of a pitcher, whistling all the while.

Given the chill outside, I know my cheeks are as bright as strawberries in the heat of the shop. The place is filled with early risers, most of them bundled similarly to me. Boat people, I'm sure. I remove my jacket and fold it over my crossed arms.

"See something you like?" Zack asks, wiping his hands on a rag.

Having come in a few times now, I've decided that his mystery drinks are better than anything I would ever normally order. "I'll take another recommendation."

"Brave woman." He grins, big and mischievous, then bends below the counter to grab ingredients. "How've you been?"

"Fine."

"Convincing," he says.

"Couldn't sleep last night."

"Oh?" He drizzles clear syrup into the bottom of a cup, raising the bottle two feet above the rim, then flips the bottle and places it back on the shelf below.

Like a therapist, he has an unassuming demeanor that makes me want to be honest. "I saw a friend turned enemy yesterday."

"An enemy?"

"I don't know what else to call her."

"It's a powerful word, that's all."

I fiddle with my key ring, rubbing one between my fingers. "Yeah, well, it was a powerful falling-out. How are you?"

He shrugs, pouring some milk into a metal pitcher. "Same old. I had a late night too. A buddy was visiting and bought me one too many beers."

"So you're dragging a little too."

Speaking louder over the hiss of steaming milk, he says, "Yeah, but I have a remedy."

"And what's that?"

After the frothing dissipates, he taps the pitcher on the countertop. "Lemon juice and cayenne."

The very thought makes me shiver. I make a face, cheeks scrunched in disgust. "Yuck."

"Does the trick, though," Zack says. "You get used to it. Like jumping into the ocean."

"In this weather?"

"Indeed," he says. "Sour, spice, and a cool dip. Good as new."

"Wait, you swam out there *this morning*?" My skin tightens. A few minutes in Pacific Northwest winter water can cause hypothermia. Even a two-second dip sounds like too long. "With a hangover?" I shake my head and chuckle a little, struck by his joie de vivre.

He shrugs. "We all have our tricks."

"That's a terrible trick."

He chuckles. Pouring the milk into the cup, he breaks the stream once, twice, three times, then moves the pitcher forward, making a perfect foam tulip. He slides the mystery drink toward me.

"Gorgeous," I say. "What is it?"

"A brown sugar latte."

"Simple," I say.

"There's a secret to it, though." He wipes the counter with a rag.

"Oh?"

He leans forward as if he's going to whisper. I lean, too, and can smell the used coffee grounds by the espresso machine.

"Cardamom."

"Cardamom?"

"And a hint of orange." He gestures toward my cup.

I sip. Sure enough, the caramel sweetness of the brown sugar is balanced with the bright herbal spice and subtle haze of citrus. "Wow."

Satisfaction flickers across his face. "I hope your day picks up, Abby."

"You too."

I pay and step aside, and a new set of customers takes my place; I hear Zack talking to them, asking questions. Everyone seems like a regular here, which doesn't surprise me. In the few times I've come in, Zack has always treated me like a regular—no wonder his shop is so popular.

With my prized latte in hand, I wander into the seating area, searching for a window spot to enjoy my coffee. I've found a good one, facing the water, but the sound of my name holds me back.

I turn and am met with surprise, nerves. "Robin," I say. "Good morning."

"Fueling up, I see," he says. "You ready for the day?"

"Yes," I breathe. "Excited."

"It's a small group scheduled, but there have been gray whale and minke sightings last night and this morning, so it should be a good trip. More intimate with fewer people."

"Intimate?" I don't like the idea of being so on the spot my first day.

"Don't worry. I'll talk you through the motions." He inches toward a two-person table where a book and a half-finished coffee reside. "Want to join me?"

"Sure," I say, a little disappointed not to have the morning to myself. I had hoped to gather my nerves *before* I saw Robin.

We sit, and he rearranges the table to make room for my cup. "How do you know Zack?"

"I don't," I say. "Just from here. I've only been in a few times."

Robin seems to ponder that. "Seems like you've known him longer."

"Isn't he like that with everyone?"

Robin glances toward the bar as if to confirm. "Well, yeah."

"The coffee is stellar."

"Can't argue there." He takes a sip. "The whole marina loves him."

"Has this place been here long?"

"Zack opened it a few years ago, but he's been doing coffee for over ten," Robin says. "He needed a job after his accident, and none of the other companies would hire him, so he learned coffee. People in town thought he was so good they rallied to help him open his own place."

"He had an accident?"

Robin leans forward, speaking low. "He used to work on the Alaskan fishing boats. Something happened up there one season, and he came back with dark eyes and a bad limp."

I glance toward Zack, who's laughing and gesturing with a group of people. He takes their cash and opens the till, finding change, but when he hands it back, they wave him off, and he places the extra dollars in the tip jar. A smile of thanks pokes through his beard, crinkles around his eyes. The deep dips below his cheekbones are hidden beneath his hickory-colored, uniform whiskers. I'm struck by the sense of community, of belonging. Even in California, I was never close with the research team. In the Point Hudson Marina, it seems everyone is close.

"You'd never know now," Robin says, finishing his coffee.

I take a sip of my own. The flavors are balanced on my tongue, bright and warm.

Robin and I chitchat about whales and town. I tell him about my time at the Salish Science Center, the first time I saw orcas, and my passion for the ocean. He tells me more about Sound Adventures. It's a family business, going back two generations—his grandparents started it as a ferry to Canada, but after seeing so many whales, they started offering tours. In the next few years, his parents will hand him the reins.

It has been about forty-five minutes when Robin checks his watch. "Want to walk over?"

He gathers his things and buses his dish while I slip into my jacket. We both wave at Zack on our way out. The morning chill is strong against my cheeks, especially after my acclimation to the warm coffee shop. Robin and I walk together down the cobbled pathway, taking in the morning. I hear him sigh, and I breathe deep, too, listening to the soft knocking of the docks against pylons. The *Glacial Wind* glimmers in the morning light, squeaky clean. We climb aboard. The white deck beneath my feet, the salt air, and the foggy cold feel like home.

Robin walks me through the morning routine: brewing coffee, setting up little vases of carnations on each table, and bringing out the gray whale books from the big stack in the wheelhouse. I check to make sure the bathroom has extra toilet paper in the cabinet, and I'm glad to sense that my mishap with the head is history, though I'm still surprised Joanne didn't say anything.

Meanwhile, Robin checks the engine, starting the *Glacial Wind* for a few minutes before powering down again. He explains to me that we get gas at the end of the day, which makes for a quicker morning start. He also explains how the morning will go: the guests will arrive and congregate outside, I'll greet them and lead them down the dock, Robin will help them aboard, I'll make sure they're all seated, he'll do a safety briefing, and then I'll describe the area and our plans for the day while Robin helps Captain Kim get underway. It's a well-oiled process, and I try to memorize every word, determined to ensure things go without a hitch.

I'm in the middle of placing laminated baleen whale charts on each of the tables when Captain Kim comes aboard carrying a pink box, and I pause at the sight of her. "Good morning," I say.

"Abby," she exclaims. "Happy first day."

Robin pokes his head in from outside. "Doughnuts?"

Kim places the box on one of the tables and opens it to reveal white-powdered jellies, long tan maples, apple fritters, and more. "Welcome to the Sound Adventures team, girl."

Without hesitation, Robin goes for a jelly. "Best morning ever," he says through a bite.

I grab an apple fritter. "Thank you, Kim. This is so nice."

"Just buttering you up before the long day," she says.

"Why'd you get a dozen?" Robin asks.

"Small group today, remember?" Kim selects one of the plain glazed doughnuts and breaks it in half. "Figured the guests would want to share in the first-day fun."

For a moment, nibbling on the fritter, I'm overcome with joy. The few reservations I had about working for a tour boat are melting fast. It's hard to believe this is happening, that a kind team would welcome me so heartily. I use the doughnut to distract myself from an impending flood of happy tears.

"I'm so glad to be here," I tell them.

"Hold on to that feeling when you clean the toilet later," Robin says.

Kim snorts with laughter. "C'mon, it's time to load up the group and shove off."

~

The tourists are glad for the doughnuts, which makes them glad it's my first day as a naturalist on the *Glacial Wind*. Thankful for Captain Kim's idea, I relax into the motions of the morning, following Robin's earlier instructions to a tee. I watch him introduce himself and wave to the crowd when he points to their new naturalist, Abby Fisher. He walks them through basic safety, and then he's out the door, helping Kim maneuver out of the marina.

All eyes shift to me.

The sudden spotlight gives me a spike of adrenaline, bordering on panic, but then I remember Zack and the mystery coffee, the first-day doughnuts, the fact that Robin and Kim are counting on me, my passion for the Puget Sound, and how much I want to share that passion with the guests. I spot Mary and Becca among the few tourists, and they give me four thumbs up.

"Welcome," I begin. "How many of you are from the area?"

Only Mary and Becca raise their hands. A trio of tourists mentions Canada, and another three say Oregon.

"All right," I say. "Under your table mats, you'll see a map of the Salish Sea, which spans the inland marine waters between Washington and Canada. The islands and deep channels were carved out by glaciers ten thousand years ago." I hold up my own map and point along with my explanation, helping them get their bearings along with a mini history lesson. I add that gray whales were spotted about forty minutes away and delve into whale facts.

While I'm up there talking, time flies, and then Robin returns, and it's time for a break. I wander over to Mary and Becca, ready for some familiar faces, and ask them how they're doing.

"Just wonderful," Mary says. She looks a little pallid but cheery. "You're doing great, Abby."

"Oh, thanks." I'm glad to hear it. "How are you, Becca? No school today?"

She shakes her head. "Parent-teacher meetings are this week, so we have half days, which are practically useless."

"So we're playing hooky," Mary says with a wink. "Where are the whales today?"

"It looks like they're traveling down the strait toward us, just south of the San Juans," I say. "Have you seen gray whales before?"

Becca shakes her head. "Only minkes and humpbacks, plus orcas and porpoise."

"Slinky minkes." Mary leans close. "Do you think they're boring too?"

I lean in conspiratorially. "Don't tell Robin I said so."

Mary laughs.

"I like them," Becca says. "They're elusive. I respect that."

"That's a good point," I say, glancing around. "I should mingle more. Do you want any snacks?"

"Later," Mary says. "Go do your thing, Abby."

I take orders, putting together baskets of chips and jerky, pouring coffee into mugs, making small talk with the other customers. Captain Kim calls from the wheelhouse something that I can't quite make out, and the boat slows considerably.

I poke my head through the door. "What?"

"Gray whales at eleven o'clock," Kim says. "I'll angle us closer. Can you bring them out onto the bow?"

"Yes." I come back out and tell the group about the whales. "Captain Kim is going to get us a little closer. Why don't we all head outside?"

I remind them to use the railing as they go, then hold the door while they all shrug into warmer layers and file outside, congregating on the bow. We're all looking toward eleven o'clock when, of course, the whales pop up at nine, startling everyone with their spouts. A bumpy nose pokes out of the water while the long back of another slides seemingly endlessly along the surface, until finally the flukes lift, angle up, and slip underwater. Everyone peers over the railing, fingers clutching the cool metal, gasping with each surfacing.

The whales go through numerous sets of deep dives, and I mingle with the tourists, offering information as well as excitement. While I might know more facts, I revel as much as they do. The group's collective interest makes them all more relaxed and chatty—with me and each other. I glance at Robin once or twice throughout the hubbub, and he smiles to reinforce my good job. It's a relief, really. And the whales—eliciting such a rush to my veins, a joy like nothing else—give me a sense of belonging.

It's not unlike spotting whales with Dr. Perez, only here, there's no need to record, place a tag, or do anything other than enjoy the whales' grace. Here, I get to witness people's first-time awe. It's humbling, heartening. Minute by minute, I see their appreciation growing, their reverence expanding. Each guest has the opportunity to make change, and I'm glad to help instill that urge.

After an hour watching the whales surface, plus a detour to watch sea lions basking on a nearby outcrop, we usher everyone inside. Kim maneuvers us southeastward, picking up the pace to return to Port Townsend. Mary and Becca are the last indoors, and I help Mary step over the threshold. She's weaker than this morning, and I give Becca a concerned look.

"How you doing, Mom?" she asks.

Mary's cheeks are rosy from the cold. "Do I look that bad?" She pulls a tissue from her coat pocket and dabs at her nose. "Just a little winded is all."

I help Mary and Becca settle into their booth again. "Can I get you two anything?"

Becca and Mary share a mischievous glance, then grin widely. "Hot chocolate?" Becca asks.

"Done," I say. "Two?"

"Oh yes, don't leave me out," Mary says.

I nod, feeling a tug of worry as I walk off. At the snack station, I mix up some Swiss Miss. Robin sidles up next to me.

"How's she doing?" he whispers.

"She looks weak," I say. "Is that normal?"

He shrugs. "It seems to ebb and flow," he says. "Is Becca in good spirits?"

"Yeah."

"That's a good sign." He grabs a cup. "I'll walk over with you."

While the other tourists munch on snacks, use the restroom, and flip through whale books, Robin and I sit with Mary and Becca. They've removed their warmest layers, though Mary still wears a thick sweater and a pullover. Mary has kept her hat on, but Becca removes hers, revealing dutch braids like mine, a little frizzy. I learn that Mary used to be a school principal, back when they lived in New Mexico. Becca skipped sophomore year and is a junior angling to become a chemist.

"A chemist?" I ask. "Does anyone else in your class like chemistry?"

"No way," Becca says. "All the girls want to be lawyers or hotel managers or something."

I laugh. "Hotel managers?"

Becca shrugs, lifting her cup to her lips.

"She has a good chemistry teacher," Mary adds. "They do a lot of hands-on stuff."

"It's the best," Becca says.

"She's going to break all kinds of barriers, this one," Mary says. "She's always had an eye for science. And she's usually the only girl at science camp."

"I can relate," I say.

Becca grins.

"And how have you been, Mary?" Robin asks.

"Oh, Robin. Always redirecting the conversation back to me," Mary says, though her tone is light. "I'm fine, you worrier." She shifts in her seat. "Can you let me out, Becca? I'd like to use the head."

Becca slides out of the booth, then slides back in, watching her mother make her way slowly toward the restroom.

"How is she?" Robin asks, serious.

"This round has been rough," Becca says. "They changed her program again, and she's been sick a lot."

"Have you missed any school days?"

"Only today," Becca says. "She'll let me skip for whale watching, but never for her sake."

I ache on her behalf; Becca's strength astounds me. Even now, I can't imagine the emotional toll of taking care of my mother the way Becca must—let alone when I was a teenager.

"I really liked the gray whales," Becca says, changing the subject. "They have cute noses."

"All knobby and freckled with white," I say, agreeing with her assessment.

Becca nods, and the conversation takes a happy turn. Mary returns and offers her own opinions about the whales today, their hulking size and those lovely wide tails. Robin leaves the table shortly after that, standing to address the group again. He offers more facts about the whales and answers eager questions.

Once we've docked in Port Townsend, Robin and I help the tourists off the *Glacial Wind*, taking special care with Mary, the last one off. Robin and I watch Becca walk Mary up the ramp toward their car. She's patient and deliberate, her thin arm wrapped around her mother's frail shoulders, gesturing with her other hand. They both laugh, a sweet sound that fills the marina.

Robin touches my arm. "Nice job today," he says. "Ready to clean the toilet?"

"Ha. Sure."

"Seriously," he says. "Kim and I will get her gassed up; you tidy the inside."

Realizing he's serious, I embarrassingly sober up. "Right, yes."

"It won't take long." Then, again, "You did good."

"Thank you," I say, the weight of my sincerity drawing out the words.

"Thank me *after* the toilet," he says, clapping my back.

It's nearly four by the time we've finished prepping the boat for Wednesday's tour. In step with Kim and Robin, heading toward the parking lot, I'm tired and energized all at once. Chrissy and Nick insisted on my coming over for Thai takeout after work, and I'm eager to tell them about my day.

Digging my keys out of my purse, I say, "Well, see you later."

"Oh, no you don't," Kim says, catching my arm. "It's your first day, and you've yet to go through initiation."

"Initiation?" A pulse of anxiety hits me in the chest. "You already bought me doughnuts."

"Those aren't *initiation*," Kim says.

"You wish," Robin adds.

"We're getting drinks tonight, the whole team," Kim says. "The Manatee at eight."

I shake my head. "Oh, I don't know. I have plans with—"

Kim points at me with her own set of keys. "Mandatory."

I relent, my chest still tingly with nerves. "Fine, fine."

"It'll be fun," Kim says, dropping the intimidation act. Her eyes squint with a smile.

"It *won't* be fun," Robin says, staying the course. He looks me in the eye. "At least the hangover won't."

I laugh, warming to the idea. Meeting the whole Sound Adventures team sounds a little overwhelming—and with alcohol, a little risky—but they seem like a family, and after having such a positive day, I yearn to be a part of it. "I'll see you at eight."

2012

Eli was nowhere to be found for another ten days, and then one Friday, my spirits buoyant with the long week finally behind me, I ran into him again while getting coffee. I'd opted for a latte on my break; the weather was dreary and rainy, the water obscured by mist. Eli was sitting at a table by the window, overlooking the bay, and he set his book down the moment I walked in. Had he been waiting for me?

Drink in hand, I walked over. "Fancy meeting you here."

He gestured to the open seat. "Join me?"

I hesitated. He was clean shaven today, stripped down to a T-shirt, a sweater and jacket bunched and cast aside on the window ledge. Having mostly seen him in long sleeves, I studied his tattoos for a moment. Molecular structures of little hexagons with letters and connecting lines dotted his right forearm. Up over the swell of his bicep, the structures had flowers and vines tangled among them, congealing into trees. A forest of evergreens ringed his upper arm, their tops hidden under the edge of his sleeve.

I recognized those molecular structures from school, though I couldn't remember what they were. Curiosity lowered me into the open seat.

On his left arm were familiar equations: equal signs and square roots and even the elegant curve of an integral. The numbers grew more complicated, twisting into a Fibonacci sequence above his elbow that looked like a giant snail shell.

I gestured at his tattoos. "Those are interesting."

He stretched his arms forward so I could look closer.

"I remember those structures from my undergrad. That's advanced stuff." I paused. "I don't remember what they actually are, though."

His brow wrinkled, pensive. "The biggest one is oxytocin."

"The love hormone?"

He nodded. "Plus adrenaline, among other things."

I didn't know how to phrase my next question, so I stumbled through it. "Why . . . I mean what . . . does it mean something?"

He pointed to the beginning of the tattoo, down by his wrist. "Life starts with adrenaline, instinct, then"—his finger traced up his inner arm—"lust, love, labor." His fingertip passed over the flowers, into the trees. "Us, nature, everything—we're all just molecules."

"I love it."

He cracked a smile. "It keeps me grounded."

"And all the math?"

"Proofs of equations." Reading my confusion, he added, "I went to college to be a mathematician. Same concept as the molecules." He extended his arm, pointing. "The world is made up of numbers and patterns."

"Fibonacci," I said.

"Exactly." He sat back, seeming impressed. "Not many people get it."

"Well, I was a nerd in school too."

"Me? Nerdy? What are you talking about?"

I laughed, leaning forward to slip out of my coat. "A mathematician seems like a rare profession."

"I'm not here to talk about calculus. Tell me about marine biology."

So he *had* been waiting for me. I wasn't necessarily glad. "What's there to tell?"

He spread his hands, inviting.

I gestured to his tattoos. "When I was a teenager, I saw seawater under a microscope, and that was it. The life contained in a single drop of water . . ." I shook my head, dizzied by the thought. "It's astounding."

"Oh?" he prompted.

"Absolutely. Phytoplankton, the tiny plants, they're the beginning. They turn the sun's light into energy. They're everywhere, giving us oxygen, life." I took a sip of my latte, watching his face. He stared back at me with interest and understanding. I hadn't talked about my passion for so long.

He said, "Go on."

"The zooplankton—little animals like crustaceans and larvae—they prop up the entire food chain." I tapped my finger on the table for emphasis. "It all starts with that single drop of seawater, all the way up to the blue whale, the biggest animal on earth. So big you could swim through its aorta. It relies on the plankton. We all do."

"Scope," Eli said, nodding his head slowly.

"Take orcas, for instance. They're incredibly intelligent. They have family structures, language, and some argue they even have culture. We humans—we have no idea the type of intelligence that lies in our oceans. We've only scratched the surface."

Eli grinned, revealing a set of perfect teeth.

"What?" I asked, self-conscious.

"You love it like I love photography," he said. "Raw passion."

He definitely understood. A flood of relief spread through me. How long had it been since I'd gotten to talk about my interest? Eli's understanding was something I hadn't known I craved. A thirst I hadn't noticed until the cup tipped toward my mouth.

"So why are you working at the bank?" Eli asked.

The question was a thunderclap, a sudden darkening of the sky. Just the thought of the bank drained me and left me weary.

"I was on a research trip in Alaska, and my husband had to have emergency heart surgery. After that . . ." I shrugged. "There aren't many opportunities in town, and I don't think I could leave him again." I felt a tug in my heart, a gentle yearning to see Dennis right then. That horrible plane ride home, wondering if he was alive or dead in each moment that passed, had been a true nightmare. The thought of experiencing it again made me want to cry out.

"So you settled." Eli's words had judgment in them.

"I made a choice," I said, defensive. "The bank is temporary."

Eli crossed his arms, leaned back. "What's your plan, then?"

I didn't have an answer. I sipped my coffee, which was growing cold.

He leaned forward. "Take it from me, Abby, from one misunderstood, nerdy, passionate person to another. Do what you love."

Feeling like I was suddenly under a microscope, I checked the time. "I should get back."

"I'll walk you over?"

I shrugged into my coat, thinking of Riya. "It's all right. Enjoy your afternoon." Then I added, "Thank you."

"For?"

"The conversation." I meant it. Talking about science had jumpstarted a dormant part of me; I buzzed with newfound energy.

"Again soon?" he asked.

And as much as I felt guilty for spending time with a man who wasn't Dennis, I reminded myself that Eli had a wife. He wasn't interested in anything more than friendship. And besides, it was only coffee. Only conversation. "Definitely," I said.

2018

Chrissy and Nick were a little disappointed that I couldn't stick around after dinner, but we resolved to meet up again at the end of the week. Aside from my eagerness to meet my coworkers at the Manatee, I was glad to escape the baby talk. I've always known that to some degree I'll lose Chrissy when she starts trying to get pregnant, but I didn't expect to face that now, not while my life is so unsteady.

It's five past eight by the time I've finally parked downtown. I've changed into black jeans and one of my nicer tops, a green blouse. The evening is especially chilly. A crisp breeze slithers up from the water. My hair is braided back, the hollow of my neck exposed, and the next gust sends shivers wiggling down my back. As I reach the building, I glance up to the top, where wide bracketed cornices crown the roof and high windows with molded window caps line the upper floors, a mess of twigs and bird poop on the intermittent ledges. All the buildings in town look like this: old, crumbly, but with restored features, faded but colorful paint, shrugged up against the shoreline.

I turn under a wooden manatee-shaped sign. The door blinks with a neon **Open** sign, buzzing in the small foyer when I step in from the cold. My only option is to head up a narrow staircase toward the raucous chatter and the unmistakable clanging of glasses. The Manatee is a popular place. In the entryway, for a few glorious moments, I'm anonymous—but then someone is calling my name, and my nervousness returns.

But it isn't someone from Sound Adventures—it's Zack.

"Fancy meeting you here," he says from the bar, which is a curved half moon to the left of the doorway.

I wander over, relief spreading through my limbs; I find him mostly effortless to talk to, and his presence puts me at ease. "How's it going?"

He takes a long sip of orange-brown liquid in a rocks glass. "Oh, you know." His cheeks are ruddy underneath his beard. "Meeting someone?"

"Many someones," I say. "The whole Sound Adventures crew."

He shakes his head. "Initiation?"

"How'd you know?"

"It's a long-standing tradition." For a moment, his eyes meet mine, and then they flicker past me.

I turn around; it's Kim.

"Abby," she says. "We're in the big booth over here."

Zack tips his glass, smirking. "Have fun."

My comfort dwindles as I wonder what exactly initiation entails. Kim leads me through the main room to a side area with large booths. A few familiar faces are mixed among others at a ten-person table. Drinks already have waned to half their fill, and everyone cheers when we walk up.

"Robin, get her a beer, would you?"

He shakes my shoulder in greeting, walking past me toward the bar.

"IPA," I tell him.

He offers a thumbs-up without looking back.

"Everyone, meet our newest naturalist, Abby," Kim says.

"Hi, Abby," everyone calls.

"Abby, meet everyone."

I give a little wave. "Thanks for having me."

A barrel-chested man says, "Don't be shy; sit down!"

A row of people scooch closer in the booth, making room for me to squeeze onto the bench. Linda, whom I met in the Sound Adventures store, is across from me. The man next to me introduces himself as Henry, Linda's husband and Robin's father. Kim sits down and conducts more introductions: Bob and Carol—the ones who started it all—are Linda's parents (I do the math, and they must be in their eighties, but they don't look more than sixty). Kim found them through Henry, who was her old boss, before she got her captain's license. There's another captain and two more employees, but I don't catch their names over the noise.

The only other familiar face is Joanne's, and she's seated at the opposite end of the table. Even talking with the others, she wears a perpetual tight-lipped frown. She doesn't bother to acknowledge me, and I'm a little relieved. After the issue with the head, I'm thankful I won't be working with her on the tours.

Robin comes back with my beer and drags a chair to the end of the table so he can sit. I take a quick swig, eager to catch up to everyone else. After a round of cheers and laughter, everyone falls back into their respective conversations, except for Robin and Henry and Kim, who look at me expectantly.

"Thanks again for having me here," I say, shrinking under their attention.

Henry shifts beside me. "Robin says you have a degree?"

"Yep," I say.

"Then what are you doing with the likes of us?"

Kim laughs, as does Linda, glancing over. "Don't give her a hard time, Henry," Linda says. "Abby, dear, we're happy to have you."

"She's the most educated of all of us," Henry says.

"I'm sure I have the least experience too." I sip my beer, the hops tingly on my tongue.

Henry laughs, nudging me with his shoulder. "We'll fix that."

The conversation meanders after that, and I'm glad. I interject occasionally, but otherwise, I simply listen, feeling the edges of my shyness soften with the beer and camaraderie. An hour goes by, and Kim tells a story of how a tourist lost his toupee off the side of the boat; I respond with a toupee story of my own, describing how a professor's slipped off and floated down the river, and how a student taking a piss on the riverbank found it but didn't tell the professor ("I'm doing his wife a service," the student said).

My second beer is waning; when Kim notices, she asks, "Another?"

Before I can answer, Robin interjects. "Initiation time."

Cold anxiety overtakes the warmth of beer in my chest. I never understood the point of hazing. I'm tempted to bolt, but my need for the job overpowers my worry. I silently pray that initiation is just a string of flaming shots or something silly like hitting on the bartender—fun stuff, not frat-pledging stuff.

"All right, what do I have to do?" I ask, bracing.

The whole table laughs at my acceptance of the inevitable.

"Buy us a round," Henry says, and they cheer again.

"That's it?" I ask.

"That's it," Robin confirms.

I take drink orders, assessing my bank accounts in my head. If I use two separate cards, I'll be just fine.

"You'll need help carrying it all back," Joanne says, standing.

"Thanks for the help," I say, trying to keep things light, but she doesn't respond.

At the bar, I look around for Zack, but his chair is now occupied by someone else. I order everyone's respective drinks: white wine for Linda and Carol, beers and well drinks for practically everyone else, and whatever Joanne wants.

"Laphroaig," she says to the bartender. "A double, neat."

Scotch—really? With me buying? I try not to take offense, but then Joanne leans close and says, "Clog any toilets today, Abby?"

A ball of anger rages through me, but I'm too sober to call her out; I don't want to risk my new job. Joanne and I wait side by side in silence.

"IPAs," the bartender says, sliding three pint glasses across the counter toward us.

"I'll take these back," Joanne says, balancing all three in her hands and leaving before I can protest.

I wonder if she told Robin about the toilet. Anger turns to embarrassment; I recall that tampon—not even mine!—showing up in the bottom of the bowl. I grip the bar counter, my head swimming with an uneasy, squirmy feeling. I should've told her the truth right then and there: that it wasn't my fault, that I'd only used a tissue. If I tried now, she wouldn't believe me. *Remember, Abby,* I tell myself, *you got the job. It's no big deal.*

But maybe it is a big deal. Joanne could hold this over me. She could tell the lot of them, and they could fire me before I've had a chance to prove my worth.

Joanne does two more table trips, and by then, I'm boiling. The bartender places two glasses of wine on the counter, and now he's pouring the Scotch. I can't let her hold my job security in her hands. I have to say something.

When Joanne returns, I turn toward her. "Why didn't you tell Robin about the toilet thing?" I blurt. "If you hate me that much, you could've just told him I fucked up on my first day, and that would've been the end of it."

At first Joanne looks confused; then she takes a sip of the Scotch the bartender just poured. "I don't hate you," she says.

I shift on my feet, resisting a hiccup. "Yes, you do."

"I don't," Joanne says. "I hate newcomers. The new dynamics and personalities." She waves her hand, sipping more. "And I *did* tell Robin. He didn't care. Kim just laughed."

"You . . ." Anger flares in me again. "Just like that, you threaten my prospects at a job? You don't even know me."

"You were a shoo-in. I didn't threaten you." She finishes off her two shots, at least twenty bucks down the hatch.

"And that Scotch!" I exclaim, steaming with indignation. "That was unnecessarily expensive. I buy the whole group a round, and you take it as an opportunity to drink whatever the hell you want?"

She surprises me then by cracking a wide smile. Without answering, she takes up the two wineglasses and walks back to the table. I almost yell after her, but I don't want to make a scene. As I fume, my tipsiness burns off quick, sobering into a silent, brooding frustration.

The bartender slides two final beers toward me. "Do you want to open a tab?"

"I'll pay now."

Once the damage is done, I sulk back to the table. Slumping into the booth again, I pick up my fresh pint and take a long, slow pull.

Robin has a strange grin on his face. "Joanne tells us you passed your initiation."

I don't understand.

"You're officially in the gang!" Kim says, exuberant.

I shake my head. "I don't . . ."

"The Scotch?" Robin says.

"What about it?" I ask.

"That was the test," Kim says.

"You all are cruel," Linda interjects.

"It's a time-honored tradition, Mom," Robin says.

I'm sweating through my blouse. "What?"

"You called me out on the Scotch," Joanne says from down the table. "That's the test. You have a backbone."

"You aren't afraid to speak up for what's right," Robin says. "That's a quality we need on our team."

I digest their words for a moment. "You weren't being rude on purpose?" I ask Joanne.

"She's always rude on purpose," Robin says. "But you didn't let it slide."

I almost did. Had it not been for the alcohol or the news that she'd told Robin about the head, I might have. But I don't say that; I simply down half my beer.

"Cruel," Linda repeats.

"Welcome to Sound Adventures," Kim says. "You're a true part of the team now."

"Is someone at least going to pay me back?" I ask.

They all laugh.

"This is a tradition?"

"My father pulled that trick back with Henry," Linda says, giving Bob a sideways glance.

"Then Henry pulled that shit on me," Kim says.

"Then I did it to Joanne," Robin says. "And Joanne has done it to all our new hires since."

"Has anyone ever let it slide?" I ask.

Robin shrugs. "Only a few, but they didn't last." He gets serious, looking at me square in the face. "This is a family, Abby. We tease, we beef, but we always have each other's backs."

"Linda's right—that *is* cruel," I say.

Linda flashes me a set of straight teeth, tipping her wineglass in my direction.

"We did have the courtesy to loosen you up with a few drinks first," Kim says.

"Good thing," I say, and Robin chuckles.

"We're glad to have you, Abby," he says.

I nod, still a little dazed by my dissipating anger and confusion. Despite the whole trick, I suppose I like the sentiment—to be a marine biologist, a conservationist, you need to stand up for what's right, even if sometimes it makes you uncomfortable. That was a quality I admired in Dr. Perez. I'd always wondered if I'd stand up for the whales the way she did—I guess tonight was a clue. At least with enough beer first.

"If you ever have something to say, speak up, all right?" Kim adds.

Without thinking, I say, "That wasn't my tampon."

For a moment, everyone is silent, and then the whole table erupts in laughter. They must've all heard the story.

"It's true, it's true," I say. "I've been on tons of boats—hell, I'm a functioning adult. I know better. It wasn't mine."

"Excuses, excuses," Robin says.

"I went in there to blow my nose; that's it. Next thing I know, the damn thing spits up the tampon."

Kim takes a breather from her howling laughter to say, "That's true: the *Glacial Wind*'s head *does* have a habit of spitting things back up."

"See?" I say.

"I don't believe it," Robin says. "It's too embarrassing to be an accident."

"I believe her," Joanne interjects. Her persistent scowl breaks into a smile. "You all should've seen her face when I found it. Pure white."

Kim is back to laughing, and this time, I join in. Joanne was right: Robin doesn't care, Kim only thinks it's funny, and judging by the rest of the table, it's no matter at all. With everything out in the open, I feel myself easing up again, the IPA dulling any leftover nerves. By the time Kim launches into her own head story—it actually *did* overflow once, with a tour group of fifty on board—I've forgotten about my worries altogether.

2013

Eli and I made a habit of our coffee meet-ups. He told me stories about his trips—the time in the Rockies when he ran into a mountain lion, the trip to Spain when he went to a nude beach that actually wasn't a nude beach, the time in India when a macaque stole his money belt—and I told him stories about growing up in town—drag racing on dirt roads, helping my father birth a calf, hot-wiring tractors at age fourteen, and the many instances when I saw whales. He asked about my time in Alaska, wanting to know where I'd hiked and how close I'd come to orcas. I asked if he ever missed mathematics.

"I got to a point where all my options pointed toward teaching," Eli said one afternoon in early June. "I didn't want to teach, so I picked up the camera again. It'd been a hobby when I was a teen, and then all of a sudden, this part of me was reawakened." He smiled at me from across our usual table. "So I saved up as much as I could and started doing it full-time."

I envied his willingness to take a turn like that, to jump into a new career with both feet. "How's trip planning, by the way?"

He tipped his head back, eyes darting toward the ceiling in a show of both excitement and frustration. "I think I've finally decided on Morocco. I was so set on Egypt, but you know, the political unrest makes it seem a little dicey, and Molly wouldn't have it."

My gut clenched, as if I was doing something wrong—and maybe I was. We only got coffee, only ever on my lunch break, and when I said it out loud to myself on the drive to work, it sounded inconsequential. Not worth mentioning.

And yet.

We rarely mentioned our spouses, as if we'd made an unspoken agreement. I still hadn't told Dennis about my lunches with Eli. Dennis had never been the jealous type, but something halted me on nights when I thought I'd casually mention it. Guilt gripped my tongue—but guilt for what? Eli and I weren't physical, yet we talked with intimacy, and perhaps that was where the line became blurry. You didn't keep a friend from your husband. You didn't keep secrets unless they were potentially harmful. And could this harm Dennis?

"I can understand why Molly would worry about you," I said. "I wouldn't want Dennis going there."

Eli flinched, though I wasn't sure if it was because I'd mentioned Dennis or because I'd agreed with his wife. In my own way, a way I didn't like to acknowledge, I cared about him, too, and wanted Morocco to be the winning choice.

"I guess she's right," he said, pushing his hair back. "Anyway, Morocco. I've already started planning where I want to go for dunes. And of course the architecture. I'd like to buy a new lens, too, but it's expensive."

I smiled.

"What?"

"Nothing, just your excitement. It's contagious."

He smiled, too, relaxing into it. "It's nice to know someone who understands. We speak the same language."

"I guess we do."

His forehead creased. "I get so stir crazy—Molly hates that."

I glanced down at my fingers, which were laced together in my lap.

"I've been meaning to tell you: I have a new showing on Saturday, during Gallery Walk. It's at the Greenwater Gallery."

"Congratulations," I said. "More beach photos?"

He shook his head. "Now that the weather is warming up here, I wanted to show off my cityscapes. It's still Cuba, but vastly different from what has been on display the past few months." He leaned toward me, speaking the next words like a secret. "You should come."

I'd gone to the Hannon Gallery after work on my own, once, just to see his photographs. They'd blown me away, the detail and color so vivid I'd felt as though I were sitting on those beaches. I'd spent two hours admiring his work before Dennis had called, wondering why I was late for dinner. The next time Eli and I had met, however, he'd wrinkled his nose. "You should see my *real* work." I knew that his invite for Saturday was big.

He continued, "I had them printed on aluminum, and I love how they turned out. The metal really brings out the color."

"Will Molly be there?"

He couldn't blame me for wondering—I had a strong sense that, like Dennis, Molly didn't know about our lunches.

Eli frowned slightly, only for a moment, and the expression looked out of place on his ever-jovial face. "No. She's out of town visiting her mother. She's seen them already, though."

"Oh." His answer might've made me glad, but instead, I felt a twisting in my chest, as if someone were grating a screwdriver against my sternum. "She's out of town" made this feel dangerously close to *sneaking around*—which this wasn't. I tried to reframe my thoughts, telling myself, *It's just friendship*. Even, *It's just a crush*. There was no denying that eight months of conversations had caused Eli and me to grow close—but Molly's absence had a subtle stink to it. Was our friendship heading somewhere new? The invite frightened me.

"I'm really proud of this show, Abby," Eli said, sliding his fingers around the curved bowl of his coffee mug. "I'd love you to see my real work."

Staring at those hands, I said, "I'd be happy to see it." I raised my gaze to his. "I'll be there."

He sat back, relieved, his forehead no longer creased. "I'm so glad. It'll be fun."

That night, when I got home, Dennis had dinner ready. I dropped my purse on the floor and locked my arms behind his neck and kissed him, and he squeezed my waist, lifting me ever so slightly, the heels of my shoes rising off the hardwood. But there was a difference in his touch: a dullness. It was similar to the dullness I felt at work.

"How was your day?" he asked. He smelled like sawdust and caulk and sweat—a familiar scent.

"Fine," I said. "You?"

He kissed my nose. "Good."

"Let me change out of my work clothes; then we can eat."

In the bedroom, I removed my skirt and blouse and slipped into an old T-shirt and pajama shorts. I wondered how to broach the subject of Saturday with Dennis, apprehension wiggling through my veins like an eel.

Back downstairs, Dennis was sitting at our table. He'd made steak and potatoes, which wasn't something I was in the mood for, but it looked good, and he did have a knack for cooking my steak exactly the way I liked it, a tender medium rare with a black pepper sear.

Dennis wanted to know if I had any hopes for how we should spend our weekend. We always discussed the weekend on Thursdays, as if our days off had finally come into sight, on the horizon. Dennis worked most Saturdays, but he was off Sunday and Monday, and we liked to spend our one overlapping day off together.

"Maybe we could get dinner Saturday night?" he asked.

"Can we make it Sunday?"

"Sure," he said, chewing a bite of steak. "How come? You have plans?"

Just tell him. "Yeah, in the evening," I hedged.

"Chrissy?" he asked.

I nodded—why did I nod? Then the lie was coming out before I could stop it. "Yeah, just some girl time. You mind?"

"Not at all," Dennis said. "We can get dinner on Sunday."

"That sounds great." I took a big bite so I could avoid digging myself into a deeper pit of culpability. I had never lied to my husband—not technically—and the ease with which it came to my lips terrified me.

Dennis launched into a story about a job he was working on, and I tried to swallow the Saturday issue, chewing it up and forcing it down with my steak. I couldn't bring myself to back out. He didn't suspect anything, and more importantly (I curtly reminded myself), he didn't have anything to suspect. Eli might as well have been a coworker with an overlapping lunch break. Right? Right.

In Dennis's work story, his client, an older woman, kept accusing his guys of leaving beer cans around, when the true culprit was her deadbeat son. Dennis had finished the job today and was relieved to get the hell out of her paranoid life.

"To just assume that level of unprofessionalism," Dennis exclaimed, shaking his head. "It's insulting. Especially to Eduardo. Half our clients assume he's here illegally."

"That's outrageous," I said.

Eduardo was Dennis's site manager on bigger projects—and, more importantly, one of Dennis's closest friends. He'd been living in town longer than most of the retirees who suspected him, and I felt Dennis's anger—focused on it, even, to get my mind off Eli.

"He was really beat up over this one too," Dennis went on. "That woman was a real piece of work. Always criticizing him behind his back. She never wanted to discuss anything with Eduardo—she'd call me instead, even when he was there on-site. She didn't even try to hide her racism."

"Jesus," I said, disgusted by the thought.

"I missed a consultation because of her," Dennis said, worked up. "I had Jackie bill her for all that extra time we spent arguing over the beer cans and invisible problems."

I took another bite of my dinner while Dennis kept talking, answering reflexively as the conversation continued. If he were Eli, we'd be talking about travel or science or unanswerable existential questions. Dennis and I used to talk about those things, but those topics had dwindled into more practical matters. Dishes. Work. Scheduled weekend activities. It felt so repetitive, so banal compared to Morocco and whales and life's passions.

Later that night, after a couple of hours of TV, I slipped into bed while Dennis brushed his teeth and turned out the light. The mattress tipped when he climbed in, covers ruffling and whooshing in the darkness like the whisper of waves along the shore. I felt the warmth of him settle beside me, close. His hand slid over my thigh, hip, waist, shoulder. He brushed the hair from my neck and kissed the ticklish flesh, his stubble like sandpaper. I heard him breathe deeply, smelling my hair. His hand grew more daring, sliding underneath my T-shirt, but I pulled away. Dennis didn't push but instead traced a line down my back, as if he could coax the desire out of me.

Every time I closed my eyes, trying to focus on Dennis's touch, Eli appeared in my head. The more Dennis touched me, the more I thought about Eli. I hated myself for that.

Finally, as Dennis grew more passionate, I squeaked out an excuse. "D, I'm tired. Another night?"

His hand froze where it had been stroking my hip. "Sure, Abs, of course." He kissed my shoulder, and then the warmth of his body slipped away, back to his side of the bed, which could have been a mile away from me, for how far it suddenly felt. When once Dennis's love had been enough to make up for my lack of career, our growing apart had reminded me of the walls I'd built around myself. He was comfortable; I was suffocating.

APRIL

2018

Throughout my first month of tours, I go out with the Sound Adventures crew for drinks a few times per week. The grandparents, and even Robin's parents—though clearly avid fans of drinking—don't come often, leaving the bar scene to Robin, Kim, Joanne, myself, and occasionally the other captain, Megan, and one of the girls who works the shop, Trish. Zack is there on occasion as well, telling his own crazy stories (I see him in the mornings, too, for prework joe). I flip-flop between dinners with Nick and Chrissy and drinks with my new coworkers, and for a little while, I feel as though things are finally falling into place. There are some days I don't think of Dennis or Eli at all.

The tour schedule grows more rigorous as time carries on, approaching summer. By mid-April, we're seeing orcas on a regular basis, and we start scheduling daylong tours on the faster catamaran vessel, the *Bobcat*, and double half-day tours on the *Glacial Wind*. Most days, my schedule is wild: a morning tour starting at nine a.m. and an afternoon tour starting at two, which means I'm at work by eight in the morning and don't go home until almost eight at night. Kim and Robin and I survive on trail mix, PB&Js, and the occasional box of microwaved takeout, eating in shifts while the others tend to the guests.

These are some of the best days of my life. Between the time I wake up and the time I go to sleep, between idle conversation with my coworkers and fun facts with cheerful guests, I see whales. Many of them. Each time I spot that first flash of a black fin or spout of breath, a rising excitement pulses through me like a drumbeat. Tourists ask if I ever tire of the whales, and my answer is always no. Day after day, I am enamored.

In late April, I have my first day off in eight days, and after sleeping for twelve hours straight, I awaken to Taffy begging to go out. Her high-pitched, nasal meow pierces the still late-morning air, like helium escaping a balloon. I roll out of bed and crack the door. Taffy darts out, bounding through the garden and around Gwen's house.

In the doorway, I breathe in the freshness of the morning. The sky is blue with little wispy clouds, and the air that trails through the open door is crisp but not unpleasantly chilly. The ground is wet with dew, and the spiderwebs strung throughout the garden—bejeweled with drops of water—glisten in the sunlight. Gwen's planter boxes were abloom with crocuses and primroses back before I moved in, but now her spring bulbs have exploded: butter-colored daffodils, scarlet tulips, pink hyacinth, and the first purple bobbing globes of alliums. Even the rhododendrons outside my cottage are budding, the tippy-top blooms already open to the sun.

My phone buzzes, coaxing me back inside before I'm ready. I latch the door with a gentle click and turn on the coffeepot to brew while I check my messages.

It's my mother: Day off? Come visit.

I have errands to run, but then a second text convinces me: We have to talk about something important.

My mother is never vague, and I fear the worst. The image of Wendy and my father embracing in the barn flashes in my mind. "What did she say to you?" my mother asked. Staring at my phone, the coffeepot gasping, I wonder, wonder, wonder, until my pulse is whooshing in my eardrums.

What's wrong? I text, but I don't send it. Instead, I write, 30 min?

Mom says, Great.

On edge, I shower, braid my hair, and get dressed. I speed out to Chimacum, my hands shaking on the wheel. I imagine everything my mother could possibly want to discuss, imagine hearing words I can't bear to even consider: *Wendy and your father* . . . I know how my parents used to fight, and while they seem fine lately, I might've missed something while I was in California. My father is charismatic; I can't fathom him straying, but what else is there to explain Wendy? A whirlpool of shame and fear and anger and disbelief swirls inside me as I drive, my mind chasing half-formed thoughts in circles. Nothing adds up, but I guess I'll find out soon.

I arrive at my parents' house just before noon. My father's truck is not in the driveway. When I walk into the house, Mom is sitting at the kitchen island with a plate in front of her, only the fallen scraps of a sandwich remaining.

"Sweetheart." She gestures for me to sit down, while she herself stands, carrying her plate to the sink. "Can I get you water or lemonade?"

"Nothing right now," I say. "What's wrong?"

She doesn't answer; she returns to her seat.

"What do you want to tell me?"

Her face stiffens, forehead creasing, mouth pressing into a slight frown.

I feel a question burning in my chest, and I start to sweat. It's a warm day. The kitchen window is cracked, and a breeze slips in through the curtains. In that moment, I'm certain it's an affair—what else can it be? It explains so much: my father's current absence and my mother's pained expression.

"It's about Wendy," my mother finally says, breaking the silence between us.

Before I can stop myself, I blurt: "I know about the affair."

My mother's face changes, then, from creased tension to a wild, wide-eyed surprise. "You . . . what?" she whispers.

"I know," I say, reaching for her hand in comfort, but she draws back.

"Did your father say something?"

"No, but I—"

"It was years ago, Abby," my mother says in a rush. "How are you finding out now?"

"What?"

"I want you to know, dear, that he was a brief mistake. I love your father. And we're stronger than ever now."

My mouth opens, but no sound comes out. This time, my mother reaches for me, and I'm the one who pulls away. I don't understand what she's saying or what this has to do with Wendy.

"It was years ago," she repeats. "Shortly after Dennis's heart surgery."

"What are you saying, Mom?" My voice sounds distant and high pitched.

"The affair," she says, her voice turning up into a slight question. "You asked about the affair."

"You . . ." I take a deep breath, the next words rotten on my tongue. "You cheated on Dad?"

"That's not what you were referring to?" she asks.

I pinch the bridge of my nose, fingers quivering. "I thought Wendy . . ." I can't finish the sentence. All this time, I thought my mother was the victim—but it's Dad. How could I have suspected him? I'm as angry at myself for the assumptions as I am at my mother for her unexpected confession.

"You thought . . . Wendy?" she asks.

I stand up, suddenly too close in proximity to her. How can their true love, their perfect relationship, be so flawed? I recall those turbulent times, the arguments I overheard. Was I a blind newlywed? Should I have tried to help my parents when I heard their fights?

"I need to get out of here."

"Abby, wait," my mother says, reaching for me. She catches my sleeve, but I yank it away.

"How could you?" I ask.

"We've worked through it, dear. We're fine now—better than ever."

I storm outside; she's close on my heels.

"Abby," she calls. "Just listen—"

I slam my car door, fuming, aching, shocked.

When I was growing up, my parents were the ideal. Chrissy's mom always had a new man sleeping on the couch at noon; Nick's parents were passive aggressive and tense all the time; but *my* parents . . . they were the ones who taught all three of us how to love and be loved. They held hands at the movies and stayed up late laughing and always seemed like such a *team*. Maybe I'm a hypocrite—I've known temptation myself—but I always thought my parents were the higher standard. The goal. The example for the rest of us.

Was all of that a lie?

"I need to go," I say.

"Let's talk about it. Please?"

"I can't believe this," I say to myself, starting the car. Yanking the stick in gear, I back out of the driveway. My mother is standing where I left her, calling after me, but I can't hear her through my own sobs. I speed away, back toward town.

2013

The evening of Gallery Walk, I donned a black dress and jean jacket, kissed Dennis good night, and drove into town to find Eli. It was balmy for June, a crisp breeze wafting up from the water. I parked in a gravel lot by a beach, on the eastern end of Water Street, and hurried toward the Greenwater Gallery, a new space that I hadn't explored before. Port Townsend always had a new gallery, owners swapping spaces and artists doing showings in as many locations as they could.

Gallery Walk was just that: a jaunt from gallery to gallery, sipping free wine, ogling well-lit displays, and stashing complimentary cheeses in your pockets for later. On my way, I recognized a few bank customers among the wandering groups of people, but I was invisible. It felt strange to know such intimate details about them—how they made their money, how much they had, how many of them were merely trust fund babies—and yet they didn't even recognize me on the street.

I pushed work from my mind. It had a way of creeping into my thoughts like a worm, and I hated how much *a part* of me it was becoming. Dennis had said it would be temporary, yet here I was, two years later, approaching my thirtieth birthday with nothing to show for my interest in marine biology.

Eli hated that I worked at the bank. He'd said, "You should be doing what you love." But I couldn't. While Dennis's work was better than ever, I still contributed to our income, and having something steady had removed some pressure on his mind and, more importantly, his heart. I still perused job listings on Saturdays, while Dennis was out of the house, but I'd long ago exhausted my options. Either I was rejected, or the opportunity would take me too far away from Dennis, or he'd protest the hours, or . . .

Dennis had once said, "Don't let the what-ifs interfere with what you want." But how could I not? The bank felt like a necessary sacrifice: for convenience, for us, for Dennis.

My dress billowed with a chilly gust of wind, and I smoothed it down, hurrying past a crowd of art lovers. Tonight, I didn't have to think about any of that. My heart skipped with anticipation, whirling as if it were caught up by a tornado. The Greenwater came into sight, its forest-green sandwich board announcing **Eli Fonseca, photographer.** People mingled in the doorway, crowded inside, and I paused on the sidewalk to take a deep breath.

Track lighting illuminated images in the huge storefront windows. I stepped closer, mesmerized. Two photographs, each three feet in width, were hung with wire from the ceiling. The images were as iridescent as tropical fish scales, shimmering as I shifted in one direction or another. The first photograph was a street view: pastel buildings, a wide sidewalk, and a teal 1950s Chevy pickup parked out front, loaded with produce.

The second image caught my breath. The view was from atop a roof. Right below, shabby houses—painted sea-foam green, orange, and electric blue, with roughly tiled tops—lined a curved cobblestone street. A four-tiered bell tower stood in the far-right corner; on the horizon, mountains spread into the distance, and above, a dappling of puffy clouds was contrasted by a sky of solid blue. But the setting, while breathtaking, was not the subject. In the bottom center of the image, a tan-skinned boy in a polo shirt played on the street below. He was alone, midstride, heading away from the camera toward a blurry ball. In his left hand, the boy held a magenta bougainvillea flower.

I stepped closer to the window, observing every touch of color on the giant aluminum print. I could picture Eli there, on some balcony, just him and his lens. Briefly, I closed my eyes, imagining the hot sun on my face, the sweet-smelling Cuban breeze. I imagined the boy's squeal of delight, the chatter of men on a porch somewhere out of view. I imagined the snap of Eli's camera. How strange that he was able to capture scent, temperature, movement.

Peeling myself away from the image, I pushed into the gallery, eager to find him. A large snack table just inside explained the blockage of people at the door. I snagged a piece of cheese and wandered farther in, the gallery opening up once I got past the food. More images adorned the walls, varying in size. Most were horizontal, but a few intimate verticals caught my attention: a closer image of the bell tower, two girls walking hand in hand down a long empty street, a woman smoking on a stoop.

I finally spotted Eli in a nook toward the back of the gallery. He wore dark jeans and a long-sleeved black V-neck. About six people were crowded around him as he told a story from his trip. People chuckled, and an older woman kept saying "Oh *my*," as if every detail was a surprise.

". . . until I realized the guy was only being polite," Eli was saying. He laughed along with his audience. Behind him was a photograph of a horse and cart parked beside a pink, chipped building. The horse looked a little worn, but its ears were forward. A man stood beside it, holding the reins and grinning right at the camera.

"And *then*—" Eli continued, but he spotted me and said, "Actually, can you excuse me?"

He pushed past the crowd, coming toward me, and the people dispersed, viewing more images or heading toward the front for more antipasto.

Eli stepped close. "You came. I'm so glad."

I spread my hands, gesturing to the images all around. "These are breathtaking, Eli."

"So much better than beaches, no?"

"It's all amazing," I said. "The one out front . . ."

"*The Boy with the Bougainvillea*?" He smiled. "I saw you through the window looking at it."

I shrugged, showing my loss for words. "It's . . ."

"Yours," he said.

"Oh, I couldn't possibly . . ."

He touched my elbow. "I always give away one image on the first night of a show, for luck. I look to see who's deserving."

"Well, what about—"

"It's yours," Eli said. "I'm the artist; it's my decision."

I took in a quick breath. "I don't know what to say."

With his hand still on my elbow, he guided me toward the back of the gallery. A glass-paneled door led to a courtyard and, beyond, the beach. The moon was out, waxing.

Eli released my arm. "I'll steal some champagne and cheese, if you scope out a spot to sit."

"Shouldn't you be mingling?"

"I've already sold my two largest pieces," he said. "That's three months' mortgage. I think I've mingled enough." He ducked back into the main room, beelining for the food table.

I slipped out the door and into the gauzy moonlight. My heart raced; what was Dennis doing right now? Watching TV or reading? Having a bowl of ice cream on our couch? Grocery shopping?

I didn't know where this night would go with Eli or why he'd invited me in the first place. His intentions frightened me. Lately, when I was in close proximity with Eli, a desirous heat would spread through me like a tidal wave. It had the power to knock my feet out from under me. This crush I'd been nursing—the flushed feeling I got when I saw Eli enter the coffee shop or already sitting there waiting for me or sauntering into the bank as if we hadn't just had lunch—I thought those feelings were minor, and nothing reciprocated. But as I wandered through the garden behind the Greenwater Gallery, I grew uncertain.

A bench was located at the end of the stone path, right beside a three-foot drop to the beach. It overlooked the water. Silver light glimmered on the surface, a single sailboat interrupting its path. The triangle of the mast bobbed back and forth. I sat, staring out at the shadowy ripples, listening to the soft whooshing of little breaking waves and shifting pebbles on the beach.

Maybe I ought to go. Maybe being here was a bad idea.

A dark shape interrupted the calm ocean, close to shore. A seal. I watched its head bob along the surface, shiny in the moonlight. Then it ducked under, its blubbery back curving out of the water before it disappeared completely.

"Something out there?" Eli asked, sitting down beside me.

"A seal," I said. "Maybe it'll pop up again."

"Let's hope."

Tonight was no different than any other day with Eli: two friends talking. But it *felt* different in an indescribable, alluring way. I considered leaving, telling Eli I needed to head home, but when I tried to speak, I wavered.

He set a little plate of food between us on the bench and handed me a plastic flute of champagne. "Cheers."

"To?"

"A successful opening," Eli said. "And good company."

We clanked glasses and sipped. The bubbles stung my tongue, and I shivered.

I couldn't believe he'd offered his photograph to me. If he'd sold two large pieces for months' worth of house payments, that meant the biggest prints were over a thousand dollars each. I couldn't be indebted to him like that; it was too generous. Not only that, but how would I explain the piece to Dennis when I brought it home?

"Are you sure about the photo?" I asked. "I know it's worth a lot of money."

"Not another word." He rolled up his sleeves and arranged a piece of cheese onto a cracker from the plate between us. "My ultimate goal with any of this is to be understood. And granted, I only saw you through a window, but the look on your face . . . that's what I want from anyone who views my photography." He ate the cheese and cracker, chewing thoughtfully. "That's what I strive for."

I wished we were in Cuba, far from anyone. "What amazes me is your ability to make me feel like I'm there. How do you do that?"

"Magic," he said, finishing the last of his champagne. He handed me a prepared cracker.

I bit into the flaky crisp; the cheese was gouda. "Seriously."

"Seriously? A combination of formal expertise and passion," he said. "For instance, the viewer often wants a sense of where the photographer is standing. That way, you feel grounded. Having that grounding quality is part technical skill, part instinct. It's not just point and shoot. It's a combination of staking out the right spot and then letting go."

"Interesting." I watched the way the moonlight made shadows of his features. He'd shaved for the event, and his face looked naked. "And the unique perspective?"

"That's just a matter of thinking outside the box and being a little bold," he said. "*The Boy with the Bougainvillea* was actually taken from the roof of someone's house. He wasn't sure of me at first, but when I showed him my camera, he reluctantly acquiesced. I almost fell off that damn roof, but the guy was impressed by the images I got."

"No way," I said, finishing my champagne.

His eyes were on the water. "Homero. He was a nice guy. Not a lick of English, but we had dinner that night. Best *vaca frita* on the whole trip."

"That's—"

"Ah! The seal," Eli exclaimed, standing.

Sure enough, the seal had surfaced again, perhaps twenty feet from where I'd seen it duck under. It paddled slowly along, its head like a rubber buoy.

"You act like you've never seen a seal before," I said.

Eli watched in silence until it disappeared with a little splash. "Well, it's not like I see them all the time."

I chuckled at his excitement.

He sat back down. "You're the marine biologist; aren't you supposed to get excited?"

"I *do* get excited," I said.

"Oh?" Eli asked, twisting on the bench to face me. His arm rested along the back, and his knee bent toward me, bumping against the cheese plate. "What about just now?"

"Well, it's not a childish excitement," I said. "Like seeing something for the first time."

"Are you calling me childish?"

I met the interruption with a dismissive raise of my eyebrows. "I get excited in a different way. Like seeing a family member after a long while apart. It's not *Oooh, look at that!* It's *There you are; I'm so happy to see you.*"

Eli nodded, pensive. "That's how I feel about getting a good image."

"Like coming home."

"Then why don't you spend more time on the water?" Eli asked, touching my arm. "There's got to be something you can do around here."

I shook my head. "Either I'm not qualified, or it's a volunteering gig—and that won't pay the bills."

"I refuse to believe that," Eli said.

"Yeah, well . . ." I shrugged, remembering the latest listing I'd seen: a marketing director position at a nonprofit that helped seabirds. I could classify any birds they brought in and research migration patterns, food habits, anything—but marketing was a whole other skill. I was just being realistic.

"And you can't move? If you're truly as miserable as you say you are—"

"It's not just me," I said. "My husband—"

"He wouldn't move for you?"

His insinuation made me stop short. Dennis would do anything for me—at least, I believed so. However: "I couldn't ask him to uproot his business. His whole life is here. *Our* life is here."

"But is it the life you want?"

My face felt hot. To stall, I made a little cracker-meat sandwich and shoved the whole thing in my mouth.

"I don't mean to pry," Eli said, facing forward again, stretching his legs out in front of him. "I just believe we should all do what we want with our lives."

I swallowed, chilled by the breeze. Looking out toward the water again, I spotted the seal bobbing along. There must've been a good school of fish out there. Meanwhile, the sailboat had twisted and now faced in the opposite direction.

"Thank you for coming tonight," Eli said. He ate the last cracker and placed the plate on the ground, scooting closer in the process. "I'm so glad to know someone who appreciates my work."

I felt the heat of his leg close to mine. "Judging by the crowd, a lot of people like your work."

"Yeah, but you seem to actually *get* it. Even at lunch—I never have to explain a feeling to you. You just know."

A little shy at his words, I said, "I can't wait to see what you capture in Morocco."

"Me too."

"Do you always go alone?"

"Mostly," he said. "I met Molly on a trip, actually. In Mexico. She came on a few after that, but I get more work done when I'm solo. She hasn't come with me since Kira was born."

"I'm guessing they're not going to Morocco with you?"

"Molly wants to wait until Kira is a little older. I travel cheaply—hostels, camping—and sometimes venture into sketchier areas. Not the best for a little one."

He rested his hand on my thigh, electrocuting. It wasn't a damning gesture—no stroking, no squeezing, just resting lightly, almost as if to get my attention—but it wasn't innocent. I almost slapped it away, but a small part of me ached for his hand to explore elsewhere. The result was my doing absolutely nothing at all, pretending I didn't notice.

"Have you done much traveling?" he asked, a whisper. How close he was, his breath on my ear.

"I've never made the time."

"There he is!" a voice called from the gallery. The back door cracked open, spilling buttery light into the courtyard.

Eli's hand slid off my leg. He stood. "Veronica, just enjoying your courtyard."

I stood, too, a little dazed by the interruption. Eli led me back toward the gallery and into the loud heat of the building. In the narrow back foyer, Eli, Veronica, and I squeezed into close proximity with another woman, gray haired and inquisitive looking behind red-framed glasses.

"Eli, dear, I wanted to introduce you to Ava Kirkland," Veronica said.

"Oh yes, I've heard a lot about you." Suddenly in professional-artist mode, Eli stepped forward and shook Ava's hand. He wore a modest grin as she raved about his pieces, detailed her interest in a showing at her own gallery, and discussed the purchase of one of his smaller portraits.

Meanwhile, I shifted uneasily, trying to keep my shoulder from grazing Eli's. A black dress and colorful knit shawl were draped over Veronica's narrow form; her earlobes sagged with the weight of large handmade earrings. She looked incredibly artsy, eclectic, and unique. Compared to her, I must've looked like a girl on date night. I shrank under her curious gaze.

Finally, the conversation faltered enough for Eli to pivot the discussion. "Veronica, have you met Abby Nelson?"

"Can't say that I have," Veronica said, taking my hand. "Are you enjoying the show?"

"We were just discussing Cuba," Eli said. "Abby is taking home *The Boy with the Bougainvillea*."

"Oh, lovely." Veronica's suspicion seemed to dwindle under the promise of a sale. "That was a favorite of mine too."

I looked at Eli. "I ought to get going."

"We'll sort out the photograph on Monday?" Eli asked.

I knew he was talking about lunch. "Sure," I said. "Nice to meet you, Veronica."

I slipped away from them, pushing past the lingering art lovers and the ravaged food table and hurrying out through the front of the gallery. I barely registered the street, the sidewalk, the evening, until I got in the car. Inside the safety of the cab, I let out a little cry of horror. Why had I not pushed his hand off my leg? What would have happened had Veronica not interrupted? I couldn't bear the thought. How far Dennis had been from my mind, guilt like a faint whisper holding me back, indistinct and weak. How long would it have held out against the shout of Eli's allure?

Perhaps his gesture hadn't meant anything. He'd touched me before. On the hand or arm or back or shoulder. Was a leg so different?

I checked my phone, surprised to see a few missed calls from Dennis, plus a voice mail from Chrissy. I held the phone to my ear.

"Hey, Abs, it's Chrissy. Listen, Dennis called looking for you, said you weren't picking up. He thought you were with me, and I covered for you. What's going on? Call me."

I swallowed hard, then dialed Dennis.

"Abby?" he answered. "How's girls' night?"

I stuck the keys in the ignition, the car clock coming on. It was close to ten. "Did I wake you?"

"No, just reading," he said. "On your way home?"

"Yeah," I said. "Sorry I didn't see your calls."

"Chrissy said your phone died."

I thought for a moment. "Yeah, I'm in the car, and it's charging."

"Well, don't drive and talk; you'll get pulled over."

Touched by his concern, I said, "I'm parked."

"I was at the store. Did Chrissy tell you? She said you'd like waffles."

Welling with tears, I said, "Waffles are perfect. See you in fifteen?"

"Can't wait," Dennis said. "You're not too drunk to drive?"

"Not at all," I said, my voice thick.

"See you soon."

We hung up, and I buried my face in my hands. Biting back the sour remorse, I texted Chrissy: Thanks for covering. I'll explain tomorrow.

Her reply was quick: Better be good, with a winky face.

I drove home tearful and hot faced. The house was dim when I came through the door. I slipped off my shoes, my jacket. Dennis was asleep sitting up in our bed, snoring. His book was draped over his lap, and the bedside lamp was on. A whole new rush of tears sprang, and I ducked my head, tiptoeing into the bathroom to wash my face.

I closed myself in the bright room, Dennis's snores muffled through the door. I looked in the mirror; my eyes were red, and my eyeliner had smudged below my lower lashes, making me look tired. I *was* tired. Tired of working a shit job, tired of feeling stuck, tired of wondering what my life *could* be. Dennis had once been my anchor, steady and grounding, but now he'd become wedged on the bottom of the sea, keeping me submerged.

As I glanced around the little room, a twinge of irritation replaced some of my shame. His uncapped shaving cream canister had leaked, and the gel had dried sticky around the bottom of the can. I sighed, wetting a washcloth to clean up the goo. A large and thundering snore made me cringe. I could never understand how he managed to sleep through that sound. He was especially congested tonight, and I suspected he'd eaten the rest of our ice cream after all. It always made him snore extra.

In that moment, I despised his snores; they were like the crash of a dinner plate on hardwood, a shattering that made my shoulders involuntarily hunch. The thought of getting into bed with him and trying to sleep, after the night with Eli—it made me want to take the couch. Instead, I scrubbed at the shaving cream; it'd hardened and wouldn't come off.

Another guttural inhale, this time waking him. "Abby?" Dennis called.

"In here," I responded.

I heard the bedsheets ruffle, then his feet on the carpet. He opened the door, brushed past me, and lifted the toilet seat. While peeing, he said, "You have fun?"

Focusing on my scrubbing, I said, "Yeah."

He flushed, then shuffled back into the bedroom. "You coming to bed?"

"You didn't lower the toilet seat," I said.

The mattress squeaked as he flopped back down. He turned off the lamp. "Come to bed, Abs," he called.

I scrubbed at the counter even after the last of the blue guck had transferred to the washcloth. Dennis started snoring again, and I lowered the toilet lid and sat down. My reflection stared back at me in the large bathroom window.

2018

Chrissy picks up on the second ring. "Hey, lady, what's up?"

"Do you . . . are you free now?" I ask.

"Are you all right?"

"My mom." My voice goes high and squeaky. "My mom cheated on my dad." The words are so ugly I close my eyes, and I would keep them closed if it weren't for the road flying by. I wipe away tears and stare at the car in front of me, trying to focus. I'm almost to the mill; I could be at Chrissy's house in less than ten minutes.

"What?" Chrissy asks. "Are you sure?"

"She told me."

"I didn't know they were having problems," she says.

"It was years ago," I say. "Before Dennis and I—" I don't finish that thought.

"They worked through it? That's very big of your father."

"Chrissy, are you home? Can I come over?"

She sighs, rattling the phone speaker. "Abby, I'm sorry, I'm heading to work. I have a late shift."

"Oh."

"Tomorrow?"

"I have work," I say, remembering how life continues.

"After work? We'll eat tubs of ice cream, and you can tell me everything."

I laugh at her stereotypical yet tempting plan. "Maybe."

"We're doing it," she says. "We'll pour Baileys on it."

"Now you're talking," I say, feeling a slight rise in my mood just talking to her.

"I'm sorry, Abby," Chrissy says, getting serious again. "At least they're still together."

When Chrissy was little, she desperately wished her parents had married—but that's not always the answer.

"I'll let you go," I say.

"Hang in there," she says. "I'll see you tomorrow. Love you!"

"Love you." We hang up.

Somehow, I've ended up on Dennis's street, and when I drive by, I peer at the tall hedges lining the road, as if I might see him through the tangled branches. With a stab in my heart, I don't allow myself to stop. After nearly five years apart, I still find myself drawn to old habits, old comforts. I might've come home for my family and friends, and I might linger by Eli's gallery, but when I let myself go on autopilot, I fly to Dennis.

At my apartment, I put on pajamas, climb into bed, and watch nature documentaries on my laptop. I order Chinese takeout and find comfort in the sound of David Attenborough's voice, watching hour after hour of animal stories, from hunts to mating rituals. Meanwhile, I try not to think about my mother's secret, my father putting up with it, and how it all happened under my nose while I was falling in love and getting married and . . .

I always thought my parents were different—better somehow. They were an inspiration to my own life; with Dennis, at least early on, I built toward that future. My parents' example was my North Star. And now, hearing about my mother's lies, it's like the sky is falling. I can't stand to think that they're just as messed up as everyone else—because if they are, there's no hope for me.

2013

The next morning, I woke up late, and Dennis was already out of bed. Throwing a long cardigan over my pajamas, I went into the bathroom and dragged my hair into a bun. I still felt irritable but also guilt ridden. Things had gone too far with Eli last night. The stray touches, the closeness, the way he'd looked at me in the moonlight. The way Dennis had briefly disappeared from my mind, a distant twinkle in the vastness of my sudden lust, while Eli burned like a star up close. I'd dreamed of Eli last night, and not for the first time. I had this nagging feeling of his hands on me as I walked downstairs.

I forced myself to focus on waffles. Dennis hadn't made Sunday breakfast in a while, and his call last night to Chrissy suggested he'd planned to make it this morning. The scent of buttermilk wafted over me when I reached the bottom of the stairs, and I licked my lips. The stagnancy of our marriage wasn't just Dennis's fault. The monotony of work and chores had taken over our romance like ivy; I could barely see our foundation anymore.

I still burned for him, I told myself. It was a smolder lately, but still alight. Waffles were proof that he still tried.

"Good morning," I said cheerily as I walked into the kitchen.

Dennis wasn't there. The sink was crowded with dirty dishes, and the waffle iron was crusty and unplugged on the counter. A syrupy plate sat beside it, just one. Had he eaten without me?

I spotted a glass measuring cup on the counter with a paper towel draped over the top. Inside the cup, the waffle batter had a cracked top. How long had it been sitting out? The oven clock told me it was ten—Dennis must've made himself a waffle hours ago. My head pulsed with frustration, disappointment. The old Dennis would've brought me breakfast in bed or at least waited until I got up. It was a stupid thing to be mad about—like I needed my husband to make me Sunday breakfast—but I'd been eager for it. And beyond that, it stood for so much more. What had he done lately to show that he cared? I'd taken that lousy bank job for him, and he didn't even seem concerned that I despised it. I'd fallen silent in my dissatisfaction, and he'd let me.

"Dennis?" I called, wandering through the house.

I found him outside, on his back, under his truck. A pool of grease had spread into the fresh gravel. A slimy bucket had been cast to the side.

"What are you doing?" I asked.

"Changing the oil," he said. "Damn bucket had a crack in it."

"You didn't notice that before you put it down?" I asked, hugging myself in the chilly morning. The sky was overcast.

"Well, it's not like I meant to get oil everywhere," he said, clearly already frustrated.

But I was frustrated too. "The batter was all gross."

"What?" Only half of him stuck out from under the truck.

"The waffle batter. It was all dry. Why didn't you just use it up and stick it in the oven to stay warm?"

"I thought you'd want it fresh." He groaned, his body wiggling as his arms worked at something underneath the truck. There was a clang, and he grumbled, "Damn it."

"I thought we'd have breakfast *together*," I said.

"You seemed tired. Besides, we're having dinner tonight."

"We can't have two meals together in the same day?"

"That's not what I'm saying. But anyway, I've been needing to get this done."

My arms tingled in the chilly breeze. I waited for him to say more, but he didn't.

Then, as I was walking away, "Abby?"

I turned, hopeful. "Yes, Dennis?"

"Can you see if there's another bucket in the garage?"

I sighed. "Sure."

While rummaging around in the garage, I got a call from Chrissy.

"Hello?"

"Hey, lady," she said. "You owe me lunch and an explanation."

"I owe you?" I pinned the phone between my shoulder and ear and dug through some old cleaning supplies. Behind where we kept the riding mower, I found a few gas containers and our weed whacker but no bucket.

"Yeah, how incriminating was my covering for you last night? Are we looking at some community service, or is it more like ten years to life?"

Giving up on my task, I cradled the phone in my hand. "Can we make it brunch? I could meet you in a half hour."

"You sound serious," she said, her tone shifting. "Is there something wrong?"

"Otter Crossing?"

"I'll be there," she said. "See you in a few."

"All right."

"Oh! Can I bring Nick? He's over here drooling."

"Can we make it just us?" I said. "Tell him it's no hard feelings. I just—"

Chrissy, for all her joking around, understood perfectly. "Sure, Abs." Then some mumbling on her line. "Nick says we have to bring him something to go."

I snorted. "Fine by me."

We hung up.

Back outside, I told Dennis, "I'm meeting Chrissy for breakfast. I couldn't find a bucket."

He crawled out from under the truck. He had grease on his blue T-shirt and in his hair. "Didn't you just see her last night? I thought you wanted to hang out today."

"Well, you're working, so I figured—"

"No, it's fine," Dennis said, turning toward his toolbox on the ground. He bent, putting some strewed tools back in their rightful spots. "Can you get me a bucket while you're out?"

"Sure." Surprised by his soreness, I asked, "Do you want me to stay home?"

"You don't seem like you want to," he said, not looking up.

My fists clenched. "Well, why would I? It didn't seem like you wanted—"

"I was letting you *sleep in*," he said, exasperated.

"Well, should I call Chrissy? Should I tell her—"

"No, go." Dennis slammed his toolbox shut. "I have plenty of work I can do. It's not like I do anything else lately."

"What was that?" I said, stomping a little closer. "At least you *like* your work. At least it doesn't make you want to blow your brains out on a daily basis."

"What are you talking about?"

The fact that he didn't know made me even more livid. "The bank!"

"I thought—"

"It's soul sucking, Dennis," I said. "How can you not know that?"

"I thought it was going better."

"I'm a marine biologist," I said. "Depositing checks for people couldn't be farther from how I want to spend my day."

"Then find something else."

"Oh," I said, throwing my hands up. "Why didn't I think of that?"

"What, there's just nothing? No jobs that you'd like better?"

"The last time I tried, you—" I broke off and searched his eyes for understanding, a sign that he felt my frustration—or at least sympathized—but his expression was creased with impassivity. "I'm meeting Chrissy. I have to go." I walked back toward the house.

"So what are you saying, Abby? You want to completely turn our lives upside down just because the bank is boring sometimes?"

I slammed the front door behind me, not willing to listen to him anymore. When I came back outside with my purse and keys, ready to leave, I half expected Dennis to be waiting. He was always the one to throw water on a fiery argument. He was always so much more level-headed. But he wasn't there. The riding mower was gone, and he was a small dot in our perimeter field, bouncing along, uncaring that I got in my car and left without apology or reconciliation.

2018

It's dark outside when the *Planet Earth* music blares and the credits roll. My phone has six new messages from my mother, plus a voice mail, but I don't want to look. I'm not ready yet. Two take-out boxes rest on the nightstand, one upright and one on its side with a fork handle sticking out. I blink at the dark screen of my computer, wondering what to do [illegible]

I unfold my legs, tingling and achy, and pad over to the door. Taffy is waiting for her dinner, which she's made a habit of eating at my place. She darts inside, meowing in cascading, forceful pleas. The weather has taken a turn, the rain pitter-pattering on the waxy rhododendron leaves outside. I pop open a can and dish up Taffy's dinner, and a hush falls over the cottage again as she eats, save for the rain and the smack of the cat's tongue.

What now? Without Chrissy, I'm alone with my thoughts, and I get the urge to leave the cottage altogether, else I'll go crazy.

I dress in leggings and a sweatshirt and catch a cab to the Manatee. Beer and superficial socialization seem like second-best alternatives to the more mature option of talking through my feelings, but I can blame Chrissy's work schedule for skipping that.

It's past eight when I get there, and the place is fairly full. I find a seat at the bar, and Brian, the bartender, slides an IPA toward me without asking. I'm surprised I don't see any of my coworkers, but still, the relative anonymity is a comfort.

I hunch over my pint, letting the hops chase away the sharper edges of my shattered mood. People gab all around me, and I watch the little groups, the flirtation and the friendship. Some push right up next to me to flag Brian down for more beers, more wine, more martinis. Some are more forward than others; I'm amazed by how long one guy stands politely by the bar, waiting for Brian to notice his need. The people watching is a welcome distraction.

"Abby?"

Upon seeing Zack, I get a strange flutter of relief in my chest. I'm glad to see someone familiar after all. "Hey."

"Waiting for someone?" He's wearing a soft-looking V-neck sweater with the sleeves rolled up.

"Nope," I say.

"You're here alone?"

I shrug. "I needed a drink."

"Ah, one of those days?"

"You can say that again."

He slides onto the stool next to mine, raking his long hair out of his face. "So is the drink helping?"

"It's too early to tell."

Zack waves to Brian, an effortless gesture that catches the bartender's attention right away. "Mind if I wait with you?"

"Of course not," I say.

"I'm meeting a lady friend," Zack says, "but she's chronically tardy, so I have time for a drink or three." Brian delivers Zack's usual—an old-fashioned with rye—and Zack turns toward me, giving me his full attention. "So do you want to talk about it?"

I sigh and guzzle a few gulps of beer.

Zack chuckles. "That bad, huh?"

"Just—my parents."

He fiddles with the maraschino cherry in his drink. "One of those *my parents are real people* moments?"

I stare at him. "Precisely."

"An educated guess," he says, reading my surprise. "As a barista, I'm like a morning bartender. Which is basically a therapist."

"Solid logic," I say, and he chuckles. "What's your diagnosis?"

He gestures at my near-empty glass and grabs Brian's attention again. "A second beer will fix you right up."

Brian comes over. "You two drinking together?" he says, then turns to me. "Be careful, Abby; he's a heavyweight."

"Not lately," Zack says.

Brian rolls his eyes. "IPA?"

"Yeah," I say, glancing at Zack. "Bring one for him, too, on me."

"Kind lady," Brian says, finding a glass beneath the counter. He walks down the length of the bar, toward the taps.

"Not necessary," Zack says.

"It's the least I can do." With honesty, I add, "The company makes me feel better."

"Mission accomplished, then." He slides off his stool, as if to go, but then, seeing my stupid expression of disappointment, comes right back. "I'm kidding."

"It's fine. I know you're here waiting for someone."

He touches my arm, gentle fingers sliding along my sleeve. "I'm kidding," he repeats. Then he removes his hand, checks his watch. "Besides, I came here half past our agreed time, in anticipation of her lateness. Now she's going on an hour. I think I'm officially stood up."

Brian delivers our beers with an unexplained grin.

"I'm sorry," I say to Zack.

"I'm not." He turns toward me, his elbow resting on the bar. "You're better company, anyway."

I suppress a smile. "Who is your mystery date?"

"Not a date," Zack says. "A friend from a previous life. Her name's Adrienne. We get beers when she ports here, but she's a flake."

"She works on the Alaskan boats?"

"Good guess," he says.

"Not a guess. Robin told me you used to do that kind of work." Immediately, I regret mentioning Robin—I don't want Zack to be angry with him for sharing such a detail.

But Zack doesn't seem angry. "So you're likely caught up, then."

"I just know you worked on the ships and left because you got hurt."

"That's the CliffsNotes version."

"What's the unabridged?"

Zack takes a long sip from his rocks glass, the ice clinking. "You got all night?"

"I have until your friend shows up," I say.

"Fair enough." His eyes crinkle with a smile, little lines forming beside them and more still down his cheeks, faint but there beneath his beard. Thousands of smiles have made those little wrinkles. "Do you know why I limp?"

I shake my head.

"It's my hip and my knee," he says. "I have metal rods in there now, which ache when it rains. I'm like an old man." He finishes his old-fashioned and moves on to his beer, an excuse to pause.

I lean closer. "Metal rods, really?"

So he tells me about his accident. It involves a storm and a pitching boat and a friend's foot tangled in a rope. Big waves across the deck, man overboard, and a desperate struggle against the weather. Zack did what he could, and so did Adrienne. Tossed an orange flotation device into the mess of gray water, reeled him in. Yet it was the heavy crates on deck—sliding, crashing against the railing—that ultimately killed the man.

"He was crushed," is all Zack says of it. "So was I, but just my lower half, hence the rods."

I touch his arm. "I'm so sorry."

"It was years ago," he says, finishing his beer. "Another?"

"Yeah."

He asks about California, and I tell him about the research program. How inspiring Dr. Perez was and how every moment of that work was meaningful. And because of the beer, I tell him about how I thought the distance would provide some much-needed therapy.

"But it didn't," Zack says, not a question.

"Nope," I say. "Turns out you can't run from a feeling. I thought it was this town, but it was *me*. When I hit a breaking point, I came back."

"And what was that? The breaking point?"

I think for a moment, flooded with that same feeling I felt in California when I learned that Eli was getting a divorce. It was a guilty, rosy feeling. A feeling I pretended wasn't there. A feeling tangled with the familiar regret and longing for Dennis, the feeling when I saw the birthday post. Maybe it was desperation—or hope. Hopefulness in getting my life back on track; hopefulness that not all was lost. Hopefulness that if I came home, I could . . . what?

"A man I know . . ." I stop, drink. If it weren't for the beer, I might've not even said that much, but now, Zack seems to fill in the blanks.

"Did you reconnect?"

I shake my head.

"The way I see it," Zack says, "you'll always wonder if you don't."

His words slug me in the chest. "It's not that simple."

He touches my shoulder. "It never is."

"Zack, you lady killer," a raucous voice calls.

We both jump back, breaking contact. A woman with short salt-and-pepper hair slaps Zack on the back.

"I thought we had a date?" she says.

"Adrienne," Zack says, confirming my suspicion. He stands up and gives her a bear hug, the two of them rocking and squeezing, with Adrienne chuckling all the while. When they pull apart, Zack says, "You're drunk."

"Fuck you," Adrienne says. "Some buddies bought me a couple. I couldn't refuse."

"So that's why you're late?"

"'Late' is merely a construct of time, and time is like the government—always trying to regulate."

I laugh at her logic.

Zack gestures toward me. "Adrienne, this is Abby."

"Keeping him busy?" Adrienne says, shaking my hand. "You're braver than I."

"He called you a flake," I say, and Zack gives me a wild-eyed *shut up* expression.

Adrienne chuckles, big and deep, and elbows my side. "I like you, Abby. Zack, I approve."

I shake my head. "Oh no, this isn't—"

"You're not my mother," Zack says to her.

Adrienne makes a face, her tongue sticking out.

He adds, "So are we drinking or what?"

"We've *been* drinking," Adrienne says.

"Just not in the same bar."

"Now you're getting it." She turns to me. "You in?"

"Oh no, I have work in the morning. I should go."

"Nonsense," Adrienne says. "C'mon, one more. I'm buying."

I look at Zack, who waggles his eyebrows. Laughing, I say, "All right, all right, just one."

My answer is met with a loud whoop from Adrienne, who quickly tracks Brian down and orders a pitcher. Then the three of us find a small round table amid the busy bar, sliding into seats just as another trio is leaving. It's nearing ten thirty, and things are really picking up; someone has turned the music up by a few notches. Compared to the quiet, close conversation with Zack just minutes ago, it feels like a different bar, a different night entirely.

Adrienne and Zack launch into gossip about people I don't know, and for a while, I listen, sipping my beer, trying to take it slow. But then Adrienne turns to me, asking questions, and soon all three of us are laughing, telling stories, and drinking. One round turns into another, and then the next thing I know, everything is spinning, and Zack and Adrienne are helping me down the stairs and out onto the street. The sidewalk tilts with each step, and the wind is as cold and shocking as ice. I'm glad when a cab arrives.

"I'll go with her," Zack says to Adrienne.

I don't hear her response.

Closing the door, Zack asks me, "Where do you live, Abs?"

I try to remember Gwen's address, but all I can recall is my parents' house and my social security number.

Seeing my strain, Zack asks, "What's it near?"

"Aldrich's," I say, adding, "ish."

The cab lurches forward, making my spins worse. I crack the window, letting the cool air whistle over my face. I wonder what Eli is doing. I wonder if Dennis knows how sorry I am. Dennis, Eli—they're a knot in my stomach, tight and gnarled. With my head resting against the half-open window, I cry little tears that dry quickly from the wind, my nose running. I hope Zack doesn't see. I hope no one can see this knot I've tied, this knot that might never come undone.

2013

Over breakfast, I told Chrissy everything: my hatred for the bank, my lunches with Eli, and how last night, I'd gone to see his photography and we'd gotten caught up talking. She listened with few questions, barely touching her veggie frittata. I even told her about arguing with Dennis less than an hour ago.

"I didn't know you were this unhappy," she said finally.

I shrugged, feeling a little better having talked about it. "I didn't think I was, until I added it up just now."

"So this Eli guy . . . have you . . ." She tipped her head.

"I haven't cheated on Dennis, if that's what you're asking," I whispered. The restaurant was abustle; I didn't want to risk anyone overhearing.

"Okay, I wasn't saying you did," Chrissy said. "But did you want to?"

The question sent a cascade of shamefulness through my body, so powerful that I was forced to take a deep breath. I knew the answer. It screamed in my ears louder than my own pulse. And by my lack of words, Chrissy seemed to know my answer too.

"Why didn't you tell me before?" she asked, speaking low.

I couldn't answer that question either.

"Of course you didn't," she said, meeting my eyes. "It's an impossible thing to admit."

"What do you mean?" I asked, picking up my fork again, pushing my ham scramble around on the plate.

"Well, you want a divorce, don't you?"

I choked on a bite of eggs. Divorce hadn't crossed my mind. With Dennis's heart condition, I should've been savoring my time with him. I should've felt lucky to be with him—and I *did* . . . except lately it didn't seem to be enough.

"I still love Dennis," I said, hanging my head.

I couldn't bear the thought of not seeing him, living with him, talking to him. Yet the thought of going home that afternoon made me want to throw up. I couldn't stand him sometimes, but I couldn't stand to leave him either.

"So you're not going to . . . ?"

"No, of course not," I said, not even sounding sure enough to convince myself.

"You'll break up with Eli, then?"

"I'm not seeing him."

"Aren't you, though?"

"It's just conversation; it's just lunch and coffee. I do that with you," I said, but I knew the difference as I spoke.

"Conversation can be more intimate than anything," Chrissy said, taking a bite of her breakfast.

We sat in silence, eating, chewing. A young waiter—no more than eighteen—came by to replenish our coffees.

I couldn't imagine breaking it off with Eli. His company during my lunches was the only thing that kept me sane throughout the workweek. But even if I didn't meet with him anymore, he'd still come to the branch. He couldn't be cut out of my life for good. I'd dread the bank even more then.

Of course, breaking it off with him also meant admitting that I wanted something more from him, and what would he say to that? What if I'd been reading into the whole thing? Then I would lose a friend and have nothing to get me through the day. No, I couldn't imagine telling him we couldn't talk anymore—we hadn't done anything wrong, really.

But was Chrissy right? Could talking be worse than sex? You could sleep with someone and still not know what they thought, what made them cry, what they loved most, and what their childhood was like. You could talk to someone and still find intimacy—so had I cheated after all?

I considered the alternative: Tell Dennis about Eli. Own up to it. Possibly separate—or get divorced. I'd always considered Dennis to be the love of my life. When had things gone sideways? Would he be blindsided by my confession, or would he have seen it coming? Neither answer made me feel better. I had the urge to weep right there at the table. What a tangled mess I'd gotten myself into.

Chrissy touched my arm, her mouth drawn down in concern. "Whatever you end up doing, I'm here for you," she said.

And that was it. With her words, I did start crying.

The rest of brunch was a mess of tears and napkins and Chrissy's attempts at comfort. She ordered a short stack to go for Nick, and when we finally walked out into the sunshine, we were stopped dead in our tracks by a family coming up the restaurant pathway: Eli, Molly, and Kira.

For a moment, Eli and I just stood there, staring. Chrissy and Molly had no clue what was going on. I'd found Molly on Facebook once, so I knew what she looked like, but face to face, I was still surprised by her beauty. She had large eyes and curled eyelashes, smooth skin, and a well-proportioned frame. I caught a flash of her wedding ring when she shifted Kira on her hip. The sight of her made me want to bolt.

Finally, Eli had the presence of mind to say, "Hi, Abby."

"Eli," I said, and Chrissy's expression turned from confusion to horrified shock. I had the urge to wipe my face again—it was most certainly red and snotty from crying—but I didn't want to call more attention to my distress.

He blinked. "This is my wife, Molly," he said. "Molly, Abby was at Gallery Walk. She's taking home *The Boy with the Bougainvillea*."

"Oh, lovely." Balancing Kira in her arms, Molly reached out toward me, and I took her offered hand. We shook. Her palm was silky with lotion.

"I'm Chrissy, Abby's best friend," Chrissy interjected.

"Nice to meet you, Chrissy," Eli said. I'd mentioned her before, so he knew who she was.

"Well, have a nice brunch," Chrissy said, stepping out of their way. She dragged me by the arm so they could pass.

"Nice to meet you," Molly said. She had a kind, singsong voice.

Kira waved, and Chrissy waved back. Following Molly into the restaurant, Eli glanced over his shoulder at me, his forehead creased. I was utterly bedraggled, and if it weren't for Chrissy still pulling me toward the parking lot, I would've crumpled to the ground.

When we were by our cars, Eli and Molly indoors and out of earshot, Chrissy pulled me close and said, "Oh my *God*."

I drew a shaky breath.

"Oh my God," she repeated. "*That* was Eli?"

I nodded.

"He's—wow."

I leaned against the hood of her car, trying to steady myself.

"You didn't mention he's married, Abby. Or that he has a kid." Her tone had an accusatory edge, but then she touched my arm. "You have to make all this right."

"I know I do," I said, coming to terms with it.

Chrissy opened her car and dug a tissue out of the glove box. She handed it to me. "And what was that about a bougainvillea?"

"He wants to give me this photograph I saw last night."

"You can't possibly take that home."

"I don't want to," I said. "But he insisted."

Chrissy grabbed my shoulders and looked into my eyes. "You need to make a decision. It's not just Dennis at risk."

"I know."

"If you truly have feelings for this guy—" She cut herself off as a car pulled into a neighboring spot and an elderly couple got out. "Promise me you'll do something soon?"

"I'm meeting him tomorrow," I said.

"Do you have any idea . . . ?" She spread her hands in question.

My heart ached, but I couldn't tell if it ached for Dennis or Eli. I shook my head.

2018

I wake up with a sour mouth and a pulsing headache not unlike being underwater, the pressure immense—and buzzing?

I roll over, and the buzzing sound intensifies. The skylights in my cottage are foggy and dark, and the clock on the nightstand reads 5:23 a.m. Curious, I pick up my phone to see a local number I don't recognize.

"Hello?" I croak, closing my eyes again, hovering on the edge of sleep.

"Come to the marina."

I recognize that voice. "Zack?"

"Are you still drunk?"

"I don't know, maybe? I feel like shit." I blink, testing my aching head, but I don't feel dizzy anymore. I remember throwing up in my bathroom. I squeeze my eyes shut, and the pressure in my temples increases.

"Can you drive safely?"

"Without falling asleep behind the wheel?"

He doesn't respond, but was that a laugh? I can hear the muffled crackle of air in the speaker.

"I *can* drive," I relent. "*Must* I?"

"Come to the marina," he says, breathy, and the line cuts out.

For a moment, I lie on my back, thinking. The dull ache of my head has intensified, but I don't think I have any painkillers in the cottage. Then I remember: my parents, the Manatee, that cab ride home, crying. Heat coming to my cheeks, I sit up. Why does Zack want to see me at this ungodly hour?

Another thought: I have work today. Oh, what a terrible day it'll be.

I roll out of bed and place my feet on the cold hardwood, a shiver trickling from my ankles up my spine and into my neck and shoulders. I'm wearing a bra and jeans, and the waistband digs into my bladder. I remove the jeans, use the bathroom, and tug on a pair of clean sweats, a sweater, and a jacket.

When I open the front door, Taffy appears from somewhere in the garden, her eyes squinting in the porch light.

"Breakfast?" I ask her.

Even she looks as if it's too early.

I turn back inside and fix her a plate of chicken, then feed her on the porch so she won't be locked in the cottage while I'm gone. She watches me go, a perplexed look on her angular cat face, ears swiveling, eyes wide. Before I round the bend out front, I glance back to see her eating under the glow of the porch light.

At the car, I unlock the door but hesitate outside. The stars are out, diamond white and glistening against the velvet backdrop of space. The cold has seeped through my layers, but despite the hangover—the worst of it yet to come, I'm sure—I get a gentle feeling of peace. The world is big, the sky bigger, and my smallness makes me feel safe among the early-morning streets of this sleepy town. Even Dennis and Eli seem small within the context of the universe (even if they still feel so large within me).

No one is on the road. I get a text from Zack while I'm driving, and at a stop sign, I glance down.

It says, You coming? Or did you fall back asleep?

On my way, I respond.

There are still many unread messages from my mother, but I set the phone back in the cup holder and press on the gas. I'm not ready to speak to her or process what she did. Worse, I know what it's like to be unhappy, know what it's like to have temptation, and perhaps my anger with my mother is wrapped up in anger with myself—a thought I can't bear to examine.

After pulling into the marina, I park near the coffeehouse, where Zack is inevitably waiting. I find him just outside, on a bench that overlooks the bay. The sky is lightening ever so slightly, the stars faded from the horizon but still twinkling straight above us. I can see my breath; the scent of salt water kisses my nose.

"Why?" I say, agonized. I sit beside him, close but not touching, though he rests his arm across the back of the bench.

"Morning," he says. "Here."

He hands me an espresso shot glass filled with yellow, pulpy juice and sprinkled with red powder.

"Bottoms up." He tips his own shot into his mouth. Then he sighs forcefully and hisses through his cheeks. "Refreshing."

I'm too hungover to question him, so I follow suit. The liquid goes down worse than whiskey, and my senses are overwhelmed with the burn of sour lemon juice and cayenne. I hiss, too, gagging a bit.

"That's awful," I say.

Zack chuckles. "It'll help. Have you had water?"

"I didn't have time, what with the rude awakening."

Unfazed by my attitude, he hands over a canteen. "Drink."

"Gladly." I unscrew the cap and drink half, the water a tad metallic from the bottle but otherwise refreshing.

Feeling the fuzziness in my head subsiding, I turn to him, admiring his smiling face, his beard a little scraggly from the long night. "Good morning," I say.

"You ready for part two of the hangover cure?"

I don't know what he's talking about at first, but then he's standing, stripping down. Horrified, I recall what he told me over a month ago about curing hangovers. Just the thought of swimming in that freezing water makes me shiver all over.

"No way," I say. "No, no, no."

He removes his shirt, revealing a lanky frame, with sculpted pecs and the slight swell of a beer belly. His chest is dotted with freckles and red-brown chest hair.

"You coming?" he asks, unbuttoning his pants.

I glance away, my eyes searching the empty walkways. "What if someone sees us?"

"Who? People on boats?"

I swallow. His expression challenges. His boxers—light blue—have little whales on them. Standing, I unzip my coat.

Zack claps. "Yeah, brave woman."

I remove my sweater, shoes, sweats, and shirt. The air is biting—no, worse than that: it stings. My headache rages, but I also feel a little lighter, perhaps from adrenaline. Stripped down to my plain black bra and panties (lucky they match), I suck in my stomach a little, from both the cold and self-consciousness. The breeze from the water ruffles my hair and his beard. He hesitates, which makes me wonder if we're supposed to go skinny-dipping. I'm relieved to see that Zack doesn't remove his underwear.

He holds out his hand. "Ready?"

I take it, our fingers locking.

He leads me down to the water, where the air is even cooler. White froth has collected on the beach, and we walk carefully over the stones and sand toward it, the soft lapping of the waves filling the otherwise-still morning. A foghorn sounds, soft and pleasant, and Zack grins at me. For a split second, I forget that we're in our underwear on the edge of the hypothermic sea.

Zack lets go of my hand and walks ahead of me, the waves touching his toes. He has scarring all along his left side, raised swaths of stretched skin from his waist down to his ankle, pale pink in the cold. I think of his accident, what he told me last night, how painful it must've been. It'd taken the crew nearly thirty hours to get him to a hospital.

He turns back, looking at me. "Come on," he says gently.

"How do we do this?" I ask.

"What do you mean?"

"Like, do we jump in? Or wade in? I'm not dunking my head."

"I usually wade quickly. Or jump."

"I'm not jumping," I say.

He gestures for me to come, and I slowly step into the rippling waves. The cold is immediately, achingly numbing.

"Jesus," I say, my teeth chattering, body shaking. "It hurts. It actually *hurts*."

Zack turns toward the water and spreads his arms, walking farther into the sea. Then he raises his arms into a point and dives in.

I cringe, getting hit with the splash, the spray soaking my bra.

Zack surfaces, standing in the waist-deep cold. "Your turn," he says with a chattering grin.

"No, no, no," I say, but the look of him, his beard soaked, the water billowing his boxers, the stars and the sea, it all makes me feel a lightness I've never felt. Adrenaline, probably. But pure fun, too, like letting go. I stare at the water, black and shimmering, and step out a little farther toward him. With a quick breath and clenched muscles, I dunk myself up to my neck.

"Yikes!" I yell, popping out immediately.

Zack is close, laughing, and then I'm laughing too.

Once we quiet down, I ask, "Now what?"

"We get out before we get hypothermia." He starts off toward shore.

"Thank God," I say, right behind him.

He plods out of the water, up the beach, his feet sandy, his boxers clinging. Briefly flustered, I try not to look, staring past him toward the maritime center instead. I don't want to imagine what I look like, salty and covered in goose bumps.

"Hurry, let's get warmed up," he says, and we jog the rest of the way.

Inside the coffee shop, Zack retrieves some towels from the bathroom, and we dry off by the door, the lights off. He rubs the towel over his head, chest, and legs, then throws it on the wood floor to mop up the mess of water and sand. When he's not looking, I press my own towel into my soaked bra, squeezing the water out. Then I wrap myself in the towel and bounce on the balls of my feet, trying to warm up.

"Almost time to open?" I ask.

"We have a half hour," he says softly. "Still cold?" He takes a tentative step closer, his eyes resting on me, a faint glimmer in his pupils.

"Freezing," I say and stop moving.

He rubs his hands over my arms quickly, warming me with friction. I lean toward him a little. He has a trail of light freckles along his collarbone. Then his hands slow down, and we step together, and he's simply holding me. I am weightless and tethered down all at once. The seawater has dried, and my skin is gritty with salt. Pulling back slightly, I look up into his eyes. His gaze slips down toward my lips, and his hands come up to cradle my face.

I imagine his lips would taste like the sea; I turn away before I can know for sure. Uncertainty wells inside me—how quickly this has happened. I *want* to kiss him. Stripped down in his shop, in the dark, the close proximity, with my adrenaline still coursing, the moment lends itself to a kiss. To warmth. To body heat. But what then? I haven't kissed a man or even wanted to in nearly five years. I can't in good conscience kiss Zack. Not on impulse. Not when I don't know what I want.

He deserves an explanation, though. "I can't," I whisper. He deserves a *better* explanation, but my thoughts tangle.

His hands fall away from my face, the warmth and comfort leaving with them. He steps back, his forehead creased in thought. "It's another man."

"No—" I rush. "Well, yes, but no."

He waits.

"I feel ridiculous being undressed. Can I?" I gesture toward the outside bench, where our clothes remain.

He waves his hand dismissively, stooping to tend to the floor. I duck outside and gather my thoughts, our clothes. In the privacy of the outdoor hall, I quickly remove my soaked panties and step into my sweats, then shrug into my shirt. Is there any way to redeem myself after rejecting him? The shame would keep me outside, but my need to make things right lures me back inside. I can't leave things like this.

Zack is behind the counter, flipping switches on the espresso machine, unwrapping plastic-covered trays of cookies. When he sees me, he points at the ceramic dripper and asks, "Coffee?" His face is an emotionless mask.

I nod, setting his clothes on a chair. My hangover is returning. I feel tired again.

Still in his dripping boxers, Zack gets a kettle boiling. I watch him retrieve a filter, select a roast, grind the beans. I don't know what to say to him, how to explain the confusion swirling inside me.

"Do you need me to get you some dry clothes?" I ask—neutral territory. "You can't work in wet boxers all day."

"I have clean ones in my truck," he says, not looking up from his task.

I begin to apologize but stop myself. "Want me to get them for you?"

He shrugs. "Red Toyota. It's unlocked."

I slip outside once more. The air is a damp, bone-chilling cold. Hurrying to his truck, I scold myself for how poorly I handled things. And oh, how desperately I want to know his mouth. When did that happen? Until last night, I didn't know him much at all. Only the feeling I get when I'm around him—a sense of warmth and acceptance. A feeling that energizes me. A feeling of being less adrift.

Inside his truck, an old coffee cup rests in the cup holder next to an empty prescription bottle, plus a few used food co-op containers on the floor. A fresh set of clothes is folded neatly on the back seat bench, and I retrieve them. Closing the door, I check my hair in the reflection of the driver's-side window. I look like hell, my hair in salty disarray, somehow frizzy and matted at the same time. I sigh, trying to fix my curls a bit, then give up and go back inside.

Zack is sprinkling a touch of cinnamon over the tops of two steaming cups. When I come through the door with his clothes, he looks up, a strange expression on his face, like a mix of relief and dispiritedness: bright eyes, pressed mouth.

"I thought you would split," he says.

A pang of sorrow emanates through me like a ringing bell. I slide his clothing across the counter toward him. "Cinnamon?" I ask.

He half smiles. "It complements the nutty vanilla notes of the roast."

I glance over my shoulder, out the windows toward the sun, which has just broken over the top of Whidbey Island. "Watch the sunrise with me?"

The half smile spreads to three-quarters. He collects his clothes. "Let me change." He disappears into the back, where the bathrooms are located.

I carry our pair of steaming coffee cups to the window seat of the shop, right in the path of the sunrise. The sky is clear, save for a few long stratocumulus clouds, their puffy tops flushed with pink. Separating sky and ocean, Whidbey Island is a thin indigo strip, crowned by the jagged Cascades beyond. In mirror image, a burst of yellow, orange, and pink ignites the clouds and water. Darker purples edge the view, and spreading outward from the horizon, the dome of the sky is painted in light blue. The sun is a tangerine orb, rising steadily.

I sip my coffee—perfectly balanced with flavor—and barely hear Zack approach. His sudden presence pulls me away from the view, and I set down my mug. He settles on the seat beside me, smelling of fresh laundry. His hair is a little less tousled, too, his beard combed.

"Listen, I—"

He cuts me off. "You don't owe me an explanation."

"I feel like my heart is being pulled in a thousand different directions," I say. "That's not fair to you."

He lifts his mug to his lips, his eyes on the sunrise. "Fairness is a fallacy anyway," he comments. "I'm not going to pressure you."

"I'm sorry."

"Don't be."

We drink our coffees in silence until the sun has risen and Zack's early customers have arrived, and he's swept into the workday. I hover for a little while longer, not wanting to leave, but my skin begins to itch with salt, and my bra is still damp. He offers only a glance as I leave; I need to shower and change before I report to the *Glacial Wind*, a full day of tours ahead.

Here's what I should've said to Zack: *This is the best morning I've had, ever. This is the first time I've felt so liberated. And this is the last time I want to break a man's heart with my own uncertainty.*

MAY

2018

For the next month, I get my coffee elsewhere. The whale watching tour schedule becomes hectic. Mary and Becca continue to come, and I'm pleased to learn that Becca is taking a Running Start marine biology class through the community college; in the evenings, I help her with her homework. I avoid the Manatee when I can and suggest corner booths and back room tables when Robin and Joanne and Kim insist I come out. Chrissy and I meet occasionally, but she's busy with work and baby fever. My mother calls, but aside from a few text messages confirming I haven't perished, I avoid my parents too. It's a busy spring but a lonely one.

In late May, Chrissy convinces me to go to the Rhody Festival with her, a teenage tradition that died with adulthood. Saturday's Grand Parade was once a scene of high school flirtation, gossip about the Rhody princesses, and snacks at Aldrich's Market. Nostalgia convinces me to go. In local fashion, we even stake out our seats on Lawrence Street the day before, tethering camping chairs to a sidewalk tree with a bike lock.

It's an abnormally warm day for May. I walk to Aldrich's to meet Chrissy out front, and we hug.

"Knocked up yet?" I ask.

She gives me a scolding look, then bursts into a smile. "Today is going to be fun."

We splurge on Italian paninis, potato chips, and lavender sodas. A fat, chocolate-drizzled cream puff catches our eyes in a pastry case, and we buy that, too, hoarding extra napkins at the cash register for the inevitable mess. It's noon, an hour before the parade, and the street is packed.

When we get to our spot, a young family has infringed on our space, our chairs clearly shifted back toward the sidewalk, the bike lock stretched as far as it'll go. Without saying anything, Chrissy hands me her lunch bag and sets our chairs back up in their original positions, uncomfortably close to the family. They shift over, red faced but not willing to make a stink.

Plopping down in her seat, Chrissy whispers, "Rude."

I giggle at her passive aggressiveness. Once, in high school, some boys hid our chairs in someone's yard, dumped in a hedge. She was furious, but with a straight face, she found the perpetrators (including one who, later that year, took her to homecoming) and forced them to apologize to the owner of the house for damaging the bushes. The owner, an ornery old woman, gave them quite a piece of her mind, and Chrissy was smug the whole rest of the afternoon. She even convinced me to buy her carnival tickets for it, and we rode the Zipper four times in a row, laughing all the while.

Now, we settle in our seats and chow down on the paninis. The family shifts another foot away, and Chrissy winks, successful in reclaiming our territory. It's still a half hour until the parade, but practice melodies from the marching bands hidden two blocks north carry over the bustle of eager parade goers. Children squeal; parents chuckle and yell; dogs wag their tails and beg for scraps of lunch. While we eat, an unclaimed copper dachshund appears, his little tail tucked, and Chrissy hands him a piece of salami from her sandwich. He darts away at the sharp call of his name—*"Berkley!"*—a woman half a block away waving a leash.

"Is Nick doing the Rhody Run this year?" I ask Chrissy.

In the middle of a bite, she nods.

"You too?"

"God, no," she says. "You know I don't run."

I laugh.

"Maybe I'll be one of those ladies who walk with strollers and never even get winded."

"I hated them when I was a teen," I say. I don't want to think about losing her to a baby, to a new set of mom friends, never to drink with me past nine p.m. again.

"Didn't your mom used to run?"

Yet another topic I'd like to avoid. "That was when I was really little."

She takes a big bite of her sandwich, getting mustard on her chin. Wiping it off, she asks, "Have you spoken to her at all?"

"I don't know what to say to her."

"You're angry. You could say that."

"What good would it do?"

"All I know is bottling it up doesn't do anybody any good."

"Who says I'm bottling—"

"You always run away from problems." Chrissy bunches up her sandwich wrapper.

"I do not—"

"What was California, then?"

"It was getting my career back on track. It was doing what I *love*."

"Then why aren't you still there?"

"Because," I say, faltering. "Because I was all alone out there. Because the other research assistants were pretentious. Because I missed . . ." I trail off and meet her eyes.

"That's what I'm *saying*," Chrissy says, touching my arm. "Have you healed? Have you gotten over Dennis *or* Eli?"

I press my lips together, tears coming hot and quick.

"I'm sorry," she says softly. "But I'm your best friend. I'm *supposed* to tell you when you're being stupid. And ignoring your mom is stupid." She touches my arm, her big eyes holding mine. "This grudge is hypocritical, Abby. You're taking your frustration with yourself out on your mom, and that isn't fair."

"I never—" I stop, considering her words. "It's not the same."

"If she said they worked past it, then they worked past it." She sits back, breaking her stare. "Being angry *now* doesn't change anything."

Blinking, I look off toward the sound of the marching bands. A drum line has started, and I spot the first row of red-clad teens rounding the bend, horns and snares erupting.

"Are we going to eat this cream puff or what?" she asks, grinning.

I dab my eyes, my defenses softening. "Don't hog it."

"Have you met me?"

As the parade starts, we devour the cream puff, getting custard on our fingers, our laps, and the grass in front of us. Thank goodness we grabbed extra napkins, because between my bout of tears and the messy pastry, we use them all. The copper dachshund appears again, trailing a leash, and licks cream from the ground. The sugar patches my wounds, at least for now. Chrissy scoots close and cracks jokes, and I know she's trying to make me feel better. She has a strange way of balancing real talk and comfort.

The street becomes crowded, to the point that a few dads hover behind us, one brushing the back of my head to yell for his child not to run into the street. Just like the old days, we're glad we staked out our seats the day before. Familiar local companies and schools pass by, pop songs blasted through cordless speakers. Big and elaborate papier-mâché floats wow the crowd, while other groups walk stiffly with wrinkled banners. Dressed-up dogs trot beside their jubilant owners. People juggle, twirl ribbons, wave, and throw candy to the sidelines. Kids run past the curb, grabbing the little twisted wrappers right off the pavement.

Chrissy waves at the passing floats, chatting with me in between the loudest passersby. The family to our right offers us some bottled lemonade, a peace offering, and soon we're talking with those crowded around us too. One guy happens to be the older brother of a classmate of ours. We laugh about our own parade years, the goofy outfits, marching band, school colors.

About halfway through the parade, Chrissy and I stand up to stretch our legs. Some smaller floats are passing, and it gives us a chance to wander toward the sidewalk, out from under the looming views of the many people standing behind our chairs. From back behind the hubbub, looking down the declining length of Lawrence Street, it seems the whole town is here to watch. Six blocks of sidewalk are lined with people, three rows deep on both sides. Glancing in the opposite direction, up the gentle hill, I can see where the parade is coming from, the seemingly endless floats turning onto the main route from the neighborhood street on which they've been waiting.

The crowd is a mass of unfamiliar people, but I feel a small-town kinship with them. Most of them probably shop at the food co-op, go to the Rhody carnival, read the *Port Townsend Leader*, and stop for the fawns and does that wander into the road in broad daylight. How many of them have hired Dennis or his dad for construction or have seen Eli's photographs at Gallery Walk? Chrissy likely knows even more, working at the hospital.

As I'm musing, a group steps past Chrissy and me, heading up the hill. I move out of their way instinctively, only to realize that one of them truly is a familiar face. Seeming to have the same thought, he looks over his shoulder, and our eyes meet.

"Abby? Chrissy?" Eduardo, Dennis's best friend and construction buddy, walks back to us.

I am shocked to see him. He leans in to give me a light but sincere hug, then Chrissy too.

He asks, "How've you been?"

"Oh, well enough," Chrissy says. "You?"

My mouth has gone dry, and I struggle for words.

"Good, good, business is good." His eyes rove over me; unspoken tension builds inside me, hard packed. He's perhaps the only bridge to Dennis I didn't burn. "I didn't know you were back in town, Abby."

"She's been back for a couple months," Chrissy says, sensing my lack of words.

Finally, I'm able to force out, "You look good, Eduardo."

"Really?" His eyes crinkle with a grin. "The new baby has been keeping me up at all ungodly hours."

"The dark circles suit you," Chrissy jokes.

He nudges her with his elbow. "You're too kind." His eyes rest on me again, with sympathy. "I hope you're finding your way, Abby."

"Yeah," I say.

"She's working on the whale watch tour boats now," Chrissy says.

"Oh? That sounds amazing." After a long pause, Eduardo says, "Well, everyone is good."

Everyone. I want to ask more, but I can't form the words. I wish it were Dennis standing before me; I instinctively search the crowd for his face, but it's Jackie who appears instead. She comes over, not seeming to realize it's me until it's too late. She stops a few feet behind Eduardo, her eyes round, her jaw tight.

I must've made a face, because Eduardo turns around. In a clear effort to smooth over the stormy emotional atmosphere, he says, "Jackie, look who I ran into."

"I see," Jackie says through clenched teeth.

Chrissy smiles, helping Eduardo with the unfortunate task of making things less uncomfortable. "Jackie, it's been a while. You look great."

"Thanks." She hardly seems to notice Chrissy; her eyes bore into me.

"Are you well?" I manage to ask, repeating myself from the parking lot. I never liked that Jackie hated me so much; now, it seems like an unbearable symptom of unfortunate circumstances. We could've been friends, once upon a time. "How is—"

"Fuck you," she says.

"Hey, now," Eduardo says, and then he's actually holding her back, his arms straining against her weight. Jackie reaches for me, her face red with menace. Chrissy hauls me backward, and thank goodness, because my legs don't work. A few dads nearby have to step between us, holding up their palms and shouting, "Hey, whoa," and "Whoa, calm down."

Jackie growls, an alarmingly animal sound. But then she relents, and Eduardo guides her away. I hear him say, "Jesus, Jackie, what's wrong with you?" Her shoulders are shaking.

I slump against Chrissy, still protected by a cocoon of concerned men. Jackie and Eduardo are walking up the hill; her fists are balled, and his hand is firm on her arm. He's gesturing with his other hand, probably scolding her, but she's shaking her head, and then they disappear into the throngs of people.

A stream of classic cars rumbles in the parade, all waxed and spotless. Old men in veteran ball caps wave to the crowd. The nearby dads who held Jackie back begin to dissipate, one of them asking if I'm all right before returning to his family a few rows down. I have the desperate urge to collapse into my camping chair, but Chrissy holds my shoulders.

"Abby, you okay?"

I'm dazed. Jackie always blamed me for everything, and maybe she was right. I left for that research study, and Dennis had open-heart surgery. I met Eli and broke Dennis's fragile heart. Jackie wasn't wrong in her hatred of me, not by a long shot.

Before I can lie and tell Chrissy I'm all right, my cell phone rings. It's my mother. I waver. Chrissy sees the screen and gestures for me to pick up. Still quivering from Jackie, I consider all the bridges I've burned. All the damage I've done, the people I've hurt. My mother has bridges too. I'm one of them. I look into Chrissy's encouraging face and answer on the last ring, plugging my other ear to hear over the hubbub of the parade.

"Thank goodness you answered," Mom says by way of greeting. "Abby, dear, I feel awful. Can you visit? Can you come home so we can talk?"

"Mom," I say. "I'm at the Rhody parade. I can't hear you very well." I veer off the sidewalk and pause under the low maroon boughs of a Chinese maple at the edge of someone's yard. Chrissy follows and puts her hand on my shoulder in solidarity.

Under the quiet shelter of the tree, I ask, "What's up?"

My mother sounds desperate. "Your father and I would like to see you."

Chrissy circles her wrist in a *go on* gesture.

I take a breath. "Okay, Mom. Tonight?"

"Tonight, yes, perfect. Pizza okay?"

"Yes, that's great." After we hang up, I glance at Chrissy. "Happy?"

"Need me to come—for moral support?"

I shake my head, looping my arm through hers. We make our way back to our chairs and plop down. The parade continues. With a pang of dread, I spot Jackie and Eduardo farther up, wrangling screaming kiddos as if nothing even happened. I wish I could sink deeper into my chair.

2013

On Monday, I woke up long before my alarm. Dennis and I had barely spoken the remainder of Sunday and had gone to bed without even so much as a *good night*. We'd even skipped our dinner plans, instead ordering takeout and eating in front of the TV. Yet that morning, on the fuzzy border of sleep, I felt his arm draped over my side, and I pressed into the heat of his body, enjoying the sensation. Instinctively, he drew me closer.

Then the world came screaming.

It was a horrible moment, really. Caught in the gauzy glow of restfulness, I suddenly felt everything all at once rushing back to me: stress, regret, guilt, anger—and especially fear. Fear that I'd get up and Dennis would still be angry; fear that I'd face Eli that day and not be able to push him away like I should; fear that if I told Dennis about my unhappiness, Eli, and my misery enduring just one more day at the bank, just one more day of putting off my dreams, he'd leave. Fear that I might leave him.

I slipped out from under his hold and the covers. Cool air gripped me, and I wiggled into a robe and slippers.

Downstairs, the morning light cast the kitchen in a buttery glow. The sun had not yet fully risen over the trees; long shadows striated our front field. Deer mingled, flicking their tails, practically invisible in the tawny grass. It would be a warm day. Closer to the house, spiderwebs glistened with dew, more delicate than lace. I started the coffee maker and sank into a dining table chair, facing the window.

In Alaska, while getting my degree, I'd gone out on a little research boat with my classmates and professor. It was a routine trip, half designed to collect seawater samples for a lab class, half an excuse to spend a day on the water. We'd just eaten lunch and were making our return trip when we spotted a flurry of seagulls not far off the forested shoreline. The gulls were twisting and hovering and making a raucous commotion. We cut the engine just as a burst of dark mouths broke the surface some thirty yards away, lunging upward in a great surge. The bravest gulls descended, and then the giant mouths sank back into the ocean.

A few students hooted at the sight; I was dumbfounded into silence. Five humpbacks cooperatively feeding.

We waited for what felt like eons, watching the water. Gulls hovered, stoking our own excitement. Then a ring of bubbles simmered at the surface not far from the first lunge, the birds sank toward the water, and then the whales thrust upward, all at once in a great gray mass. Their open mouths looked like giant mussels cracked open, dark maws with white barnacled pockmarks. I could see the billowing, expanded throat of the closest humpback, filled with thousands of gallons of water and herring, the nose sinking into the depths once more.

Not in my entire life had I felt so exhilarated, joyous, or small.

This was before I'd run into Dennis in that coffee shop, before our romance had bloomed. It was, perhaps, the highest point of my professional life. The thought saddened me. As the sun rose on that Monday morning, I realized that if I didn't do anything about my unhappiness, my career would only ever be a distant memory, longed for at a kitchen table.

2018

Both my parents' vehicles are in the driveway when I arrive. I park behind my mother's car and sit in silence for a moment, collecting myself. After the parade, I spent the afternoon at home doing a few much-needed house chores before I succumbed to another long workweek tomorrow. Now, though, I'm out of tasks to put off seeing my parents. The affair is a challenge to the ideals I thought I'd been raised with. Of course I have questions, but more than that, I wrestle with Chrissy's insight: perhaps I am angrier with my own actions than my mother's. No matter how upset I am, I have no right to judge—the least I can do is hear her out.

Deep breath, I tell myself. I grab my purse and head inside without knocking.

As always, Cooper is the first one to greet me, his tail wagging so furiously it could wiggle right off his body. I stoop, petting his soft ears, tipping my chin up to avoid any licks on the mouth. Glad for the sweet distraction.

"Abby?" My mother comes around the corner from the kitchen. Her nose is red, her eyes puffy.

I give Coop one more scratch, then stand. "Hi, Mom," I say.

We don't hug. The foyer smells like pizza, and as I follow her into the kitchen, the scent of burnt cheese and greasy pepperoni intensifies.

Dad is there, the oven open, sliding the pizza off the rack and onto the stove top to cool.

"Good timing, Babby," he says, tossing the oven mitts on the counter. "You can sit down."

With reluctance, I scoot onto one of their bar seats at the kitchen island. I can feel their eyes on me. My mother stands beside my father at the opposite end of the island. Both their faces are serious, drawn into pinched expressions. They appear as a united front. When did they become these flawed people?

"You wanted to talk?" I ask, growing impatient under their stares.

"It was nine years ago," my mother says. "A onetime thing. We were struggling, you know."

"You never told me you were," I say, but then I recall their arguments back then, and I'm ashamed to realize that maybe I *did* know. Maybe I shouldn't have pretended they would be fine.

My father places his hand over hers on the counter. "It's in the past, Abby," he says. "We've already moved on from it, and we'd like you to respect that."

"I'm not perfect, dear. None of us are," she says.

I offer a single nod of acknowledgment, because it's true. No one is perfect—not even them—and it was unfair of me to expect that of them. For a brief moment, I allow myself to mourn that childhood fantasy. Then the moment passes. "You're right," I say.

My mother sighs, her mouth twisting into a half smile of relief.

Dad speaks up. "That wasn't what we wanted to discuss tonight, though."

"It wasn't?"

My mother pinches the bridge of her nose, her eyes squeezed shut.

My father says, "It's the house."

This surprises me. "What about the house?"

"Shortly after you married Dennis, we were forced to refinance," my father says. "We didn't want to burden you with the news right after his health scare. You had enough on your plate."

"How does this have anything to do with now?" I ask.

My mother bends down to pet Coop, clearly distressed. Dad is left to explain, but he falters too. I press my lips into a line, waiting. I recall Wendy, her strange embrace with my father and her abrupt departure. My pulse quickens. I forgot about her when I learned of my mother's affair.

"Wendy," I say, prompting Dad. "This has something to do with Wendy."

"She's our real estate agent. In the barn"—he clears his throat—"she was comforting me. Abby, dear, we're losing the house."

My first thought is of me at twelve years old, atop my old horse, Cinnamon. A hot July day, riding bareback with only a halter and lead rope for steering, far out in the field, the back fence overgrown with chickweed. A hawk circling overhead, a swoop, and a startled duck. Cinnamon rearing and me falling. Tall weeds and a sagging, hidden string of barbed wire. Scratched-up arms and a bruised tailbone. Cinnamon's red-gold rump disappearing back toward the barn.

I'm not sure why the memory pops into my head. The duck was so random, so unexpected. A bombproof old quarter horse spooked by a frightened bird. My mom didn't believe me when I first told her why my arms were bloody. Now, I feel like she must have felt then: unbelieving. There's no way Cinnamon, a reliable horse, would spook. There's no way my parents, ever a constant, would face this type of hardship. But the scratches are here for proof.

The kitchen is quiet, save for Coop's nervous nails tapping on the floor. He knows something is wrong, and my mother rubs his head, as if that'll help. My father waits for my response.

"The pizza must be cool by now, right?" I squeak. My whole chest aches.

He sighs and turns, running a wheel over the pie, cutting it into slices.

I ask, "Do you know where you'll go?"

"There's a place in Irondale we're looking at."

Irondale: a shabby suburb halfway between Port Townsend and Chimacum.

"And the horses?" My childhood is being ripped to pieces.

My mother stands, a hand lingering on Coop's head. "Connie Bishop will take them."

"You're not going to keep the horses?"

She shakes her head. I know better. If they're going to Irondale, they won't have property for the animals, and boarding horses is expensive.

"Cattle?" I ask.

"To the neighbors," my father says. "Everything is accounted for."

"What about your business, Dad?"

"I can still work on tractors, same as always. I don't need a workshop for it—most of the time I go to them, anyway."

My eyes brim with tears. "But Mom, your horse lessons?" It's her dream, after all. The flower department pays the bills, but the horses are her passion.

She shakes her head. "I don't know, dear. Connie doesn't have an arena. But I'm free to visit them anytime I like. It's a good arrangement for now."

"And there's nothing you can do, nothing I can do?" I ask. "Why didn't you tell me before I left? I could've used my own equity—"

"It wasn't your job to bail us out, sweetheart," my father says, circling round the table. He pulls me into a hug, strong and familiar, and it sets loose a whole flood of tears. My mother joins in. How many memories will leave this kitchen when they move out? It's the most constant thing I've ever known.

For a long while, we stand there together in each other's arms. Digesting the news, I realize: they aren't just my parents; they're adults. Adults who are stumbling along just as I am.

2013

After getting ready for the bank on Monday morning, I heard Dennis stirring and expected he'd ignore me when he came downstairs. I was slipping into my jacket when he came into the kitchen, his face puffy with sleep, his short hair mussed. He wore only his boxers and an open robe and shuffled toward the coffee maker.

"I'm leaving for work," I said, turning toward the door.

I didn't anticipate his reply: "Wait."

I turned around, and he was there, wrapping his arms around me tightly, his body still bed-warm. I stiffened, thinking of Eli and meeting him for lunch later that day, but Dennis buried his face in the curve of my neck and breathed deeply, and I instinctively sank into him. He kissed my cheek.

"Have a good day," he said, though I wasn't sure how to interpret it, given that he knew I hated my job.

I said, "You too" and meant it, because after all, he was my husband, and I loved him.

But when he held me that morning, something was different. A shift had occurred. While his embrace felt familiar and comfortable, it didn't render me weak as it once had. It didn't compel me to call in sick. It simply felt like more of the same. And that morning, I needed a different feeling to tether me to him.

JUNE

2018

It's the second weekend in June. The Cascades are unobscured, and though it's early morning, the air is already balmy, a promise of an abnormally hot day. I've donned shorts and a Sound Adventures tee and am driving to the food co-op to pick up lunches for Joanne and Captain Megan. Today, I'm serving on the Friday Harbor tour trip—not my normal post, but I'm excited for a day up in the San Juan Islands. Unlike the half-day tours, which are quick and close to home, the full-day trips are a temporary getaway. Two resident orca pods have been spotted—a guaranteed good day, something I've been needing.

I've spent the past few weeks helping my parents pack up my childhood. Garage sales, moving boxes, kissing horses on their noses and handing lead ropes and old saddles over to Connie Bishop. My parents came away with a good chunk of change, having sold most of their valuables. It'll keep them secure while they work with Wendy to finalize their new place. In between, the busy summer tour schedule has been a whirlwind of emotion; work provides solace, but only for twelve hours of the day. The other twelve are a different story.

Stepping into the cool AC of the food co-op, I turn right and head for the deli, where premade sandwiches and wraps await. I browse the cold cases, gathering a few favorites into my arms. I know Joanne has a soft spot for PB&J, so I grab her one with fresh organic jelly (according to the wrapper). Megan suggested turkey, and I find one with Havarti cheese.

I'm more indecisive, and I wander the brightly lit rows, chilled by the open refrigerated shelves. I find myself in the olive and gourmet-cheese section. I pick up a container of smoked-salmon cream cheese dip, pondering if I can get away with eating only chips and dip for lunch. Maybe I can make it healthy by buying some fruit?

"Having trouble deciding?"

I turn away from my indecision. Zack is cradling a basket full of produce, beer, and a package of steak. He reaches across me to grab a wheel of brie.

"That dip is the bomb," he adds.

His beard is gone—well, not gone entirely, but much shorter. The last time I saw him, it came down to his collarbone. Now, it's cropped short to almost stubble. His hair is shorter, too, and he's wearing a breezy-looking button-down shirt. I haven't seen him since our dip in the ocean six weeks ago, but it feels as if no time has passed at all (though somehow I feel five years older).

I look at the salmon dip in my hands, pink flecks amid a swirl of white cream cheese, a sprinkling of chives smooshed against the clear plastic lid. "Can I get away with eating it for lunch?" I ask him. "Or should I find something healthier?"

He smiles, eyes crinkling with genuine delight. "I mean, salmon has protein and omega-3s, so that dip is probably the healthiest thing in this place." He winks.

"Sold." I settle the container in my arms along with the sandwiches, freeing up my hands. "Have a cracker recommendation?"

We walk the few feet to the snack section, an awkward silence building between us. When we get to the row of chips, Zack reaches up to the top shelf to grab a bag of bagel crisps. "These are my favorite."

I manage to take the bag without our fingers touching. "Yum."

A lingering pause. "So how are you? It's been a while."

A long while, I think. Too long. Seeing him standing before me, I consider how lonesome these weeks have been. How much I've thought about him, often in the quiet moments of the morning. Imagining him there in my cottage, brewing coffee. The shameful flush in my cheeks when I catch myself daydreaming about a man I barely know, as if I haven't learned my lesson from Eli, as if I'm not still hung up on my past. "I've been fine. Rocky life stuff, but I'm hanging in there."

"I'm sorry to hear that."

"What about you?" Without thinking, I add, "I miss your . . . coffee."

His forehead creases briefly before his eyebrows rise. "Business is good, but I miss making mystery drinks for you."

I feel some heat come into my cheeks. "Certainly *someone* else must ask for your latest creations?"

"No way," Zack says. "They're just for you."

"Oh." My cheeks must be vermilion.

"You doing anything today?"

A bold question, considering I already pushed him away. "I'm working," I say, a bit to my own dismay—and clearly his. "I'm just picking up lunch for the crew."

His slight frown dissipates. "Looks like a perfect day to be on the water."

My excitement rises. "K and L pods are around, so we should see a lot of whales."

"I'll let you be on your way, then," he says. "I don't want to hold you up."

He isn't holding me up. It's still an hour and a half before the tourists will arrive. But he's making his way toward the front, and maybe I'm holding him up, so I don't protest. We walk to the checkout lines. He goes through one, I go through another, and we end up wandering out of the grocery store together, into the already-beaming sun. I squint in the sudden change of light. Even more freckles show on his forehead in the brightness.

"I'm heading for the shop. Care for a coffee before you go?" he asks.

"I'd love something iced."

"Whatever you want," he says. "Follow me over?"

I nod. As I get in the car, though, my good mood takes a dip. I don't feel ready for this connection with Zack; I'm not even sure I'm over Eli yet (despite his apparent hatred of me), let alone Dennis. It's not fair for me to flirt with Zack's feelings. When I arrive at the marina and park, he's already there, waiting out front so we can walk together into the shop. His easy smile wears on me.

The coffee shop is busy, the windows all open to accept the cool breeze off the shore. Zack steps behind the counter, moving in sync with the employee on shift, working around her to make me an iced coffee. When he's done filling two cups, we walk back out into the sunshine, finding a pair of chairs near the mouth of the neighboring pier.

I sip the drink. It's hazelnut, and I savor the flavor. "Can I pay you back?" I ask.

"Nonsense," he says. "Your company is payment enough."

"Zack—" I break off, gathering my thoughts into something coherent and gentle. "Zack, I don't want to lead you on."

He shifts in his chair, sipping his own coffee. "You're not," he says. "You already made things clear. It's my fault for putting pressure on you, for making you feel like you can't come in for coffee anymore."

I shake my head. "I wasn't avoiding you. I was avoiding my own . . ." I spread my hands. How can I tell him I still have so much baggage? "There's a lot to explain."

"You don't have to explain now," he says. "Or at all, if you don't want. But I *would* like to make you coffee again. Can I at least do that?"

I sigh. "Yes, I would like that." Maybe I should just be honest. "Zack, I miss seeing you. It's just—I don't know what I'm doing. I have a lot to work through, and I'm not ready for . . ." I trail off. "Is that okay?"

He doesn't divulge his emotion; instead, with neutral eyes on the water, he takes another long sip of coffee.

Maybe I've said too much.

After an eternity, Zack meets my gaze and answers, "Anything you feel is perfectly okay. And I like your company too."

It's the best thing he could've said, given what I just told him—I try to hide the dumb, wide, giddy grin on my face. We finish our drinks in the sun, our legs stretched out in the heat. When we're done, I stand up.

"I have to go to work," I say.

"So do I."

"But I'll see you around?"

He stands and surprises me with an airy embrace. His arms encircle me, but it doesn't last long.

He says, "Sooner than six weeks from now, I hope?"

So he was counting too. I smile. "Definitely."

2013

At work, I didn't feel brave or ready enough to see Eli for lunch. He'd probably have his photograph with him and expect me to take it home. I imagined him lifting it carefully out of the back of his SUV, its colorful face glinting in the sunlight, his arms deft. I was still shaken by running into him the other morning with Molly and Kira. But there was also Gallery Walk, that bench, and the moonlight, which shook me in other ways. And Chrissy's words: *You need to make a decision.*

I dropped the sticky notes I'd been fiddling with. "Mind if I go to lunch early today?" I asked Riya.

She shrugged as a way of response.

It was only eleven, and I guessed that if I went now, I could avoid Eli altogether. I grabbed my purse and bolted out the door without another word.

I hadn't brought a lunch, so I walked to Seashore Pizza, about five blocks from the bank. The day was pleasant, if a little hot for my black slacks and long-sleeved blouse. It was just before the lunch rush, so the single-slice pizza line was short. I bought a slice of mushroom sausage to go and ducked out into the sunshine, past the coffee shop where Eli and I liked to meet, and walked down to the beach that neighbored ours.

I settled on a log and ate my pizza, listening to the waves whooshing before me. Eli filled my thoughts: the skip in my heart when I'd spotted him during Gallery Walk, the way he'd captivated that crowd of art fans, and my nervous excitement when he'd suggested we escape out the back. Even at breakfast, the churning gloom I'd felt upon seeing him with Molly and Kira. I realized that those were the same feelings I'd had when Dennis and I had first started dating. The eager pangs in my chest, the angsty longing in my belly, the clammy palms, and the racing, lusty thoughts. Even the jealousy. When had those feelings faded from my husband? When had life begun to feel so stale?

When I was done, I brushed the crumbs from my lap. The only thing that dammed the waves of dark thoughts was the fact that I had successfully eluded Eli.

Or so I thought.

"Early lunch?" he asked, coming over.

I hesitated by the log, my heart thwacking. "I guess."

Eli was wearing a new-looking black T-shirt, a little tight. "Can we sit?" he asked.

My legs gave way, and I sank to the log again, embarrassed. Was I sweating through my blouse too? The sunshine felt oppressive. He sat close. Already, I was swept up in his hazelnut eyes.

"You didn't want to meet today, did you?"

I glanced away, out toward the gray structures of the naval base across the water. "I—" But I cut myself off and sighed.

He touched my chin, ever so briefly, so that I'd look at him. "We haven't spoken about what this is, so I thought I would." He placed his hand on my leg, like he had at Gallery Walk; I couldn't bring myself to push it off. "Abby, seeing you yesterday morning made me realize what we have, the way you make me feel. It's unlike anything I've encountered before."

"I feel the same way," I admitted, my voice muffled.

His serious, thoughtful expression brightened. "I know this is more complicated than most relationships, but I don't want to risk losing you."

Relationship. Was that what this was, truly? Hearing him say it made my head spin. I was most certainly sweating through my blouse. I tugged on the collar, fanning the fabric away from my skin. I stood, and his palm slipped from my leg.

"Eli—" I tried, but then he was standing too.

He came closer by one step, two, until I felt our attraction vibrating in the narrow space between us. My lust for him overwhelmed me; it drowned out all hope of logic. He ran his hand along my arm, then cupped my jaw, gently, sensually tipping my mouth up toward his. Like being drawn by gravity, I felt myself rising toward him. His proximity had awoken a wild craving in me. His arms drew me nearer.

Yet just before our lips brushed, I drew back ever so slightly, his stare again coming into focus. His eyes held mine; his hot breath caressed my face. Doubt gripped hold of me.

A nagging feeling made me turn my head. Someone on the sidewalk was watching our almost kiss: Jackie.

I broke away from Eli, practically shoving past him to bolt after Jackie. She was rushing away, drawing out her cell phone. I was able to reach her in time, though, and my hand clamped around her wrist with bear-trap strength. She tried to wrench herself free, but I held tight. She met my eyes with a stare that could melt glass. Desperation and shame surged through my veins, making me dizzy. Jackie yanked free.

"You have twenty-four hours to tell him," she said, slow and deliberate. "Otherwise, I will."

She stormed off, and I didn't stop her. Eli came up beside me, his hand resting on the center of my back. "Who was that?"

I recoiled from his touch, the spell broken. "I have to go."

"Abby?" His voice was shaken, watery.

"Eli—" I shook my head. Tears stung like poison on my cheeks. "This is over."

I didn't look at him as I hurried toward the bank, leaving him there on the sidewalk. I called Dennis immediately, wiping my tears away with my sleeve.

"Abby?" he answered. I never called him in the middle of the day, and there was an edge of worry in his voice.

"Dennis—" I swallowed. "Did Jackie call you?"

"What? No. Is something wrong?"

"No," I squeaked. Shuddering, I tried to compose myself. "Nothing wrong. I just ran into her, is all. Will you be home on time?"

"Yeah, but Abby, you sound upset. Did she say something to you?"

"It's fine," I said. "We can talk about it after work."

"You sure?" Voices and the steady beep, beep, beep of a truck in reverse came through in the background. He was at a job site.

"I'm sure," I said.

"All right, I'll see you tonight," he said, then added, "I love you."

I couldn't bring myself to reciprocate. If I did, would it be a lie? My lips still tingled with the promise of Eli's touch; I could still feel the pressure of his hands.

"Have a good day," I said and hung up.

I don't recall working that afternoon. In a haze of worry and self-loathing, I completed my tasks on autopilot. I allowed myself to get caught up in the monotony, like vacuuming after an argument just to avoid more confrontation. The bank, for once, was a refuge from the shit storm waiting for me. But then the doors were locked and the lights were dimmed and Riya came to me and said that I really needn't worry about tidying up the whole place before closing.

"Abby, I don't know what happened while you were at lunch, but it's almost six, and I'm going home," she said. "Are you ready?"

Only then did I look up from my task and finally accept the fact that time had continued forward without my permission. I wasn't ready, not in the slightest. "Right, yes, let's go home."

2018

My mood is uncharacteristically buoyant as I wander toward the marina—more buoyant than it has been in five years. Heat waves shimmer above the parking lot, and refracted sunlight gleams off the water. The warmth fills my bones as I board the *Bobcat*, the fast Friday Harbor catamaran vessel with a tiered-step viewing area on the bow.

Joanne notices my elevated demeanor immediately. "You get laid or something?"

Captain Megan, already in the wheelhouse, chuckles.

"What prep still needs to be done?" I ask, avoiding the question entirely.

"Oooh, so you *did*."

"I didn't, but that's none of *your* business." I shrug, my thoughts still hazy with Zack. "I just feel like it'll be a good day, is all."

"You saw the whale report," Joanne says, (thankfully) back to business.

"Two pods," I say with excitement.

"Oh, you haven't checked since early this morning, have you?" Joanne grins wide. "We have a superpod."

It's the jackpot of whale watching. All the southern resident pods coming together into one huge group, feeding and playing. It's a sight I've never seen. Where most whale watches include a few sightings, perhaps eight individuals on a lucky day, the superpod promises thirty, fifty, maybe more, depending on how spread out they are. What's more, the southern residents are an endangered group, so not only are the numbers spectacular, it's a rare treat to see them together. My heart leaps into my throat, beating wildly.

"Shut up." I chuckle with joy. "Are you pulling my leg?"

"No, ma'am," Joanne says. "We're in for a great day."

After stowing our lunches in the minifridge and prepping for a nearly full boat, Joanne wanders down the dock to usher the waiting tourists aboard. Forty-seven people file down the metal ramp from shore, the last of them coming through the open door of the Sound Adventures gift shop with swag in hand. Joanne reminds them to walk carefully across the floating dock; I stand at the stern of the *Bobcat*, helping people climb aboard. I take their boarding passes and direct them inside, where Megan awaits to guide them to their seats.

As I greet the guests, I listen for accents among the distinct little groups. A pair of couples from the East Coast (New York?), ten Canadians clearly having a family reunion, a few French- and German-speaking families, plus more local-looking tourists carrying Patagonia jackets and wearing Teva sandals, with pasty legs and hiker-thin bodies. Even the kiddos match their parents, wherever they're from, as easily distinguishable as the adults.

Mary and Becca climb up, too, and I grin as they pass, trying not to notice how skinny Mary's bare arms have gotten. She's wearing a big hat to shield her skin from the sunshine. Becca has to help her off the dock, and I offer my arm.

"Supposed to be an exciting day," Mary says cheerfully.

"You bet," I say. "Glad to have you along, as always."

Becca smiles as she and her mother duck inside.

Joanne is at the back of the line, coming toward me with the straggling guests. The last tourists pass, each taking my hand for balance. Then—someone I recognize, walking beside Joanne, coming closer. A big lens case slung over his shoulder. His daughter walking alongside him. It's as if I've swallowed a peach pit. I cough, anxiety strangling me. Out of habit, I stoop to help the girl up, practically lifting her by her arm onto the deck. Then I stand, holding my hand out for Eli.

Thank God he doesn't take it. He seems just as surprised as I am, but his daughter keeps things moving. She steps toward the threshold, and he's forced to grab the railing and rush past me to ensure she doesn't trip. Joanne swings up after him, oblivious to my fluster.

"Abby is one of our naturalists," Joanne tells him. "Abby, this is Eli."

He pauses on deck, his fingers locked around Kira's wrist.

"Eli's the photographer we hired to take new promotional photos for us," Joanne continues. "And what a good day to see whales."

"Couldn't have picked a better day," he says to her, but his tan skin has paled, and his knuckles are white. Kira squirms, and he releases his iron grip. "Thanks again for having us, Joanne. C'mon, sweetheart, let's find our seats." Without a glance in my direction, he leads his daughter inside, stepping sideways through the narrow door to avoid knocking his camera bag.

I let out the breath I was holding. My hands quake, my finger joints twitching beyond my control. A whole day on a tour with Eli? After he literally slammed the door in my face at his gallery? I'm not sure I can handle his presence, confined to this boat as we are.

"What's wrong?" Joanne asks, stepping closer.

I lean against the railing. My pulse is thunder in my ears.

"That's my . . . my ex," I say, because that's the simplest word I can manage to describe our history, our everything.

Joanne leans close. "It didn't end well?"

I shake my head, pressing my lips together. I consider bailing altogether. They probably wouldn't fire me if I feigned sickness. But no one else can fill in for my shift, and I can't leave Captain Megan and Joanne to manage a boatful of forty-plus people on their own. I think of the superpod too. The promise of an exciting trip. I refuse to let Eli ruin my good day.

Joanne pats my shoulder in consolation, then brushes past me, ready to get underway. It's my job to brief the passengers while she prepares for departure. I step inside and walk to the front, the eyes of nearly fifty passengers falling on me.

"Welcome to the *Bobcat*," I say, my voice elevated to reach all the way back. I spot Eli and a fidgety Kira sitting on the starboard side, near the window, perhaps six rows back from the front. I think about how his daughter now lives in a broken home; I wonder how she took the news, if she understood what her parents meant when Eli and Molly inevitably had to explain why Mommy and Daddy weren't living together anymore. Sorrow stabs my ribs.

"How is everyone today?" I croak, shoving my emotions down, down, down.

The passengers cheer with jubilance, oblivious to my peril. I stumble through the rest of my speech, glancing periodically in Eli's direction to see his eyes on me, penetrating. I lose all familiar wording, my awareness hovering in his corner of the room even when my gaze is elsewhere.

Megan and Joanne get us underway, and finally, as we slip past the Point Wilson Lighthouse, I have a chance to duck into the back. Joanne takes over, going from row to row to ask people if they want coffee, tea, chips, or a piece of cobbler. I hide with Megan, settling beside her in the wheelhouse.

"Off day?" she asks. I've never served as a naturalist on her boat, and she must think I'm terrible.

"To say the least."

The water is calm and alight from the sunshine. Low tendrils of fog still hug the land, obscuring the shoreline. Above the fog, however, the mountains shine purple, distant and high above the water. It's a perfectly beautiful day.

"Oh yeah?" Megan says, prompting me to say more.

"It's Eli—"

"Oh, the photographer. Isn't he great?"

"He's just about the last person I want to see right now."

She glances at me. "Shit, that's happened to me before. No wonder you were babbling up there."

I press my lips together. "That bad?"

"Not to them, I'm sure," Megan says of the tourists. "But Robin said you're amazing, and that whole time I was thinking, *Really?*"

I elbow her, and she chuckles.

"In seriousness, though, just take a deep breath and relax. You're stuck here all day."

"If I jump ship later, don't rescue me."

"If you say so," Megan says, shifting our course slightly.

I climb back down, since I ought to help Joanne. She's passing the wheelhouse as I step down.

"Some breakup," she says. "You're pale."

"That obvious?" I ask.

"Only to someone who knows you."

Eli knows me in some ways better than anyone else. He *definitely* must've noticed.

She leans in close. "It's not your kid, is it?"

"What? No," I say. "Not mine."

"Okay, okay," she says, raising her hands. "I won't pry."

On edge, I head back into the main seating area, where the rows of tourists are chatting among themselves. I give them my spiel about spotting whales: what to look for, how to alert the group, and what species to expect. I don't want to get their hopes up, so I don't mention the superpod, but I allow my own excitement to seep into my voice and fuel a quick lesson on the other animals we'll see throughout the day.

As we make our way up to Friday Harbor, I avoid the starboard side of the boat at all costs. Joanne seems to notice and covers for me over by Eli, no more questions asked. The morning carries on somewhat uneventfully. We see a Steller sea lion bull lounging in the sun on a depth marker buoy and pause for ten minutes for the kids to get a good look. A few squeal when the bull wakes up and flops into the water with a splash. I hear the snap of Eli's lens. Harbor seals and an eagle also make an appearance, but no whales. Islands, in Canadian waters. A prickle of disappointment makes my stomach clench. Megan makes the decision to head toward Friday Harbor first so the tourists can wander around and get lunch.

Rounding the outer hook of the cove, we slide through the narrow channel into the bowl of the harbor. The Anacortes ferry is loading with cars, and countless sailboats line the floating docks. Off to one side, a long pier stretches out toward the mouth of the marina on great barnacle-crusted pylons. The town of Friday Harbor, charming and colorful, is built on a slant; from our vantage, the whole quaint sprawl is in view, climbing back toward the rural hills beyond. The sun is high now, and the tourist-catered streets are dotted with people.

By the time we arrive at the pier, the guests have gotten restless; a faint air of chagrin has spread throughout the group at the lack of whale sightings. As Captain Megan maneuvers us up against the dock with the help of Joanne, I address the group with an update, telling them we'll have a couple of hours in town before going on a whale hunt this afternoon. I remind them that the whales are wild and expecting to know their every move is unrealistic. Part of the beauty of seeing these pods *is* that they're wild and happy and free.

"That's what makes us so lucky to see them when we do," I say, before detailing the location of the Whale Museum in Friday Harbor, emphasizing the allure of these creatures, as well as the important research being done to preserve their habitats.

"Return promptly by one o'clock," I remind them as they file out the door. Unsmiling with her usual pinched expression, Joanne helps the unbalanced few step off the deck, giving me a chance to hide from Eli.

Once the boat is unloaded, Megan, Joanne, and I have a chance to relax and plan the afternoon. We sit down on the roof of the boat, right in the heat of the sun, a map spread between us. I break out the lunches I bought earlier, handing out our respective meals. As Megan checks her phone for Canadian whale updates, I dig into the salmon dip that Zack suggested. Of course, it's amazing. With fondness, I scoop a large glop onto a bagel chip and chomp it all down in one bite.

The sparkling water, the June sunshine, the delicious food—I should feel content, or even joyous, but Eli has put me on edge. When I returned to Washington, I thought upon seeing him, all those feelings I'd had would come rushing back. But in his presence today, all I felt was emptiness. And shame. And guilt. Nothing approaching the yearning or excitement I once experienced. This realization fills me with sadness. My interest in Eli was fleeting; he wasn't worth the ruin of my marriage.

"Abby? Earth to Abby," Megan is saying.

"Huh?" I blink in the sunlight.

"Jeez, lost in thought much?" Megan says.

"I guess so," I say. "What did I miss?"

"We're going to head north after this," Joanne says. "They're definitely in the Georgia Strait, so here's hoping they come south so we can meet them this afternoon."

"Sounds like a plan," I say, grateful for the distraction. "Any ideas for if we don't see them?"

"Some transients were spotted off of Port Angeles, so if there's no luck, we could detour a little on the way back and hope to see them," Megan says. "Not the greatest idea, but it's an option."

"Humpbacks spotted near north Whidbey too," Joanne says, glancing at her phone.

"Another good alternative," Megan says.

I nod, munching. All those things I yearned for back when I met Eli—spending my time out on the water, the wildlife, the like-minded coworkers—I have that in Sound Adventures. How far I've come since then—and how far I fell in his wake.

If only I could get career and love right at the same time.

~

A little after noon, Megan and Joanne head into town for a few errands while I stay on the *Bobcat* to clean, tidy, and watch over things while everyone is away. I'm humming to myself, reorganizing the snack bar, when I hear the outside gate squeal, the telltale sign of someone climbing aboard. Megan or Joanne probably forgot a purse or something. I continue my task, ducking behind the counter to reach for the chip bags in the cabinet underneath.

While I rifle through the cabinet, I hear the squeak of a chair and the wispy crinkle of a plastic bag near the starboard row of seats—I realize it's not Joanne or Megan but a tourist. They often forget things on the boat but are never so bold as to board when the gate is closed.

I pop up, startled to find that it's Eli.

He jumps. "Jesus."

"What are you doing?" I ask.

Kira, thankfully, is preoccupied with his phone, her feet dangling off her chair. His backpack sags open on his own seat beside her. I glance out the window, hoping to see Joanne and Megan walking back down the pier, but they aren't there. Seagulls line the visible railing undisturbed. We're alone.

"I couldn't find my wallet," Eli says.

"Oh." I point toward the floor, where the base of the chair is bolted down. A lump of brown is resting atop the metal bar. "That it?"

He stoops, leaning to retrieve it. I watch the muscles of his back stretch beneath his shirt as he reaches. The gentle, familiar swirl of his Fibonacci tattoo pokes out from under his T-shirt sleeve. When he stands, he fiddles with his wallet, not looking at me. I turn to continue my snack chore—or really any chore to avoid him—but then he speaks, halting me in my tracks.

"You're not at the bank."

I look around, knowing exactly what he means. My mouth goes dry, and I swallow.

"I'm happy for you," he adds, confirming my thought. "It suits you."

"You're getting a div—?" I break off, glancing toward Kira.

He nods solemnly.

I shake my head, regret filling me up to my neck, a sickly feeling. "I'm so sorry, Eli."

"Don't do that," he says. "Don't look at me with pity."

"I don't—"

"Yes, you do." He holds my stare with tempestuous eyes. "You might not have been invested in us, but I was."

Heat flares in my chest, a swirl of shame and frustration. "Invested? We never defined what this was."

"Don't play stupid," he says. "Maybe we didn't fu—" He breaks off, glances at Kira, then lowers his voice. "Maybe we weren't physical, but we had something."

His words bring our lunch dates into more focus, a wider perspective. I chose to doubt Eli's feelings out of convenience—as long as I didn't know for sure, I didn't have to feel guilty. But now, faced with the reality of our relationship, I'm struck by the wretchedness of the whole thing. How was I so selectively blind? How did I not see the truth in his gestures, the way he used to cradle his coffee cup, touch my arm, glance at my lips? The way he spoke, so softly that I couldn't help but lean toward him across our usual table? Now, the truth is all I see, shining in my eyes like a lighthouse strobe, showing me how close to the rocks I sailed.

I glance at Kira, wondering how much she's heard, but she's preoccupied with her game, the phone screen flashing bright colors.

“I never wanted you to leave your wife,” I say coolly.

“Yes, you did.” His tone is low but sharp. He grabs my wrist and guides me to the opposite side of the boat, farther out of earshot of his daughter but still within sight. “Admit it, Abby. You’re no better than I am. In fact, you’re worse, because you refuse to own up to it. You *wanted* this. You wanted me. And even now, years later, you’re still bullheaded enough to deny the whole fucking thing.”

I flinch at his language. “I *didn’t* want you,” I lie. A familiar lie—one I’ve been telling myself forever.

He chuckles, an ugly, taunting sound. “I don’t buy that for a second.”

“What do you want from me, Eli?” I ask, exasperated. “What do you want?”

The hard lines of his face soften then, surprising me. Suddenly, he looks so defeated. “Tell me this wasn’t all in my head.”

His words shoot through me like hot water through ice. “Of course I felt something,” I say. “Of *course* I did. But if you want me to say that it was all worth it . . .” I shake my head. “I would give back every minute with you, if that would undo all the damage done.”

His jaw clenches, and he nods, a harsh and singular motion. His lips are pursed, and his cheeks are puffed out slightly. My heart feels like a brick being eroded by the sea, wave after wave of regret eating it away into dust. Eli turns to go. He grabs the phone from Kira’s protesting fingers, gathers his bags off the seat, and ushers his daughter out into the bright sun of the hot June afternoon.

When I came home, I thought he’d bring solace. But now, having truly seen him, I realize he isn’t the answer. I’m responsible.

2013

Dennis was waiting for me in the kitchen when I got home. He was boiling water for some sort of pasta dinner, a jar of pesto and a box of noodles placed on the counter near a handful of other ingredients. I smelled garlic, tomato. When he heard me come in, he dropped his knife on the cutting board with a clatter and rushed over to me, his face stricken.

"My thoughts have been running wild all day," he said. "What happened?"

My nose was red and my eyes raw from sobbing on the way home. Exhausted by my self-inflicted agony, I shuffled past him and sank into a chair at the dinner table. He sat, too, dragging his seat closer so he could place one hand on my knee and the other over my cold and shaking fingers.

"Abby, you're scaring me."

What could I say to him? That I was unhappy? He'd only ask why, and I wouldn't be able to form an answer. I hadn't cheated, not in the true sense of the word, but Jackie had seen me come close and would tell him if I couldn't. None of it—any of it—seemed to make up one whole train of thought. All the pieces of this mess were scattered across the floor in opposite directions. He grasped my shoulders, forcing me to look into his eyes. They were pleading; they tore me up inside.

Tears brimmed, and I lowered my head, leaning forward into the solidity of his chest. We sat for a moment this way, him stroking my hair while I cried into his shirt. I tried to hold on to the feeling of his love and comfort. I tried to burn it into my mind so that even if I told him about Eli and things were never the same again, I'd still have the memory.

Burning garlic delayed my need for words: Dennis stood abruptly, stirring the smoking pan before removing it from the burner. He turned off the stove and sat back down, wiping his hands on a towel. I'd never seen his face look so pinched, so solemn. I hesitated, frantically trying to savor this moment, the moment of his unknowing. It was like memorizing the contours of a glass before throwing it against the hardwood so that maybe after the damage was done, I could remember its curvature and glue it back together. "I've been having lunch with a bank customer," I said, my voice barely audible. "A few times a week for the past seven months. He's a photographer."

Dennis's brow wrinkled, but he didn't speak.

"I wasn't with Chrissy on Saturday night; I was at Gallery Walk—with him." The words were oily in my mouth.

"You cheated on me?"

"No," I said with force. Then again more softly: "No."

"Then why did you lie to me?"

"I didn't cheat, Dennis," I said. "We only ever talked. But I started to . . ." I trailed off, looking away.

"You started to what?"

"Feel," I said.

A faint twitch of his mouth made my heart stop. Then he said, "What does Jackie have to do with this?"

"She saw us today, having lunch. He tried to kiss me." The words felt like a lie—I'd wanted to kiss Eli too. "I pushed him away before he could, but Jackie saw."

Dennis coughed; his eyes were reddening. "So, what, do you love this other guy?"

My throat swelled, and I blinked. "No," I replied, and it felt like the truth. It *had* to be the truth. "But Dennis, I'm not happy."

I watched a tear slide down his acne-scarred, clenched jaw. "Is it me? Can I change?"

I'd expected him to be angry or hurt—not desperate. "I don't know," I said.

"Is this about work, or is this about me?"

I stared out across the kitchen, toward the front door. I longed to get up and step over the threshold, out into the lavender evening. Absence was the only way I could imagine surviving the dreadful night ahead. I hated what our marriage—our lives—had become. Distance seemed to be the only answer. "Both? Everything feels numb lately."

He grasped my shoulders, his hands firm, shaking me just a little. "Numb?" he asked. "You're numb? What is that supposed to mean? Do you not feel me? Do you not love me anymore?"

I recoiled from his angry desperation, flooded with doubt. I remembered when he'd proposed, the slight hesitation I'd felt. I remembered all the little times when I'd felt apprehensive or held back or stuck. In that moment, they seemed to outweigh the good times tenfold. While I didn't want to hurt him just then, I didn't want to sink into his embrace either.

"This isn't fair to you, Dennis." The words seemed to come of their own volition. "You deserve someone who doesn't have any doubts."

"What doubts? Abby, why didn't you tell me any of this sooner?"

"It's not fair to you for me to feel this way," I said, pulling my arms free of his grasp.

"But I want *you*," he whispered. "Why is all this coming up now? Can't we talk through it? Can't we try?" He reached for me, hands grabbing for my own, but I sat back, unable to let myself succumb to his grip again.

"I want some time apart," I said.

Finally, he stopped trying to touch me. He slumped back in his chair, his face reddened but with no more fresh tears. "Is that what you really want?"

I felt so foggy, so lost. Like swimming through murky water, afraid of what might appear out of the abyss.

"Yes," I told him.

His lips pressed together, forming a white line. "I'll give you the space you need, but I'm not signing divorce papers."

I shook my head and stood. Sitting before me, Dennis represented every regret. My tanked career, my uncertainty, my lack of daring—all of it rested on his shoulders. I'd been so afraid of losing him that I'd lost sight of myself. Time apart seemed like the only answer.

Dennis said, "We can fix this together."

"I don't know if we can."

"You don't mean that."

"I do," I said. "It didn't happen overnight, but my feelings . . . they changed." I knew my words hurt him, but it was the only way he'd understand. "Things have been stagnant for so long, Dennis. Didn't you notice? Didn't you hear me? This isn't working, and it's not fair to either of us." I stepped toward the door then, grabbing my purse from the coat hook.

"You're damn right it's not fair." His chair scraped against the floor as he hurriedly stood.

I stepped out into the chilly twilight. "I'll be at Chrissy's."

He yelled after me, "How can I be sure you're not lying?"

I didn't dignify his words with a response. I threw my car into gear and peeled away. Dennis, standing on the porch, shrank in my rearview mirror. My chest constricted, so achingly upset by the whole ordeal. But more frightening was the creeping relief I felt tingling in my fingertips.

2018

I hide in the bathroom and splash cold water on my face while Joanne and Megan load the tourists onto the *Bobcat* for the afternoon. We're underway when I emerge from the head, most of the redness gone from under my eyes. Joanne is up front, explaining to the guests what the afternoon holds. I plant myself in an outdoor chair on the stern, not wanting to see Eli even from afar. The wind whips at my face, making me feel a little more alive again. I'm so battered and drained from earlier that the cold, salty air is a cleanse to my senses.

I stare out at the green-blue water, the frothy wake of the *Bobcat* unfurling white wings behind us. Despite the speed of the boat, the sun still manages to reach my bare legs with warmth. Friday Harbor becomes an emerald curve behind us, the white boats like a string of bobbing pearls as we speed away.

"Thanks for covering for me," I say when Joanne steps over the threshold.

She settles in the chair beside me. "I'll need your help this afternoon."

I give her a long, loaded glance.

"What happened between you two? Eli seems like such a nice guy."

"I know I need to buck up," I say. "I just can't stand the thought of seeing him again."

"Well, you have to," Joanne says. "We're paying for his promotional photos, you know."

I didn't realize he did gigs like this, but it makes sense. Divorces are expensive.

Joanne stands. "Play lookout with Megan in the wheelhouse for a while—I'll wrangle the tourists."

I stand, too, the backs of my knees tingly. "Thanks."

"Hey, I get it. I've been through my fair share of breakups."

She's right—everyone has. And somehow, that reminder is a comfort.

2013

I arrived at Chrissy and Nick's house tear streaked and altogether torn. My relief had faded with the distance, and now I simply felt weary. I knocked on the door, realizing that I didn't have a bag packed. I was still wearing my work clothes.

Nick answered. "Abby?" His face went from relaxed joy to a tight, concerned look of confusion.

"Who is it, babe?" came Chrissy's voice from the other room. Then she rounded the bend.

Wordlessly, I fell into her embrace, a new wave of sobs convulsing my chest. She stroked my back, and Nick closed the door, wrapping us both in a hug that swayed for a good long while in their foyer.

"Sweetheart, can you brew some tea?" Chrissy asked him finally, and he broke away, shuffling toward the kitchen.

Chrissy led me to their couch, her arm wrapped firmly around me, not slipping for a second. When I was seated, she spread a blanket over my lap and hurried off, only to come back moments later with a box of tissues. Their dog, Ginger, came over to rest her soft chin on my knee.

"Tell me all about it," Chrissy said.

I did my best, my voice shaky and broken and hiccuping with emotion. I told her about the encounter with Eli, about Jackie, and finally about how I'd told Dennis. A teapot whistle sounded, and a minute later, Nick came in with a tray of steaming mugs. He sat down beside us, and Ginger returned to her dog bed in the corner.

"I hope chamomile is all right." He rubbed my back and handed me a mug.

I nodded, burying my face in a tissue. I felt so tired, so deeply and achingly tired. I missed Dennis vaguely, the comfort of his arms—but then that realization set me off into another tailspin of sorrow. Could I live without him? Was that better than the stagnancy of staying? He'd said we could work it out, but how? I didn't see a way for us to make it work without significant compromise—without one of us being miserable. Eli had made me realize just how deeply eroded my marriage had become. While I loved Dennis, I wasn't happy.

Miles offshore from any certainty about anything, all I knew for sure was the desperate urge to get out of my wretched work clothes.

"Do you have any pajamas I can borrow?" I asked Chrissy.

She sat a little straighter. "Fuzzy, flannel, or shorts?"

"The baggiest, coziest," I said.

"Be right back." She hopped up and disappeared.

Nick patted my arm. "Cream or honey for that tea?"

I curled my legs under myself, settling beside him. "It's perfect as is."

"Love is dumb," he said softly, leaning back.

I'd comforted him similarly once in high school. He'd been dumped by Naomi Weston, who'd told the whole school that he had an STD, when in reality it was the other way around (Nick wasn't embarrassed to admit that they'd never slept together). He'd sat on Chrissy's couch, and we'd stayed up late eating raw store-bought cookie dough and trash-talking Naomi. Around midnight, after getting into Chrissy's mom's liquor cabinet, Nick had begun to cry. It wasn't just the rumor, he'd said. It was that he hadn't been man enough to date her. I'd told him, "Love is dumb." He was a great guy, and Naomi was a bitch.

So when Nick said, "You're a great person. Dennis is a bitch," tea dribbled out of my mouth. I coughed and wiped my face. Nick chuckled.

Chrissy came back into the room holding a stack of folded pajamas. "Laughter?"

"Remember Naomi Weston?" I said, blotting my shirt.

"She's a bitch," Chrissy said without pause, and we all laughed. "Does this mean we're breaking out the cookie dough and peppermint schnapps?"

"No way," Nick said. "I threw up that night, remember?"

"That is burned in my memory forever," Chrissy said, coming to stand beside him. "I almost didn't marry you over it."

He gave her a nudge.

"Why don't I remember that?" I asked.

"You were passed out by then," Chrissy said.

I sipped my tea, recalling that night and how the next morning I'd woken up nauseated. It was strange to think about those days before Dennis.

Chrissy handed me the stack of pajamas. "I brought options."

Unfolding my legs, I stood and went into the bathroom to change. I could hear the two of them speaking softly to each other on the couch, little chuckles and notes of conversation. It gave me a sad, longing, achy feeling.

In the bathroom, I thumbed through the pajamas, finally settling on a baggy old Chimacum High School tee and a pair of blue plaid bottoms. I carried the rest of the stack to Chrissy and Nick's bedroom, then returned to the living room.

"Five bucks," Chrissy said to Nick when I came out.

"Aw, c'mon, Abby," he said.

I sat back down, nestling myself in the deep corner of their sectional. "What did I do?"

Chrissy scooted closer and handed me my tea. "I bet him five bucks that you'd choose that exact shirt-and-pants combo."

"Am I *that* predictable?" I asked.

Nick was shaking his head, a grin still crinkling his eyes, but Chrissy got serious then, her mouth drawn down in a frown. I knew what she was thinking: while I might be predictable in things like pajamas and breakfast food, I was pointedly unpredictable when it came to Dennis and Eli. Her expression brought me down from the temporary high of their company and the memories of teenagerhood. Even Ginger let out a long sigh, shifting her head on her paw, her eyes drifting shut again. Nick was the last to recognize the turn in mood, but when he did, he spread the blanket over the three of us and sipped his tea.

"You can stay here as long as you like, Abby," he said, always the practical one.

"Coincidentally, I just washed the guest bed sheets," Chrissy said.

"I don't think I'll be able to sleep." I dropped my head onto Chrissy's shoulder. "I've made such a mess."

"Sometimes that's necessary for change," she said. "Sometimes a mess is better than perfect misery."

I started to weep softly again. I hated to think that I'd hurt Dennis or Eli but knew for certain that I had. In one day, I'd broken two hearts—three if I counted my own. Even then, I could feel mine pulling in two different directions. "Is this really for the best?"

Chrissy stroked my hair, and Nick took the mug from my hands, replacing it with a tissue.

"It'll all work out the way it's supposed to," Chrissy said.

I didn't believe her, but I appreciated the sentiment.

~

Around nine o'clock, Chrissy suggested I lie down and try to sleep. "You need clarity, and the only way you'll get it is by resting."

My head was pounding, so I nodded and followed her into the guest room. Chrissy tucked me in with a mess of pillows and blankets, Nick turned off the lights, and they shut the door. I closed my eyes, but even though the bed was a cocoon of warmth, I couldn't sleep. I hadn't faced the depth of my relationship with Eli until today. The look on his face, pained and confused, had shown it all so plainly. There was no going back to our comfortable but undefined limbo—what had happened today had planted my feet firmly on the ground, and there was no hiding from what I'd done.

Yet I'd blindsided Dennis. We'd fallen into a routine, and he was perfectly comfortable there. He *knew* I hated the bank job, and yet day to day, it hadn't seemed to make a difference to him. It was easier than my being more adventurous. I felt almost angry with him over his heart surgery, too—almost. I'd been terrified to do anything, go anywhere. Jackie's blame and pressure toward staying had squandered any leftover ambition I had. I refused to believe that my misery had been 100 percent self-inflicted. It was a conglomeration of fear and guilt and regret, imposed by all sides—myself, Dennis, Jackie—that'd wedged me into this tight place.

The pounding in my head grew worse. With a lurch, I recalled the good times too. Working on the house together, the afternoons making love, the laughter and Sunday breakfasts. It hadn't all been bad, had it? Memories played along my eyelids as I finally slipped toward the cushy nothingness of sleep. It all blurred together: happiness, frustration, grief, guilt, joy, and love. Teetering on the edge of sleep that night, it all seemed like such a fluke. Unlikely, wretched, yet somehow also fortunate.

2018

In the wheelhouse, I keep the binoculars pressed firmly over my eyes, searching the vast, rippling lines of the Salish Sea for a disturbance. Megan slows down as we approach Canadian waters, then swings around so we can skirt the invisible aquatic border, heading west. The sun glares from the south, a shimmering, blinding streak across the calm ocean. It's really a perfect day for whale watching. With the slower pace, tourists emerge from indoors to hang out on the bow in the sunshine.

I'm the first one to spot them, first a single black fin, then another, then too many to count. I tell Captain Megan to turn the boat, and on cue, Joanne pops her head in.

"Northeast," I tell her.

She disappears, and I return my gaze to the calm ocean.

With the binoculars lifted to my eyes, I strain to find them again. The blurry, rippling blue is hard on my depth perception, but then another fin—much closer than before—marks their direction. Megan maneuvers the boat so that the orcas will pass in front of us at about four hundred yards away—a respectful distance that puts us well out of their path. In case there are more whales in the area, Megan cuts the engines. I can tell they're southern residents by the gentle and curved dorsal fins, and this encounter gives me goose bumps. Less than one hundred individuals remain of this unique community—it's a blessing to see them.

A group of four females surfaces next, heads bobbing up out of the water with puffs of breath. I can hear tourists cheering on the bow.

"Better help her out," Captain Megan says, referring to Joanne.

"Right, yes." I hurry out of the wheelhouse, slinging the binoculars around my neck.

The heavy door to the front deck has already been swung and locked open, the ocean breeze filling the enclosed cabin. Joanne has gathered everyone out on the bow, with people pointing and squealing. As I step outside amid the hubbub of tourists, I glance around for Eli. Joanne has Kira in tow, answering questions; Eli has climbed up to the roof, crouched near the windows of the wheelhouse on the wide white expanse, his camera lens—longer than his arm—pointed toward the sea. I hear it snap. I turn my head before he notices me looking.

The *Bobcat* has a relatively small bow, but the standing bleachers make use of the space. Tourists line either side of the narrow center walkway, gripping the rails, leaning forward, craning their necks for a glimpse. Joanne is among them, carrying the ID catalog so the tourists can look. The laminated pages are filled with image after image of saddle patch markings. As she weaves through the jubilant throngs of whale watchers, she explains all this information with ease.

When she spots me, she says, "We're seeing Js and Ks." She hands me the book.

Another handful of orcas surfaces on the starboard side, close. I can hear the rain of water following their loud spouts of breath, a hiss of droplets hitting the calm sea. The whole group gasps. The piercing cry of a child onboard rises above the eager cheers of the guests. Another few whales surface and dive—my guess is ten in all, so far.

I glance at the book, having not yet memorized the whole population. A large male darts close, and I ID him as K35, nicknamed Sonata; he's followed by a female, perhaps his mother, Opus. A spunky tail slap makes me swivel left; I catch a glimpse of three J-pod whales: Slick (J16) and daughter Alki (J36), plus one more with a smoky-looking saddle patch. Across the rows of excited tourists, I make eye contact with Joanne. She grins and gives me two thumbs up.

The whales disappear, and the whole group hushes, waiting. Water sloshes along the hull of the boat, a metallic swish and plunk. In a world that is chaotic and cruel and loud, it's humbling to see a group of nearly fifty strangers fall absolutely silent in anticipation. It happens on every tour, the guests—even the children—holding their breath in wait. Then the exhale, the squeal of relief, when the orcas make their appearance once more. There is nothing as breathtaking as animals in the wild.

Everyone is surprised by a breach. Some guests probably missed it, while others clap, saying, "Did you see that? Did you see that?" Another breach has them erupting with joy. "There! *There!*"

Joanne catches Megan's attention from the bow, and through the glare of the wheelhouse window, I see Megan make a circle with her thumb and index finger: A-OK. The whales have changed directions significantly, with more coming from behind us, and I know my coworkers' exchange without being a part of it: Megan won't be able to engage the engines again until the whales are well on their way. We aren't allowed to intentionally maneuver this close, so the proximity of the whales is an extremely special accident. For the whales' safety, we have no choice but to sit and enjoy.

A little girl near me, clinging to the rail, squeals as a pair of females surfaces only twenty yards from the boat. I can see the white underbelly of a third, twisting underwater, checking us out. I stand back, a little breathless, allowing other tourists to fill my gap by the railing.

Another, closer breach sends everyone into a bout of cheers. My fun facts are silenced by the ongoing presence of the whales—I'm completely upstaged, and I'm glad. Even Mary, who looked so weak earlier, appears enlivened, peering off the rail with Becca holding her arm. The boat is soon surrounded, the whales passing under and around us. A few Canadian tour boats pause on the edge of the superpod, binoculars raised.

"Abby," Eli says from up top, pointing.

A twinge zings through my belly. Why would he call to me, after our earlier conversation? I follow his gaze, searching the water, and then I see something strange: the orangey color of a newborn orca's belly, the nudging nose of an adult female, and the fin of a third. Joanne and I lock eyes in confusion. The trio disappears. Something is wrong.

"Go up top," Joanne says, pointing toward Eli.

I shake my head. I'd really rather not, but I don't have a say, and Joanne's scowl affirms that fact. She grabs the boat microphone from inside and flips it on, narrating to the whole group. There hasn't been news of a baby, so this is fresh information.

At the mercy of the current, we drift closer to the strange trio. I climb up to the roof and plant myself a few yards from Eli, as far from him as I can. He doesn't look up from his viewfinder. I raise the binoculars to my eyes and swivel my head. Then, so close to the same place we first saw them, a female surfaces again. Then the second, the baby propped up on her rostrum. She carries it for a few beats, and then the baby slips sideways off her nose and into the sea.

The baby is dead.

The realization is a stab to the gut. A profound feeling of loss grips my throat and strangles my words. In this endangered population, every birth is significant. There are so many reasons this could have happened, but the most likely is malnutrition. The orcas are starving from lack of salmon and being poisoned by pollution. It's no wonder no calves have survived in the past few years. Yet with the scene unfolding before me, I am forced to set aside the abstractions of science—what I see now is a distraught mother. An individual in mourning.

Eli lies on his belly, propped up by his elbows. He glances toward me, concern lining his stricken face.

"Keep taking pictures," I choke out. "Researchers . . ." I trail off, horrified.

"Got it," he says, looking through his lens again.

I peer through the binoculars again, waiting. The next time they pop up, I see bite marks on the baby's tail. Recalling a similar story from years ago, I wonder if the other female midwifed the birth. I ID the nonmother as J46, Star, and spot her grandmother farther off. If the whole family group is here, the mother and baby must be J-pod whales. I rack my brain but haven't memorized the family groups enough to piece together what's going on.

Meanwhile, Joanne is doing her best to explain the odd sight. Some tourists are distracted by other orcas. We're still surrounded, too many to count, their appearances punctuating the macabre scene with the baby.

"Is it grief?" Eli asks me, a whisper. He's still gazing through his camera

"Yes."

Scientists warn against attributing human emotion to big, likable animals—but a mother nudging her baby along, pushing it toward the surface for breath, seems like it goes beyond scientific definitions and the excuse of instinct. Deep in my heart, I know these animals are capable of feelings like love and sadness. What else could this be but grief?

The whole tour boat watches in relative silence. For the next twenty minutes, the converging pods put on a display, but most of us are distracted by the mother. I wonder if the scene is too dark for the children on the tour; I hear Joanne answering Kira's questions with careful simplicity. I doubt Eli's daughter has grasped the full complexity; she seems antsy in the quiet. A few feet from Joanne and Kira, Becca catches my eye, then Mary. Their faces are solemn too. Overcome, I blink, staring toward the blinding, sun-splashed ocean to burn back my tears.

I feel a hand touch my back; Eli has come closer. His touch is unwelcome, but at the same time, I'm heartened by his gesture of comfort.

For a long while, we watch as the mother nudges her baby along. The exuberant pod members disappear first, shrinking into the distant ripples, obscured by distance. The trio gradually moves away from our boat, too, in a more erratic path. Captain Megan waits until mother and baby are well past us before engaging the *Bobcat*'s engines. I climb down from the roof to help Joanne answer more questions on the bow. Eli fiddles with his camera still up top.

"Why are the pods broken up as they are?" someone asks me. She has the look of a Portland housewife, outdoorsy with a toddler on her hip, her strawberry hair windswept.

I'm glad for an inquiry that isn't about the orca baby. "They're matriarchal family groups, broken up into smaller family clans. Offspring will travel with their mothers and grandmothers their whole lives if they can."

"What happens when a mother dies? Where do the offspring go?"

"They'll stick together." I pause. "In some cases, if all the other family members have passed, the remaining whale will join another clan. We've seen that happen a few times."

Her face turns solemn. I can tell she wants to ask about the baby. "What about when—"

She's cut off by the unmistakable thump of a fall, knees or elbows hitting the deck. Then a shriek—and not a shriek of joy. At first, I assume a kid tripped, but turning from my conversation, I see a crowd forming and push through. Mary is on her back, breathing shallowly. A bruise is already blooming across her temple. Her frail body seems even tinier lying in the middle of the deck. I crouch beside Becca and touch Mary's cheek. Her eyes are closed.

"Joanne," I call, my voice coming out much more strained and desperate than I intend.

Becca says, "Mom? Can you hear me? Mom?"

A tourist pushes through the crowd, claiming to be a nurse. She takes Mary's pulse and gently wedges a balled-up jacket under her head. Megan accelerates the *Bobcat* south toward Orcas Island. I hear someone say that there's a new clinic there—the closest option.

Amid the blur of commotion, the nurse tells Becca and me that we need to get Mary inside. Eli and another man offer their strength, and she's carefully lifted indoors. In a daze, I herd the other tourists inside as well and lock the door to the deck. Once it's closed, Megan throttles the boat even faster, the wind whistling outside.

I'm relieved to see a twitch in Mary's fingers as the nurse and Becca tend to her. My shock subsiding, I spring into action. I get the other guests seated, offer snacks, and try to exude an air of calm. Joanne helps, bouncing from row to row to check in, while everyone else's focus remains on the delicate woman lying in the middle of the floor.

I haven't spoken to Mary much on this trip, nor Becca. Should I have checked in more? Did my preoccupation with Eli blind me to a sign that something was amiss? I think of the mother whale nudging her baby. The fragility of life. The unexpected twists and turns.

Eli comes up beside me but says nothing. What is there to talk about, after this intense day? What comfort can he bring me? None, I realize. It's not possible. I thought that when I came back, I'd see him, and somehow he'd tell me what I needed to know. He'd fix things for me. But that's not the case. He may have opened my eyes to the things I'd been putting off, the things I truly wanted, but he wasn't the answer. He never was.

It's a frenzy of tense waiting as Megan navigates us to the nearest hospital. Finally, we dock, and medics are there waiting. They board and efficiently whisk Mary and Becca away. When they're gone, the whole group of us left on the *Bobcat* stands in startled silence, whispers cascading.

"Hi, everyone," Megan says when she returns from chatting with a medic. "Let's get seated now."

People settle into their chairs, sagging with a release of tension, their mouths pressed shut, save for a confused, harried child who chirps with worry. Her parents shush her until the whole cabin falls silent.

Megan clears her throat, then raises her voice. "We're going to take the rest of you back to Port Townsend. We should return on schedule."

She leaves it at that, heading to the wheelhouse to get us out of the harbor. Joanne disappears too. I'm left with all eyes on me, my emotions run ragged.

Someone asks, "Will you have to get them later?"

"I'm not sure; she may have to be airlifted," I answer.

A few tourists gasp, clearly unsettled by the idea.

"The medics assured us she'll be fine," I lie. I didn't speak to the medics at all, but it's a comforting thought, one that settles the tourists and eases my own fears just a little bit. I imagine seeing Mary later, helping her onto the *Bobcat*, her hand in mine just as always.

2013

I woke up disoriented and heavy at one a.m. to loud arguing. A man's voice—not Nick's but familiar. Dennis's voice. Dennis?

I sat up, dizzy with sleep, and placed my feet on the floor. I tried to make out the words, but they were muffled. My head felt as if it were stuffed with cotton. I stood.

In the hall, the voices were louder, and I realized that they were coming from the front of the house. Ginger was whining. I padded over the carpet and spotted Nick and Chrissy, the front door open, arguing with Dennis. Despite my grogginess, I could tell by his voice that he was drunk. I'd *never* seen him so much as sip a drink.

"I don't believe you," he was saying. "You're covering for her. She must be out fucking that other guy."

"She's trying to *sleep*," Chrissy said hotly.

I nudged between my friends, making my presence known. Dennis was red faced and smelled like beer, but his shoulders relaxed when he saw me.

"Abby," he said. "You're here. You were telling the truth."

"Of course I was," I said.

"They wouldn't let me come in to see you."

"She needs rest," Chrissy said defensively.

"Like *I'm* the bad guy. Like *I'm* the one in the wrong." Dennis turned to me again, his anger softening. "Abby, please come home. We need to talk this through. We need to work this out. You're my wife; we're—"

"Sleep it off, Dennis," Nick said, standing between us. "She's here because she wants distance. If you can't respect that—"

"Shut up, Nick," Dennis said.

I'd never heard him speak so harshly in my life. "D, I need space. Please go home. We can talk in the morning."

He checked his watch. "It's morning right now."

"*Later* in the morning," I insisted.

"So I go home, and what?"

"Sleep it off," Nick repeated.

"Can someone take you home?" I asked. "Can you call Eduardo?"

"I'm fine. I can drive," Dennis said.

"No, you're not," I said. "Call Eduardo."

Under our watch, Dennis called his friend, who agreed to pick him up. Nick had to relay their address. It would take Eduardo ten minutes to get there.

After hanging up, Dennis reached out for me. "Wait with me, Abby?" His chest seized with a dry sob. "Please, just . . . wait with me here?"

"I can wait with him," Nick said to me.

"No, it's all right. You two can go back inside." I stepped past Nick and Chrissy and sat on their top porch step; Dennis sat beside me, clutching the porch railing to steady himself—he'd spent his whole life sober, and he likely had the spins.

Nick seemed to hesitate, but when I looked up at them once more, they acquiesced and went inside, the door clicking shut. I suspected Nick would wait up, listening on the other side, but I didn't feel threatened by Dennis. I felt responsible for my husband's misery. Sitting with him was the least I could do; I owed him that much.

Dennis sighed, leaning toward me a little, but he didn't touch me. The neighborhood was still, all the porch lights off except for the one we sat beneath; rings of moths fluttered above our heads in the light like chaotic little halos. The stars were crisp and twinkling, and wispy clouds stretched low over the rooftops. The air was chilly, but I didn't dare go inside for a coat.

"How do you feel?" I asked.

Dennis was slumped against the railing, clearly nauseated. "Broken."

"I meant—"

"I know what you meant," he said, not looking at me. After a pause, he said, "There are so many fewer stars in town."

I studied the sky. It was true—the lights from town drowned out the distant layers of stars. We were used to many more, our house being tucked into the rural woods, up on the ridge and away from other sources of light.

"Yeah," I agreed.

"You can't blame me for wanting you to stay close to home," Dennis said abruptly. "The heart problems scared me too." There was water in his throat, making his voice thick and pitiful. "What am I supposed to do without you, Abby? I love you."

My insides seized. I touched his back, trying to form a response.

Dennis's phone rang. "Yeah?" he answered. "What? Oh. I think you missed the turn. I'll walk out to the main road. Okay. Yep, see you soon." He hung up and wobbled to his feet. "Eduardo's turning around. I'm going to walk to him."

I stood, too, suddenly reluctant to let him go.

"Please come home tomorrow, Abby," Dennis said, touching my cheek.

I closed my eyes briefly, and then his hand fell from my face, and he stepped off the porch. I watched him walk away, my chest torn wide open. His shoulders were hunched, and he walked crooked, straightening out every few yards. Then he went around the corner and was gone.

The night was peaceful and silent. I didn't want to leave the porch; in that moment, I didn't want to leave Dennis either. But I knew how the night could make the heart lonelier. I knew how easy it was to swim with the current, even if it was better to swim against.

Turning the knob to go back inside, though, I hesitated. I looked back once more, hoping Dennis would still be there, but the little street was empty.

~

When I went back inside, my friends had both been waiting up after all. Chrissy offered me a tissue, and I wiped my nose. We all retreated back to bed, and once I was tucked under the guest covers, I could hear Chrissy and Nick talking softly to each other in the neighboring room. For the next half hour, I tossed and turned, unable to succumb to sleep. I was desperately tired but, at the same time, haunted by Dennis's visit. I longed to see him. I longed to feel his arms wrapped around me. I longed to apologize to him, to sink back into our lives together, to find a way to make it work. And the more I tried to sleep, the stronger that longing became.

Finally, I sat up, giving up on sleep. It was 2:03 a.m. I shuffled into the bathroom, flushed, and wandered out into the house to find my purse and coat.

Nick was there, wearing only boxers, drinking water at the sink. "Abby?" he said. "Can't sleep?"

"I'm going home," I said.

He set down the glass. "You—what?"

"I need to go home," I said. "This is insane. I love him."

He shifted uneasily. The oven clock cast a faint green light across his bare chest. "You should sleep on it, Abby. There's a reason you left this evening. Why not wait until you're fully rested?"

I shook my head. "I was wrong earlier," I said. "I'm certain now."

"Well, I'm not going to stop you," he said. "Are you okay to drive? You won't fall asleep?"

"If I can't fall asleep in your guest bed, I doubt—"

"All right," he said. "Text me when you're home?"

I nodded, stepping forward for a quick hug. His arms surrounded me, squeezing tightly. "I'll tell Chrissy."

"Once I'm gone?" I said with a little grin. We both knew she'd protest my going—she was headstrong like that.

He sighed. "You're going to get me in trouble."

"Thanks, Nick," I said.

"Just text me when you're there," he said. "I hope you're doing what's right."

"Me too," I said and slipped out the door into the night.

2018

After the tourists disembark in Port Townsend and the parking lot is empty, Joanne and Megan leave to gas up the *Bobcat* and call the other Sound Adventures crew with the news of Mary. I insist on going with them, but Eli's been lingering in the parking lot. I emerge from the lower docks in no mood to talk to him, my heart achy, but I know he's waiting for me.

Walking toward him across the gravel road, I sigh. The sticky heat of the day is wearing off, the breeze tousling my hair. I meet Eli's eyes across the parking lot, and he straightens. Behind him, the clouds stretch above in hues of light-laced peach, lavender, pink.

"Hey," I say, stopping a few feet away.

"Hey," he says.

Kira's in the back seat, nestled up with his camera bags playing another iPhone game.

"I'm sorry about earlier."

He shrugs.

"I'm sorry how we keep leaving things."

He bristles. "I considered getting a charter flight home from Friday Harbor."

"Why didn't you?"

"The job," he says.

"You waited for me here, though."

"I did."

"Why?"

"I want to know I'm not crazy, Abby. I want to know that this wasn't all in my head." He holds my eyes with his, penetrating, firm.

There is no room for denial anymore, not so long after the damage was done. *Affair* is the only word that applies to those afternoons together. He knew me. He *understood* me. And worse, he understood the parts of me that Dennis never truly had. Eli and I craved each other physically *and* mentally. Though we didn't touch, we fell for each other. What else could that be, other than an affair? *We had an affair.* At least Eli was brave enough to admit it.

"It wasn't all in your head," I admit.

Eli crosses his arms. "That's a relief."

"You . . . you saved my sanity."

"I'm not a psychiatrist."

"I was in denial. Denial about what was happening between us. Denial about my marriage. Had I asked Dennis—" I don't finish that thought. "Eli, I'd convinced myself this wasn't what it was. I'd convinced myself—"

"I know." He softens then, his brow unfurrowing. "I know."

"I apologize," I say. "Sincerely. Your marriage . . ."

"It was bound to happen. Hell, it lasted this long."

I nod. "I thought if we never did anything physical, I wouldn't hurt Dennis."

"You loved him," he says. "I can understand that." He steps closer and touches my shoulder, a tender gesture.

I loved Eli too. I loved him—and yet I think I loved the fantasy of him even more. I loved his company, his ideas, his interests, but he represented something greater, and that's what seduced me. In a time when I felt the most trapped in my life, Eli stood for liberation. His travels, his stories, the way we fell into conversation and the whole world disappeared around us—*that's* what I loved most. The role he played, the freedom he taught me was within reach, if only I extended my hand. I realize this now, after this wretched day. After arguing in Friday Harbor, after his hand touched my back and it didn't feel as lovely as I thought it would. After seeing him with his daughter.

I might've loved Eli, but I was *in love* with Dennis. He was my best friend, my lover, my mountain. He stood for solidity and comfort and strength. He didn't deny me anything I set my heart on doing, but he didn't encourage me either. He didn't make me feel as though I *could*—perhaps he assumed I would stand up for myself if it truly mattered. How wrong he was; how passive I was. He held on to me so tightly for the same reason I never stepped into larger opportunities: the uncertainty of his health and how much time we had left together. Dennis represented home—and in those days working at the bank, I didn't want to be home. I wanted to escape.

Had I asked, Dennis would've escaped with me. I know that now. Had I only asked . . .

Finally, Eli lets his hand fall from my shoulder, and he takes a step back. Something dissipates between us. The evening air is thinner, my thoughts lighter.

"You're tan," I notice.

An instant grin spreads across his face. "I just returned from my second trip to Morocco. And I finally got to see Egypt too."

"Were they amazing?"

"What do you think?" he says with a flash of his old humor.

"I'm so glad," I say. "Will you be showing the photos?"

"Next month," he says. "You'd love the dunes."

"Maybe I'll swing by," I say.

With tenderness, kinship, he says, "You should." Then: "Abby, seeing you with the whales . . . I'm glad you're doing something you love."

"Thank you," I say. "Me too."

"Are you and Dennis still together?"

It's an innocent enough question—something I would want to know about him, if I hadn't heard about his divorce. But how could he not know? Can he not read it on my face? The pain. The regret. The heartache.

"Eli," I say slowly, "Dennis is dead."

2013

Normally, the drive from Port Townsend to Chimacum was fifteen minutes, and that included a few spent slowly climbing the dirt road to our driveway. It was 2:15 a.m. when I got on the road, and I laid on the gas, hoping to get home before 2:30. But past Mill Road, out by PT Mini Storage, where the road became narrow and dark from a stand of trees, I had to slow down. The single car ahead of me was braking, too, its red lights igniting the cool dark. An ambulance was parked on the side of the road, the flashers blinding. Following the lead car, I steered briefly into the other lane in order to pass the accident.

I stole a quick glance, still distracted by my urge to get home quickly. It was a little blue car—nothing I recognized—its nose down the embankment, crunched into a tree. Scooting past the wreckage and the flashing lights, I saw the lumped body of a deer in my rearview. The driver must've hit the deer and swerved off the road. The town being somewhat overrun with deer, it was a common happening. As I accelerated, leaving the accident behind, I sent a brief message of hope into the universe that the driver was all right.

I missed Dennis even more after that. As it had so many times before, my mind roved back to that dreadful news of Dennis's heart; in Alaska, I'd felt so very far away. I felt far away tonight, too, but I was getting closer by the moment.

Speeding along, almost home, the certainty that had been missing from our marriage came roaring back. Despite our troubles, we were meant for each other. The relief I'd felt earlier that evening hadn't been in leaving Dennis—it'd been from finally coming clean to him. Mending things between us would take time and work and change and compromise, but he'd been right—we could work through it. This was our chance to move forward, and I couldn't wait to sleep in his arms.

When I got home, it appeared as though no one was there; Dennis had left his truck at Chrissy's house. I burst inside to find Dennis's earlier attempt at dinner, the pasta pot still filled with water on the stove. A year might as well have gone by since he'd scorched the skillet of garlic now resting on a cold burner.

"Dennis," I called.

He was probably asleep already.

"Dennis." I rushed upstairs, into the bedroom.

He wasn't there.

"Dennis?" Had he passed out on the couch? I checked, but he wasn't there either. Had he and Eduardo stayed out after all? Or maybe he'd gone back to Eduardo's house for the night. With a dip in spirits, I shuffled into the kitchen once more. I at least had to text Nick I was home.

When I found my phone, a handful of notifications cluttered my screen. A call from Jackie, a call from an unknown number, a call from Chrissy. All in the last fifteen minutes, all since I'd started home. My phone had been on vibrate. A sinking feeling crept between my ribs and nestled there; fear made my pulse flutter. A text from Chrissy read: PICK UP PICK UP PICK UP. An earlier one read: PICK UP YOUR PHONE. And earlier still: Call me.

Glancing around the empty kitchen, I knew the messages were about Dennis. With the sting of emotion in my nose, my eyes, I selected Jackie's voice mail and lifted the phone to my ear.

Sirens. Static. Jackie's voice: *Abby, it's Jackie. There's been an accident. Where are you?* Silence.

The little blue car.

It didn't add up—but then it did. What did Eduardo drive? I refused to believe it; I ran through every excuse in my head that could possibly make that accident *not* Eduardo's car. *Not* Dennis.

Without much thought, without much of anything other than a keen focus on reaching Dennis, I grabbed my purse, rushed out the door, and barreled down our dirt road, heading back toward town. Chimacum High School, Irondale Road—hometown landmarks flew by. The engine revved as I pushed on the gas, hitting twenty over the speed limit.

I saw the lights of the fire truck first, a bright flickering through the trees. I slowed considerably, steering off the road to the shoulder, then stopped and jumped out of the car. An ambulance and police car were parked, too, a cop and fireman talking quietly nearby. One EMT was dragging the body of the deer off to the side of the road, steam emanating from the hot heap, dark blood left behind in a sticky strip. Deep down in my gut, I knew this was bad before I even reached Jackie.

She was parked behind the ambulance, tear streaked, hugging herself. Still wearing her pajama bottoms.

I rushed to her. "Where is he? Where's Dennis?"

Another EMT, packing up the ambulance, glanced in my direction. Jackie had a stricken look on her face, the paleness of her skin in contrast with the redness of her eyes and nose.

"Where is he?" I demanded, uncaring if I made a scene. Uncaring how loud my voice got. "Answer me!"

Jackie shook her head, overcome with another wave of tears. She buried her face in her hands, moaning.

I looked around, frantic. The little blue car was empty. A tow truck was arriving. The ambulance was closed, seemingly empty. Where were they? Where were Dennis and Eduardo? I rushed for an EMT, practically falling against his shirt.

"Where is Dennis?" I asked, desperate, clutching the collar of his uniform.

His face contorted; he held back from answering.

I let out a sob. "Where?"

He gulped, his Adam's apple bobbing. He looked like a kid, younger than me. "Gone, ma'am."

"Gone—what? To the hospital?"

"He . . . died, ma'am."

"No he didn't," I said. "No he didn't."

The EMT touched my shoulder. "I'm sorry for your loss."

The news swallowed me up, swallowed me whole. The ambulance lights blurred in my vision, and I sank to the asphalt. I yelled. I moaned. I bowed my head to the pavement and quivered against the hard grit. I shook with disbelief, with unfathomable heartbreak, too deep to measure. I would never see him again. I would never feel his warmth. I would never kiss him again in my life. He'd never make me another Sunday breakfast, those perfect pancakes. He'd never laugh or smile again. He'd never complain about work or tickle me or brush his teeth or hold my hand or ask me about my day.

He'd never hear me say that I made a mistake, that I still loved him.

I would never get the chance to make things right between us.

Sobbing with my forehead on the road, I longed for Dennis so hard I thought my ribs would crack open in agony.

Dennis had saved me from a car accident once. He'd carried me out and stayed with me on the ground. He'd saved me that night, changing the course of my whole life, showing me love and companionship and loyalty.

Had I been there for him tonight, I could've saved him.

2018

As if drawn by gravity, I find myself driving down Discovery Road. I pull over at Laurel Grove Cemetery. The sky is very dim now, the brightest stars starting to peek through the blue fabric of the atmosphere. I pull a sweatshirt over my head, get out of the car, and head up the hill. It's cooler outside, and the walking warms me up. Though I've only visited once, I could find him in pitch black. Gravel and sunburned grass crunch under my shoes. He's buried farther back, along some hedges. When I find Dennis, the simple stone with his name and dates, I drop to my knees.

I run my fingers over the words etched there: **Loving Husband**. My tears sting, and I run the back of my hand under my nose. At his funeral, I felt like such a fraud. Only Chrissy and Nick knew the whole story—even now, my parents are aware of only bits and pieces of what really happened—and they stood beside me in silence, dressed in black, listening to guest after guest offer their condolences. Jackie didn't speak to me, not one word. His casket was propped open, and he looked almost plastic in his wedding suit. After the burial, I threw up in the hedges and collapsed into my parents' arms, sobbing until I couldn't breathe, my lungs shriveling to the size of thimbles.

Now, in the silence of the evening, I touch the grass with my fingertips, imagining his body staring up at me through the packed earth. "I loved you," I whisper. "You knew that, right? Tell me you knew."

That dreadful night, Dennis probably died thinking the love of his life was leaving him. His last thought could've been one of heartbreak.

"Please forgive me," I tell him, curling on the ground, as close to him as I can be. "Please. You were the best thing to ever happen to me."

I hear an SUV pull into the gravel parking lot of the cemetery. I squeeze my eyes shut and fist my fingers around a tuft of grass. If the driver notices me here on the ground, lying at the base of a headstone, they decide not to approach.

I continue whispering to Dennis. "I was so stupid. I should've never taken you for granted." My whole body quivers. "I hope you know how sorry I am."

The sky darkens into a star-streaked night. I turn onto my back and watch the thin clouds float past, remembering Dennis. Our love is a movie before my tear-blurred eyes. I replay it all: the highs, the lows, and all the many small moments in between. The touch of his fingers on my cheek, the intentness of his blue eyes, the heady smell of his skin. The night is big and wide and quiet.

"Dennis?" I ask, just as I would on late nights in bed when I couldn't sleep. My voice is small and raw from crying. "I want to tell you about California. I think you would've really liked it."

Tucking my hands into the sleeves of my sweatshirt, I talk to Dennis all night, until the dampness of dawn has chilled me to the core. When I finally lift my head, the morning has broken. Pastel light pushes against the night as I walk back to my car. The other visitor is long gone.

Like the lightening horizon, I have split wide open.

2013

Eduardo said so much had happened in mere moments: a deer leaping from the brush, a swerve, an impact. Three heartbeats' worth of time, with a ripple effect the size of a meteor. The doctors said Dennis had died instantly and hadn't felt any pain. How could they possibly know that?

I saw Eduardo in the hospital, but afterward, we went our separate ways. Jackie continued the construction business on her own, making Eduardo her business partner once he was well enough. I quit my job at the bank and stayed at my parents' even after the funeral, comforted by the sounds of them going about their lives while I lay awake in the same bed I'd once fantasized about Dennis in.

I sold our house—I couldn't sleep there anymore, not without waking to a creak or a gust of wind, thinking it was Dennis, thinking he'd come back to me. I couldn't stand it, so I sold it quickly for just enough profit for me to skip town. By fall, I'd moved to California, knocked on the door to Dr. Perez's office, and landed a scut work job that turned into the research study on humpback behavior.

I thought I could leave the tragedy behind, but what I didn't realize then was that Dennis would be in my heart forever—and I couldn't run from that.

2018

After leaving the cemetery, I felt wide awake, so I went to Energy Coffee for a mystery drink from Zack—an oat milk cappuccino, which he astutely described as a comforting breakfast in a cup—and spent my morning drafting a detailed report on yesterday's orca sighting for the Center for Salish Orca Research. Around ten, Becca finally updated the Sound Adventures crew about her mom: Mary had had low blood sugar from throwing up before the tour, and the excitement paired with no food had caused her to pass out. In the Orcas clinic, she'd received fluids, then returned home. According to Becca, Mary is going into the Port Townsend hospital today to reevaluate her treatment with her doctor.

My all-nighter is catching up to me by the time I've finished narrating a half-day whale watch and arrive at the hospital to visit Mary. I'm directed up to the third floor, where Chrissy works, and sure enough I see her when I walk through the door.

"Abby?" She gives me a brief hug; her scrubs smell like plastic. When she pulls away, her face is pinched with concern. "You look terrible."

"Thanks," I say with a laugh.

"What's wrong?"

"Actually, nothing. I'm here for a patient. Mary Hodge?"

"How do you know Mary?"

"How do you?" I ask, but of course I know instantly.

"She comes in here once a week."

"She goes whale watching," I explain. "Like, all the time."

Chrissy's expression softens into understanding—then rounds with surprise. "So you were there yesterday?"

I nod.

"They said she collapsed on a tour boat, and I didn't even think to draw the connection."

"I wanted to see how she's faring," I say. "Is Becca here?"

"Running errands, I think," Chrissy says. "But Mary is still here."

She leads the way down the hall, passing a nurse's station, where she waves at some coworkers, all wearing colorful scrubs. As we round the bend, huge bay windows reveal an incredible view. The hospital is built on a high hill above the town, and I can see the whole slope of land down to the water. Some military-related ship, all gray and jagged, is sliding through the calm afternoon water toward the naval base across Admiralty Inlet. Beyond, the Cascades are ethereal blue through the gauzy veil of thin clouds.

We come upon a doorway, and Chrissy slides the curtain aside. Mary is sitting in a padded chair, hooked up to an IV, reading. Soft light comes in through the window.

When Mary sees us, she looks up. Her smile is wide. "Abby," she says. "What a nice surprise."

I bend down to give her an awkward, gentle hug. "I'm so glad you're all right."

"I'll leave you to it," Chrissy says, ducking out.

I perch on the chair beside Mary. "How are you feeling?"

"Oh, sick," Mary says. "But fine, just fine."

I'm relieved to know she's okay, but it's a partial release, like exhaling only halfway. I have other things on my mind, weighing me down.

I rub my tired eyes. "Everyone has been worried. You gave us quite a scare."

"And where is everyone?" she says in mock anger. "Seems like you're the only one who cared enough to come."

I laugh. "Everyone else is coming later. I got off early."

"Whales today?"

"Yes," I answer.

"The calf again?"

I try to stifle a frown, to no avail. There hasn't been any news of the calf—in fact, we haven't heard anything about the situation since we initially reported the sighting to the Center for Salish Orca Research.

"No," I answer. "We saw Bigg's orcas hunting a sea lion, though. Very exciting. I'm glad you weren't there."

This time, she actually pouts. "I'm so embarrassed. I can't even handle the thrill anymore."

"Becca explained that it was a perfect storm of circumstances. Don't sweat it."

Mary looks into my eyes. "My future is uncertain. I just want to make the most of *right now*." She taps her index finger on the arm of her chair with those last two words.

I take her hand, stroking her lacelike skin as gently as I can manage. Tears threaten, but I manage to swallow them down, looking out the window, unblinking, until they dry up.

Mary doesn't comment on my emotion. "Abby, if there's anything I've learned from this whole ordeal, it's to let go of regrets. Let go of the past."

I look at her then.

"I can tell you're saddled with something," she continues. "If you waste all your time worrying about what's over and done, you'll never enjoy the time you *do* have left."

"What if I don't deserve—" I cut myself off, startled by what I'd begun to say. It's true, though, isn't it? My guilt has pinned me down.

"Pishposh," she says with a sassy wave. "We all deserve love and joy and humor. That's what living is about. There's no deficit of those things. There's no score."

I spent a lot of last night telling Dennis about my life since the tragedy. Something I miss most is simply telling him about my day—we had so much to catch up on.

"I want to make things right," I tell Mary, tears brimming again. "But I can't. It's too late."

She hands over a tissue box from her side table. "Then make things right for yourself."

I wipe my eyes and then look into her kind face, noticing the little dusting of pale freckles across her nose. Yesterday, with Eli, I made a little effort—and I felt better for it. He likely did too. It's funny how honesty was able to mend years' worth of bitterness.

There's still more to be done.

"I should go," I tell Mary. "Thank you for your advice. We'll see you on another tour soon?"

"Oh yes." With a mischievous grin, she adds, "You can't keep me away."

I stand. "I wouldn't dare."

I slip out into the hall again, heartachy but motivated anew. I find Chrissy not far from Mary's room and give her a quick hug. "Dinner soon?"

Her smile falters into a more mysterious expression: creased brows, flat mouth, intense eyes. "I wanted to suggest tomorrow, actually. Maybe at your parents' new house? Nick and I bought them a housewarming gift, and we wanted to tell you—"

I know immediately: "You're pregnant."

"Shhh," she says, dragging me behind a blind corner near an empty room. "My coworkers don't know."

I expected a sickly, creeping disappointment, but after Mary's words, after the hellish few days I've had, after the years of feeling so lousy, all I have for her is joy. Chrissy will make a fabulous mom, and I know how deeply she wants this. I beam at her, excitement buzzing.

"But . . . you are?" I clarify.

She nods vigorously, breaking into a full-on smile. "I am."

"Oh, yay," I whisper, grabbing her hands. We bounce on our toes, spread our arms wide, and pull one another into a long, tight, exuberant hug. "Chrissy, I'm so happy for you."

"Stop it—you're going to make me cry."

"Hormones?"

We break apart, and she sticks her tongue out at me.

"I'm going to be the best auntie ever," I tell her. "Have you told—"

"No one yet. You know how Nick's parents are, and my mom's overseas again—I'm kind of okay with putting them off."

"So you want to tell my parents tomorrow?" I ask.

"We want a housewarming for them," she says. "But yes, we'll drop the news then."

"My mother will be over the moon," I say.

"She'll love playing grandma."

"You'd let her do that?" I'm definitely a long ways off from kids, so Chrissy letting my mother enjoy grandmotherhood is a priceless gift.

Chrissy rolls her eyes. "Of course, silly. She'll be the best grandmother the little bean has."

"Ugh, you're the best friend ever." We hug again.

"I have to get back to work. Text me later?"

"Duh," I say.

~

It used to be that I couldn't drive this road—the same road of Dennis's accident—without weeping. Now, I hold strong—but all that motivation Mary instilled in me earlier has worn off by the time I reach the Nelson Construction office. I park out front, right next to Jackie's

Escalade, and get out. The office is located just outside of town near the storage facilities, right in the shadow of the paper mill. The air has the harsh, rotten-egg smell of sulfur. Gusts from the north have blown the mill's stink overhead, the sky a little hazy above the trees. It's one of those smells that out-of-towners giggle and groan about, while the oldest locals don't even notice it anymore. To me, it's just a reminder of days spent visiting the construction office—perhaps today it's a bad omen, but I'm (reluctantly) resolved.

I walk through the jingly door. It's a glorified room for paperwork, but years ago, before Dennis's father died, Jackie insisted they have an office—even a tiny run-down one—just to keep the accounts separate from family finances and meet with clients on more professional territory. I spent many early days surprising Dennis here, with lunch or kisses or love notes left on his truck for him to find later. It doesn't look much different, save for a fresh coat of paint. The mill stink is more faint inside, mingled with the scent of wall primer.

Jackie looks up from her desk, her face moving from customer-welcoming politeness to an *I hate you* scowl. She stands, and I briefly wonder if she'll lunge at me again.

"Just let me talk," I say, holding up my hands.

Her jaw clenches.

"I know I fucked up," I say. "More than once, and in your eyes, probably all the time. But I loved Dennis. Deeply. I was head-over-heels crazy about him since the moment we met."

She flinches but doesn't speak.

"What you saw five years ago, downtown, was the lowest part of my life. I don't have an excuse, only a clarification: what you witnessed was as far as it ever went."

She rolls her eyes but keeps her mouth pressed firmly shut.

"The night of the accident, I was on my way home to make amends with Dennis. I wanted him to know how much I loved him. And he never got to hear it. And I hate that. But don't think, even for one second, that I didn't love your brother." I choke up. "He was the best thing to ever come into my life. And I just wanted to thank you for sharing him with me. Albeit unwillingly."

Jackie's forehead creases. "I saw you last night."

That's not the response I was expecting. "Huh?"

"At the cemetery."

The other car. That was Jackie? "Oh."

"I visit him every week."

"Sorry to interrupt," I say.

"How long did you stay?"

Considering the bags under my eyes, she probably already knows. "All night."

"I waited in my car past midnight, then left," she says, surprising me. "I didn't think you'd care, this long after the accident." Her mouth is still pinched, but her eyes have softened.

"Of *course* I care, Jackie. I always will."

She folds her arms. "You were always leaving."

"I was constantly trying to prove to you that I loved your brother—"

"Love isn't something you *try* or *say* or *demonstrate*, Abby. It's just something you do."

Aside from perhaps our last year together, I know in my heart that Dennis never doubted how I felt about him—but he experienced my love day to day. Jackie only ever witnessed the big moments—his heart surgery, our marriage, the accident—and I realize now that many of those moments involved me leaving or taking her brother away from her. It isn't fair of her to expect me to prove anything, but knowing what they went through as kids and what it was like to care about someone with a fragile heart, I can't blame her. If I were Jackie, I would've wanted to protect Dennis from heartbreak of any kind too. So instead of being defensive or lashing out at her with my own anger, I say, "I'm sorry."

I can barely hear her next words. "Last night was too little too late . . . but it was proof."

I didn't think I had any tears left, but now more are streaming down my face. "I miss him so much."

"He was too good for you," she says, her voice still low.

"I agree."

"He was too good for all of us," she says. "Myself included."

My brows knit together.

"I could never keep him safe from Dad," Jackie says. "Sometimes I think his heart trouble was from the stress of childhood."

"Oh, Jackie, that's not—"

She waves me off. "It doesn't matter now."

"He was so loved," I say. "By everyone."

She nods.

"I don't expect you to forgive me," I tell her. "I just wanted you to hear—"

"I forgive you," Jackie says, and I'm astonished. I bite my lip to distract myself from how weak my ankles get, how much my eyes sting.

Jackie's ever-hardened face relents, just for a moment, her forehead relaxing out of its creases, her frown softening. "None of us are perfect, and no amount of groveling will bring him back. But I have to believe that forgiveness makes things bearable."

"I like to think so."

"It took guts to come here," she says. "And if you miss him that much after five years, you must've really loved him." She sighs, as if her next words will take a lot of effort. "Maybe you're not so bad after all."

My knees are quivering, and yet I feel lighter than I ever have. It's as if she's lifted an entire mountain off my shoulders. "Thanks."

She sits back down, and I can tell the conversation is over. Her eyes—a little watery now—flicker back to her computer. "I'll see you around."

"Maybe at the grocery store later?"

She frowns and looks up again, and for a split second I fear she doesn't think it's funny, but then she laughs. "Sure."

I walk back out into the sunshine just as a car is pulling up: Eduardo. He gets out.

"Abby? What are you doing here?"

"Repenting," I tell him.

"Did it work?"

I shrug, smiling.

"Good for you," he says. "I think that's all she ever wanted."

"I feel like I got off easy," I joke.

"After all this time?" he says seriously.

I shrug, my eyes prickling all over again. I wait a beat before asking, "How did you feel better, Eduardo? Do you?"

He seems a little staggered by the question, but in a good-natured way. "It took some time. But then I thought about what his advice would've been. And of course, he would've said it wasn't my fault. We were always complaining about the damn deer together—it was practically an inside joke."

"It was?"

"Oh yeah."

Remembering that night, I ask, "How was he? Before it happened?"

Eduardo clenches his jaw, but only for an instant. "He was torn up, Abby. I won't deny that."

I nod, staring into his sincere face.

"But he also said something you might like to know. He was all slurring and rambling, going on and on about you. I remember he said, 'I count myself a lucky son of a bitch for every day she decides to spend with me.' Then he threw up on the floor mat."

I laugh. "Really?"

"It was gross." He snorts. "He didn't want you to go, but he seemed damn glad for the days you'd already spent together." He pauses, a long pause, his gaze elsewhere. A dark hardness floods his expression, and then he looks back at me, alight once more. "He was in the middle of some long Shakespearean speech about you when the deer jumped out. He was in love right up until the end."

I don't know what else to do but rush into Eduardo's embrace. He holds me tightly, smelling of sawdust and sweat, so similar to how Dennis used to smell when he got home from work. "We all gotta keep living our lives, Abby," Eduardo says into my ear. "It's what he would've wanted."

~

Once, early on in our relationship, Dennis came home late and found me on my computer listening to whale songs. He thought I was crazy, but when he sat and actually listened, he got all quiet and pensive. Staring out the window into the liquid blackness of the evening, perhaps he was imagining them. The recording gave off the slosh of water, and it swayed us there in the dark kitchen.

Orca whales don't just click and squeak for echolocation. Their high-frequency sounds are often for communication. They find each other in the vast, murky blue-green, telling each other where they are and what they're doing, like text messages pulsing through the depths. Humpbacks, with their low-frequency moans, sing for territory and for love. Whales have cultures and families and possibly even tradition. Like people, they have distinct voices. They speak and sing. They also grieve.

After the crash, I knew I would never forget Dennis's voice. People told me time would blur him around the edges, but he's as crisp in my mind as the day I last saw him.

That night, listening to the whales, he whispered, "Why do I feel like they know more about life than I do?"

"Because," I told him, "they've been around for millions of years. They've perfected the art of communication."

I know nothing compared to the whales—but I'm learning.

2018

It's my parents' housewarming, and I'm in charge of the wine. After deliberating in the Hadlock QFC for ten minutes, I find something with a nice label, grab two, and head toward the checkout stands. I keep picturing the farmhouse, my childhood bedroom, the view of the valley. I keep remembering the smell of the barn, like timothy hay and oats and horse sweat and leather and tractor grease. Effortlessly, I can walk the whole farm in my mind, during any season. The hot summer sun making the stretch from the house to the barn feel twice as long, my jeans sticking to the insides of my thighs. The bone-chilling whip of a winter wind down the valley, the three of us breaking the ice on troughs and hauling water by bucket from the pump house. The crocuses and daffodils and dusty blue-green sprigs of lavender in the spring; the apple trees heavy with fruit in the fall, limbs sagging practically to the ground.

When I think of going to my parents' house, I think of West Valley Road, their black mailbox, and the gravel drive. It's why I almost take a wrong turn once I'm back in the car, the wine bottles on the passenger seat. I have to force myself to drive opposite to my instinct. When I pull up to their new house—a little run-down suburban-looking place—I feel a plunge in my heart. Whatever is left of my youth—from horseback riding to high school shenanigans to having that scarlet crush on Dennis—is all gone. We're all adults now, and I mourn every memory.

Chrissy and Nick's Subaru is already in the driveway; I'm five minutes late. When I walk up the alien steps and turn the smallish doorknob, I brace for the feeling I had each time I walked in with a moving box weeks and weeks ago: unfamiliarity. I steel myself for the weird smell, like Pine-Sol and dust and some other family.

But when I walk inside, it's a glimpse of the future.

My mother, Chrissy, and Nick are sitting at the dining room table in the cave-like alcove to the left of the kitchen. Dad is standing over the stove, stirring something. They're all talking loudly. Dad interjects, and the four of them burst into laughter. Coop runs up to me, his nails scraping on the linoleum, a new sound, more plasticky than in their old home. I bend down to scratch his ears and breathe in deeply, pleasantly surprised by the utter familiarity of the smell: my mother's shampoo, my father's garlicky Alfredo sauce, a little mud, and the unique mustiness of their furniture.

Nick notices me first. "Heeeeyyy!" he says, waving.

I stand and step over Coop, setting the wine bottles on the kitchen counter. "Sorry I'm late."

"Nonsense, Babby." My father gives me a squeeze. "Sit down; get comfortable."

I linger in his hold, then circle the table and sit beside my mom. She pats my hand, and for the first time all summer, I don't recoil. It's taken a while to warm to her again; the house chaos was a big, welcome distraction to muffle the process, but after things calmed down, I still felt a little twinge when I saw her. I've been chewing on something my father said, too, something that only just now finally feels like a form of comfort.

Shortly after they broke the house news to me, they called Wendy to get the process going. Mom fell into packing mode, and Dad started all the outside projects he'd been meaning to tackle for years now. He fixed the wiring on the faulty barn light, cleaned the grease off the floor of his workshop, and patched fences. I thought the whole thing was a useless effort, but he refused to leave the place in bad shape for the next owner.

In mild disagreement, still bitter over the whole thing, I decided to help him with the fences. When would I ever nail up boards or fix electric lines with him again? I wanted to grab onto that piece of childhood and never let go.

I carried the box of nails, the crowbar, a level, and a hammer, and Dad hauled a few replacement boards out to a pasture corner. The horses had been using the wood as a butt-scratching station, and the weight of one-thousand-pound animals had cracked a few top boards; two more were simply old and rotten. I pried off the bad planks, the rusty nails squeaking and honking as they tore free. Dad held up the first board, and I tacked it on.

I was still so baffled by my mother's confession, and while I sought a simpler time that afternoon, I couldn't help but ask my dad how he'd been able to stay with her afterward. "How could you trust her again?" I pressed, handing him the hammer. A part of me wanted to know how Dennis might've trusted me again, had he not died.

Dad secured the board on his side; the level that rested along the top of the board wiggled precariously as he struck the nail. "Marriage is like a fence, Abby. Just because there are a few broken boards or rotted-out posts doesn't mean you tear the whole thing down and burn the lumber. You repair the weak spots. You move on."

I didn't accept his words then, but as I sit at the dinner table in their new home, his sentiment finally sinks in. I'm so like my mother, in a way. When things went sour with Dennis, I wanted to run. And he was like Dad: willing to fix the weak spots rather than burn the wood. Now, I'm proud of my father for his thinking; I feel a bit of kinship with my mother, finally seeing things from her side. She was wrong, of course, but she knows it—just as I know my affair with Eli was wrong. And if I can't forgive my mom, how can I forgive myself?

"So how are you settling in?" Nick asks my mother now.

"It's actually really wonderful," she says. "The smaller place is so much easier to keep clean."

"Not to mention the yard," my father says from the kitchen. "It takes me less than ten minutes to mow the sucker."

"And work?" Chrissy asks. "The horses?"

"John's actually been busy this summer," she says. "And the lack of a workshop hasn't really affected things, right, dear?"

"It's even better," he says, straining noodles, steam billowing. "Again, less to clean."

"I've been visiting the horses on my days off," Mom says, answering Chrissy's other question. "I miss them terribly, but I've been able to sneak some quality time. And Connie appreciates the help with brushing."

"That's great," Chrissy says.

"What kind of wine did you bring, Abby?" Nick asks.

I stand. "No idea, but I'll open it."

My father hands me a corkscrew, and I get the glasses out. While he sets our dinner plates at each place setting, I pass out the wine, skipping Chrissy. Finally, we're all seated, and I'm taken back to the pizza-and-chicken-nugget dinners we had as kids, begging my parents to let us eat on the couch in front of the TV. They always forced us to eat dinner at the table, much to our dismay, but now there's nowhere I'd rather be.

"Dinner looks amazing, John," Chrissy says.

"Yes, thank you so much," Nick chimes in.

"This was a great idea, Chrissy," my mother says.

"We wanted to celebrate this new chapter," Chrissy says. "We're glad you're settling in."

"The house certainly feels more like a home with all our favorite kids in it." Mom touches my hand again, and I squeeze her fingers briefly before picking up my fork.

"I almost forgot . . ." My father stands, retrieves something from the oven, then returns. He sets a steaming foil bundle onto an empty dish and opens it up to reveal his famous garlic bread, fat cloves cooked into a crisp baguette with more butter than a nurse like Chrissy could condone, but she's the first one to grab a piece.

"God, this is so good," Nick groans.

I sip my wine, and Mom seems to realize that Chrissy doesn't have any. "Oh dear, Abby forgot your glass."

"Actually, that's the other reason we wanted to have dinner with you guys," Chrissy says. She and Nick lock hands and grin at each other.

Mom knows before Chrissy can say anything, squealing so loudly that Dad drops his fork.

"What is it?" he asks, confused.

"We're pregnant," Chrissy says.

My father's face lights up. "Congratulations!"

My mother is standing, circling the table, hugging Chrissy and Nick both. "I'm so happy for you," she says. "I'm so, so happy."

We cheer and laugh, and finally Mom sits back down.

"I remember you three on the couch watching cartoons," Dad says. "Like yesterday."

"We definitely want to repeat history with the baby," Chrissy says. "She needs to know what a good chicken-nugget cook you are."

My dad chuckles. "You know you can buy them in the frozen section?"

"Not the same," Nick says.

"She?" Mom asks. "You know the sex already?"

"No, just habit," Chrissy says, touching her stomach. "I hope it's a she."

"What about you, Nick?"

"Me too."

"You sure?" Dad asks. "Daughters are trouble."

"Hey!" I say.

My mother places a hand on her chest. "Whatever it is, it'll be so, so loved."

"We're counting on that," Chrissy says. "Now, do you guys prefer classic Grandma and Grandpa, or do you want to go the Nana and Papa route?"

My mother's eyebrows shoot up, her mouth rounding into an O. "What are you saying?"

"Well, my mom is always MIA, and Nick's parents are in California now, so we'll need some honorary grandparents here."

"Oh, my dear Chrissy," my mom says, fanning tears.

Dad simply smiles, his face red.

"This is the best housewarming gift of all time," my mother cries.

"Happy new home," Chrissy says.

"It's a good thing," my father finally manages. "We'll have plenty of new memories to fill this house with."

I nod and sip my wine, holding back my own sudden flood of happy tears. I wonder, mildly, what the baby will remember most from this house. Will it be Coop's nails on the linoleum? Chicken nuggets and veggies dipped in ranch? Or completely new memories I can't even fathom yet? Friends like Chrissy and Nick who haven't even been born, schoolteachers who are still in college, cartoons that have yet to be drawn. Pets yet to be adopted, summers yet to be sweated, and snow days yet to freeze her little fingers—and the five of us adults, yet to drive them to the animal shelter, yet to set up the sprinkler in the backyard, yet to brew hot cocoa for when the snowball fights cease.

Maybe the house and Chrissy's pregnancy and this new life path are for the best after all.

JULY

2018

On July 14, my thirty-fifth birthday, Chrissy, Nick, and I get ice cream at Pete's like the old days. My banana split comes out with a candle on top, and they sing me "Happy Birthday" and hand over a gift certificate for a much-needed massage and facial. Sitting in our big, cushy booth, I blow out the candle.

"What'd you wish for?" Chrissy asks.

"I'll tell you if it comes true," I say.

After we demolish our sundaes, they show me paint swatches for their in-progress nursery. Chrissy and Nick already seem like parents. The nursery will be blue with a white crib, dresser, and trim. They've bought practically all the parenting books in existence. My parents have already dug out my old toys and onesies to give to the "little bean," as we've been calling her. Chrissy and Nick also show me pictures of the puppy that awaits them at the animal shelter. He's another doodle like Ginger, too young to leave the shelter yet, but they bought him a new leash and bone and have dusted off the old dog bed. Our spools of thread, our lives, have (mostly) untangled, and I'm grateful for the days we spend together.

Eli's dune photos are premiering at his gallery tonight, and after Pete's, the three of us make our way down Water Street toward his space. It's Gallery Walk, and we stop at each gallery on the way, feasting on cheese and crackers even though we're already full from the sundaes. When we finally make it to the Fonseca Gallery, we walk into the brightly lit space and stop our conversation short.

The walls are adorned with incredible, sweeping images of golden-orange dunes. The photographs border on abstract, long slithering peaks in the sand and windswept ripples like water. They're images of shadow and light, but with Eli's signature color. He's printed them on aluminum, and some must be five, maybe six feet in width.

"Wow," Chrissy says, disappearing into a conjoined room, where I spot a few images of the pyramids and camels. Nick follows her, holding a plate of cheese (he's never been able to resist free cheese).

I wander in the opposite direction, studying the up-close grains of sand, near-pixelated but shimmering on the aluminum. One image strikes me: a ridge of sand stretching away from the camera like a spine, with wind ripples down the sides like ribs. I can see Eli's shadow in the foreground, the arms bent up toward the obscurity of his head, a camera strap hanging down. The name of the photograph is *On the Back of the Beast*, and I can practically feel the hot wind tugging at my T-shirt.

"You like?" Eli asks.

I tear my eyes from the warm-toned wonder. "These are breathtaking."

He folds his arms, his lips quirked. "Appreciate it."

"Have you sold any yet?"

"Yes, three six-footers, believe it or not. Who knew Pacific Northwesterners would like barren scapes?"

"It's well deserved," I say, happy for him.

Together, we walk into another offshoot room, where blue walls are tiled with many small images of Moroccan architecture: huge arches, domes, fountains, courtyards, all in vibrant indigo and white and stucco ocher. Each image centers on a set of mosaics more intricate than the last, flowery backsplashes of cobalt, teal, and faded red. Blooms and patterns with minuscule detail.

"Wonderful, aren't they?"

"Truly," I say.

"Come this way." Smile lines deepen around his eyes. He leads me through a door, into a back room. Frames, track lighting, and paint cans are piled up in one corner. A desk, computer, and wastebasket are opposite the door. "I'm almost done editing the promotional photos for Sound Adventures."

He sits down, and I peer over his shoulder. A floating screen saver of Kira at the park blinks away, and his computer awakens to reveal a gallery of orca photos. He scrolls through iconic images of breaching black-and-white bodies, misty-blue snowcapped mountains in the background. They're postcard worthy. Some from a different tour even feature the new Sound Adventures catamaran—the debut Edmonds vessel.

"They'll love these." I point to a picture of a spy-hopping orca with evergreen land and snowcapped Mount Baker behind it. "This one is perfect."

"Good eye," he says.

He scrolls further, and the images grow more dismal. My heart is wrenched by the memory of that baby orca, its mother nudging the carcass to the surface. The telescopic zoom of Eli's camera has made it possible to see every detail in crisp clarity: The delicate, limp body of the baby propped up on the tip of her mother's nose. The yellowish underbelly and little teeth. The eye of the grieving mom.

The scene made national news. The mother, J35, carried her calf for seventeen days before abandoning her dead newborn. To bolster my written report, Eli sent his images to the Center for Salish Orca Research, which tracked the mother from there. His photos headlined articles from the *Seattle Times*, the *New York Times*, and the *Washington Post*. The ordeal inspired many to do better by the environment: avoid single-use plastics, vote in favor of protecting key habitats, and so on.

More unexpected was my own experience—after reading my report, the Center for Salish Orca Research offered me a job. Their offer arrived the same day I learned that Becca's school had raised nearly $8,000 for orca research; the day another tourist divulged that she was a Seattle restaurant owner who'd recently taken salmon off her menu; the day Robin and his parents, the owners of the Sound Adventures tour company, announced their partnership with the Washington State Orca Task Force, working to regulate tour laws to satisfy public interest while keeping our waters quieter and safer for the southern resident orcas; and the day I was asked to be the Sound Adventures conservation representative, working alongside advocacy groups and speaking on behalf of the tour company to convince average citizens to do their parts. Effecting change at their level. While I mourn with J35, I also see her story as a turning point. The tours I've narrated since her plight have been filled with concerned, thoughtful tourists wanting to know how to help.

I declined the CSOR's offer. I might be a skilled researcher, but I'm also a damn good tour naturalist. I might know how to read and record data, but convincing citizens to care and take action is a whole other challenge. It's a calling I never knew I'd love, and it's where I'm meant to be. I only wish I'd figured that out before I lost Dennis.

In the Fonseca Gallery, the computer screen goes black, and Eli stands. "I have something for you." There's a large print leaning against the wall, shrouded in a sheet. I know what it is before he reveals it: *The Boy with the Bougainvillea.*

"Oh no, I couldn't," I say.

"Wow, where was this taken?" Chrissy asks, coming through the doorway.

"Cuba," Eli answers. He angles the photograph in her direction, and Nick trails in, equally captivated.

"What's it doing back here in the dark?" Chrissy asks.

"Abby was about to take it home."

"Actually, no—" I say, but I find my fingers curling around the raised edge of the wood backing, where the hanging wire is kinky and loose.

"You *have* to," Chrissy says. "Your cottage could use some color."

"See?" Eli says, grinning.

Then another woman pokes her head into the office, and I recognize her as Eli's cashier. "I have another large sale; do you want to meet the buyer?"

"I should get back out there," Eli says to us. Then he turns to me. "Don't be a stranger, Abby."

"I won't," I say.

I'm not sure if I'll see him again, but I won't avoid him either. I even ran into Jackie at the grocery store again and nodded in her direction. I don't have the heart to hide from anyone anymore—Dennis wouldn't have wanted that. He would've wanted me to heal, move forward, never forget him, but never let him hold me back either. And that's exactly what I wished for when I blew out my birthday candle.

~

The sun is on the rise; nearly five a.m., and I can already tell it'll be a nice day. It's chilly now, but the cloudless sky and slight humidity promise a scorcher. I wiggle into some shorts, pull over a loose Sound Adventures T-shirt, and tuck my hair under a ball cap. After feeding Taffy on the porch—she's officially adopted me as her co-owner now, at least on the days I wake up earlier than Gwen—I get into my car and dial the number on the way.

Zack picks up, groggy, his voice gravelly with sleep. "Hello?"

"It's Abby," I say.

"I know; I have caller ID."

"Get up and meet me at the marina," I say.

He begins, "Do you know what time it—" but I end the call.

I roll the windows down and sing to myself all the way there.

When I pull up to the coffee shop, Zack is standing there shirtless in a pair of sweatpants, his arms crossed. I get out, and he calls, "I'm not jumping in."

"Yes, you are," I say.

"The bolt in my hip is achy. I'm not jumping in," he says.

I'm not sure whether to believe him or not. "Buzzkill."

"I have an alternate idea."

"Oh?" I ask, stepping closer.

He grins and takes my hand.

We walk toward the water, away from the coffee shop. Too soon, he lets go of my fingers, and we file down the metal ramp to the floating docks in the marina. He glances over his shoulder every once in a while, just to make sure I'm keeping up. A bell on a boat nearby gongs, and hulls bump gently. Seagulls are already awake and chattering, lifting into the sky. A pair of otters leaps off the opposite dock, tumbling together with frenzied, playful splashes. The sun has painted the calm water golden, barely a ripple to disturb the liquid light. Thin tendrils of fog hug the shoreline.

We arrive at a sailboat, and Zack hops aboard, gesturing for me to follow. I hesitate.

"Don't worry; it's mine," he says.

I climb aboard, holding the metal railing. I follow him down some narrow stairs and duck below. The slim interior is basically half bed, half kitchenette, with a tiny bathroom door open by the stairs. Two mugs of steaming coffee are already resting on a strip of a table by a bench seat opposite the kitchen sink. He opens a minifridge tucked under the counter. "Cream okay?"

"I'm good with black." I scooch onto the padded bench. A little window above the sink reveals a limited but pretty view of the marina, the triangular lines of sailboats swaying, crisp white in the sun. The curtains framing the window are a tad dusty, a little frilly, quaint.

"It's better with cream," he insists.

"Then why'd you ask?"

He chuckles, splashes our coffees with cream, then returns the carton to the fridge and sits beside me. "See? Isn't this preferable to jumping into the freezing ocean?"

"I never once said otherwise." I take a sip and relish the perfect chickory coffee; Zack was right about the cream.

"Good?" he asks, smugly watching me.

I don't give him the satisfaction of an answer.

I realize how close we're sitting, how secluded we are. It's only us on this tiny boat. I glance toward his bed, the covers rumpled from sleep, three pillows lining the pointed back wall. His mattress is contoured to match the shape of the hull, a cozy-looking space. I take another long sip of coffee. He's still shirtless. I realize I haven't been this intimately close to—and alone with—a man since Dennis.

"So what's with the rude awakening?" he asks.

"I just felt like seeing you."

"And you couldn't wait until I opened the shop?"

"I wanted you to myself."

"Oh," he says, smiling over the rim of his mug. "Well, you got me."

His words have a *now what?* edge. I don't know how to answer the unspoken question.

"It just seemed like a good way to start my day," I say. "Good company, that is."

"I can agree," he says, looking into my eyes.

I glance at his lips, noticing the swell and curve and knowing that if I tasted them, they'd taste of coffee.

He catches me looking but doesn't poke fun anymore. "How do you like it?"

I realize he's talking about the coffee, not his company. "So good."

"It's a New Orleans favorite," he says. "A newbie at the shop. I just got a case."

"So I'm your guinea pig?"

"Yes."

"Well, good, because you're mine," I say.

His forehead creases in wonder. I look at him and think about the vast love and life I built with Dennis. He will always be a part of me, but I have companionship yet to offer. Part of moving forward is letting go—not of his memory but of the guilt that saturates it. He would've wanted me to know warmth and company and compassion and understanding and humor again. He would've wanted me to love again.

"My husband passed away five years ago," I explain. "I have all this emotional baggage. All this . . ." I wave my arms, searching for the words. "All this shit to work through. I'm just beginning."

Right now, I don't know who Zack will become to me. I don't believe there will be any comparison to Dennis other than, perhaps, romance—and that's a good thing. There's a spark between Zack and me, sure and glowing, and I'm compelled to fan the flame.

"I'll tell you about it, if you want," I offer meekly.

He stands up, worrying me for a moment, but he's simply refilling our cups. "Only if you'll hear mine," he says with a smile. He sits back down beside me, resting an arm along the back of the bench. I can feel his body heat against me. I glance at his lips again, skin tingling.

"We all have baggage," he goes on. "Haven't you realized that's what the coffee is for? It facilitates conversation. It gives us the energy to unpack."

"Oh," I say.

He looks into my eyes. "Tell me what's been on your mind."

I nestle into the shelter of his arm. I take a long sip, breathe deeply, and dive in.

AUTHOR'S NOTE

The role that whale watching boats play in the Puget Sound's marine habitat is a complicated one. I am not a scientist or expert—I don't pretend to know if or how our endangered southern resident population can be saved from extinction. What I do know is this: whale watching companies, research organizations, and citizens across the Salish Sea cherish the southern resident killer whales deeply.

I would've never fallen in love with our local marine wildlife if it hadn't been for seeing them in their natural habitat. I was five years old the first time I boarded a whale watching boat, and it changed my worldview forever. Some may not agree with Abby's stance on whale watches, but let's continue to have those respectful conversations—that's how we learn, grow, and continue to do better by the environment.

Researching this book inspired me to ask questions and alter my habits—and I continue to change as I learn more about the natural world. My hope is that this book might inspire you to make changes on behalf of your own cherished habitats. For an incomplete list of ways we can all live more sustainably, plus my favorite eco-friendly products, visit my website: jennifergoldauthor.com/oceans.

ACKNOWLEDGMENTS

Writing a novel can often be an isolating experience, but without the input, expertise, love, and support of the following people, I would've never been able to put these words on the page.

First and foremost, many thanks to Alicia Clancy for the care, insight, and enthusiasm throughout the entire editing process. It takes a special kind of editor to make an author genuinely look forward to getting their book picked apart. You take my work to the next level. Thanks, also, to my entire dream team at Lake Union Publishing. I am one very blessed author.

Michelle Richter, your trust and belief in my ability as a writer mean the world to me. I couldn't have wished for a better agent to have in my corner. Never stop sending me cat photos.

Special thanks to Sue and Pete Hanke and the entire family at the Puget Sound Express for answering my questions and giving me a glimpse into your kindhearted, tight-knit community of whale watching enthusiasts.

To the staff at Velocity, Port Townsend: Thank you for keeping me caffeinated throughout many, many editing sessions. Thanks also for sharing your expertise and providing much of the inspiration for Zack and his coffee shop. You all brighten my days—the great lattes are just a bonus.

I would also like to thank two real-world counterparts to the fictional marine organizations featured in the book: the Center for Whale Research (which inspired the Center for Salish Orca Research) and the Port Townsend Marine Science Center (which inspired the Salish Science Center). Since I was a child, these organizations have nurtured my interest in and appreciation for the natural world. Not only did they serve as real-life resources for this book, they instilled in me a great respect for the Salish Sea. Visit my website at jennifergoldauthor.com/oceans for more information about how you can support these wonderful organizations.

When I was itching to learn more about the southern resident whales and the Puget Sound as a whole—literally on the precipice of a total career change just to satiate my interest in marine biology—my mother said, "Why don't you just write a book about the whales?" Thanks, Mom, for the idea. Thanks for Taffy too.

Dad, thank you for being my writing role model, cheerleader, critic, and friend. I love our "book talks."

Sue and Steve Gillard, thank you for being such superfans.

Finally, to my husband, Joe: It will take me a lifetime to properly thank you for your unconditional love and support. I'm so glad to be your wife. Thank you for tolerating all the nature documentaries, fun facts, and science center visits. I love you more than whales, which, as you know, is a whole darn lot.

BOOK CLUB DISCUSSION QUESTIONS

1. Abby sacrificed her career on more than one occasion in order to remain close to Dennis, but she ultimately resented him for it. Was it selfish of Abby to want a different career than the bank? Had she been more honest with Dennis about her career goals, do you think he would've supported her in the pursuit of the career she always wanted?
2. Abby, Chrissy, and Nick have been friends through thick and thin, but with her friends' recent decision to start a family, Abby struggles with a fear of being left behind. How have you weathered the evolution of friendships? What would be your best advice for Abby as her friends enter this new stage of life?
3. Do you think Abby was wrong to start having coffee with Eli without telling Dennis? Would you define what she did as cheating? Had Dennis lived, do you think he would've forgiven her?
4. Do you think Abby treated Eli fairly throughout their relationship? Why or why not?

5. Abby's idolized vision of her parents was turned upside down with the realization of her mother's affair. Do you think Abby's anger toward her mother was justified? Do you think her parents had a strong relationship? Do you believe a couple can come back stronger from infidelity?
6. At the end of the book, Zack acknowledges that "we all have baggage." Do you think Zack's emotional transparency is good for Abby? Do you think they end up together?
7. Throughout the book, Abby struggles with the meaning of *home*: her hometown, her childhood house, and the sense of belonging she feels when she's with the people she loves. What is *home* to you?
8. Abby cares deeply about the Puget Sound. What habitats do you value? What small changes can you make in your weekly routines to benefit the environment?

ABOUT THE AUTHOR

Photo © 2019 Pinto Portrait

Jennifer Gold believes love is sweet and life is messy, which is probably why she has a passion for writing about the relationships of career-focused women. Having grown up on the Olympic Peninsula of Washington, Gold has a deep appreciation for the orcas, humpbacks, seals, and other marine wildlife that inhabit the Puget Sound and beyond. When she's not writing books, Gold can be found cleaning horse stalls, drinking coffee, and spending time with her husband and two cats. Find out more at http://jennifergoldauthor.com.